CHLOE HODGE

COURTING THE FAE CAPTAIN

ROMANCING THE REALMS

COURTING THE FAE CAPTAIN

CHLOE HODGE

Courting the Fae Captain

Copyright © 2025 by Chloe Szentpeteri

First edition: August 2025

Paperback ISBN: 978-0-6453849-9-4

Hardcover ISBN: 978-0-6453849-8-7

E-book ISBN: 978-0-6453849-7-0

Special thanks and acknowledgement to:

Copy Editor: Emily Morrison Editorial

Cover artist: Selkkie Designs

Formatter: Jade Church

Find me at: www.chloehodge.com

Instagram: @chloeschapters

TikTok: @chloehodgeauthor

Facebook: Chloe Hodge Author

AUTHOR NOTE

Courting the Fae Captain is a standalone instalment of the romantasy series, *Romancing the Realms*. If you like fierce females with feminine rage, high-stakes action, fated mates and spice, you will devour this addictive, swoony novel.

Please note: This novel contains content that may be triggering for some readers. This book includes explicit romance, mature language, violence, death, blood and gore, murder, attempted murder, assault, attempted sexual assault and reference to off-page sexual assault. This book is intended for readers 18+.

For all the women who have ever felt broken, beaten, or worn down by society. I see your labour and your love. I see your strength and your wisdom. I see your rage and your wrath.
This is for you.

Soul's End
The Soul Court
Kraitor
Vistyx
Domeratt
Ryvia's Rest
The Bone Court
The Shadow Court
Necropolis ruins
Strait of the Sea Serpent
Dievar Downs
Devil's snag
The Blood Court
Aremoor

COURTING
THE FAE
CAPTAIN

THE COURTS AND CLASSES OF MITHRIA

THE SHADOW COURT
Spell Weavers
Masters of Shadow can manipulate the dark for combat or stealth. Wielders of dark magic can use spells to create objects.

THE SOUL COURT
Soul Speakers
Spirit Mediums can communicate with the dead.
Fae in this class can also become powerful Seers.

THE BONE COURT
Bone Cleavers
Necromancers can reanimate the dead.
Lesser Magics include manipulating bones for small periods.

THE BLOOD COURT
Blood Mages
Blood can be manipulated into objects or spells.
Healers can purify blood and cure wounds.

BEFORE

It would take many years before the lord would understand the meaning of regret. He had never had to ask for anything in his life, short-lived as it was. Everything he had was handed to him on a silver platter, and when your cup was constantly full, it left little room for wanting.

No, regret was a foreign concept used by nameless males with no purpose or position in society. Highborn males didn't regret or feel remorse. Especially not amongst necromancers. Powerful males had little use for the sentiment when there were empires to rule and enemies to fight.

Besides, the lord had the blissful crutch of nobility on his side, there to lean on should he ever need. For his was a powerful bloodline, with generations of ancestral lords. So, when it came time for him to marry, the young lord was more than eager to meet his new bride.

Of course, marriage in the Shadow Court was not without its traditions and tribulations, especially when it came to lords and ladies of noble blood. Fae lineage was a precious thing, and it was his solemn duty to sow the seeds of a healthy, strong bloodline in a healthy, strong female.

That's where the Wedding Rite came in—a ceremonial affair that any would-be wives entered when vying for the male in question's hand. It was a female's greatest honour to participate. And only one female's triumph.

The Rite was viewed as outlandish and outdated by some of the other Courts in Mithria, but the Shadow Court was home to a segment of the continent's most powerful armies. Its ruler commanded the largest naval fleet and the only real port of trade for international and local waters. The Shadow Court had several of the greatest leaders the nation had ever seen, and it was for this reason alone that none dared argue against its traditions and ceremonies.

These trials were but a small price to pay for a female hoping to end up on the arm of a lord as powerful as this, which was also why they were only hosted when a member of one of the Court's most notable families was concerned.

Blood. Magic. Strength. Power. Money. They were all anyone worth knowing really cared about in the Shadow Court. Such things were worth fighting for—worth dying for.

And the female who had conquered the Rite to win his hand? Oh, was she a fiery little thing. She did everything right, won every ceremony, and bested every other female in the fight for his hand. Then, when it came to marrying her, he took her hand and heart and claimed her as his own.

It wasn't until their fifth wedding anniversary that he began to feel that ugly little thing called doubt. Fae could take a long time to conceive, but her failure to produce an heir was unacceptable. If he didn't have an heir soon, his position—his very future and perhaps his bloodline itself—would be at stake. Mithrian Fae were always in one conflict or another, and denizens of the Shadow Court were always vying for more power and titles.

"Every female is tested before the Wedding Rite," the male had hissed to his wife one day as he paced the extravagant marble floor of their bed chamber. He turned to her, furious. "I was assured you were fertile. You promised me a son."

"I'm sorry," she replied while placing a delicate hand on his arm. "I am trying."

"Not hard enough." He lashed out, his backhand slamming against her cheek. His wife crumpled to the floor in an instant. The male stared at her in shock. Not just against the act he had committed, but at how much he liked it.

He hadn't meant to hit her. Not really. But it stirred something in him, filling his veins with adrenaline and lust. The smack of his hand against her cheek, the position his wife lay sprawled in as he looked down at her ... the fear in those beautiful blue eyes.

Yes, the male thought. *This would do quite nicely.* If his wife continued to fail, he would condition her until she performed adequately. He considered her a beautiful creature—it's not as if he didn't enjoy trying, but her body was only worth so much if it didn't entirely work.

"You *will* give me a child. I will have you checked by the healer weekly. And for each week you fail to achieve this task, you will be punished accordingly."

A single tear slid down the female's face. "Please, I—" She swallowed, then tried again. "I love you. I want a child, too. You know I do."

He held his hand out to her and could barely contain his excitement as she flinched at the sudden movement. But he kept his features neutral as he helped her up and tucked a strand of hair behind her ear. "Shh, my love. It's alright. I forgive you."

Her body stiffened almost imperceptibly, and she inhaled once before she straightened her shoulders and looked into his eyes. "I will do better, I promise. I will give you an heir the likes of which this Court has never seen. An heir who will change the course of history."

"Good." He nodded, pleased with the shift in attitude. "I would settle for nothing less."

The casual violence that day was one of many occurrences that would follow in the years to come. Eventually, his beloved did provide a male heir, who died in the birthing bed that very same day. The male could barely tolerate her after that, and day by day, his wife's joyous glow and bright eyes began to fade to reflect haunting loneliness and despair.

Until one day his wife produced another heir, healthy and whole.

A female.

This was an outrage that the lord could not accept. She had failed him in all the ways that counted, had made a mockery of his kindness and love.

She was punished for it for several years, until the lord deemed his child of an age to care for herself. And then, with his power and influence, he simply removed his wife from the equation. It wasn't until many years later that the lord would come to realise that his heir would, indeed, change the world, just as his wife had promised. And years later, he would understand, finally, what it was to regret.

CHAPTER ONE

'The Mithrian Fae are among the most ruthless species recorded. Unlike their elemental brethren across the seas, theirs is a race that reveres bloodshed and darker power. If you cross them on a bad day, don't expect to see another.'

The Trials and Traditions of a Mithrian Fae

I had always known I'd never outrun fate … that didn't mean I couldn't try.

Lightning forked through the sky as I made my way inch by careful inch down the rain-slick slate beneath my bedroom balcony. Thunder roiled, and a large crack made me flinch so violently I nearly lost my grip, which kept me from the precarious drop below.

My heart bashed against my ribs. I'd done the climb many times before and was no stranger to the risk, but my fingers were so cold, it was an effort to curl them into the narrow ridges of stone. My only saving grace was that it had yet to start raining. But one wrong move and this foolhardy endeavour would all be for nothing.

I had to go. My father would ship me off to Domeratt tomorrow to join a host of other would-be-wives hellbent on marrying the city lord's son—a captain of the Shadow Court's vast naval army, or so I had heard.

Frankly, I couldn't care less what the male's titles and achievements were. I had no desire to vie for his attention. Stories of how highborn Fae treated their wives in the Shadow Court had often floated past my ears. The servants in my home liked to gossip over juicy scandals and female misfortune. From their seemingly endless chatter, there was a lot of that in my homeland. When one was born into a world of immortal necromancers and dark magic wielders, one was bound to get a little more comfortable with death or other ill-fated fortunes. Hence, the abundance of misfortune that often went unchecked.

There were four courts in the Fae land of Mithria, each with their own class of magic wielders—Spell Weavers, Soul Speakers, Bone Cleavers, and Blood Mages. Though these classes were not exclusive to each court, the four belonged predominantly to the Shadow Court, the Soul Court, The Bone Court and the Blood Court, respectively. I belonged to the Shadow Court, though my magic had yet to reveal itself, but I didn't plan to be anywhere near the Shadow Court when it did.

I frowned, pressing myself flat against the stone as one of the castle servants reached out to tackle the banging shutters of a bedroom window beside me. Halfway there. Just a few more balconies to navigate and castle guards to avoid. I'd prepared myself, though. This was a climb I'd timed more than once, considering patrols, guard rotations, and any other disturbances one might find when scaling a damn building as tall as this one.

Ironic that I was the picturesque damsel locked atop my father's tallest tower. Only, he had no idea the kind of extracurricular activities I got up to when he wasn't looking. Take rock climbing, for example. Not very demure. Not very ladylike.

A slow smile spread across my face. The conditions were less than favourable, but I'd trained enough times in hazardous weather to know the grooves and footholds as well as the back of my hand. Besides, this was just the kind of challenge that made me feel *alive*. The only other time I felt like this was when tinkering with potions and brews.

Alchemy. *That* was my true passion. Something I had done under my father's nose since I was a little girl. Thanks to his courtly duties and long trips away, I'd been afforded the time to discover my skills, and I had no plans of stopping. Which was exactly why marrying some pompous noble who thought of females only as breeding vessels was not on my list of things to do.

I neared the lower levels as my fingers were turning blue with the cold, but I'd have time to lament their stiffness later. Just a little further and—I froze. Just below me, bundled up in furs and staring out from the balcony edge, was one of the ladies of court. Melania, judging by the ginger hair wisping out of her braid. And that female? The only thing she loved more than herself was money and power. Or any means by which to get it. If she spotted me…

I sucked down a breath and forced my teeth to stop chattering as I waited. All she had to do was look up. Why in the hells was she outside anyway? The winds were bitter and howling, the cold sinking deep beneath my bones. This also wasn't where her rooms were located. In fact, I was sure they belonged to … oh.

A male strode onto the balcony, gathering Melania in his arms as he turned her and claimed her lips. My body went taut. It wouldn't be any real scandal or surprise to see a noble getting cosy with another member of the court, but this was not a male whom any female had a right to covet. *That* was Declan James, Blood Sword of my father's and, more importantly, a married male. Scandal, indeed. If word got out about an affair, Melania would be finished. She would be seen as adulterous and unworthy to wed—utterly dishonoured. Declan would receive no real punishment, but that's the way it always went with the male Fae in Mithria. Bastards.

My muscles screamed as I held onto the wall for dear life, and sweat bubbled over my back, forming little rivulets that dribbled down my spine. *Please, please, just go inside and go back to bed.*

He whispered something in her ear that made her laugh and blush prettily, then he pulled her back towards his chambers. She protested coyly, and it took everything in me not to roll my eyes. I'd bet my left tit she was already naked beneath those furs.

Five steps.

Four.

Three.

Two.

I almost heaved a sigh of relief when they took one last step, their heads nearly disappearing beneath the threshold, when something changed. Maybe I'd done something to piss off the gods. Maybe it was the boot that slipped ever so slightly out of the groove it was jammed in, but right before that last step, Melania-fucking-Harron raised those pretty blue eyes and gasped as she found me staring right back at her.

She took in my clothes, the braid, the gaiter pulled up over my face, before her eyes slowly moved to my own. Recognition set in before the bitch smiled like it was the best day in her miserable little life.

Melania whispered to Declan, who looked up with piercing blue eyes of his own. He'd always given me the creeps. That male was colder than the deepest frost or the most bitter of winds. And I knew as soon as he looked at me that I was as good as dead. He swore and stepped indoors briskly, though his face remained a mask of calm.

I fucking moved, hightailing it across the wall as fast as I could go. My shot at escaping this hellhole just dropped by half, and the odds were never great to begin with. Declan was not a forgiving male, nor would he forget. He had always hated me. Even if I made it safely back to my rooms, I knew he'd eventually come for me and make it look like an accident. Maybe even pay some lowlifes to do the job for him.

My heart thumped, and my palms were slick and clammy. I could either continue down the wall and run for it, putting as much distance between me and him, or I could go back inside and find a public, populated place to lie low in, hopefully blend in and appear like nothing was out of the norm. There was no way he could harm me in plain sight of the castle patrons, even with our backwards gender laws.

I looked longingly at the ground. My future was at stake. My freedom. But what chance did I have of making it out now? If I escaped and was caught, the dishonour could cost me my life. My father would be furious with me after Declan informed him what he'd seen, but if I returned without complaint, my father wouldn't do much more. Not when the Rite was coming up tomorrow. Everything would be swept under a rug and kept hushed. Then I'd be forced to compete for a male I didn't want and a marriage that would rule me. I'd have my life, yes, but what was that really worth if I was never free?

Fuck it. I bypassed the closest balcony and continued my descent. At the same time, the heavens finally opened and rain poured down in a sudden torrent of rage. My hair was sodden within seconds, and my visibility drastically decreased.

I blinked back the water in my eyes just as Declan reappeared and nocked an arrow to a bow. My heart dropped into my stomach. He wouldn't take me out on the wall, surely? The fletching on his arrow could be traced back to him, and then where would he be? My father may not have wanted me, but he would not permit the murder of his only child. And yet that evil male looked down at me, took aim, and *smiled.* Terrible and cold, and joyful with the hunt. Oh yes, he fucking would. Perhaps he was a greater asset to my father than I'd realised. Perhaps my father would turn a blind eye for his precious Bloodhound. Declan had never liked me. Maybe covering the affair was just an excuse to shoot me down.

Declan drew back his elbow, ready to release the arrow. A scream tore from my lungs and thunder cracked in answer, swallowing any sound. I took one look at that arrow, prayed to any god who might be listening, and the second before the fletching passed through his fingers … I jumped.

CHAPTER TWO

'An acolyte's ascension determines both the class of magic and the court one is most skilled to serve. Deny the ascension, and one faces a fate worse than death.'

It was like a thousand sharp blades sliced into my skin as I hit the water. Not from the fall itself, though that alone might have killed a mortal, but from the frigid temperatures that raked over my skin like knives through butter. The breath fled my lungs as death wrapped icy fingers around my throat, hoping to claim me for herself. An involuntary gasp had me swallowing water, and then I was drowning, thrashing uselessly while all coherent thought left my brain. I sank deeper below the surface, my arms slowing as the cold made my limbs feel like stone and my head feel like pins were pricking every inch of me. Panic quickened my heart, my pulse racing against time as I dropped. But this couldn't be it. I was a good swimmer. I had spent much of my youth by the seaside to avoid my father. Cold water would *not* spell my end.

It took everything I had to collect myself and kick for the surface, to keep moving before I became a frozen husk at the bottom of the river. Just as well that it was too early in the winter for ice to have claimed the waterways, else my body would have been a broken, bloody puddle across the surface. Not that it made any difference if I couldn't get out of the water.

My muscles groaned, protesting every kick or slice of an arm through the water. It was dark down there—so very dark until a dazzling bolt lit the way. Thunder continued to roar as I broke the surface, gasping and clawing for purchase. Brindere, God of the Elements and Good Fortune, must have been looking out for me. I hadn't had the time to calculate the jump from the wall into the water, so I knew luck had to have been on my side to make it to the river. It had been a risk, but one that paid off. One that was better than the alternative.

My head was still coming to terms with the fact that Declan had fired at me. My father's blood dog had fucking fired at me like I was an enemy of the realm or an animal in need of a merciful end. If I ever made it out of here alive and saw him again, he'd have worse things to face than a scorned wife.

The rage I felt roaring through my system at the thought of Declan won out ever so slightly against the cold seizing my bones. It was enough to spur me to the riverbank, scrabbling for purchase against slippery vines or gauges in the ground— anything to help my exhausted body onto land. I'd barely made it onto firm ground, crawling and turning onto my back as I heaved and hacked wretchedly, when a sound rivalling even the thunder broke the night.

It was a horn, long and mournful, sounding my doom. The river current had taken me down only a short way, so that I was still able to glare up at the balcony where I'd fallen from. I searched for my opponents, expecting to see Declan with another arrow knocked. To my surprise, he was gone, likely having scurried off to warn my father of my disobedience and escape. But Melania … she stood there still, her hair a bright red banner blowing in the wind. I knew she was smiling, still plotting her little power schemes while I lay with my tail between my legs. I imagined she wanted me to flee, wanted to hear of my death on the run. With me gone, Melania would have nothing to worry about after all. She'd continue clinging to Declan and receiving whatever benefits he bestowed on her in turn. Honestly, a part of me couldn't blame her. Life was tough for female Fae. Unfairly so.

My gaze shifted from Melania as braziers flickered to life inside the keep's many windows, along with the odd shout of a guard. They knew. And they were coming. Fae were a vicious company to keep. Mithrian Fae were another league altogether … Especially when on the hunt. And what does one take to sniff out the prey?

Baying rent through the night, and my blood, though still slow and sluggish in my veins, drained from my already white cheeks. Speaking of bloodhounds … With wide eyes and a galloping heart, I returned my gaze to the balcony and searched the rampart for Melania one more time, who, in her cruel enjoyment, was still standing in the torrential rain. My heart quickened as she smirked wickedly and mouthed a single mocking word, *"Run."*

I turned, forcing my heavy boots to move and my weighted legs to propel me onwards. I was sodden and barely clinging to life, each step a too-heavy footfall in the mud. Good thing I was a stubborn ass, because curling up and letting the cold claim me was altogether too tempting right now. But if the Rite wasn't enough to get me running, it was the thought of those dogs ripping me to shreds should Declan find me first. Hounds were loyal creatures, and those howling from the keep followed his every whim. Death by dog was not on my to-do list for tonight either.

The woods were a twenty-metre dash across the field. Any other night, I might have thanked the rain for erasing my steps, but the ground was sludgy, sucking my soles up greedily as I fought to make my way to the darkness. Excited yips and howls burned my ears. Too slow. Too slow and feeble.

Move, Aeris!

My lungs burned, every breath a broken rasp as I hauled myself to the trees. I could climb them and lose the guards. But then, that wouldn't work. The dogs would catch my scent, and I'd be surrounded. And that's not accounting for any Spell Weavers and their dark magic. No choice but to keep moving. And I wasn't entirely without some tools of survival.

The maze of trees was a blur as I bypassed gnarled roots and thorny bushes, aiming for a familiar tree that was half-bent with age and the weight of its boughs. In its depths, nestled in a large hole that had once been the home of an indignant barn owl, was a satchel. I had buried it in anticipation of this day, adding stolen supplies day by day for when I would leave long before the Rite. But my father had taken measures to keep me close and out of trouble. The closer that day came, he'd doubled the guard and lumped me with lessons from multiple tutors to keep me too busy to leave when I'd originally planned. I'd had to dose my last tutor's tea with a sleeping draught to get away, and that tincture's effects would not last long.

I opened the satchel quickly, giving a cursory glance over the contents. Water, dried food rations, a change of clothes, precious few potions and tinctures, and knives. Blades were not my forte, but I wasn't entirely without knowledge on how to wield them. My Potions Master had been thorough in his teachings. Even if the old bastard wasn't around any longer, I knew he'd be proud that I was taking fate into my own hands. My chest seized. Another reason to leave. Another person to avenge.

Avadir had spent most of his elderly life mentoring me in the shadows. He had been more of a role model to me than my father ever was, until my dearest dad discovered us sparring one day, a forbidden activity. Avadir was quickly whisked away while the guards restrained me. My father had made me watch as four guards beat him bloody before my eyes. The sound of wet punches and crunching bones still haunted me to this day, as did the guilt. Were it not for Avadir taking me under his wing and tutoring me in all manner of things, even the ones against societal norms, he would still be here. That's what a kind male reaped in this gods-awful court. What a good and courageous male received for daring to equip a female with knowledge and skills. As if treating a female as an equal was such a loathsome act.

The barking hounds sounded closer. If I didn't make it out soon, the city guard would be alerted, and then the whole town would be on lockdown. *Fuck.* I took advantage of the canopy's shelter and slipped out of my soaked clothes into dry, warm ones as quickly as my stiff, useless fingers would allow. It wouldn't stave off hypothermia, but it was better than nothing. I felt the exhaustion set into my bones, and my vision became hazy as I blinked back flickering dots and darkening clouds. I'd heard what could happen if hypothermia set in.

Already, sharp pain was forking down my veins and firing through my nerves.

I'd be lucky if I didn't pass out within the hour. The potions I'd packed would be of no use, either. With that discomforting thought, I strapped on the knives and satchel and made haste, gritting my teeth with every painful jolt of my boots as they slapped against the mud.

There was an underground tunnel not far from here, ancient and tucked away beneath a hidden trapdoor. The passage wound beneath the castle walls and deep into the sewerage system underneath the city proper, right up to the docks. Before long, they'd be checking every ship leaving the shore if they failed to capture me now. My only hope of getting off this coastline had a very small window, but I could still hide in the city for a time if that window closed. If I made it that far.

My legs slowed, my muscles so stiff with tension and exhaustion that I stumbled into a nearby tree, scraping my jaw as I fell. Stars exploded behind my eyes, and I rolled, pain racking my senses until I could barely make out the ground from the sky.

A long howl sounded nearby. Too close. Too fucking close.

With every inch of willpower left, I forced myself to half-crawl, half-run towards that trapdoor until I swept aside the leafy debris and clenched the frame of the door. It felt impossibly heavy in my current state, but I managed to swing it open just enough for me to slip inside. I'd never been so excited to see a dank, dark passage in my life. *Freedom.* It was so close now.

I began to climb into the hole when pain exploded in my calf. I screamed, shrill and too loud for my swimming head as my body splattered into the mud. The door slammed down, shutting off my means of escape. My eyes darted down to my leg, where a bolt was nestled snugly in the flesh. The blood from the wound sluiced down my pants and into the muddied water. Yet still I was determined to get through that door, wincing and shouting as I clawed at the frame, my energy wholly spent. I tried. Until the very end, I tried, but my body was done. I collapsed into the mud, staring at the lightning still forking the sky. Declan would arrive any moment, and then I'd meet my maker. If this was the show Ryvia put on before my death, at least I'd know I went out with a bang.

Declan's dogs surrounded me, their jaws snapping, drool and saliva spitting as their gleaming teeth flashed before my face, but they remained restrained thanks to their training. One word from their master and I'd be torn to shreds, though. I blinked the rain out of my eyes as a male stood over me, casting a deeper shadow over me. My gaze travelled the legs, the strong frame, until finally I was looking into the face of my enemy.

Only, it wasn't Declan who stared down at me with a murderous glint in his eyes as thunderous and steely as the sky, but my father. And in his hand, hanging loosely at his side, was the crossbow that ensured I would never dare to dream again. Then, everything went black.

CHAPTER THREE

'A skilled herbalist is a fine friend to keep. A skilled herbalist *and* Blood Mage with healing magic? One couldn't wish for better company when travelling treacherous roads.'

An Alchemist's Guide to Herbal Remedies

"I see I haven't managed to wring the stubbornness out of you yet." My father's rich tone roused me from a state of sleep I was none too keen to wake from. Every aching muscle protested at the slightest movement, not to mention the shooting pain spearing up my leg from the arrow wound the asshole had inflicted.

But I was warm, and I was alive. No hypothermia and no confusion-addled brain. A few bleary blinks later, and I soon recognised the familiar trappings of my room through a curtain of matted golden strands hanging over my face.

Cream and gold accented dark wood furnishings that had

been hand-carved by artisans much more talented than this keep deserved. My room had always been a haven for me, but in the last few years, it had felt more like a prison with my father watching my every move around the castle. It was a good thing that a hidden passage led to the chambers where I could practise my alchemy and hide if necessary. Father didn't know about it, else he'd have destroyed all remnants of my happiness long ago. As it was, what remained was hanging on by a thread.

I licked my lips, then spied a carafe of water on the bedside table. The pain in my leg flared as I tried to sit up, only to find a heavy chain binding my wrist to the bedpost.

"Are you *fucking* kidding me?"

My father's gaze met mine, cold and unyielding. A cruel smirk tugged at the corners of his lips. "Did you really think you'd get away so easily, dearest? I must admit, your determination surprised me. I had every exit covered, expecting a final escape attempt, but I didn't think to have eyes on the walls."

"Extreme measures had to be taken, though I see now that runs in the family." I looked pointedly at my leg before glowering at him. "You could have killed me." The arrow in my leg had been removed whilst I was asleep, but a gaping, ugly wound had been left in its place. They hadn't even bothered to bandage it. *Pricks*.

He flicked his wrist impatiently. "The bolt to the leg was a calculated shot and far from life-threatening. I would do it ten times over if it meant you one day learned your place."

"And by that, you mean beneath you. Little better than a worm under your boot."

His nostrils flared, and he sighed. "You've a knack for testing my patience, Aeris, but fleeing the castle before the most important event of your life is beyond my limits. Like it or not, you *will* do your duty to this family."

"You don't need me to enter the Rite," I seethed. "You have enough wealth and power to preserve your position in this realm for many lifetimes. Why must I be bartered like paltry goods and treated like damn cattle? I am not property, Father. I refuse to be sold like it."

"That's exactly what you are, Aeris. Most females in your position would be overjoyed at the prospect of a safe and comfortable future on the arm of a powerful male. You will want for nothing. In return, I will gain everything."

The wound in my leg burned as I shifted suddenly, pulling at my restraint as I bared my teeth at my father. "Safe? That's rich, coming from the male who would send his only daughter into a viper's nest. I don't know what the Rite consists of, Father, but I do know the females who lose are never heard from again. How will you feel about losing your 'asset' then?"

He eyed me distastefully, like he was bored with this discussion. "I would be disappointed, but losing you is a risk I'm willing to take."

The words hit me like a ton of bricks. He'd always been a cold, hard male. He'd never shown me love or affection, only pain and suffering. Even now, after everything he'd done, there was a part of me that had hoped he'd one day change. Yet to hear him talk about my life so nonchalantly...

"You're a monster. Worse than a monster. It's no wonder Mother—" His knuckles cracked against my jaw before I could finish the sentence.

"Enough! You embarrass me, and you embarrass yourself. This childish notion of freedom ends today. Tomorrow, you will be shipped off to the Rite, where you will perform admirably and win Captain Windaire's hand. Disobey me or concoct any other foolish plans, and I will see you remain in chains permanently."

Blood welled from where I'd bitten my tongue, and I spat it on his pristine white shirt with a defiant grin. His blue eyes narrowed to slits as he rose and towered over me. I half expected him to strangle me then and there, but a timely knock sounded on the door.

He gave me a warning look before smoothing his hair back and straightening his shirt. "Enter."

A pretty girl strode in, curtsied to my father with practised grace, and planted her gaze firmly on the floor before him. I didn't fail to note her careful avoidance of the blood on his shirt, nor the evidence of it dribbling down my chin. "You rang for a healer? I can come back at another time if it pleases you."

"No," he said calmly, all traces of his prior rage gone. "Go about your work. See that she is unmarked. I want her to look radiant before she leaves in the morning."

She nodded. "As you wish."

He left with a final threatening glance at me. I supposed there wasn't much else to say. Not much else I would ever want to say to that gods-awful male. He had fired a bolt at his own daughter, had locked me up like a criminal and taken away any hope of me ever leading a life worth living. No, what he'd done to me was the final nail in the coffin. If I never saw him again, it would be a blessing. I would mourn the life he stole from me, but if the gods struck him down, I would not mourn him.

I'm not sure why I ever bothered to hope for a miraculous attitude adjustment. I'd been imprisoned long before he'd wrapped a physical chain around my wrist. I didn't love the male. Ever since my mother left all those years ago, and Avadir had been taken, I hadn't felt any semblance of the word at all. I was alone. Truly and utterly alone. Not that I was going to let myself drown in self-pity. I might have lost the battle today, but I was sure as shit not going to lose the war. Father wanted me to endure the Rite? Fine, I had been playing games all my life, anyway. What was another?

"Does he do that to you often?" The healer's lovely voice seemed too loud in my chamber. Too … daring. She'd be whipped or worse if anyone heard her boldness. And these walls surely had eyes and ears this night, keenly lurking and listening.

I shrugged. "Sometimes. Behind closed doors, when no one can see him for what he truly is. You could be hanged for even asking that, you know."

She smiled. "If they executed every outspoken healer, there'd be no one left to mend them. Not much use having fancy estates and positions of power if one isn't around to use them."

I smirked, then winced at the bruise already blooming under the tender skin of my face. "To need mending would require the owner of said finery dirtying their hands in the first place. That's what lackeys are for."

She snorted, rather unladylike, and bent over my leg to assess the injury. "So, what did you do to deserve this?" The flourish of her hand did not match the disgust painted on her face. "The castle is in an uproar, so I've heard whispers, but I'd like to hear it from you."

Her blonde braid tipped over her shoulder; her brown eyes focused wholly on inspecting the wound in a calculating manner. She couldn't have been much older than me, which meant she must have been very good at her work to be attending the lords and ladies of the likes of my father's status. An ambitious one. I liked that. I wondered if her powers had anything to do with it, not that healing was a common gift among my kind. Our creators were dark creatures of chaos. The goddess Ryvia delighted in the spilling of blood, not preserving it. Still, magic worked in wondrous ways, never failing to surprise with its uniqueness among individuals.

I contemplated the four courts and their classes. The healer was likely a Blood Mage, if her power had any bearing on her profession. The fact that she had no supplies on hand only supported that theory.

"I tried to fly," I answered softly. "So he clipped my wings."

She remained silent, so I watched in fascination as her hands cupped over my wound. Her lids closed, her brow furrowing as she concentrated. Red flared from beneath her palms, highlighting the veins pulsing under my skin before fading once more. When she removed her hands, the skin was as smooth as a baby's. I marvelled at her work, seemingly so effortless, but a closer look at her face showed the slightest hint of fatigue from the act.

"Incredible," I whispered. "You could change the world with a gift like that."

"Someday, I mean to," she said matter-of-factly. The brightness of her brown eyes showed she was confident of that, too. "Look, I know I'm a stranger, but I'm no stranger to the kind of treatment you receive here. I've met many girls in similar positions."

"Have you met any that came out of the Rite alive?"

The light in her eyes darkened at that. I knew before she even spoke that her answer would be no. Instead, she surprised me. "A barbaric tradition," she hissed. "One that should have been abolished long ago. One day, someone will bring about the dawn of a new age. One where the impoverished and downtrodden have the strength to stand up to their oppressors." She inspected my leg one final time before pulling the covers back over me. Then she pinned me with a fierce look. "I hope to see the day when our world will learn what equality can be, where wisdom is power and death no longer rules as the rhyme or rhythm of our existence. We may be dark wielders or necromancers, but we are so much more than that."

I stared at her a little dumbly—this confident, beautiful young female. "Wow. You should be a motivational speaker." I shook my head. "Honestly, if what you say is true, we could all use a little more of that hope."

She laughed. "We all have a voice. We just need the means to use it."

"Let's hope we get the opportunity to."

Her brow rose. "You're competing in the Rite, I take it. Why not be that person?"

I frowned. "How do you mean?"

"I mean, win that bloody competition and show those bastards that you are more than what rests between your legs. I've heard the captain is a good male. A fair one. If you marry the captain, you'll have more power than most in this province, hells, even in all Mithria. So use it."

"That's…" It was brilliant, that's what it was. And also highly improbable. "That would require winning in the first place. You're a smart female. I know I'm not the only one who noticed none of the losing Fae are ever heard from again. You can't tell me every noble house just tucks them away, never to be seen again, out of sheer embarrassment."

She pursed her lips. "No, I wouldn't presume to. There's absolutely nothing normal about what happens in the Rite or to the losing females. Which is why you're going to find out and stop it from ever happening again."

I cocked my head. "You're serious, aren't you?"

She smiled a little evilly. "Deadly."

I leaned back and contemplated. My father might have

stolen my freedom of choice, but once I was in the Rite, he had no jurisdiction or say in my actions or schemes. I didn't give a shit about marrying the captain, nor what such a position would provide, but maybe I hadn't been looking at it the right way before. Still…

"Even if I won and did marry the captain, who's to say he would listen to any of my ideas? He's still male, and ultimately, they seem to be the only ones in power in this court."

"Can I give you some advice?" The healer crossed her legs and leaned in. "I have been posted among all the courts at one point or another. There are power-hungry males in all of them. But that's why we females need to stick together. That's why we need to make a stand. Why do you think I'm so comfortable being so open with you? Why I'm not afraid of any consequences? They *need* us. Males could never survive without the fairer sex. The damn fools would tear each other apart without a voice of reason. It's my skills as a healer that make me indispensable. It's what gives me *power* over them. Find something that gives you leverage in the Rite and use it. Use them."

The healer was right. I wasn't without some skills. If I played my cards right, if I won … The cogs were already turning in my mind. These males had bartered with our lives for far too long. I refused to become another victim, lost and forgotten. There was a good chance I was never leaving the Rite … or leaving it alive, but that didn't mean I couldn't cause a little chaos along the way. And if I did? Father had only ordered me to win. He said nothing about how or what to do when I did.

I held out a hand. "I didn't catch your name, healer."

She smiled deviously. "A wiser female might not give it. My name is Dreena."

"It's a good thing, then, Dreena," I said as she shook my hand, "that we're only as wise as the company we keep."

Her laughter tinkled like a bell. "You remind me of someone, you know. A good friend of mine. Someone I believe will do great, terrible things."

I tipped my head, pleased with the comparison. "To changing the world, Dreena."

She swiped a finger over my jaw, healing the bruise there in an instant. "To great and terrible things."

CHAPTER FOUR

'There is no public record pertaining to any Rites, past or present, nor to the names of those who participated in them. The identities and fates of all but the winning females remain unknown.'

The Trials and Traditions of a Mithrian Fae

There was no polite way to put it. Travelling by cart was a bitch. The pace was slow, and the carriage they'd stuffed me in was windowless and dreadfully boring. A small candlelit sconce lit up the interior, but I would have much preferred to see the world as it passed me by. Instead, I was stuck, chained, no less, to a fucking nanny.

Roslin was my attendant, actually, but she may as well have been a babysitter. She hadn't even minded when they'd stuck a chain around her wrist linking me to her. At her ripe old age, I supposed she wasn't spared any indignities.

"You're going to love the castle," she prattled on, her withered hands tucked into her lap. Her wavy grey hair was tucked back in a neat bun, her gown a simple shift. The tight bun and sombre grey of her dress did little to hide the paleness of her white, leathery skin. "It overlooks the sea, with a view of all the grand ships docked in the Soul Court's base."

Unsurprisingly, Roslin was excited about my admission into the Rite. I would never understand her acceptance of the way females were treated in this world. My father had looked after her, though—even given her some semblance of finery—and it was perhaps for those reasons that she remained so loyal to him. She had never protected me from his wrath and had even punished me herself multiple times when I was a child. She often seemed to enjoy it. Perhaps she thrived on fleeting dominance. But as far as I was concerned, she enjoyed being oppressed.

"Any view is better than my current one," I said, looking at the four walls.

"It's for your own good," she admonished. "We can't be too careful with you." Roslin clicked her tongue. "Climbing the castle walls and such. No wonder your father, Lord Lockhart, kept you under such a tight leash all these years! Not tight enough, if you ask me."

There was no point trying to explain why I would have done anything to escape. She had never understood and wasn't about to now. "Can I ask you a question, Roslin? Do you think my father respects you?"

"An impertinent question," she said. "But if you must know, yes. I have looked after you and your father for many years now. He trusts me. We're like family."

I sighed. That couldn't be further from the truth. "If only you knew how one-sided that loyalty is. Roslin, please. You could help me before it's too late. Before my father throws me to the wolves." My voice rose in desperation. "I might die in there!"

She was silent for a moment, her eyes searching my face as she considered. But then she levelled me with a look that made my heart fall. "Participating in the Rite is an honour. One you don't deserve."

Gods, she was evil. Always had been. And maybe it was the pain and suffering I'd felt from her hands all these years or the frustration of my current predicament but I couldn't help it as I said, "You want to know why my father will never give two shits about you? He doesn't respect you because: A) you have the indecency to have different genitalia to him, therefore making you the lesser sex, and B) you are a peasant living in a world of pompous asses. He considers you the help, Roslin, not part of the family."

Her cheeks blazed, her sharp nose turning up. The slightest hint of dark magic flared black at her fingertips, gone as quickly as it came as she composed herself. "Rude girl. You won't gain the captain's heart with that kind of behaviour."

I rested my unbound hand on my cheek. "Oh? And what do you know about the captain?" I didn't know much about him, but then again, I was never one for castle gossip and had never cared to ask.

At this question, Roslin brightened, shifting her bony ass on the cushion-lined seat beneath her. "*Well.* I have heard he is quite handsome. Not even you will be able to deny that, Aeris. He's also an excellent swordsman and has a knack for strategy and warfare, as his position requires. He is, of course, a skilled mariner."

"So he's an overachiever, then," I stated. "And did his dear old daddy pave the way with bribery and coin, or did the captain earn his position himself?"

Roslin pursed her lips. "The captain went through his

training like every other soldier. He's very regimented." She scooted closer and folded her hands primly in her lap once more. "Apparently, he's rather fond of reading and sketching. I've heard he loves animals, too. Especially his hounds."

Okay, gossip or not, I could work with this. It wouldn't hurt to learn all I could about the captain. Information was like bargaining chips. Still, every other female would be angling for the same thing. I was hoping for more personal interests, but what did I expect, really?

"What next? He loves long walks on the beach? This isn't going to help me win any favour, Roslin."

"Oh, ungrateful girl! But I suppose you will need every advantage if *you're* going to win, and winning helps your father." She pursed her lips again, which aged her at least a decade, but her frown lines quickly relaxed back into excitement. "Okay, keep those ears open because this one's a goodie." She looked around like some lurking gossipmonger might spread the news any second … like someone was going to jump out from the blankets in a neat pile in the corner.

"Waiting with bated breath," I said with a poor attempt at cheer.

"He lost his mother recently. It's said she died of the sudden onset of sickness, but no one really knows what happened to her. And that's not even the interesting part."

I must admit, she had my attention. I leaned closer. "Go on."

Roslin grinned. "I'm friends with the castle cook at Domeratt, whose family has been cooking for the Windaire family for generations now. He says Lady Windaire was taken in the night and whisked away to an asylum, and says only Lord Windaire and his trusted advisors know where it is. The servants are all getting excitable trying to guess how mad she is. What rubbish." She rasped a low laugh and shook her head.

"Incredible, the kind of stories these bored old servants will concoct. If Lord Windaire says she died, then the poor female died, and that's the end of it."

Indeed. Only, this wasn't the first time I'd heard a story like this. The first part, anyway. My own mother disappeared rather suddenly when I was little. There one day and gone the next. The difference being that I was told she left my father of her own will. Not that she died or was mysteriously whisked away in the night, but that she had simply chosen to escape that pitiful excuse of a male she called husband and abandoned her daughter in the process.

Interesting … and certainly worth noting. "Do you know of any asylums Lady Windaire might have been taken to?"

Roslin's eyes crinkled in thought. "There are some facilities throughout the court, but if someone of noble blood was staying in one, you can be sure the news would have spread. No, it's just a silly rumour, girl. Nothing more."

Rumour or not, I tucked that little kernel away for later. Perhaps it would come in handy down the line. "You've been most helpful, Roslin. Thank you." I meant it, too. Which must have come as a shock because the old girl was giving me a suspicious once-over.

"I know that look. What are you plotting, Aeris?"

I winked and made a show of looking around the carriage. "Oh, just the usual. Escape and freedom." It wasn't entirely a lie. I was always hunting for ways to escape, and being at the Rite would be no different. Only this time, I was also looking for answers. Answers that the captain may very well be seeking, too, given the disappearance of his mother.

Roslin gave me a disapproving look before shaking her head. "Honestly, child, how your father has put up with you all these years is beyond me."

"I could say the same thing," I grumbled.

She released a long, world-weary sigh and lay her head against the wall.

"Oh, lighten up, Ros, we've a long way to go and this carriage is awfully small." I lay against the cushions and closed my eyes, still smiling. I might not be getting out of this box anytime soon, but when I did, I wouldn't miss the nanny. Not for a second.

A jolt of the carriage had me lurching awake with a start. I grumbled, wiping the drool off my face with the back of my sleeve, before glancing at Roslin. Fast asleep and snoring her head off as the carriage trundled to a stop. Well, it seemed tomorrow was already here. *Fuck.* I wasn't the slightest bit ready for what lay in wait … which was gods only knew what.

Would they throw me into an actual vipers' nest? Would the females in this dreadful contest be forced to fight in a pit, swords and shields and bloody murder? Or would this be more of a beauty pageant with bitchy gossiping and a handful of nails to the eye? I wasn't sure which was worse. Actually, yes, I was. The bitchy nobles, definitely. I'd take the swords or vipers any day. Better yet, the vipers could fend off the bitchy nobles. Now that would be a sight to see.

With that comforting notion in mind, I smoothed out my dress, rolled my neck, and took a deep breath. The carriage came to a stop, followed by the voices of various males floating back to me through my cubic prison.

"This is it. The beginning of the end," I whispered.

The door swung open, revealing a male dressed in crisp, cream slacks and a white shirt with an insignia of a sea serpent wrapping around a sword embroidered on the chest. He was handsome, in an altogether too clean kind of way, with a shaved face, slicked-back blond hair, and green eyes. But it was his smile that captured my attention. Too big, too … trying.

"My Lady," he said with a bow. "Welcome to Castle Windaire. I trust your journey here has been a comfortable one?"

I raised the wrist, still tethered by chains to Roslin's resting arm, which dangled rather comically from the movement. "Exceptionally. A freeing experience."

The servant didn't bat an eye. "I'm so glad to hear it. And I'm so very sorry."

My nose crinkled. "Whatever for?"

"For what comes next." He stepped to the side, and I hardly had time to let out a pitiful squeak when two large goons rushed forward and shoved a pungent bag over my head, causing me to fall backward into the carriage where Roslin startled awake. There was no air for screaming. No thought for escaping. As the smelling salts filled my nose and mouth, there was only oblivion, which took me gently in her arms.

CHAPTER FIVE

'Precious little is recorded on the Waifling. These vicious creatures hunt in packs and live in dark, quiet locales. It is said they are blind, though I wouldn't test the theory.'

Hunters of Mithria: Volume I

Darkness. Impenetrable darkness and a cold, hard floor greeted me as I came to. As was becoming all too common lately, my head throbbed, rattling my skull as I slowly sat up. The faintest aroma of smelling salts still lingered in my nose, the hairs in my nostrils all but burnt after those thugs had knocked me out. At least the servant had been polite enough to ask how the journey was. *What a lovely gentlemale.*

My lungs swelled as I inhaled deeply. The air was musty and dank, like someone had closed the door on this place and never looked back. My knees wobbled as I reached out, bracing myself against a stone wall. Cobwebs clung to the callouses on my skin and wrapped around fingertips, forming gloves of dirt and dust. The grooves in the stone beneath my palm were somehow reassuring. Every line and indent, every crack, was an ode to the brokenness in my heart. Because I was here, in this dark orifice of hell, instead of sailing the seas to a wider world beyond this nightmare continent and its warmongering Fae.

A piercing shriek echoed off the walls, causing the hairs on my neck to stand on end. Goosebumps prickled my skin as every nerve jumped to attention. Another scream followed, this one farther away. It wasn't a stupid prank or a playful initiation. It had to be the Rite. *Silly me, thinking we'd start small by trying to woo the captain. But nope. Those screams weren't the good kind.*

Panic flared as self-doubt crept in thick and fast. I wasn't just fighting for the captain's hand; I was fighting for my life. The revelation was incredibly stupid, given my circumstances. I'd been so fixated on *where* the losing females were taken once the competition ended that I hadn't considered *how* they might be transported. Dark Fae didn't do body bags or coffins. We burned our dead to protect our souls from Bone Weavers who might reanimate our corpses, or worse still, the *aimless*—creatures desperate for even a lick of magic. Having our magic consumed by those things was not a fate I would wish on anyone, and certainly not something I'd like to be on the receiving end of, even if I wasn't alive to feel it. Gods only knew what it meant for a dead one's soul in the afterlife.

A shiver slithered down my spine before the discomfort coiled around my gut and constricted, leaving me slightly breathless. I was so woefully unprepared for this and, for once, it wasn't a comfort to know there were others in my position. Not when lives were at stake.

I needed to move. Whatever the circumstances, I was alive, and I damn well liked my body in one piece and breathing. Gritting my teeth, I held my hands out, edging around the room for any hint of furniture or something I could use as a weapon. Nothing. A growl of frustration escaped my lips. *Okay. Breathe. What would Avadir do? He'd tell me a weapon was an extension of myself. That I was the real weapon.* And, fair, I wasn't entirely without skills. He'd probably also tell me to pull my finger out and fucking *move*, which was entirely valid.

I pulled a couple of pins from my hair and ran a finger along their edges. Sharp, but they would only serve so well if a real threat approached. My muscles were stiff, my jaw locked, so I rolled my neck and loosened my bones, shaking myself out like a dog.

"You've got this."

The wall was my constant companion as I brushed one palm along the cold stone. If the room they'd dumped me in was bare, I'd hazard a guess that the underbelly of this place was much the same everywhere. Some kind of prison or maze, if the unending passages were anything to go by. I just had to keep the wall on my left and keep fucking moving. Eventually, I'd make my way out … unless someone or something found me first. I pushed the thought away and continued moving.

Soft, Fae lights flickered on suddenly, lighting up the path every ten metres or so. The green light was so dim, I could barely see several feet in front of me, but it was better than the pitch black of before.

I kicked off the pathetic slippers I'd been ordered to wear. I'd be much more comfortable barefoot and quiet. Not that my flowing chiffon gown made that easy. All was still, not a sound to be heard within the dark depths but for the gentle whisper of my dress along the ground. I rolled my eyes suddenly at the irony. I was so glad my father had the maids buff my skin raw, style my long blonde hair to coiling perfection and puff the ever-living hell out of my face with powder for this. I huffed. Bastard probably knew this was coming and had a little laugh with the other soulless ghouls who ran this archaic tradition.

In the silence, I noticed the sound of another's feet finding their way in the dark. The steps increased in frequency and volume as their bearer ran frantically closer to where I stood. I wanted to scream at them to stay quiet, to keep still, but the sound of heavier steps became clear behind the smaller ones. Something large chased the girl, its claws intermittently scraping against stone.

A scream ruptured the silence moments after, as what sounded like two bodies collided. My pulse raced as it died just as quickly as it began. Something growled, and then a gurgling filled the air. I squeezed my eyes shut, pressing against the stone to make myself small as I waited for what happened next.

The dark made it difficult and disorienting to know what was happening. All I saw was the rush of a shadow, followed by a sound I could only describe as *ripping*. I put a hand over my ears. It was all I could do to shut out the sound and swallow the whimper rising in my throat. But I still heard the bones crunch and flesh tear. This time, I did gag ever so slightly before I clamped my hands over my mouth.

The creature stopped its feast, followed by a slight rumble in its throat to inform me of its shifted attention and gradual approach. Tears filled my eyes, my stomach clenching in fear. I had no idea what it was or what it could be. I had no idea how to defend against it or if I even stood a chance of fending it off. But as the seconds passed and I remained standing, it led me to believe this thing was either blind or simply curious. If it couldn't see, then it would be able to track its prey another way. Regardless, I was still royally fucked with no clue what to do or where to go.

Slowly, I slid down the wall, moving carefully in the opposite direction of the creature as it searched for me. I took another painstaking step and was suddenly affronted by warmth pooling between my toes. I realised I had crept to the dead female's blood. I put a searching hand out to check if she was alive, and was immediately sickened. This thing had destroyed her so thoroughly, it felt like she was becoming one with this place, seeping into the very cracks in the floor.

An idea came to me as I considered how animals tracked prey. The idea made me sick, and I wanted to cry as I carefully scooped her blood and smeared it over my face, my hair and my dress. It wasn't enough to completely mask my scent, but it might be enough to confuse it. The heady scent of iron hit me, but I didn't dare breathe as the creature sniffed and—

Nothing happened.

Gods, it worked! The creature couldn't find me. I was no longer a breath of life to snuff out, but a mask of death it had already discarded. A blooming decay of a freshly caught meal. I felt its hot breath huff over my face, startling me with how close it was suddenly, and I clenched my nails together, forcing myself to become a living statue. I refused to die down here, shredded into a forgotten tapestry of death.

It felt like an age, but eventually the thing snuffled and returned to gorging on the female. I waited, still and silent, until even the creature grew tired of its catch and sauntered off in search of other prey.

I remained still for minutes until I was certain it was gone. When I was sure, a gasp shuddered out of me, then tears fell, hot and heavy. My chest heaved, and my body trembled with shock and disgust. My cheeks were too warm, too taut, as if a blanket was suffocating me, like I couldn't breathe as I wore the female's blood as a second skin. I didn't know how long I stayed like that, too stricken to move. I was horrified at the thought that there might be more than one creature. Would this death paint work on another? I didn't want to test it.

"Don't give up. Not now," a voice whispered in the darkness.

I flinched, raising my pins like little swords as I shifted into a crouch with my back against the wall. The shape of a body appeared, though I couldn't make out her face. "Don't come any closer," I warned.

"If I wished to hurt you, I'd have done so already." Her tone was matter-of-fact, if slightly amused. "I'm simply curious to hear how you survived that thing."

"Morbidly," I replied. "And I'm not sure 'simple' applies to our current predicament, but you're welcome to stick around and find out."

She laughed a little awkwardly. "You're feisty, for a lord's daughter."

I stiffened. "Says the female laughing after another was just brutally murdered."

"You're right, I'm so sorry. I, ah—I laugh when I get nervous. And say stupid things." At my silence, the female cleared her throat and continued. "A terrible trait, I know. But I'd very much like to stay alive, if you can see where I'm going with this?"

The tension in my muscles eased. Socially awkward females, I could deal with. But placing my trust in others was not natural for me. I'd made the mistake before and been burned for it. Who's to say she wouldn't stab me in the back the moment it was turned? Or that she wasn't pretending to play nice? I was her competition after all.

I realised she had been so light on her feet that I hadn't sensed her approach. Quiet and calm ... Perhaps she could be useful. But her scent gave her away. Jasmine and sandalwood, with something light and playful lacing the top. Blissful, and entirely too noticeable. I sighed. I wasn't in a trusting mood, but I had already witnessed—in all bodily ways except for sight—someone else's death. I wasn't in the mood to be around for another.

"They're blind. Stay quiet and keep still, and you'll be fine. Also, your scent gives you away. You'll need to, um, mask it."

"Mask it? With what? There's no mud or … *Oh!*" I heard her take a step and slip slightly on the stone … or rather, the blood coating it. Then it dawned on her. "Oh."

I cringed. "I'm not a monster, I swear."

"Better to become a monster than the meat," she said after a pause. Somehow, that made the ice in my bones thaw a little. The survival instinct was oddly grounding. "I'm Sherai, by the way. I wish we were meeting under better circumstances, but here we are."

"Aeris," I offered. There was no harm in a name, and if we got out of here, she'd learn it soon enough anyway. I didn't bother to wipe my tears as I shuffled to the blood. "Come. I'll help you." She squatted beside me, and the warmth radiating off her small frame was admittedly comforting. "I'm sorry for this."

I dipped my fingers into the blood to smear it over her cheeks. This close, I could see the outline of her face and feel the angles and curves as my fingertips swept over her cheeks. She was beautiful. Bow lips, high cheekbones, arched brows. Her frame was delicate and feminine. But then, I'd expected most, if not all, of the females in this competition to be pretty. It would be an insult to our overbearing fathers to be anything less.

"It's still warm," she said softly.

"Try not to think about it. That female is gone now. We're still standing."

"Didn't think my first friend here would be made while finger painting like some crazy blood ritual," the female said, a little lighter.

Gods, her sense of humour was dry, which was kind of perfect for our current situation. I couldn't help but grin. "Honestly? I didn't think I'd meet anyone friendly at all. We're all here for the same reason." I added under my breath, "Mostly." She didn't say anything to that, so I finished up my work and sat back on my haunches. "You're good to go. We should probably get out of here in case there are more of those things stalking these halls. They might come back to continue snacking."

"You know, we now have the smell of their lunch on us, right? Are you sure this is the way to go?"

I shrugged. "It worked the first time. Besides, there's a difference between something fresh and hot and blood that's turning foul. Let's get moving. I guess we'll find out on the way."

We stalked through the dark at a snail's pace, me with a hand on the wall, her with a hesitant hand clasped over my arm. Surprisingly, her presence was a comfort. Her steady breathing kept me hyper-focused as my ears strained for any sound and my eyes blinked back at the unending dark for even a hint of light to guide us. The occasional scream or howl rang out somewhere distant, making Sherai hold on tighter. My heart would race again, but nothing ever came of it, so we pushed on.

We walked for some time until soft snarls broke out ahead of us. A squabble of some sort between not one but two or three of the creatures, from what we could tell. I grabbed Sherai's hand and we flattened against the wall. They fought for a time, the occasional sound of flesh ripping the only time their growls and grunts halted.

"What do we do? They're right in the middle of the path," Sherai whispered in my ear.

Indeed. But we couldn't go back. There was nothing to return to, and there was no knowing if anyone would come for us. I guessed that anyone who didn't make it out would be eaten alive or left to rot. "We have to keep going. We'll never leave this place if we don't. If we can't get through quietly, we just run, okay?" Her body shivered beside mine, so I squeezed her hand reassuringly. "Trust me."

We advanced cautiously, padding along on tiptoes while the beasts ranted and raged, fighting over whatever trappings of 'meat' they'd landed on. Whomever they were fighting over hadn't stood a chance. Hells, our odds of getting through were slim at best.

If only my powers had decided to show their face. I hadn't mastered them. Hadn't been able to flick that switch inside that allowed my true form to come to light. My mother used to tell me I'd be powerful—that my bloodline meant I was destined for great things, but she couldn't have been more wrong. My magic had not awoken, and I failed to see it doing so now. Avadir, as much as I'd loved the old boy, was the only other person who'd come close to setting them free. But he was gone now, and the progress I'd made when attempting to wield with him had long receded into the dark depths of my mind and soul. My ribs were a cage, binding that essence in tight, keeping them trapped beneath the surface. Perhaps it was for the best. I'd only ever had my wits to rely on and that had been just fine … for the most part.

"I don't suppose you can wield?" I asked Sherai in a low voice.

"Um … not well," she admitted. "I'm from the Soul Court

anyway. I don't think reading fates or prophesying will be of much help here."

"Unlikely. Onwards, then."

My nose crinkled at the offending stench of blood and entrails as we crept forward. I held my breath, pressing up against the wall once more and sliding sideways. I almost gasped as something flicked against my leg—a tail, I realised. It whacked against my skirts, and I stood there, mortified, until the beast moved unbothered and I was free to continue. The creature in question must have made a bold claim on the body because the other two growled suddenly, followed by fresh chaos as the three clashed together again in violent delight.

It happened so fast. Claws scraped against stone, the smell of death and decay ripe in the air as fangs gnashed and giant bodies bounded around the space. It was instinct, perhaps some kind of sixth sense, that told me to duck as a mouth full of razor teeth sliced through the space I'd been standing. It didn't stop the claw that sank into my shoulder, though. Blazing heat seared through me, like a lance of molten fire. And still I did not scream. Sherai grabbed me as I faltered. We stumbled out of the fray and into quiet solitude as we crept far enough away to take a breath. Only then did I let myself hiss in pain and slide to the ground. Nausea bubbled in my stomach, and the darkness spun a little, making it even more dizzying and disorienting.

"We can't stop Aeris. We have to keep moving."

The girl was a goddamn taskmaster. Couldn't I have a second to heave in peace? "I just … need a … moment," I wheezed.

I felt the movement as Sherai shook her head. "You don't understand. Your blood is in the air now. They have your fresh scent!"

I froze. My scent … Godsdammit. One body between three creatures was little more than an appetiser, so the promise of another one would be driving them mad. The second they finished with their entrée, they'd be ready for the main meal … Which meant they'd be after us any—

Howls and roars and bloodcurdling growls. The sounds of a twisted hound catching the scent. I jumped to my feet, ignoring the stabbing pain in my shoulder. "Run. Fucking run, Sherai!"

To her credit, she didn't immediately sprint to safety and leave me behind. Instead, she pulled on my good arm and practically dragged me along as she hauled ass. Each step was agony as the wound in my shoulder jolted. A bolt of electricity, striking again and again until I was cradling my arm and biting my lip so hard I drew blood.

"I see light!" Sherai called breathlessly. "There, at the end of the tunnel!"

I'd never been happier to see anything in my life. Pain be damned, I was getting the hells out of this place. The thought of freedom egging us on, we increased our pace. I gritted my teeth as blood dribbled down my gown, spattering the lilac silk and chiffon with artful drops as we ran. Not long now and we'd be out of here. So close, so—

A dash of movement, and I was knocked off my feet. I tumbled to the ground, my shoulder barking in pain as I hit the stone hard. My gown ripped, the delicate strap snapping, and the bodice tore halfway down.

Brown hair fell into my face, and I spat it out of my mouth in disgust, realising it was indeed *hair*, not fur. The light was bright enough now that I could vaguely make out a female's features as she lifted her head and glared down at me. And oh, she was not happy. Perhaps not even sane, judging by the crazed look in her eyes.

She shrieked and raised something sharp and curved into the air. A blade? No, a bone. That was a fucking Fae bone she was about to impale me with. And by the looks of how pale and clean it was, it had been down here for some time. Gods, how many females had died in this place? I was wrong. We weren't in a maze. We were in a fucking crypt.

The air whooshed out from between my teeth as I grabbed her hand and curled my fingers, clenching my nails deep into her skin. The bone lowered, the makeshift blade dropping dangerously close to my eye.

I couldn't even call for help, not as I dared a split-second glance at Sherai, who was battling her own attacker.

Gods help us, we were not one day into the Rite and females were already turning murderous. Is this really what we were reduced to? A pack of starved dogs in a wild frenzy as they battled over the only prey? I knew what wild things did when cornered. Kick a dog enough, and eventually it loses itself to basic survival instincts. It bites, it mauls, and it tears its attacker apart.

The captain wouldn't know what hit him. Or maybe he would revel in the brutality of this game. The basic instincts and the primal hunger that lived in all of us. And yet, the thing about the circle of life is that there's always something stronger. Always a bigger fish. And today that fish was me.

I pushed all my energy into my core, twisting her hand just enough to slip out of harm's way. The bone struck the stone where my head had been, and she hissed as I twisted and punched her in the throat. She uttered a strangled cry as she choked, her hands grasping at her windpipe. The creatures could be heard down the tunnel, no doubt curious about our tussle. I didn't hesitate to grab the makeshift bone knife, but I did freeze as I looked down into her eyes. Wide and green and not full of anger or hate, but … fear. She was afraid, and fear made people do irrational things. I couldn't bring myself to slide the knife home. It would have been so easy to slip it beneath her ribcage, to angle it just so. A mercy, even, compared to the beasts that prowled this place. Or I could be the bigger person. I could reach out my hand.

"I'm not going to hurt you," I said softly. "We can leave this place together."

Some of the feral glassiness in the female's eyes left, a look of relief easing her features, but then she glanced over my shoulder, and that fear came right back.

"Aeris."

The name was a garbled plea, and I looked to find Sherai in a rear chokehold from the female behind her. The look in that one's eyes? That was altogether different. Determination and indifference. *She* was not someone to cross, but I took one look at the hopelessness in Sherai's eyes and knew I'd stop at nothing to get her out of here.

"Let her go," I said slowly. Authoritatively.

To my surprise, the female listened. She bared her teeth, her brows raising ever so slightly as she took in a second threat. "Aeris?" she asked. "Aeris Lockhart?"

Alarm bells rang inside my head as she cocked her head, her lips thinning as she seemed to look at me in a new light. Well, that was comforting. I didn't let her see my concern. Not as I grinned and saluted her. "The one and only."

Her eyes narrowed, and she shifted her stance. The female barely spared my weapon a second glance. No, this one was certainly no stranger to combat. I adjusted my own stance, lifting my weapon, ready to lunge if necessary.

I'd shifted my focus so completely onto the females that I forgot about the very thing we'd each been running from. A massive shape leapt from the darkness. I saw it from the corner of my eye and frantically spun, shifting out of the way as it landed on the female behind me. She screamed, the sound immediately silenced as the creature found her throat and ripped the whole thing out.

In the light, I finally saw what it was we'd been trying to escape. It was a monstrosity. Patchy brown fur, milky eyes, and a maw full of rows upon rows of rotting brown fangs. It resembled something akin to a wolf, but twisted, somehow. As if even the gods couldn't work out how to finish making it. The grizzly head turned, and even blind, those eyes met mine, as if seeing into my soul. There was a sound further back down the tunnel, and I knew it had to be the other two beasts on their way.

I glanced at Sherai, at the door looming just out of reach, then back to my opponent, silent and watchful. She grinned slowly as she caught my stare, and I knew there was no getting out of this. Not with a beast on both sides.

There was only one option. I looked at Sherai again, trying to convey my plan, and miraculously, she dipped her head almost imperceptibly back. This was it. The last mad dash. Without waiting, I threw the bone blade at the female's feet, who hissed as the weapon clattered loudly in the silence. The beast roared, thundering past me as I squashed my body against the wall before launching back into a run.

Sherai bolted at the same time, and we grabbed for each other's hands, sprinting as hard as our legs would carry us. Golden light spilled out from the cracks around the door frame. It groaned and clanked as we slid the bolts back and hefted the heavy thing with all our might.

Behind us, snarls and the female's shouts broke out. I could only imagine how that struggle was going, but I couldn't afford to turn back. Finally, the door widened enough for us to slip through, and then we were almost falling over ourselves in the rush to get in and get the door shut. We'd just about got the unbelievably heavy door closed again when a bloody hand grabbed the frame and shoved with surprising strength. I grunted, my shoulder too spent to put any more weight into the task, and a moment later, the female slipped through the crack, helping to close the door forever on the beast on the other side.

We slid the bolts home, and I had a momentary thought of whether we'd just sealed any other females left inside forever. But I was too afraid to risk leaving the door unbolted, even if it was ridiculously heavy.

The beautiful female who'd attacked us turned around and smiled with bloodied canines. "Welcome to the Rite, ladies. May the best female win."

CHAPTER SIX

'Sea Serpents, while majestic and mystical beasts, should be given a wide berth at all times. If you come across one, the chances are you'll be dead within minutes. Steer clear and never underestimate their power. Alone, they are mighty, but in groups, they are unstoppable.

Hunters of Mithria: Volume I

Fifty females had originally participated in The Rite. Sherai and I had learned that after being escorted from the underground passage into what appeared to be an opulent sitting room. Having come from the dark and dingy dungeon we'd awoken in, the place seemed overly bright, with its merry fire crackling away and numerous velvet chaises dotting the room. But it wasn't the furniture that piqued my interest, nor even the occasional female in mirrored disarray to my own ghastly appearance. It was the gilt-framed mural spanning the length of the room, nestled comfortably above the fireplace.

Fifty female portraits adorned the parchment, each detailed with names, bloodlines and titles. And of those 50, 12 portraits had violent red lines gauged through the middle. It didn't take a mastermind to understand why. It was clear that fewer than 50 females stood in the room.

I glanced across the room at the female who'd tried her hand at killing Sherai and me. She watched me from her position by the window, her blue eyes shining with the promise of death. Despite the blood splattering her slim frame, she still seemed put together, with her glossy raven hair and perfect poise. I wondered what her father had promised should she win the Rite. Or if the ambition—the violent determination—was all her.

There were others dotted around the room who seemed cloaked in that same darkness, but mostly the other females looked shocked and utterly devastated. All were beautiful in their own way. And all were decidedly alive. Fighters. Survivors. If tonight had proved anything, it's that we were all capable of brutality when our lives were at stake. I supposed that was part of the point.

Had the hosts of tonight's delightful entertainment been watching us this whole time? Laughing as we fumbled in the dark or fell to teeth and claws? I bet they gambled on our lives, too. Like we were simply horses in a multi-round race to the finish. The thought sent white-hot rage roaring through me. I was a number to them. Not a name or an identity but a price tag. My life was meaningless to these people. And yet, there were females in this room who would still do whatever it took to gain the captain's hand.

Was the male part of all this? Was he watching, too? So much of The Rite was steeped in mystery. I swallowed back the bile rising in my throat. It was sick. *Vile.* And if I ever made it out of here and was forced to marry that bastard? I'd kill him the very same night. Such violent thinking, but it brought an idea to mind. A very dangerous, very reckless thought. The more I dwelled on it, the more room it took up until the roots of something bigger began to take place. So, as I sat against the wall beside a tired Sherai, her head drooping with every passing second, I began to plot. Her face eventually plopped onto my good shoulder. The closeness was uncomfortable at first—or rather, allowing my guard to drop so thoroughly was—but I let her sleep. She'd proven an ally tonight. For now, that was enough.

I shifted slightly, studying the female as I gently cradled her head down to rest on my leg. She snored lightly, a little bit of drool escaping her full lips. She was even prettier than I'd thought. Beneath the blood, her skin was smooth and brown, and her long hair was tawny and coiled. Her ancestors might have been among the first Fae who'd sailed centuries ago across the Strait of the Sea Serpent—a stretch of water named for the deadly scaled beasts that frequented those depths—and found themselves in the Shadow Court. I found my thoughts drifting, streaming through unconscious musings about such places.

Most Fae avoided those waters for obvious reasons. They'd claimed countless ships that now rested in pieces at the bottom of the ocean. Pirates and other unscrupulous sorts still tried their luck from time to time—a calculated, if rather stupid, attempt at ferrying black market goods or, worse, slaves, from port to port. No one would dare attempt such a thing around Domeratt, though. The city soldiers and the captain's naval officers kept a close eye on all ships coming and going from their docks. The city had come a long way since olden times, of course, but the great passage from the Fae of old was still a feat continually respected and admired.

I recalled stories told of the battles waged between the Shadow Court Fae and those of the western lands. Numbers were lost on both sides, until a pact was eventually formed and the Yuranai tribes were given lands and titles worthy of their proud people. Now, the descendants of those Fae were seen all over Mithria, though many remained in the Shadow Court and populated the seafaring capital of Domeratt, where I now found myself.

My tentative ally snorted loudly, startling herself awake and cutting through my stream of consciousness. "What?" she asked, alarmed. She sat up straight. "What's happening?"

I smiled. "You're safe. We're inside the castle."

She sagged in relief and wiped her mouth, her cheeks reddening as she quickly shifted off me. When she was settled with her back against the wall beside me, her eyes moved around the room, falling on the female who'd tried to kill us underground. "I won't feel truly safe until we're long gone from this place."

"Didn't realise what you signed up for?"

"Didn't sign up in the first place," she corrected.

"Ah." I ran a hand through my matted, bloodied hair and grimaced. "Let me guess, your father forced you into this mess against your will?"

She frowned. "Aunt, actually. My parents are dead."

My heart panged a little. "I'm sorry."

Sherai shrugged. "Don't be. They died when I was young. My aunt is cruel and cold, but she's looked after me all those years when she could have thrown me to the wolves."

"So, she offered the bare minimum of common decency, then." Sherai looked away, and I realised I'd struck a nerve.

"Sorry," I said. "I'm not very good at this. My father made it a habit to … remove anyone I ever got close to."

She looked at me and smiled tentatively. "We have that in common. And really, I should be thanking you. You could have left me back there. You had the opportunity to run when you had that knife; instead, you stood up for me. It's likely you've now painted a target on your back with stabby pants over there."

I chuckled as I glanced at the female in question, who seemed to sense the attention and made a point of hissing and showing me her canines. "Stabby pants would have made her mark eventually. That one doesn't care about the sanctity of life or others. She sees only obstacles in her way. Be careful around her, Sherai. We are never safe in a place like this."

Sherai considered for a moment. "In the crypt, when she said your name … she seemed to know you. Or know of you. But you didn't seem to know her. What's that about?"

I grimaced. "I have no idea. But I'm betting nothing good."

Sherai nodded at a mural I'd been studying earlier. "A rather macabre piece, don't you think? What do you make of it?"

"I think," I said slowly, "that the first test we survived was just a taste of what's to come. I think I'm happy to have an ally moving forward."

"An ally," Sherai said with a nod. "And a friend?" The tone of her voice lifted at the latter, almost like she was asking for confirmation.

"Sure." I smiled and, for the first time in a while, the notion felt genuine. Natural. I held out a hand. "Friends."

She took it tentatively with hands that were soft and smooth, and relatively clean. It felt like a sin, somehow, to take that innocence in my bloodstained hands. Gods only knew what the other females thought of us right now. I'm sure we looked quite gruesome, with our faces painted scarlet. Our battle armour, of sorts. A mask to hide the real fear that lingered beneath. Because, as comforting as it was to have a friend in this place—to know I wasn't alone—I couldn't ignore the portraits that had been struck out on the wall. And to know that there was a very real possibility that I could be next.

I must have dozed off at some point because I woke to find males in black robes flooding the room, their faces covered with their cowls. Each of us was plucked up from our resting places like spring chickens and dragged out of the room, some kicking and screaming. My instincts told me to fight them, but Sherai shook her head subtly. She was right, of course. Best to comply for now. There was nothing we could do except allow ourselves to be guided wherever we were led.

I took note of every room we passed and every turn, just in case. The place was gigantic, but the exits were few and far between, unless you counted the windows, which I, for one, did. Eventually, we were deposited into a large foyer, lit by decadent chandeliers and overlooked by an arched balcony above two grand staircases curving down from either side. The guards took up residence around the room, watching us with dark and glittering eyes barely perceptible from beneath their hoods.

The obvious wealth of this castle made my father's look like a hovel by comparison. Lord Windaire and his son were clearly not wanting for anything except, oh, I don't know, a harmless bout of bloodletting and butchery. *Fuckers.*

My eyes remained glued to the balcony while the other females shuffled awkwardly or huffed with impatience. I saw no reason to be impatient. Any second, and the hosts would make their appearance. Sure enough, five figures seemed to appear out of nowhere, their bodies swathed in robes, their heads also hooded. But hiding their faces were golden masks depicting various animals. A sea serpent, a lion, a wolf, a bear, and an eagle.

The sea serpent stood front and centre, breaking from the phalanx to stand at the balcony edge. He took a long minute to study us, our faces and dishevelled states. I felt his eyes like a scourge over my body. Cold and glittering, making my skin crawl the longer they lingered.

After another moment, dark shadows seeped out around the four other males from where they stood, drifting down the stairs like it was fog. I almost rolled my eyes at the display of magic. This waiting game was a purposeful show of drama and intrigue, and I didn't care for it. My body was exhausted, my mind felt frayed, and my heart was feeling a little heavier than yesterday. *We've already had enough excitement for one night. Get on with the fucking show already.*

"Fifty females entered this sacred Wedding Rite, hoping to win the hand of a lord of noble blood and powerful magic. 50 of you entered, and only 38 remain after the first test. The Blood Rite. Many more of you will fall. Some might say the Blood Rite is a barbaric and unconscionable act, but we know better than to take stock of hearsay from common folk and lesser Fae. This is tradition. Strength. And there is none other than this great test to judge the merit, intelligence, and strength of its participants." The male's voice carried the slightest hint of pride. There was no doubt he believed every word he was saying.

'Common folk and lesser Fae'. I almost snorted. If I weren't in said Rite, I might very well have laughed. But there wasn't anything remotely funny about this. Not for me and the 49 other females who had been forced to participate, nor the many who came before us. How many had been lost to the Rite? How many beautiful, strong, wonderful females had fallen because of a group of evil, egotistical Fae getting off on the pain and suffering of others?

Fuck them. Fuck all of them. I looked at the male with the serpent mask and decided at that moment that before this was done, I would stand over his dying body and *smile*. I would root out the whole nest and destroy them all. Someday, somehow, they were going to pay. They wouldn't be spouting this nonsense about tradition and merit if the tables were turned. They wouldn't be saying anything at all.

The sea serpent looked down on us, the gilded mask glinting as the chandelier's light reflected off it. "You have all done well to survive the first test, but know this: today was but the first of several to come over the winter and thaw. You will be fed, watered, and clothed, with comfortable quarters during your time here, but you will also earn your keep. You will each be assigned castle duties and will spend your days working and undergoing combat training in equal measure. Tardiness, dissent, and complaints will not be tolerated. These are your only rules. Listen to your masters and give your all in the Rite, and you will do well."

He dipped his head once before swishing his robe and striding out of the room. The other masked males followed like silent wraiths, and then we were left once more with the guards. I hissed as one suddenly grabbed me roughly by the arm. But I allowed myself to be escorted once more. I tried to keep Sherai in my sights, but she was soon lost in a sea of grumbling females and surly guards, so I focused my attention once more on my surroundings. The castle spanned on and on, each room full of grandeur and wealth I'd never dreamed of.

It was a decent walk to reach the wing dedicated to the contesting females. The guard led me up a staircase spanning several floors before we finally came to a stop in a wide hallway with doors lining each side. He slid a brass key from his pocket, opened the door before us, then not so gently nudged me inside.

"Easy on the goods there, handsy," I said with a wink.

He glared momentarily, then slammed the door in my face and locked me in.

I sighed and pressed my forehead against the cool wood. This was going to be a long few months, but perhaps that was a blessing in disguise. Time was my ally. Time allowed me to do some digging on the mystery surrounding previous participants and the so-called asylum, or, at the very least, the next few tests. It made perfect sense that the hosts would want to keep everything about the Rite hush-hush. Locking females away, never to be seen again, was the perfect way to do that. Of course, they could simply throw all the losers in those underground tunnels and solve their problems that way, but droves of sudden disappearances would probably cause more questions than not. It was something to ponder.

I also had the distinct impression I wouldn't be wandering around the castle freely anytime soon. Not if they had guards assigned to each of us. For now, the best thing to do was simply what they told us to. I had no issue with earning my keep or training my body. I desperately needed the latter if I were honest. I wanted to be able to protect myself as best as I could.

The hosts weren't the only threats in this castle, but they were the biggest. I bet that this applied especially to the leader —the one with the sea serpent mask. He was no doubt running the whole thing. The others would likely look to his approval and leadership. Which meant if we really were in a viper's den, then there was one simple solution to my conundrum. I had to cut the head off the snake.

CHAPTER SEVEN

'There has always been five leading the Rite. Five males, five hidden identities, creating a leadership known simply as the Pentad. In the years since conception, assassination attempts have occurred on numerous Pentad members. None have been successful.'

The Trials and Traditions of a Mithrian Fae

The room my newfound friend had locked me in was lavish. Obnoxiously so. I'd expected some kind of sick torture chamber or love dungeon to spend my days in upon arriving. Instead, I'd been dumped in the height of finery.

What. The. Fuck?

The room was bedecked in cerulean and emerald accents, with gold trimming, over a tasteful ocean mural on the walls. Silk comforts adorned every corner. Ornate brushes for hair and makeup lined a gorgeous pearl vanity, with jewels, accessories, and everything a noble lady could dream of thoughtfully laid out, as if in supplication.

I gasped as I took in the view from the floor-to-ceiling glass windows overlooking the ocean on one side, unable to hide my awe. The view was mesmerising, if a little frightening. The castle had been moulded into the cliff face, carved from the very rock it nestled upon. Likely, the foundations were more solid than they looked, but it was still alarming to see such a drop before me. Above, the starry night swirled with mist from the ocean spray far below, circling jagged rocks that poked up like toothpicks from the water's depths. I loved the ocean and had spent much of my youth by the beach, but I never tired of its beauty. There was something so powerful about the ocean. It ebbed and flowed. It crashed before it calmed. It gave permission to let go of every awful thought or memory, washing them away forever. I loved the ocean … and I hated it.

For all its beauty and might, it always reminded me that I was not in control and never had been. My father had seen to that long ago. For a while, I accepted that as the way things were … until he took Avadir from me. And now more than ever, I wondered if he'd taken my mother, too. More mysteries. More heartbreak to unpack.

I threw one last glance at the jagged rocks and paused. I hadn't noticed it at first, but tucked behind an outcropping, just barely peeking out, was a dock. It was a tiny thing, suitable for nothing bigger than some rowboats. Anyone coming and going would need to navigate treacherous rocks, and those waves were coming in *hard*. Still, it was the perfect little spot to ferry someone—maybe a few someones—out under the cover of darkness. *Interesting.*

I turned, tucking that information away as I scanned the

rest of the room. Everything was unnaturally perfect, and I wondered as I strode through the chamber if all of the rooms looked like this. I jumped on the bed, notably free from any chains, and groaned as my head pounded in answer. *Assholes couldn't let us have one night to rest before dumping us straight into the competition? Captain what's-his-face was off to a great start.*

The bed, on the other hand, was the epitome of comfort. I groaned again, only this time out of longing, tempted to bury my face within the covers and fall immediately to sleep, before thinking better of it. I was covered in grime. The bed didn't need to wear it as well. With a huff, I sculled the glass of water left on the bedside and hauled my ass up. I was almost afraid to check the giant wardrobe across the room, but … curiosity got the better of me.

It was true that I enjoyed experimenting with deadly potions and a spot of blade play or rock climbing in my spare time, but a girl could just as equally enjoy the finer things in life, too. And oh, did the wardrobe deliver.

"By the gods."

The most beautiful dresses stared back at me as I gazed inside. I squealed a little, gathering them in my arms. Each one was a masterpiece, thoughtfully detailed and carefully lined with beading, embroidery, lace and—*oh?* Some had armour, while others were lined with scales, feathers and the like.

I checked the drawers, curious to see what treasures awaited inside. To my disappointment, there was little in the way of practicality. A combat suit and some boots for physical training, but beyond that, there were no weapons within the vicinity that I could see. I would search every nook and cranny for something sharp, just in case.

A knock sounded suddenly at the door, followed by a flash of paper slipping inside. The people here were big on invisibility, it seemed, and less interested in chitchat or exchanging pleasantries. Fine by me. I trudged to the envelope and ripped it open without ceremony. The letter read:

Your presence is requested for a Midnight Masquerade. You will find evening wear in the wardrobe, along with a mask in the bottom drawer. A servant will collect you before midnight.

Remember, this is a game only one can win. Ride the swelling tides or sink beneath dark depths. Merciless is our ocean. Murderous are her makers.

I rolled my eyes. Pretty prose, but it was just another threat to keep us uncomfortable.

A masquerade ball was the last thing I felt like after today's events, but it was highly probable that the captain would be there. Hells, it was worth attending just to get a glimpse of the male we would be dying for. Besides, I imagined the 'request' so kindly mentioned in the letter was anything but. I had no choice in the matter.

Fine. They'd seen us with blood on our hands and grime in our hair. Now they wanted beauty and pageantry. I smiled slowly as I ran my fingers down a silk dress, an idea coming to me. *They want a show? I'll damn well give it to them.*

CHAPTER EIGHT

'Males are like predators. Dangle some prey in front of them
and they'll pounce at the first opportunity.'

I hated to admit it, but the ball was spectacular. No extravagance had been spared, and I couldn't help but stare in awe at the vast hall filled with countless wonders. Chandeliers lined the ceiling, which was supported by marble columns running the length of the room. From those, pine furs mixed with lilac and baby-blue florals hung in garlands or twined around the walls like the ivy. A fire crackled in a huge grate on one side of the room, warding off the chill of the crisp evening air.

The scent of roasted meats and gravies climbed my nose as I stood gazing at the scene, and my stomach grumbled in earnest, reminding me I hadn't eaten for a day. The exotic spices, notably from the western lands across the sea, only made it worse, causing my mouth to water. That's when my gaze fell on the jellies, candied fruits, and other desserts calling my name from the dining table. It spanned the length of the damn room and was topped with enough food to feed a town. Most of the food would likely go to waste, and I doubted our hosts would be so kind as to offer it to the city folk who would appreciate it more. This kind of excess could save lives, but then, a bunch of murderous males didn't seem like the philanthropic types. This ball had been carefully crafted like a winter wonderland. It was almost easy to forget that predators stalked the room at every turn, waiting to sink their teeth into fresh meat.

I smoothed out my dress, a multi-faceted green gown that changed shade depending on the light and angle from which one regarded it. The silk was heavenly against my fingers, and the cut was exquisite, with a sweetheart neckline and a tight bodice that flowed out from the waist. The real treasure, however, was the intricate details—and the fierce ones. The bodice was covered in small golden scales, hard like armour and shining like a beacon. Gilded pauldrons shaped like small wings lined my shoulders, tied to the bodice with tiny gold chains that looped over the bare skin of my arms. My shoulder injury, which had been tended to but not healed entirely, stuck out as an angry mark on an otherwise perfect vision of femininity.

I wore a fox mask that covered half my face and tied back my golden hair that I'd styled in soft curls cascading down my back. My lips, I'd lined in red to catch the eye. The mouth was a female's most well-regarded—and often dismissed— weapon, depending on how it was used. Compliment a male, shower him with praise, offer pleasure with lips and tongue. But a female's mouth can just as easily be a male's downfall.

"Aeris?"

My gown swept across the polished floor as I turned to find Sherai peeking out from her swan mask. She was stunning. Her gown was dove-white with the barest blush hue tipping the feathers that lined it. Dainty little cords of silver swooped down the bust, matching the pearl beads that tinkled together throughout her coils. Her makeup was natural and soft, accented by her rosy lips and cheeks.

"You are…" She sucked in a breath and whistled. "It's just unfair, really."

I laughed as she handed me a goblet of wine. "You'll make me blush. Careful, Sherai, or I might start to think you're buttering me up for something."

Her cheeks turned a brighter shade of pink. "No, I—"

"Oh, alright, you've convinced me. I'll dance with you."

"I—what?!"

I dragged her to the dancefloor, still sputtering and protesting, and flopped her arms around me. We garnered several stares from around the room, but that didn't bother me. I had no problem with attention. It was *whose* attention I gained that was important.

"Do you see him?" I asked as we spun to a lively beat.

"Who?" Sherai asked. She gripped onto my waist for dear life, and I got the distinct impression she hadn't danced before. Her feet tripped, and she stepped on my toe. "Shit, sorry."

Yep. Not a dancer. "The captain, obviously. Don't you think it's weird we haven't seen him yet? I would have thought they'd be dangling him before us like a prized pony."

"Everything the hosts do is planned. They'll make a show of his arrival. Make us feel enamoured by him by building the suspense. You know, everyone wants the mystery of what they can't have."

She had a point. I tilted my head, studying her feathered mask, then jerked my head, indicating the others in the room. "What do you think of the other females?"

Her eyes narrowed as she looked over my shoulder while we danced. "I think many of them are scared and putting on a brave front. Many of us won't survive this."

I shook my head. "You do not fit in that category. We're going to get out of this, and we're going to do it together. Deal?"

She chuckled. "How do you know I'm not playing you? That I won't stab you in the back when you least expect it?"

I smiled at that. "Honestly? I don't. Call me crazy, but I feel I can trust you. And I think we can help each other. You're quick and you're quiet. And you're obviously observant and brave. Don't forget you could have left me back in the crypt, too. I was hurt, but you didn't leave me."

She sucked in a breath. "I might be all of those things, but I'm not a fighter. I used to spend my days with the company of books. Not fending off hungry creatures and determined females." She stopped dancing and buried her face in her hands. "What am I even doing here? I can't do this. I don't want to do this."

"Hey, keep it together, okay?" I said gently. "People are watching. Don't let them see you doubt yourself."

Sherai lifted her head and looked me in the eyes. "How are you so calm, knowing what awaits us? Unless you have some amount of physical training, which would make sense from what I saw in the crypt, and you seem intelligent enough..."

I laughed. "Um, thanks? I guess?" It was true I had received some training from my former mentor, both physical and intellectual, but it was never completed before Avadir's untimely removal.

She shook her head vigorously. "No, that didn't come out right."

The timely groan of two obscenely large double doors opening at the end of the room drowned out the awkward apology Sherai offered. The hosts glided in, again wearing their long black robes and gilt masks. Silence reigned across the ballroom as each host, save the sea serpent, took their seats at a table on a small platform at the end of the hall. Probably so they could spy on us from their little position of power. The leader took a goblet from a servant, then raised it high, gesturing for us to follow suit.

"This feast honours the dead, may their souls rest with Ryvia, but let it also be a reminder to the living. Here and now, you are safe. But tomorrow offers no such promise. Rest tonight. Drink and eat your fill, then be sure to show up every day hereafter with a sharp mind and an even sharper body. For these are your weapons now. Use them wisely." With that, he took a long drink and sat, those cold eyes making my skin crawl as they skittered past me.

The servants ushered us to the tables, where we were all but forced to take our seats, too. I sat with a scowl at being forced to abide, then, unable to resist, helped myself to heaping portions of food. Oh, gods. It was an effort not to moan as I tasted the first morsel. I was several mouthfuls deep when I noticed Sherai staring at me from where she sat on my left.

"What?"

"How can you eat at a time like this? My stomach is in knots."

My brow raised. "Dinner time, you mean? Sherai, we don't know when we'll get a chance to eat again. They could lump another surprise on us at any moment. We need our strength."

Her lips pursed. "What if they poisoned it?"

"And where would the fun be in poisoning all their guests? Doesn't make for much of a show." I didn't add that I was well-versed in poisons and had made a point of examining everything I ate before it made it into my mouth, or that I knew well enough how to counter most common poisons.

"Not to mention the cleanup required," a girl said from across the table. She grinned and held out her hand. "Akira," she offered. "I couldn't help but overhear, but I'd have to agree it would be pointless to kill us off so simply." Akira was stunning. Long, straight black hair and lily white skin. She had a small nose and lips, with skin like glass. I stared at her in admiration and a small amount of envy. That unmarked fairness suggested she spent most of her time indoors or perhaps underground in one of the many temples or necropolises in the four courts. Her features also hinted at ancestry from distant lands, though I wasn't sure where.

I turned back to Sherai. "See? Akira agrees with me. Now eat."

Sherai huffed and took a bite, then groaned quickly after, proceeding to chow down in a rather unladylike fashion.

"Aeris," I said to Akira. "I'm from the—"

"Shadow Court," she finished. "I know who you are. Who your father is."

I waved a hand. "Don't hold it against me. And your family?"

"The females from the temple I lived in have long served Valere, but they are not my family. I was taken from my true blood as a child when Mithrian Fae raided my homeland and stole many of us away across the seas. The religion and path the people of that temple walk is one I may have been raised in, but it is not one I chose to follow. Don't, as you said, hold it against me."

I cringed inwardly. Valere, God of Torment, was known by

all as a cruel and hateful creature. It was said he gained his power through Fae sacrifice and dark ceremony. Those who followed him were often regarded as extreme cultists and were given a wide berth. Once someone was inducted into their ranks, it was almost impossible to get out, and many were sacrificed before they got the chance. From what I knew of their practices, Akira would have endured a hard life and much suffering. And it was likely going to get worse. Valere didn't release his worshippers to participate in marriage rites. It was a life 'calling', which meant…

"You ran away from the temple," I said softly.

She raised her shoulders. "I took my life into my own hands before they could take it for their own. My sister was…" She took a composing breath. "I couldn't save her in time."

"I'm so sorry. I can understand why you'd run. But why run here?"

The hand resting on her fork tightened until the knuckles went white. "My adopted brother's work. He assisted my escape under the pretence of helping me. Little did I know he'd bartered my life for a healthy sum to set himself up far away from the temple's clutches. He might have saved me from the temple, but he condemned me to the Rite in its place. I traded fire for brimstone, I'm afraid."

"My gods," Sherai whispered. "So much pain has followed your footsteps. I will pray the light of Falane finds you here." Falane was the Goddess of Nature and New Life. One of our more benevolent gods. It was said her light healed and purified all it touched, if one was so lucky.

Akira's eyes narrowed. "It would be wasted breath. They stopped listening a long time ago, if they ever did, and do not care for the likes of us. The gods shroud me in darkness, so I learned to live in the shadows."

I shook my head. "I'll drink to that," and I drained the

whole glass. Akira was interesting, and Sherai was lovely, but I was better off not getting too attached. At the end of the day, we were all pitted against each other, whether we liked it or not. I didn't want the captain's hand, but I sure as hell wanted to keep my life. I liked these females, and that was a problem. I couldn't afford distractions. "Excuse me, ladies, I'm going to get some air."

I slipped out of my seat and headed for the gardens beyond the balcony doors, curious if the burly guards standing by would even allow me past. To my relief, they said nothing as I made my way outside, taking the stone stairs toward the gardens. More guards surrounded the perimeter, no doubt. Trying to escape would not be easy, but that didn't mean I couldn't assess my chances for another day. The air had a sharp bite to it, the flesh on my arms instantly prickling from the sharp lick of an ocean breeze. The first snow had not yet fallen here, but it wouldn't be long before the castle grounds would host a blanket of fresh powder.

It was too cold to be wearing such a flimsy gown, but discomfort was far from my mind as my slippered feet crunched over the pebbled path. The castle grounds were beautiful, with perfectly manicured lawns and trees, and a lake dotted with elaborate fountains of sea animals. The stubborn remnants of wisteria vines clung to a long pergola covering a walkway to the east, which I headed towards casually. Anyone could be watching through the large windows from the banquet hall, so it wouldn't do to appear suspicious, even though I was using this time to evaluate the area.

A wall snaked around the exterior of the grounds, effectively keeping everyone out—and all the females in. Not a problem, given my knack for climbing, but I knew guards would patrol it night and day, which meant if I were to attempt fleeing, I'd have to learn their schedules. Annoying, but not a complete barrier to freedom … My real obstacle would be the hounds the lord most certainly kept on the premises somewhere.

I turned towards the ocean and grimaced. I already knew the castle foundation was built into the very cliff, descending upon jagged rocks and rugged coastline on either side, but this angle revealed the lack of options this provided. There was no dock leading out, and even if there was, the waves were so violent I wouldn't get far. At least not farther than the island out at sea. It wouldn't take long for the lord to notice my absence and send soldiers to come and collect me. This was their turf, and I was not a skilled sailor.

My gown swished over the pebbles, gently brushing some out of their bumpy bed. As I meandered around the grounds, pretending to explore and appreciate the flora to any assuming onlookers, I hummed a lilting beat, one my mother had sung to me as a girl. I was close to the end, nearing a large, bent tree with a hollow in its centre, when voices drifted toward me on the breeze. I stopped humming immediately and listened. They came from around the corner of the manor, and they were headed right toward me. *Shit.* I jumped into the tree hole without thinking. I cursed beneath my breath as a spider crawled over me and skittered out the entrance, leaving goosebumps over my skin.

"We used the Rite as an opportunity to search beneath the castle proper," a male said in a gruff voice. "Nothing but blood and bones from those damned beasts your father keeps. The only prisons we found were pens for the Waiflings. If your father is holding them, it's not here."

Waiflings? That must have been what the creatures in the crypt were called.

A frustrated growl followed, along with the scraping of boots on gravel as the small group came to a halt. "If he's holding her ransom, he'd want her close by, not to mention any others."

"We can keep trying Domeratt," another younger, eager voice said. "He could have made a deal with the pirates."

"My father, make a deal with those thugs?" The second husky voice scoffed. "Thieves and murderers, the lot of them. He'd sooner slit my mother's throat than allow one to lay a hand on her. Besides, they can't be trusted not to extort him afterwards. What better person to publicly barter than the Lord of Domeratt's wife?"

Holy shit. Am I hearing straight? My heart beat a little faster, because surely they weren't talking about the lord of this castle holding his wife captive? *Mother. Father. Lord Windaire.* Gods. My skin prickled once more as I realised one of the males right outside my hiding place was the captain himself. *Fuck. If he finds me...*

"We'll keep looking," the first male reassured. "We have soldiers checking every ship headed out of port and others scouring every nook and cranny in the city. We'll find her Raithe."

The captain sighed. "Sooner than later, I hope. I can't let them do this, Killian. I won't stand by while she withers and dies."

"Don't even think about doing something stupid," the first male said. "You do anything to interfere with the Rite, and your father won't hesitate to kill her. Try to help *any* of the females he's brought here, and your father will have them killed for sport."

"You want me to let this play out and marry the victor? I am not in want of a wife. Especially not one who would volunteer to be here. I'd sooner stick my cock in a clam. But you, Killian ... I didn't take you for a coward."

"And I didn't take you for a fool. I have many years on you, boy, and I know your father well. He is a ruthless male, but he is damn smart. He will be watching you carefully, testing your loyalty. Don't give him a reason to doubt it. You play the game and you play it well. If you're clever enough, you might just be able to bend the rules without consequence."

"I'll help you, Raithe," the younger one said. "We'll get through this."

"'Atta boy," Killian said. "Keep this one in line for me, Jaren. I need to get back or someone will notice my absence. You should return to your post, too, or the master will have you whipped." A moment of silence followed, then he spoke up again. "Heed my words, Raithe, for all our sakes."

Two pairs of boots crunched into the distance, and I waited in anticipation while one male remained, pacing in agitation before the tree I'd concealed myself in. The breeze ruffled my hair, and I twitched my nose as strands tickled my nostrils. The pacing came to a sudden stop.

"Are you going to hide in there all day? I can smell your perfume, and you'd best believe I heard you singing."

I froze, not uttering a sound as Raithe's deep voice pierced the stillness. The primal timbre of it had my hair stand on end, my body recognising danger instinctively. Begrudgingly, I clasped the bark and crawled out of the hole to find the captain towering over me. In an instant, he shoved me against the tree, slamming my injured shoulder against the harsh bark as his fingertips dug into my hip. In his other hand was a dagger glittering in the soft ray of moonlight that filtered through the branches, held just an inch from my throat.

Beneath the kraken mask covering the top half of his face came a smile that was anything but kind. "There you are, little lark. Now give me one reason why I shouldn't make you sing."

CHAPTER NINE

'Never turn your back on a Fae. They have centuries to imagine stabbing you in the back. Don't allow them the opportunity to make it a reality.'

The Trials and Traditions of a Mithrian Fae

Raithe's blade pressed against my throat as he shifted his free hand up to lean on the bark beside my head. I swallowed, all too aware of the close proximity of the enemy before me.

"Your father won't be pleased if you kill one of his playthings without an audience to witness it," I said with more confidence than I felt. It was only too typical I'd found myself in this position on the first damned day at this goddess forsaken place.

"My father would probably be proud," Raithe said, flashing

his teeth. The tip of the blade pressed firmer, drawing a drop of blood that trickled down my neck. "Try again."

I glared up at deep blue eyes as I squirmed beneath the cool tip of metal. He seemed to be giving me the opportunity to talk my way out of the situation. "Okay, fine. You're looking for your mother, right? And other females? I can help you."

The pressure of the blade on my skin softened ever so slightly. "Go on," he allowed.

My mind worked quickly, scrounging for something, anything, to keep me alive and convince him I was an asset. "Maybe you're looking for your mother in the wrong places. People talk, Captain. Servants certainly have a lot to say when they think no one is watching. Before my arrival, I already heard whispers of what rumours your help is entertaining, so imagine what I'll learn now that I'll be working alongside them during my stay. I can report any useful gossip back to you." I took his silence as contemplation and hurriedly continued. "Who better to feed information on what truly happens during and after the Rite than someone participating in it? The females from prior years must have stayed here. Maybe they left clues behind, Captain. A bread trail leading to your answers."

"And how do I know I can trust you not to spill my secrets to the Pentad? Perhaps it is in my best interest to remove you now. I could, you know. I would be well within my rights."

I lowered the tip of his blade and stepped forward, reclaiming my space and placing us on even ground. "And whyever would I do that? I am here for your hand, after all. It wouldn't be the most promising start to an amicable marriage."

He shoved me back against the tree effortlessly, his hand curling around my neck. "If you were really here to court me, you would be back at the ball, charming your way into the inner circle of the Pentad. But here you are, alone, hiding in a tree at the first sound of a male to come upon you." His eyes drifted to the wall beyond the tree, as if keenly aware of what I'd really been doing out here. "I wouldn't recommend scaling it, little lark. The guards would surely clip your wings before you could take flight."

"Then this little bird will peck out their eyes before they dare try," I hissed. "But one way or another, I am getting out of here, lord. Try and stop me."

He laughed at my challenge, but to my surprise, he released me and stepped back. His arms folded as he looked down at me, the picture of male arrogance. "You'd better get back to the ball if you plan on surviving long enough to try. They won't accept your extended absence as an innocent loss of time."

My brows knitted together. "You're letting me go?"

He adjusted the buckle looped over his navy coat, then smoothed out his tunic before gesturing towards the ball. "For now."

"You knew I was here all that time, yet you didn't stop your company from continuing your conversation. Why?"

His brow rose. "Maybe I require a little bird to spill the castle secrets. Maybe I was curious why a female would be out here in the first place. Or maybe I was just bored. I guess we'll see now, won't we?"

I glared at him once more, then started back toward the ballroom with as much grace as I could muster. Before I could escape him entirely, though, he called out.

"Oh, and little lark? Tread lightly. I may be a fair male, but I can also be unforgiving. Do not give me reason to regret letting you live."

I looked over my shoulder to find shadows misting along the ground towards me. His entire aura seemed to darken, and my heart raced as I felt the weight of his power. The age of it. I wasn't able to see his face behind his mask, beyond a chiselled jawline and those deep blue eyes, but he couldn't have appeared much older than 30 by the lunar year. In truth? He must have been hundreds of years old, if this sheer power was anything to go by. *Fuck.* And here I was, a mere 24 lunar years old, yet to discover what my power even was.

I turned my head and willed my feet to take one step, then another, until I was walking rather rigidly back to the castle. When he was well and truly behind me, I took a shuddering breath, the plume clouding before my face. It was only then that I realised I was shivering, whether from the threat of his existence or the cold, I didn't know. *What in hells had I gotten myself into?*

It took a while, but with the aid of a few glasses of wine and the distracting chatter of Sherai and Akira, I was able to gather my wits once more … until the captain appeared in the ballroom. The obscene doors of the great hall once again groaned open to announce his entrance. My head snapped to the far end, where the hosts now stood, their glasses in hand. Time for the Pentad's big reveal.

A herald preceded him and bowed, announcing loudly, "Captain Raithe Windaire, Lord of Cliffscote Castle and Soldier of the Shadow Court."

I almost rolled my eyes. They certainly liked to inflate their egos here. But it seemed effective on the others. A few gasps echoed around the room as the captain entered, one of them coming from Akira of all people. I glared at her, and she shrugged.

"What? Just because I was forced to be here doesn't mean I

can't appreciate the merchandise. We're fighting for it, after all."

I snorted. It did help to think of the captain as a shiny object to fawn over, rather than the commanding and somewhat intimidating male I'd met earlier. Without a blade at my throat, I could actually take a moment to drink in the sight of him. And this time, he was maskless.

The captain was tall and broad, with short, tousled black hair. A scar cut through his left eyebrow, which somehow only enhanced his handsome features. The jawline was sharp as a blade, the lips full, the nose straight. But the eyes … they were the blue of storms and angry ocean swells. Those eyes had seen murder and malice and had weathered it. They were *hard.* I hadn't yet decided if they housed the soul of a cruel male or simply a stoic one.

Though given his acceptance of this entire charade, even if somehow coerced or forced into it, I'd have to hazard a guess that he was not the kind of male one would want to wed. He was a captain of the court, for goodness' sake. Not a thing easily achieved by those with any moral compass. As I considered it, I realised it was odd that his father still held his seat.

Captain Raithe strode through the hall with ease, taking his place up on the dais beside the leader of the Pentad. His father, presumably, though there was no way to tell. The lord of this castle hadn't officially revealed himself, mask or not. "Welcome, ladies, to Cliffscote Castle. It is my pleasure to host you, alongside these great leaders, and I look forward to becoming acquainted with each and every one of you." He smiled, flashing white teeth, and I bristled at the sigh some of the females uttered throughout the room. Were they really so vapid as to fall for his false charm at a first glance? It seemed to come so easily to him, as if he weren't standing among monsters. The only reason to doubt he was wholly one of those cruel males was the fact that he was searching for his mother, and I presumed the other lost females. It proved he cared for the well-being of at least one female, which was more than I had yet to witness from any lord. Maybe the captain was a good male, as Roslin had said.

I slumped in my seat and blew out a breath as his grandiose speech continued. When his piercing gaze passed over me, I smiled like a good little girl, but I knew he'd see it for the mockery it was. I paid no attention to his sugar-coated words. I didn't buy into any of it anyway.

When he finished speaking, the tables were cleared and we were ushered onto the dance floor, waiting like sitting ducks while a score of male nobles, presumably invited as guests, picked which females they would like to dance with. My skin prickled as the Pentad member wearing a lion mask crossed the hall and took my hand. I smiled, but my insides writhed with disgust. It felt like a thousand bugs skittered over my skin where he touched me. His other hand moved to my back, skirting lower than was courteous, and all the while, I smiled and batted my lashes.

His dark eyes raked over me as we danced. My stomach somersaulted with fear, my instincts on alert as we moved. He was a good dancer. Precise and near perfect in every step. I didn't dare allow myself to make a single error. Everything we did was surely measured. Calculated.

"Beautiful," he whispered as he dipped me, taking a moment to lift his mask ever so slightly to kiss the tender hollow at the base of my throat. I almost flinched, the primal creature within me wanting to roar and lash out at the indignity of it.

These males … they thought they owned us. Thought they could use our bodies as they saw fit. Would he try to claim me for the night? Surely the captain wouldn't be too impressed if his future bride was touched by any other first... Or maybe all the males present would have their pick of the losing females once the Rite was over. I forced my lips to curl into an embarrassed smile. As he lifted me again, I found Raithe at our side.

"Such a pretty one, Lion," he said in that husky tone of his. "I might have to steal such beauty away from you." The only acknowledgement the male gave was a stiff nod before he let me go and stalked off the dancefloor. "Making friends, I see," Raithe said as he took my hand in the lion's place. It was calloused and warm, not at all like the cold and controlling grasp from the gardens.

"Is that a hint of jealousy, I detect?" I responded sweetly.

His laugh was dark and low. "Sweetheart, it would take a lot more than that to make me jealous. You are pretty, but you are just a tool to me."

"And yet here you are, the hero rescuing a damsel in distress."

"You have no idea how your night would have gone, do you?" His grip tightened on my hand to the point of pain. "I just saved you from spending a long night wishing you were dead. The lion always picks a favourite, and if the tests don't kill his pick, the females end up killing themselves."

Bile rose in my throat, but I didn't give the satisfaction of thanking him. "You seem to know enough about the extra-curricular activities of our hosts."

"I wouldn't be captain of this court if I didn't pay attention."

I smiled. "Well, feel free to commandeer your ship of male murderers and rapists and ram yourselves onto some rocks in the middle of the ocean for us."

"Such sweet words out of that pretty little mouth. I'll

remember them the next time I consider stepping in to save you. Remember our deal, lark. You are only worthwhile so long as you hold up your end of the bargain."

I hated the way he spoke to me. I hated that I wasn't even a person to him or any other male here. I hated all of them. "I swear to Ryvia, Captain, if I survive this place I'll kill the Pentad and I'll damn well kill you."

"I'm shivering in my boots," he said drily. "What's your name, girl?"

I made sure to step on one of said boots as I pirouetted. "Aeris, not that you deserve to know."

"Aeris," he almost purred. "I'll be sure to remember it."

"See that you do," I said softly. "It'll be the last name on your lips before you die."

He opened his mouth to reply when a scream rang out from a corridor adjoining the hall. I shared a glance with him before he yanked me none too gently by the arm and shoved me behind him. I snorted, then pushed past him to run to the door alongside several other females.

"Aeris," he snapped.

"Yeah, yeah, curiosity kills and all that. Go choke on a big fat—"

I stopped speaking as I pushed to the front of the crowd and found the source of the commotion. A female with long blonde hair much like my own lay sprawled on the ground, her eyes wide and glassy as she stared at the ceiling. A doe mask lay discarded beside her, broken and torn, as if it had been ripped off in frustration. Blood spread the floor around her in a giant pool, growing larger by the second. And where her throat should have been was a gaping hole of torn sinew and raw pink flesh. I glanced across the half circle to find Sherai, who made a pointed look to the side of the hall, where the female we'd fought in the crypt stood.

Our eyes met, and she grinned with her sharp fangs, which were coated dark red. She took a sip of her wine, and the next minute they were back to sparkling white. I glanced back at the dead girl—at the golden hair fanning out and the build much like my own. When I looked back at the fanged female, she nodded subtly, as if confirming what I'd concluded. The female on the ground was not the intended target of this attack. I was.

CHAPTER TEN

'There is no right or wrong way to wield. The smallest trickle of power may produce the greatest of ripples. Practice and nurture this gift, and you will do great things.'

The Trials and Traditions of a Mithrian Fae

Nearly a week later, Sherai sat with me at breakfast, eyeing me from her seat. "So, I can't help but notice there's a tension between you and the captain that's somewhat … frosty."

Thankfully, there hadn't been another incident since the murder at the ball. Our days were spent waking at the butt crack of dawn to scarf down breakfast before physical training, then either helping in the laundry rooms or the apothecary. The work was hard, but it gave me time to think. And time to snoop, not that I was making any headway on finding any information worth passing to the captain. I was thankful that I hadn't needed to speak to him or even see any of the psychotic Pentad leaders since the ball, which meant that the other females and I were safe from the Rite for the time being. Unless one counted the fanged female who had it out for me. She was a ticking clock counting down to my doom.

"Whumf?" I swallowed the lump of toast in my mouth and tore my eyes away from where Captain Raithe sat enjoying his own morning meal. He'd spent the entire morning ignoring my existence whilst other females did their best impressions of a wilting flower as they tittered and fawned over him. *Ugh, please.* "I don't know what you're talking about," I said aloud to Sherai.

"Oh, I'm sorry. How foolish of me." Her voice dripped with sarcasm. "I'm not sure how I managed to misinterpret what I thought were scowls and constant eye stabbing between the two of you for the past week. It must have been one hell of a dance you shared."

"Eye stabbing or eye fucking?" Akira mumbled before tearing into her eggs and sausage.

Sherai's tight ringlets fell into her eyes as she tilted her head toward the former sister of Valere. "Is there a difference?"

I gaped, shifting my eyes between the two of them. "There is absolutely nothing between the captain and me beyond mutual disdain, trust me." They shared a look, then turned to me and raised their brows in unison as if to say, 'we're not stupid'. "Okay, fine," I admitted. "We might have an agreement of sorts. Not that I really had a say in the matter."

"And?" Akira pressed. Her long black hair tumbled over her shoulder as she leaned forward, her dark brown eyes focused. "Do we need to beat it out of you?"

I grimaced and nodded over at the fanged female, whose

name I'd since learned was Portia, not in fact stabby pants as we had affectionately called her up until then. I avoided her at all costs, even if it seemed like she'd made it her personal mission to taunt me from afar. She was currently eyeing me as she whispered to her newly acquired allies. "You could do that, but I'm sure there will be plenty of beatings at training."

Akira looked at Portia like an annoyance and waved her off. "Ignore that murderous creature. Details. Now."

I pursed my lips. Whilst I enjoyed the two females and was building a sort of kinship with them, I was still careful to only give them general details. No specifics. After all, this affected all of us females; having them on my side was doubtless better than going it alone. "Rumours are going around that the females from prior Wedding Rites are being held captive somewhere. The captain is … interested in finding them."

Sherai's cutlery clanged violently onto her plate. "They're alive?" she asked a little breathlessly. "But I thought all the losing females had simply died. None of them were ever—"

"Heard from again?" I cocked my head. "Intriguing, isn't it?"

"Why would the captain care?" Akira asked. "Assuming his father is part of the Pentad, and given our accommodations here, I would think he'd be all too aware of what goes on."

I stabbed my eggs, watching as the yolk dribbled over my toast. "Let's just say he has a vested interest in a certain asset. He knew, or knows, one of the females missing."

"Curious," Sherai said, looking at the captain like he was a puzzle to be solved. "And what does he have on you to ensure your cooperation?"

"The power to end my life." I sighed. "I kind of owe him, given he saved me from an apparently horrific night with one of the Pentad."

Akira's eyes narrowed. "They give me the creeps, all of

them. I'd sooner put my fork in their eyes than dance with one of them."

"Wouldn't we all. But they certainly like to ensure we have no choice," I said drily. "Come on, we should get ready for training."

Sherai groaned. "I'm not cut out for this. Can't I just … watch from the sidelines?"

"Up," I commanded. "We gotta get some muscle on your body or you might not last a minute in the next test. Come on, we need to be prepared for whatever they throw at us, or throw us into."

"Oh, great. Now I'll have that looming reminder to stress about all morning."

"You're welcome," I said cheerily. "Now move your bony ass. You know you want to watch the guards train while they get all hot and sweaty."

Her dark cheeks flushed with colour. "It doesn't help, Aeris. Not one bit."

Akira slammed me onto the mat for the third time in a row, forcing the breath out of me. We'd only been at combat training for around twenty minutes, going through the motions of hand-to-hand combat, and I already felt like my bones had turned brittle. My mentor would be turning in his grave if he knew how easily I was being bested. Of course, practising alone only got me so far, and after Avadir's disappearance, I never received a replacement mentor or sparring partner. In the Shadow Court, it was generally deemed inappropriate for females to train in physical combat, and my father had laughed at the mere notion of my doing so.

I was sorely out of practice and my shoulder was still stiff from the injury I'd gained in the crypt. Akira had a natural skill, or had learned a few tricks in her homeland as a child, and was intentional and quick in her movements. She stood out against the many court females who had grown up practising embroidery or music—probably forced to, if their fathers were anything like mine—instead of learning how to protect themselves and fight back. I thought I'd have an upper hand compared to them, but that didn't seem to count for much against my fellow females. *Most* of the females, but not *all*.

I felt eyes in the back of my head from every angle.

Our training was held in a courtyard outside the western wing of the castle, where the arena was open to the elements and a side veranda offered scant shelter or warmth. Many of the castle's guards had trained before our session began, but a few continued their workout on the other side of the courtyard. Which meant we got to watch as the elite males wielded their weapons with ease and precision. They must greatly underestimate us females, to be so arrogant as to think we wouldn't be watching their advanced techniques. I paid special attention to their routines, not that it would do me much good. The Fae here were well versed with spears and long swords, and neither of those were weapons I had any clue how to defend against.

They also trained their magic for defence and offence purposes, which was yet another reminder of my apparent lack of it. I had already undergone my ascension—my coming of age being a mere twenty years old, as is customary—but that was four years ago now, and my power had yet to reveal itself. I'd expected a spark, even a whiff of something seemingly useless by now, but it didn't seem to be in the cards for me. Here in the Shadow Court, power can come in so many forms. But it was all dark magic, mostly, malevolent spells or manipulative incantations to create or control all manner of things. The rarest form was ironically the power over Shadows. Despite being the court's namesake, it was a rarer form of magic that more commonly manifested in powerful bloodlines stretching back over a millennium. A bloodline just like the captain's. Just another reason to be cautious around him.

Captain Windaire had apparently decided to train alongside us today. The good luck continued, it would seem. I'd only seen him in the courtyard once before this occasion. Which meant he either didn't make it a regular habit or chose to do so at another time of day.

I looked away from the captain and watched several soldiers spar with their magic. They wielded daggers and spears made from dark magic that soared through the air, their opponents blocking and parrying with walls of dark energy or even a slice of shadow magic. The few that could wield shadows seemed capable of creating them from nothing, whereas those wielding dark magic seemed to draw from the dark to manipulate or manifest their dark weapons. I imagined the latter would be tiring and inefficient, if there was little darkness around. A shadow wielder, on the other hand, had no such limitations. A powerful and seemingly inexhaustive gift. I sighed wistfully at the literal extensions of their abilities and focused my attention back on my opponent, who had been stretching while giving me a breather. Akira was small, but she packed a sure punch in that strong frame of hers. She had muscles in places my body couldn't even fathom.

"I thought you were a priestess, not a fucking fighter," I grumbled as I rubbed my head.

She grinned and held a hand out to help me up. "A priestess from a temple that worships Valere, God of Torment and Terror. Bodily pain is part of the average day of the week. Still, they did teach me one thing I agree with. Your body is a weapon when sharpened. Only you can decide what will break you. Now get up, I'm not finished sparring yet."

"You're enjoying this way too much." I sent a pleading look to Sherai, who was too busy avoiding the punches of another heavyset opponent to notice. There was grace and lightness in her steps. Perhaps she would make a good dancer or lithe warrior someday after all. With a bit of training. I winced as her opponent clocked her in the side. Okay, a lot of training.

"Halt," our instructor, Jaren, called. He had been one of the males I'd overheard speaking with Raithe a week ago. Turned out, he was a lieutenant stationed at this castle, but a relatively green soldier. Even by Fae standards, he was young and likely untested in the field. He was too cheery to be anything but. It also explained why he was chosen to oversee our training, instead of a duty worthy of his rank. He was damn handsome though, so there was that. Short brown hair, brown eyes, and a face that could have been chiselled by a sculptor. He was also a huge flirt and seemed to enjoy his current job immensely, regardless of having to stoop to teach females.

"I've been assessing your skillset over the past week, and it's downright deplorable. You're about as competent as a pack of blind puppies, but with some hard conditioning and a whole lot of training, you'll be in better shape before you know it." He scanned us all, his eyes lingering on me momentarily before he turned on his heel. Not for the first time, I wondered if Raithe had told him about our encounter. "You'll be placed into groups of similar skillsets. These will be your primary training squads for drills. The only exception is one day of the week, when you will duel a random opponent with no set rules. This will determine your skills' progression."

Whispers broke out among the females, with more than a

few shuffling on their feet. All of this was entirely new for some of them, and most didn't appear to enjoy the thought of a weekly duel. I wasn't too keen on it either, but I kept my gaze trained on Jaren. *Kill or be killed. Show no fear, offer no mercy.* That's the only way I'd survive here until I could hatch an escape plan and find out what happened to the females from previous Rites.

Jaren ushered a servant over, who handed him a scroll bound with leather. Jaren untied it slowly, seeming to enjoy the building tension as we hopped from foot to foot in our sweaty gear. Exposed to the cold weather, we'd be lucky not to die of hyperthermia with the slick combat suits sticking to our skin. At last, he began reading from the list. I watched as, one by one, those with the least skill were ushered by the servant to form rows to one side. I was in the next group.

I didn't fail to notice that Portia was in the elite squad. She grinned and winked at Jaren as she sauntered over to her place. He didn't bat an eye. Bonus points to Jaren for having some taste.

I glanced at Sherai, who stood in the first group, and winced. Not a good place to be. Especially when everyone else was eyeing them off like a fucking buffet. I wasn't particularly pleased about my spot either, but at least being in the middle meant we were simply average. Not an easy target and not a huge threat to those vying for the captain. Akira was with the elites, looking none too pleased about it and putting more than a little distance between herself and the rest of her group.

I frowned. Typical. The only two allies I had in this place, and we'd been separated. I'd rather keep them close, but I guess we'd have to adjust. If I counted the captain as an ally, of course, that would make three. But there was absolutely no reason to trust that the son of my enemy wouldn't change his mind about gutting me at the first opportunity. My usefulness to him would only last so long if I didn't offer any new information soon.

As if on cue, his dark eyes met mine across the courtyard. He didn't even blink as he parried his opponent's sword without looking, then turned and knocked the other male back with a savage kick, sending them sprawling. He shifted his gaze to the next opponent.

My eyes trailed Raithe's body as his muscles shifted and rippled like water. He was shirtless despite the frigid air, which was just showing off at this point. Well, fuck him, because it was working. I found I couldn't look away as he fought multiple opponents at once, fending them off with ease. Gods, he moved like the wind, his blade slicing through the air with a fluidity that reminded me just how deadly this male was. A ship captain, bending the sea to his will. It was clear he could kill me in a heartbeat, and that wasn't even taking into consideration his shadow magic. He caught my gaze again, his eyes narrowing, and I looked away quickly.

"That, ladies, is what comes from years of hard work and training," Jaren said. Startled, I whipped my head to look at him, only to realise I hadn't been the only one staring at the captain. "And in case you needed a reminder or some extra motivation, he's also the reason why you're here. Marry that male and you get to see those chiselled abs and rippling muscles every day."

Raithe threw Jaren a withering glare across the courtyard, but our instructor just grinned. "Right. Enough chatter. Clear the mats and form lines on either side of the square here."

"Giving our captain a clear view of the worthy females?" Portia said. "He'll soon know which of us deserves to be on his arm." She sneered pointedly at me.

"I guess that leaves you out then," I bit back.

Akira snorted, and Sherai covered a nervous laugh with a cough.

Jaren's eyes darkened momentarily as he eyed off Portia. "The captain is more than capable of deciding that for himself. Now clear the mats and get in line. We're finished with hand-to-hand drills today. This is your weekly combat hour."

The servant from before ran up to his side, then cleared his throat theatrically before reading from his scroll. "Aeris Lockhart and Portia Cope, step forward."

My heart beat like a drum at the sound of my name. *Please. Anyone but her. Anyone but the murderous little …* Portia stepped forward, and any hope I'd had wilted as the fanged female took one look at me and smiled a death promise.

I was royally screwed.

She strode into the middle with an emphasised swish in her hips, making sure to give the captain a sultry look before she turned on the spot. I knew he was watching, but I didn't look. Not as I stepped into the middle with my heart in my throat. Certainly not as I spotted the small dagger sheathed at Portia's hip. I had no such weapon.

Jaren stepped between us and raised a brow. "I'd like a clean fight, and I'd prefer it if both of you remained breathing at the end. Remember, there are no rules but one. *No wielding.*" He nodded at us both, his eyes catching mine before he turned. "The square is yours. Good luck."

As soon as he was clear, Portia lunged. My breath caught in my throat as I leapt back, ducking a jab to my head. She struck out again, her fists lashing out in a flurry. It was all I could do to keep my guard up as my boots slid along the muddied stone.

"Don't let her corner you," Akira yelled. "Push back!"

Portia's fist cracked into my nose, and my head whipped back as burning pain flared. Blood dripped from my nostrils, and I wiped it with the back of my arm. My opponent took a moment to look for Raithe's approval, giving me the perfect opening. I dropped, swiping her legs out from beneath her before diving onto her chest. She hissed, caught off guard as I landed a few hits to her ribs. Then, she grasped my wrists mid-air and maneuvered my body to kick me over her head. I landed on the ground with a thud, the breath leaving my lungs in a rush.

"Behind you!" Sherai cried.

I rolled just as Portia's blade sank into the mud. *Well, it didn't take long for her weapon to come out.* But I still had hope. Even if I was a little rusty, my mentor had taught me to find the chinks in my opponent's armour. Portia was a good fighter, but she was cocky, and she put too much weight into her punches, which unbalanced her. She was also easy to read … and if my guess was correct, to rile. If I could just wear her down, I might just survive this thing.

"What's the matter, Portia? Not used to fighting your victims head-on? I guess stabbing them in the back is more your style."

Her snarl drifted towards me. "For you? I'm going to enjoy watching the light go out of your eyes as I kill you."

I flicked my fingers in a come-hither motion and offered her a smirk. "Come on then. Maybe you'll get it right this time."

Her features screwed up in rage as she charged, which was exactly what I had counted on. I ran towards her, sliding over the mud and kicking her knee in. She screamed as she went down, but I should have known the stubborn bitch wouldn't give up easily. She grabbed my braid, yanking me back with such force I had to wonder if she'd torn my hair from the scalp. When her face leered above mine, she grabbed my head and bashed it once, twice, thrice into the mud. The blade in her hand flashed as she raised it, ready to plunge it into my chest.

"Justice for my people," she whispered.

Justice? I didn't know what she meant, and my head was too groggy to work it out. I was running on instinct now. Stars burst before my eyes, but I lifted my knee and thrust it into her stomach, allowing me to gain the upper hand as I rolled and straddled her. I twisted her hand, causing her to yelp and drop the weapon. I retrieved it quickly and held it to her throat.

"Yield," I hissed.

She thrashed and grunted, writhing beneath me. I let that blade nick the sensitive skin of her throat until she finally fell still. Liquid fury raged in her blue eyes, but I had the win, and she knew it. *No mercy,* I told myself. *You should offer no mercy and end it now.*

But I wasn't a killer. Not yet. "Yield," I shouted in her face.

"Okay! I yield."

Applause rang out from the surrounding females as I rose to my feet. Even some of the guards in the square gave crooked grins as though it was impressive for a female. And Raithe … I couldn't decipher the look in his dark eyes. He didn't smile, didn't even nod. I wasn't sure why that stung slightly. A feeling to decipher later.

Sherai and Akira ran towards me; their faces alight with huge grins. It was only when Sherai's face shifted into shock that I knew something was wrong. "Aeris!"

I turned in time to see a blade made of blood hovering in Portia's hand. *Blood Court magic.* Her face was the epitome of smug as she looked at me, ready to make good on her promise. Her arm raised, and I shifted, ready to dive out of the way, but the attack never came.

Shadows launched at Portia, prowling up her legs and

wrapping around her arm until she was held in a vice-like grip, making her magic sputter out and drip back to the ground. The next moment, Raithe towered over her, his eyes stormy and his jaw tight. "We have one rule for duelling. One. You. Do. Not. Wield." His shadows squeezed, until Portia screamed and something audibly snapped in her wrist. When he let go, her arm dangled limply. She cradled it and instantly retreated, her eyes wide as she gaped at him.

"The next time, it will be your throat my shadows seek." Raithe's eyes swept over every female in attendance. "We fight with honour in the Shadow Court, and we follow orders. Fail to follow the rules your instructor sets, and you will have me to deal with. Follow them, and you will flourish. Do not disappoint me again." With that, he strode off without a backwards glance, his shadows trailing the ground like mist behind him. I stared at his retreating form long after he disappeared from view.

Ryvia's wrath. He just broke her fucking wrist. A chill swept down my spine that had nothing to do with the cold. He'd saved me. Again. Debts were racking up quickly around here, and I had the feeling if I didn't find something to report to him soon, that would be my throat his shadows crushed. I had to get out of here. I would escape this castle one way or another. I damn well refused to die in it.

CHAPTER ELEVEN

'The herb is only as good as its master. Nurture it, and a fine potion one shall procure.'

An Alchemist's Guide to Herbal Remedies

The castle apothecary was blissfully quiet, sequestered in the eastern wing in a ward that was scarcely travelled by anyone other than the occasional servant. The healer was a no-nonsense female who ran a tight ship, but despite her regimented routine, Margaery had a softer side, too. I could see the care she put into her craft—felt her love for it, like I loved the science of alchemy. Being down here in the quiet calm was much more preferable to the chaos of the castle beyond.

I still couldn't believe what Raithe had done to Portia. How casually he'd snapped the bone. How cold and calculated he'd been, as if his punishment was just a slap on the wrist. But I supposed with a father like his, he'd probably faced much worse growing up. And I couldn't forget how old the captain was … all the things he must have seen and done.

I sighed as I gathered some valerian root and mint from the bushels drying in a row above the bench, then set them in a mortar and pestle. The tincture, once ground and made into a tea, would help some noble male or female sleep better, or at least ease their nerves. I could have used a cup myself.

The steady grinding as I twisted the pestle was a comfort as I looked around the apothecary. It was generously supplied, with all manner of herbs and spices from Mithria and beyond. A dream—my dream, in fact, to have such a store one day. There was something to be said for the quiet, easy rhythm of plucking herbs and amplifying their properties. The most unassuming herb could be the deadliest foe. The most beautiful flower could be an enemy's downfall. I wasn't only curious about the poisonous types, of course, but I'd learned their uses from my mother when I was a child.

She'd also loved working in the apothecary, but Father had put a stop to the hobby after a time. Perhaps he'd grown paranoid that she'd poison him. I wouldn't have blamed her.

Shit. My stomach did a little somersault as the thought popped into my head. My mother, who had once participated in the Rite and who had likely been in this very room long ago, perhaps even preparing the same tincture. I dumped the mortar and pestle onto the workbench and rushed to a shelf where Margaery kept all her records.

She'd have me reprimanded if she caught me snooping, but it was worth the risk. I ran my finger over the tomes. Purchase orders, recipes, several books about herbs and their uses, and stocktakes. I grabbed one of the latter. It pried open with a creak, and I glanced down at the first page. Name, date, item… Yes, this was exactly what I needed.

With a snap, I shut the book and popped it back on the

shelf, then scanned the date of the journal on the spine. We were in Adamantium Age VII now, but Mother would have been here sometime in Onyx Age VII. Each of the five Ages lasted 100 years and represented the cycle of life—the Bronze Age, which represented birth; the Silver Age, which represented growth; the Golden Age, highlighting prosperity; the Onyx Age, representing calamity; and then the Adamantium Age, finishing off with death. The cycle restarted with the Bronze Age. Each full cycle of 500 years was counted numerically as I.

Past records must be stored somewhere, though, given the lifespan of a Fae, it would need to be a large space. And given the Rite was an ancient tradition … I frowned. There must be hundreds, thousands of tomes to go through. *Fuck.* I didn't need to find a small library. I needed to find a damn archive.

"Working hard, I see," a husky voice said in the stillness.

I jumped, then tilted my head as I turned to its owner. "Tending to our court's many needs, I see."

Raithe smiled as he prowled into the small chamber. "I've been waiting for a report, Lockhart. I don't like waiting." He advanced, forcing me to retreat a few steps until I bumped into the shelf.

"I've been a tad busy trying not to get killed," I replied a little breathlessly. Gods. This male and the way my body wanted to bend in fright before him.

"Ah, yes, the fanged one." He smirked. "You're welcome, by the way."

My brows lifted in surprise. "Your little show of power, that was for me?"

He stepped closer again, until all six-foot-something of him was towering over me. "Despite what you might think, I don't go around breaking females' limbs for the fun of it."

"You wouldn't be the first male to do so," I pointed out.

"I am not the Pentad," he said in a low voice. "I do not condone the killing of females for sport. I would have thought that was obvious by now, given my mission. I don't want to hurt any females; I want to help them. I will, however, do what I must to protect my interests."

A tendril of shadow seeped out from his finger, curling around my body in lazy but tight spirals. I eyed off the threat slowly, then looked him in the eye. "Before you decide to get all murderous, I might have a lead." I cocked my head, considering. "First, have all of the past Rites taken place at this castle?"

Raithe lifted a hand to his stubbled chin. "For a long time, yes, but not always. The earliest Rites were held in nature, back when our kind had not long sailed to this land, and the courts weren't yet established. We hadn't met our gods then, nor did we have our dark powers."

I waved a hand. "An astute history lesson, but in the last 200 years, for example, they took place here at Castle Cliffscote?"

"I believe so. Why is this important?"

"My mother took part in the Rite," I said softly. "She would have been at this very castle fighting for her life."

The creeping shadow seemed to pause, then loosen ever so slightly, almost like it was caressing me now. "I would have been training in the navy whilst her Rite took place..." Raithe cocked his head. "I've had the unfortunate pleasure of dealing with your father multiple times, given his command over the merchant routes in Domeratt and thereby the seas in which my navy resides, but I don't recall meeting your mother."

"You wouldn't have. She disappeared when I was a child. I haven't seen or heard from her since."

Raithe's eyes darkened. "You don't say."

I took a deep breath and brushed the pain aside. I couldn't

go there right now, least of all with a stranger, so I redirected the subject. "I need you to show me to the castle archives."

His brow raised. "You're hunting for evidence from when she was here? To what end?"

"My mother loved working with herbs and tinctures, so I'm betting she would have been posted in this apothecary. There might be something useful in the records. She also—"

"Records which have no bearing on the present," he interrupted, his shadow pulsing in warning. He stepped closer until his chest was flush with mine, then curled a wave of my hair around his finger. "My patience is wearing thin, little lark."

I glared up at him. "If you'd let me finish, you big brute, I was going to say she also liked to journal. She would hide them in a panel beneath her bed back home so Father wouldn't find them. If my hunch is right, she would have kept a journal here, too. I'm betting there'd be some interesting observations in it." At his blank expression, I continued, "I need to find out which room she stayed in so I can search for her journals. Journals filled with helpful information, perhaps even secrets the Pentad wouldn't want known. If we're really lucky, possible locations for enslaved females?"

"You're reaching." His shadows receded, but he tilted my chin up. "But consider my interest piqued. I'll take you to the archives, but if your search comes up empty…"

"I'll have you to worry about," I retorted, slapping his hand away. "You've made your point. Now, which way to the archives?"

Raithe laughed. "Oh, no, little lark. This isn't a trip we can take during the day. Too many eyes watching. The guards would search you on your way out, not to mention the questions that would arise from my accompanying you. The Bridegroom isn't supposed to have favourites. Not at this stage of the Wedding Rite, at least. I'll come for you at midnight. Ensure that you're ready."

"How do you—?" He was gone before I could finish my sentence.

With an amused shake of my head, I finished making the sleeping tonic, taking the liberty to craft a special vial for myself.

CHAPTER TWELVE

Fennigal Root is a hardy little herb that thrives in mossy, moist conditions—often hidden beneath rotting roots and stumps. Take care when administering, else the consumer might find themselves missing more than a mere few hours.

An Alchemist's Guide to Herbal Remedies

The knock on my door came at midnight on the dot, and I let Raithe into my room wordlessly, closing the door behind him. His lips curved as he apprised me from head to toe. "The leathers suit you, little lark."

"You're not so bad yourself," I admitted softly.

He really, really wasn't. The captain was dressed in all black, the occasional silver glint gleaming off his sheathed blades from the light of my bedside candle. In the low firelight, his muscled frame looked softened somehow, like this was the male without his mask.

I stiffened as he stepped closer, his hand reaching for my braid, and ran it down the blonde locks just once. He chuckled at my reaction, but his face turned serious as he looked me in the eyes. Gods, why did it have to feel so intimate when he looked at me like that? So close, with eyes like sapphires. A silly, illogical part of me wanted to know their secrets, but I looked away, careful to gaze at anything but his face as he tucked my braid under the hood of my tunic.

Oh. I had thought touching me was rather forward, but it was out of practicality. I guessed he preferred not to have any identifiable traits showing, should I be seen. My cheeks burned, but I bit my tongue and kept a straight face. When he was finished tucking it away, he held my shoulders, capturing my attention once more. "There will be guards patrolling the castle, with two posted at the archive entrance. You ready for this?"

"I can manage sneaking around, but why do you need to? Sneaking doesn't really seem like a captainly thing to do."

Raithe raised a brow. "I enjoy a little light reading, but the archive stores records from across many ages. Our history is in there, along with artefacts and scriptures that my father and the Pentad guard closely. They would certainly notice if such texts went missing or became public knowledge and would mercilessly punish whoever had taken them. I would like to see what exactly they're hiding. Besides, scribes meticulously record all who enter the archive, including which texts they peruse and lend. It would look a little suspicious for me to suddenly take an interest in borrowing books about Rites and its participants, don't you think?"

"Who said anything about borrowing?" I said coyly.

He grinned. "Hence the sneaking."

I smiled back. "Seems our captain is a bit of a rebel."

"My father would say more of an anarchist. But I prefer revolutionary."

"Careful, Raithe, you almost sounded wise there. But a revolutionary isn't any different to a rebel."

His eyes lit with surprise. "The little lark has a sharp beak." A smirk formed. "And I do so like the way you say my name."

Oh. Was he flirting with me? I bit my lip, wondering what had caused the shift. It could just be a show of rebellion, seeing as he wasn't supposed to have 'favourites'. Or perhaps it was the excitement of sneaking around and actively working together. Our truce felt easier than usual, regardless. He felt relaxed and was not so intimidating. Like we'd both lowered our guard, even if only temporarily. I rolled my eyes and tried to squash the smile on my lips. "Archives, *Raithe*. Now."

His shadows did a little flourish as he gestured for me to exit the room first. "After you."

I felt his eyes drink me in as I stalked past him. I didn't have time to unpack the playfulness of that exchange. Not when we had a mission to complete, and especially not when he still very much held my life in his hands. The door opened with a gentle crack as I peeked out. Empty. I nodded at Raithe, then waited as he took the lead.

His shadows cloaked us in darkness every time we flitted under a light or past an open window. The castle was quiet. The odd servant trundled down hallways with tired steps, not noticing our presence as we hid behind statues or in nooks, but our progress was unhindered as we snuck through the castle and down to its lower levels. Only when we neared the kitchen did we hear voices. It sounded like an argument. I wondered what kind of food preparations required kitchen staff to be here so early or so late.

Raithe suddenly swept me into the shadows of an adjacent alcove, pinning me against the wall as he covered us in darkness. Interestingly, the shadows did nothing to hinder my vision, and I peered around his broad shoulder to see three bodies moving in the kitchen. I couldn't see their faces from where the doorway partially hid them from view, but I recognised one voice easily enough.

My eyes narrowed. *Portia.* Raithe must have recognised her first and decided that we should listen in.

"There are no rules, Christine," Portia snapped. "We can keep killing them off without any consequence. No one will be the wiser."

"You made the last kill pretty obvious," a smaller, softer voice said. "And then you drew attention to yourself by wielding at training yesterday. I don't think we should keep doing this. What if it gets us in trouble?"

"Coward," the third voice spat. "You're just too afraid to do the deed yourself."

"It's your turn, Christine," Portia said. "We made a deal, remember? The three of us stick together to take out the competition. Do I have to carry the load for all of us?"

"I just…" Christine's voice trickled off. "I've changed my mind. I don't want to go ahead with this. It's not an honourable thing to do, and the captain seems to value honour a great deal."

"Honour?" Portia laughed harshly. "What a lovely moral to have in a game of death. It's all well and good for him to speak of honour when he's not the one fighting for survival. Fine. If that's the way you want to play, go play it on your own. Liv and I are willing to do the dirty work."

"Run along now," Liv added.

The one called Christine left the room in a hurry, but before she could escape, a knife point emerged from her stomach. I let out a squeak of surprise, and Raithe quickly clamped his hand over my mouth.

"Did you hear that?" Portia's face appeared behind Christine, whom she unceremoniously shoved to the ground as she stepped out into the hall. Liv joined her, searching the darkness. Gurgles filled the silence, as Christine's blood pooled over the navy carpet lining the hall.

I looked at the two females' faces, then at the female on the floor. They'd called her a coward, yet Portia had stabbed her in the back. Christine never stood a chance. By the time a healer found her, she'd be long dead. Even if I ran to get one now, it would be too late. My hand curled into a fist, but Raithe placed his hands to the wall above my shoulders and shook his head. He blocked my view, and all I could see were his eyes, drilling into mine. I could feel the steady rise and fall of his chest, the way his body had ensnared me, shadows surrounding us. I wondered if he could feel how fast my heart beat in my chest.

Footsteps sounded, then backtracked moments later. "There's no one there," Liv whispered.

"Probably just a cat," Portia said with a sniff. "It doesn't matter. Christine's no longer a liability. Next on my list? The Lockhart girl."

"Aeris," Liv said. "She's the Master Mariner's daughter."

"I know who she is," Portia said darkly. "I've known that name most of my life."

My stomach tied in knots as discomfort and confusion settled in. I had no idea who this female was, but she sure seemed to know who I was. What could I have possibly done? Did my father have something to do with whatever grudge she was holding?

"You still haven't explained why she's the top of your priority list. What did she do?" Liv asked, echoing my thoughts.

"Another time. Her days are numbered; that's all that

matters. Merchant daughter or not, she's dead. Let's get out of here before anyone smells the body and comes looking," Portia said as they strode away.

We waited until they'd passed, then I toed Raithe's boot. "You can release me now."

He shifted, giving me a full view of Christine's body. I did my best to ignore the way her lips were parted in shock, her eyes frozen. "Keep moving, little lark. There was nothing you could do."

"We could have killed them," I suggested.

"Is that what you want?" his voice was deep as he took the lead once again.

Yes. No. Maybe? I didn't have an answer to that, so I stayed silent as we pressed on until we'd descended several stairs and were now underground. The air was cool and dry down here, which was the perfect condition to store priceless and aged books.

"Ahead," Raithe said with a nod.

Two guards stood at the archive entrance, as he'd promised. "And how were you planning to take out the guards?" I asked. We halted and stood behind a large stone statue.

He shrugged. "A knock to the head should sort them out."

"Don't you think they'll remember who did that when they wake?" I shook my head. "Why not use your shadows?"

Raithe shook his head. "The entrance is well lit. While my shadows can hide us, they would notice the imperfection of light."

I blew out a breath. "Okay. I have a better idea."

"What are you—Aeris!" he hissed as I walked confidently towards the guards, whose body language instantly shifted from half asleep to alert.

"A little late for a leisurely stroll, don't you think, miss?" one guard asked.

"The archives are off limits to female participants," the other sneered. He licked his lips and smoothed a hand over his bald head. "But I could be persuaded if you'd like to have a little fun."

Ew. Pass. I slid my hand into my back pocket and palmed the vial I'd stuffed there earlier, then shifted on my feet as I smiled coquettishly. The stopper flicked off easily from my thumb. "I'm always up for a little fun."

The guard placed a hand on my waist, pulling me close. I leaned in, then blew the dust from my palm into his face, quickly doing the same to the other.

Both pawed at their eyes and noses, then collapsed over each other within seconds. I turned and beamed at a bewildered Raithe as he approached. "Slumbercap mixed with Fennigal Root in powdered form induces immediate sleep and will erase the last few hours from the user's memory."

"I'm impressed. But won't the healer notice such valuable ingredient stock missing?"

I grinned. "Just a pinch of this and that. There are new supplies coming in every week. She won't notice a few trimmed leaves, and vials get broken in transit all the time. I made this handy little concoction earlier today on a whim. Never know when it might come in handy, especially with a certain someone hellbent on my death."

"On a whim," he said with a chuckle. "The clever fox is always one step ahead."

"Even a clever fox can be caught in a trap," I replied as I wiped my hands on my slacks.

After pulling the guards behind a stack of crates away from view, we entered the archive, which immediately lit up with warm Fae light. I blew out a breath as we faced row upon endless row of towering bookshelves. It would have taken years to sort this place, not to mention a team of scholars and librarians to keep records up to date.

"There must be a catalogue somewhere," I said.

"Already on it." He ushered me over to a desk with a ledger that kept record of all the borrowed books, just like he'd said. A quick search revealed a catalogue on the shelf below it.

"Look for 'H' then 'R,'" I suggested.

He flipped the pages of the giant tome with surprising care as he searched.

I stopped him at the page I'd had in mind. "Herbs and remedies, aisle 28, section 24. I'll start there. You look for anything on the Rites."

"Meet back here in 30," Raithe said. "I don't want to push our luck, especially with two unconscious guards out there."

I nodded. We split up, heading to separate parts of the archives. My strides were purposeful as I counted the rows, almost stopping more than once as a section caught my eye. Alas, reading for pleasure was not on the cards tonight. We had a job to do.

The aisle on herbology and potion making was a big one, with tomes dating back centuries, detailing the earliest practices of Fae magic and healing. As necromancy and darker magics were our way of life in Mithria, healing had been a slow learning curve. It was a rare gift indeed to be granted healing powers at all, and even then, we had adapted from learnings made across the seas in other continents.

Our power awoke after our ascension—a ceremony in which Fae youth died, only to be reborn with our newfound gifts, should the Goddess Ryvia grant them. Anyone who failed to pass her judgement was destined for an eternity of torment, even in death. I shivered. It was a cruel ceremony, but one every acolyte faced. To avoid this ceremony meant a long life spent being shunned by society ... or killed for cowardice.

I remembered the utter cold of the escix. The waters of that sacred pool felt like death itself, but they merely held our bodies afloat while we passed briefly into a realm in between until Ryvia passed judgement. Once the goddess deemed us worthy, she would decide the court best suited to our power. Then, according to our aspirations, we would join the court we aligned with. Unluckily for me, she had decided The Shadow Court best suited my talents ... which meant I had remained stuck with my father and had still not discovered what my power even was.

I shook my head. Now was not the time to wallow in my frustrations. I glanced along the rows of books until I saw a series of stocktakes and other apothecary records with Onyx Age IV imprinted on the spine, along with the subsequent years. I continued scanning until I came across Onyx Age VII, then picked up a book. It struck me that I didn't actually know how old my mother was. I'd been too young to think to ask, and then she'd disappeared, and I'd never had the chance.

My eyes narrowed. She'd left me all alone with that monster I'd called Father. Who ensured I had known no love or kindness. Had never had anyone to share my deepest thoughts with or share a hug. There had been males, yes, but those quick trysts had never filled the ache or the emptiness of truly being alone. Not when you're a female. Not when you were the only child of one of the more powerful lords in the court. And yet, despite my anger towards my mother, a part of me still wanted to find her. To know any part of her soul that might be jotted down in ink and buried in the lines of a book.

I flipped through the pages of the records I'd selected, scanning the dates and signatures of the persons on duty in the apothecary. Nothing. I searched another, and another, until I'd scanned so many with nothing to show for it that I was about to give up. Then, in a well-worn book, a feminine scrawl caught my eye, the letters looping daintily. Signed, Marion Chambers. My mother's maiden name.

My heart skipped a beat. I knew she'd been a participant in the Rite, but seeing her name and knowing she'd been in my position made my stomach roll. Had she feared for her life? Did she try to escape the castle, or had she entered into the Rite willingly? Dust plumed out of the pages as I turned them, looking for a note or a hint of personalisation. Nothing. I tried the next book, just in case, but her name wasn't listed. Bitter disappointment filled my chest. Why would it have been? The Rite couldn't have lasted more than a few months. The Pentad wouldn't drag out their sick games too slowly, or else they'd grow bored with the entertainment.

I opened the original book up again and stroked a finger over her name. She was here. And she'd worked in the apothecary. *Just like me.* Which meant she likely stayed in one of the rooms on my level of the castle. If I could find out which one and have a look inside, I might find a hidden journal somewhere. Maybe we even shared the same room. My eyes watered, and I swallowed back the lump forming in my throat. I would *not* cry over this right now. With a grunt, I kicked the shelf, annoyed that I was still so affected by the past.

A small, tattered book plopped to the ground, its pages landing open on the floor. I leaned forward curiously. No title, no name. Just a plain leatherbound book with yellowed pages. And as I turned it over in my hand, my heart leapt, because every page contained that same looping handwriting, full of numerous entries journaled by my mother. *This was it.*

"Thank you, Brindere," I whispered to the God of Elements and Good Fortune, with a quick kiss to the book's cover. I got up and ran back to the entryway, where I found Raithe waiting.

"I found something!" I said with a beaming grin.

His gaze lingered a beat too long, but he smiled too as he waved a few books in the air. "I'm not sure yet, but I might have, too." He nodded at the journal I held. "Your mother's?"

I nodded. "They must thoroughly search every room; otherwise my mother wouldn't have hidden it down here. There must be at least a couple of months' worth of entries in here. There has to be something useful here. I can feel it."

"Let's hope we both find some answers. For now, we should get you back to your room. Here, take this."

My brows lifted as he unsheathed a handsome dagger. The edges of the hilt curved like a rolling wave; a single sapphire was embedded into the centre. "It's beautiful," I sighed.

"It will keep you safe in case Portia or Liv decide to pay you a visit. I'd be sorely disappointed if someone else took your life. Keep your wits. Bar your door at night and do not trust anyone."

"Including you?"

His eyes danced with amusement. "Especially me."

I took the dagger and squeezed my mother's journal tightly in my other hand. "Thank you." I slid the weapon into my boot, turned, then headed for the door.

"And Aeris," Raithe said softly. I looked over my shoulder and saw a small smile on his face, even as sadness glimmered in his eyes as he followed behind. "I'm glad you found something about your mother."

Well, that was new. My stomach did a little flip at the kindness in those words, which, for some reason, stayed in my mind long after he'd seen me safe and sound back to my room.

By the time I got to bed, my eyes were too bleary to read,

so I made a makeshift hiding spot in my armoire and slid the journal away for safekeeping. As I fell asleep, I thought once more of Raithe and his quest for his mother. I dreamed of the sadness in those eyes when he'd looked at me. Worse, I dreamed of how those eyes might smile when he found his mother.

CHAPTER THIRTEEN

'If you're reading this journal, you're either very nosy or very desperate for help. The good news is this: I serve my tea hot and my advice with a side of cold-hard truth.'

I rose with the sun, basking in the golden rays as they beamed down through the frosted glass windows. Outside, the ocean tides were calm, unlike the violent swirling of my stomach. It was excitement, yes, but also trepidation. What would I find on the pages of my mother's journal? What horrors might she have inked that I was yet to face?

I sucked in a lungful of air, blowing it out on a sigh as I grabbed the journal and settled down beside the window on the parquet floor. I flipped through the book, procrastinating, when a torn page caught my eye. I slid my finger over it to mark the spot, and my heart jolted with excitement. A folded note had been squashed between the pages; the parchment aged with time and stained with blotted fingerprints. It gave the impression of being hurriedly scrawled. With another deep breath, I opened the note and read:

Dear reader,

If this journal is in your possession, then I am likely dead, and you are no doubt next. I have done everything they asked of me. I have killed under duress. I have survived countless attempts on my life. I pray that it will be enough, but there is a feeling in my gut… an instinct that my life will not be long-lived, even if I survive what comes next.

The Wedding Rite is barbaric and not what we have been led to believe. I hope if you have found my journal that it can aid or comfort you should you also face the Rite and soon look upon your death … or worse.

We thought the females who failed in the Rite all perished. But not all of them do. Some of them, many of them, are taken. I have discovered what they do with them, and I know where they are taken. Gods, if this note has been found, it means I couldn't help them.

Our sex has always been treated as lesser. We have always been pitted against each other. But we must stop allowing the males to divide us. We need each other. I beg of you, find them. Save the ones who are lost and free them from their iron prisons. Let there be an end to this empire of madness.

I must hurry. The drumming has begun. We females are being herded, and the guards will be coming for me. I'm so afraid. But the blood has not stopped spilling, and the Pentad must slake their thirst.

Go to the place where wooden teeth lead to still waters and look not at the ground but what's beneath it. There you will find them at the beginning of the end.

Good—

I scanned the abrupt end to the letter in dismay. No. *No.* There had to be more. There had to be something other than a cryptic riddle and a doom-filled farewell. I knew, realistically, that this letter wasn't the last thing my mother ever wrote. But it was the last thing she'd written *here.* Had she intended to come back for her journal once she'd won the Rite and freed the females? Obviously, she never had the chance. Father probably had eyes on her at all hours. It seemed like keeping her imprisoned in the castle was the kind of fucked-up thing he would do. But then … how did she ever escape him in the end?

Fuck. Raithe needed to see this. As much as I wanted to read my mother's diary entries, this was important. But I still hadn't completely ruled out that the captain could be involved with the Pentad. He was the captain of the Shadow Court navy, after all. True, his motivation seemed genuine, and despite this tentative alliance being forged with my life as a bargaining piece, I felt bad for him. He only wanted to have his mother back. I understood that feeling well. But was it the whole truth?

The more I considered, the less I felt like I could trust him. I needed to think of myself and the missing females. If I could get out of here, maybe I could find someone to help me, someone who had nothing to do with this place and no connection to the Pentad. At the very least, I'd be safer. After all, I wouldn't be able to help anyone if I was dead. Yes, that's exactly what I needed to do. I needed to escape. Now.

A dozen scenarios ran through my head, all of them crazier than the last. Scaling the castle walls, rock climbing down the cliff, stealing a horse and charging through the gate —*yeah, good luck with that one, Aeris*—hiding in a merchant cart. Oh, praise Falane, that was it! One of the servants was heading into town today to barter goods. A large shipment of herbs was being delivered to one of the healers in Domeratt. Margaery, the castle healer, would never allow me to go, of course, but if I could hide in the cart when no one was looking…

The journal fit nicely and snugly at the small of my back in the waistband of my pants. I dashed to don a cloak before creaking my door open and listening for any sign of movement. Nothing to be concerned about. This wing of the castle remained relatively quiet in the early morning. Servants went about their work once the females had started training, and most seemed to get as much precious sleep as they could before starting the long day of chores and gruelling body work.

No one batted an eye as I descended the stairs. I paused at the mid-level landing, looking out the tall window to see a merchant cart nearly at capacity already. *Shit.* My window of opportunity was quickly closing. I raced down the steps and through the corridors of disgruntled servants and females who were still waking up and in search of breakfast. I reached the apothecary and finally slowed my steps, forcing my breathing to become even as I stepped inside casually.

"Aeris? What are you doing here?" Margaery looked down her nose at me, her glasses sliding down the bridge, as she weighed a bag of what looked like cloves and checked her stock list. "Your shift doesn't start until after training."

"I couldn't sleep," I lied. "Thought I'd help with the shipment."

"Well, who am I to turn down the help?" She turned to a crate of vials filled with various concoctions. "Take this to the cart and be careful! Those are expensive. If you break a single one, I'll—"

"You'll have me whipped or you'll twist my ear off?" I

grinned, picking up the crate. "I'm sure you'll find a punishment worthy of the crime."

Margaery smacked her list onto the counter and removed her glasses. She looked even more stern without them as she pursed her lips and straightened her brown hair in its bun. "I'm going to pretend you didn't just talk back to a superior and instead tell you to move before the driver leaves. That is the last crate."

"Yes, ma'am," I said with a nod. She threw me an exasperated smile before waving me off absentmindedly.

It was a short trip out the apothecary door to the inner courtyard where the cart waited. My heart sank when it came into view. Servants bustled around the thing from every side, and the driver was carefully loading every single item, paying close care and attention to each. There was no chance of sneaking onboard.

"Another one?" The driver groaned as I approached. "It'll be hard enough to fit everything in without squashing anything. That female's going to be the death of me."

I smiled apologetically. "You could do a second trip?"

He side-eyed me as he took the crate. "Cheeky thing. Go on with ya." Then he turned to look at one of the laundresses. "How many more on your end?"

I turned to walk away, my heart sinking deep into my stomach…

"Two chests. They're rather large. Then you're free to go," the female said.

"Thank Valere," the driver said with a sigh. "Hurry on now. I'll make room for them. The weather is turning, and I'd like to be in Domeratt by sundown."

"Would you like us to bring you something to drink before you go?" the female asked him, which led to the driver asking what kinds of things they had on offer.

I used the opportunity to quickly change course. *The laundry rooms.* With one last hopeful dash, I strode purposefully to the other servant's door near the kitchen and laundry and ducked through the throng of people too focused on their duties to notice me.

A few turns later, and I was in the laundry room, facing two large chests. The room was blessedly empty of any servants, likely still talking or bringing the driver something to eat or drink. *Now or never.* I took one quick look in each chest. The first was overflowing with bolts of fabric. The second was lined with beautiful garments fit for a queen. I treated them as anything but while I snatched several out and hid them under some dirty washing. I wasn't about to question why they were sending fabric away from the castle. Maybe it was excess after the 12 died in the crypt. Either way, I stepped into the chest and folded my body into an uncomfortable ball. I popped a few dresses over me and closed the lid right before the laundresses returned.

I heard them remove the other chest, then waited with bated breath as they came back for the one I was squashed inside. A few minutes later and I could hear the bustle of the courtyard.

"Ooof." The driver's voice was muffled as he groaned, and the chest was placed down and then lifted clumsily again. "What in Ryvia's name do you have in here?"

"Very valuable artefacts that are worth more than your life," I recognised the head seamstress snap. I could tell by the feminine trill that it was her. "Now use those muscles of yours —"she paused, and I imagined the cursory look she must have granted his skinny frame—"wherever they may be hiding, and get on with it."

"Yes, ma'am," he responded miserably.

Then I was hefted up, the chest swaying violently as the

laundresses and the driver carried me onto the cart with a resounding thud, causing me to bump my head. I bit my lip, then narrowed my eyes at my invisible carriers. The likelihood of Margaery's vials smashing just increased exponentially, based on how the driver treated these goods. He *really* wanted to get to Domeratt before sundown.

Voices carried as the driver bid the staff goodbye and clucked for his horse to get moving. The cart slowly rolled out, and I breathed a sigh of relief as I shifted the gowns from my face and took a breath of air. It was stuffy in here, and I was not looking forward to a long voyage crammed in this godsforsaken thing. But I was here. I was getting *out.* If there was room, I'd kick my legs in excitement, but as it was, I'd be sporting one hell of a migraine and an aggravated back in a few hours based on the crick already forming in my neck. All I could do was listen as the cart journeyed on. No guards stopped us, no one inspected the cart, and the gate, mercifully, rolled open with a loud groan that allowed us through.

About twenty minutes of journeying along the road, and a voice called out, causing the cart to halt. Whomever it was, the driver seemed amicable towards them—even pleased. I held my breath as the males spoke, then hastily covered myself with the dress as boots sounded on the gravel path. Was this another checkpoint I didn't know about?

The chest lid opened, and I froze as the garment was swept aside. Above me, Raithe stood with the most damnable fucking smirk on his face as he looked at his catch. "There you are."

CHAPTER FOURTEEN

'Spell Weavers, most commonly residing in the Shadow Court, are masters of shadow and dark magics. Wielders from this court are widely renowned for their ability in combat and their prowess in clever magic.'

The Trials and Traditions of a Mithrian Fae

I blinked back at Raithe, silently pleading for him to let it go. For him to pretend he hadn't seen me. We'd developed some kind of alliance, hadn't we? He didn't condone the Rite. Hated the very idea of it. He could understand why I had to leave. But … No, at the end of the day, he was a male and would see this as a betrayal. If he didn't have enough of a reason to kill me before, he did now. As expected, the smirk on his face vanished, replaced by a darkness in his eyes and a clenched jaw. My stomach twisted at the sight of it.

"Gunnar," Raithe said calmly without looking away, "one of your wheels is looking a bit wobbly. You might want to tighten it before you continue. Wouldn't want to get stuck out here with one wheel with the storm coming." To me, he spoke beneath his breath, "Get out of the cart before I tear you out. Wait in the woods. If you even think about escaping, I will hunt you down, and you will not enjoy my mercy. But believe me, I will enjoy the chase."

I looked him dead in the eye as he hauled me out of my box. "So, you really are just like the Pentad. Of course you are, you're male. I will not forgive this, Raithe. And I certainly won't forget."

That charming smile returned for the driver, even if his eyes flashed at me with warning. "Good. Hold onto that anger. You'll need it."

He walked around the side to show the driver the allegedly loose wheel, which gave me the time needed to dash into the woods unseen. I didn't stop running, though. Fuck what Raithe had said. He could kill me if he caught me, but I wasn't squandering this opportunity. I wouldn't stay a prisoner in this fucking Rite.

As I ran, the birds chirped in branches overhead, and a squirrel dashed across the path, enjoying the sunshine before the storm and cold kicked in. My boots sank into the muddied ground as I skirted roots and vaulted over fallen logs and the occasional boulder. My breath was steady, despite the adrenaline racing through me. I was doing it. I was escaping. I would find help before finding the missing females. I'd help all of them—including the females still participating in the Wedding Rite. Even that fanged bitch. We didn't deserve to be treated like livestock, not even her.

I kept turning these thoughts, my goals, my mother's goals, over and over in my mind. It took me a few minutes to realise the forest had gone deadly silent. I slowed and crouched next to a tree, palming the blade still hidden in my boot. Then I froze, closed my eyes, and used my senses to truly *listen*. He didn't make a sound, but I felt his presence the moment he stepped out from behind a tree.

I whirled, tossing the dagger with precision towards him, the blade flying true to his chest. Raithe's eyes widened, registering the attack with alarming speed before he shifted and plucked the blade mid-air.

Impossible.

He eyed the weapon, then those deep blue eyes drifted to me as he smiled. "You're going to regret that."

"Fuck you." I could have run—should have run—but instead I charged, the anger I held for the mistreated females and myself fuelling my body. I jabbed once, twice, with my fists, then reared out with a high kick.

He blocked every move effortlessly, then grabbed my leg and spun. I fell back into a tree with a snarl, his hand no longer wrapped around my calf. I charged again, lashing out with a flurry of punches and kicks. I was throwing everything at him, and yet I could tell he was holding back and still managing to deflect perfectly.

"You need to look for a weakness," he said as he blocked and sidestepped another blow. "Simply striking and hoping a punch might land is futile."

"Shut up," I hissed. "I do not take lessons from my enemy."

He shrugged even as he batted my arms away. "What a foolish thing to say. How do you expect to defeat your enemy if you know nothing about the way they fight? You can still hate someone and heed their lessons. The two are not mutually exclusive. I can help you."

I stared at him, aghast. "You just took away my chance of

freedom. If that's the help you're offering, I emphatically decline."

Raithe's face dipped into a frown. "That's an odd way to say thank you."

"You don't get it, do you. This is just a game to you." Rage moved through me in rolling waves, heating my skin and electrifying my veins. My voice was low, my body still but ready. "Are we all just names on a list for you to cross out? How much is mine worth, Captain? A fancy new ship? Or perhaps a new estate for you and your new bride, whomever she may be?"

He took one step closer. Shadows plumed at his feet, and I blanched, my spine locking up. My body acted on instinct, locking up at the proximity of a threat. I had been in this position too many times, cowering while I waited for the blow to land. This was it. I'd disobeyed the captain, and now he was going to end me himself just as he'd promised. But I wasn't going to grit my teeth and take it. Not today. Not anymore. "Don't come near me."

"Do you really think I am so like them? So cruel as to shackle you and all the rest to this castle myself?" He stepped forward again, and I retreated until my back smacked into a tree trunk.

"It doesn't matter what I think. It matters what you do … and what you allow to happen," I retorted. The plumes around his feet snaked farther along the ground, and that rage inside me reared its head again. Something else glimmered awake, too. Something deep, deep down. "I told you not to come closer."

"Despite what you may think, I am not one of them. I will *never* be one of them."

"If that were true, you would have let me go. You would

stand up to the Pentad. But I guess the Windaire blood runs strong. You *are* your father's son," I spat back.

His eyes hardened to ice, and the cold fury in them was chilling. I felt that ice and his shadows grip me, trying to make me cower into submission. A muscle ticked in his jaw, and then he advanced slowly. "So, because of my blood, I should bear the weight of my father's sins? Do I need to remind you of your lineage? Or are generational sins only forced upon males? You get a free pass for your victimhood."

I flinched at the verbal blow, but as he moved into my space, something inside me simply snapped. Any restraint I may have held thawed entirely, until that slumbering beast inside me woke and clawed through ice and shadow holding me, barrelling to the surface finally. Magic. Power.

"Stay. The fuck. AWAY." My power burst from me, crashing over Raithe like waves in an ocean storm. His shadows reared up to protect him, but mine sliced through them, bearing down on his body without mercy. He stumbled back, and my jaw dropped at the ripple of energy that blasted from my core, leaving me a little lightheaded. *My* shadows. Just as quickly as it happened, I felt them pull back and up into my fingertips, as if once again leashed. I looked at my hands in awe, turning them over slowly, then looked to Raithe, who was panting.

"By the gods," I whispered as our eyes met.

His face was full of cunning amusement. "So, you're a Shadow Wielder after all. Welcome."

I pushed off the tree and blinked at him. "That's my power? It felt so strong. That was incredible."

"That was your magic awakening. It always manifests at its most powerful. But you'll need training to reach that level again ... I didn't realise you were a virgin, little lark."

"I—what?" I stared at him indignantly. "That is none of your ... I most certainly am *not*—"

He smirked, as if I'd walked right into his trap, which I realised I had. "Relax, love. It'll be our little secret."

I blinked at him again. At the too-familiar term and the casual calmness with which he spoke to me. "You're insane, you know that, right? I don't understand you. Don't you want to kill me? I betrayed you. I ran. We're supposed to be fighting. How can you act like everything is fine? I wanted to kill you for what you did. I should still kill you."

He put a finger up. "You couldn't kill me, even if you'd actually tried. I have a couple hundred years on you, and while your magic is spectacularly powerful for someone so fresh, it's clearly tied to your emotions. Secondly, if I wanted to kill you, I would have already. Instead, I actually saved your life. All shipments from the castle are checked upon entering Domeratt." I opened my mouth to reply, but he waved his finger. "Had you managed to escape *before* arriving, you would have been caught in the storm, which is predicted to be wildly dangerous tonight. There are no towns nearby aside from our seaport, and Domeratt closes its gates at sundown. Where would you have gone? Are you familiar with these areas at all? Did you consider any of this before your foolishly impulsive decision?"

His barely concealed anger took me off guard. He seemed to be more affected by my leaving than was necessary for someone in his position. "I ... I would have survived some bad weather." I lifted my chin and admittedly felt foolish for not learning more about the workings of this area before escaping to them. "You give me no credit."

My indifference to the dangers seemed to be the thing that tipped him over the edge. "Because you deserve none!" The sound of his voice carried through the woods like thunder, causing a couple of birds to take flight. I gaped as he ran a hand through his hair and took a visible deep breath. Composing himself, he continued more softly, "The Pentad would have hunted you to the ends of the earth. They have their hounds. They have far more powerful magic. With the storm to slow you down, they would have found you within a day and made an example of you to all the other females. Your death would have been slow—drawn out for months, even. And after they were done torturing, assaulting, and mutilating you, they would have mounted your head on the castle walls. You're just a female to them. You're so far beneath them that you're lower than even their dogs. You said you wished to find out what happened to the missing females, and yet you risk a fate worse than theirs for what? Dignity? Pride? Dying doesn't help anyone. Running away doesn't stop the cycle. You say you don't understand me, but I cannot fathom how you could be so selfish."

My stomach churned, my clothes suddenly feeling too hot, too tight. I hadn't thought of escaping the castle as running away for good. From his perspective, I could see how it was selfish. How it looked like I was turning tail and leaving the females to fend for themselves. And, sure, maybe I was primarily getting out of there to save my own hide, but was that so wrong? I bit my lip, then felt shame wash over me. He was right. Running away wouldn't solve anything. It certainly wouldn't help us find the missing females. I'd spent so long looking out for myself that it had become second nature, but what was going on in the Rite was so much bigger than me. Bitterness soured my tongue as I sagged, but I didn't convey all my thoughts.

Instead, I said quietly, "They are going to kill me anyway. Kill all of us. If not directly themselves, then by a female in their stead. But you're right. I was rash and I was wrong. If it makes any difference, I was going to write to you when I was free and recruit help where I could. I found something in my mother's journal. Here."

He took the letter I handed him, read it carefully, then closed his eyes as he lowered the parchment. "So it's true, then. What we'd only suspected is confirmed by your mother. The Pentad has been holding females hostage for years now, perhaps centuries. My mother is likely among them."

Despite the anger still thrumming through me, my heart panged. I took a step closer, despite myself. "I'm sorry Raithe. I was hoping to investigate this somewhere far away from the Pentad's eyes and grasp, but I can admit when I'm wrong. It's difficult to accept this fate when my freedom has been taken from me twice now in so many weeks. It seems you're no freer than I, though." I sighed. "I'm … sorry … for misjudging you. I'm not used to someone being in my corner. The only people who ever were … they were taken away from me, too."

Blonde waves fell into my face as I bowed my head. For some reason, I didn't want him to see the tears that sprang to the surface. I purposefully kept my secrets under lock and key. Pain. Sadness. They were useless emotions that muddied the brain and confused the heart. They had never served me. Only anger did.

Raithe's boot crunched on the fallen leaves, stepping into my view of the ground. "We won't let them win, Aeris." Raithe took my hand, and I inhaled sharply as he brushed a thumb over my knuckles. "I'm sorry. But you cannot let them win. You cannot run away."

I turned my tear-filled eyes to his. *When had he taken another step closer?* His face was so close, his chest brushing against mine as he surveyed me. Those sapphire eyes softened ever so slightly as he tucked a strand of hair behind my pointed ear.

"Do you think I stand a chance?" I whispered against the wind.

"I know you do. Because I'm going to help you, Aeris, and because I get the feeling that you're too stubborn to let them win. You take your fate into your own hands, which is admirable. Besides, I'll be looking out for you the whole time."

I snorted. "Even you can't control all the shadows of the castle. Portia—"

"Will get what's coming to her," he said. "But there is another way I can keep you from further harm."

"Oh? And what's that?"

"Yule is fast approaching, which means Castle Cliffscote will be hosting a feast. It marks the official occasion when the Bridegroom can single out a favourite in the Rite. By Yule, the females have usually made alliances and friends, and the competitiveness plateaus. Revealing a favourite amid everyone feeling more comfortable stirs up drama, jealousy, and spilled blood, you see. And I can't very well be Captain of the Shadow Court navy without a date, can I?"

My eyes widened. "So … what? You don't want to pick a favourite, and your solution is you want me to be your arm candy for the night?"

"Not just the night. I want you to be my favourite," he said with a grin. "It's normal for lords of these Rites to pick a favoured female, it's usually seen as a try before you buy, or a means to stir up a more heated competition. But sometimes it's genuine and is used to better get to know each other. A sort of wooing, if you will. Of course, it's still all a part of the game, but this would afford you some protection from the Pentad and any other males visiting. Unfortunately, I am strictly forbidden from interfering with any participant disputes, regardless."

I laughed in disbelief. "Raithe Windaire … Are you seriously asking to court me?"

His smile did something to my stomach as white teeth flashed and a dimple popped on one cheek. "Yes, Aeris Lockhart, I believe I am."

I laughed again, and this time it felt truly freeing. Genuine. Even if his so-called 'claim' on me was a sham, it was certainly an entertaining one. What an unexpected ride this morning proved to be. "Then I guess I'm courting the Fae Captain. My answer is yes."

"You have no idea how sweet that music sounds to my ears, little lark."

CHAPTER FIFTEEN

'There are no second chances when it comes to the Rite. You survive, or you die.'

Journal excerpt, author unknown

I planned to wake early the next day so I could dive into my mother's journal before breakfast. But I never got the chance. Instead, hands clamped over my mouth, silencing my waking scream as my eyes shot open. I bit down hard, causing the attacker to swear as I kicked and thrashed. In the darkness, a second person joined, pinning my body down and shoving a bag over my face. My breaths came short and sharp as the scratchy material blew back and forth against my lips.

Then, I was picked up and set on my feet, followed by a male voice whispering in my ear. "If I were you, I'd cooperate, or you'll spend the first portion of the next test unconscious and vulnerable to the other females … as well as everything else. It's your choice."

My heart sank. The next test was already here? I hadn't had a chance to prepare. To even get a glimpse of my mother's findings. She might have mentioned what to expect or what to avoid. I gritted my teeth as I thrashed against my attacker. "Fuck. You."

A chuckle followed. "She's a feisty one. My money's on her lasting longer than the others."

"Nah. That fanged bitch has got some real grit. She'll win for sure."

"I'll bet you 50 silvers."

"Make it 100."

I should have stayed quiet. Should have kept a low profile, but the way they were talking about us females like we were horses in some race … I snapped.

"I raise you both 100 silvers," I breathed through the fabric, "that I'll kill the two of you before I leave this place."

"She's got a mouth on her, too," the first one said with another laugh.

"I know a couple of ways to shut it," the other added.

A flash of fear skittered down my spine, but I snarled, managing to escape the tight grip of the second kidnapper and elbowed them, presumably, in the face.

"Bitch broke my nose!" He punched me in the stomach, and I bent over double as the air rushed from my lungs.

I laughed between gasps as I straightened. "I'll break more than that by the end."

"Say one more word," the first male said, "and I'll end you before we even get to the test. A little push down the stairs ought to do it. No one would bat an eye over a clumsy female. Or maybe you'd prefer we give you to the Pentad. They'll do far worse, you know."

Anger flooded my veins like a river, but I kept my mouth shut as we walked. The sound of boots on polished timber filled the air as more guards entered the hall with their kidnapped victims in tow. It seemed silly to march us all to our location instead of just drugging us again, but then, I supposed it was all part of the act. All designed to incite fear and chaos. And it was certainly working.

Females shouted and screamed as they were dragged from their beds, and judging by the answering yelps and thuds, more than a few males quickly silenced them. That river beneath my skin turned into a torrent, surging through my blood. My flesh tingled, and that same feeling of something awakening inside me followed. My power cracked an eye, as if awoken by pure intrigue. But as quick as the notion came, it was gone again, leaving me simmering and helpless.

Eventually, the females were all brought to heel, and we were marched in silence for what felt like an age. Despite having the bag over my head, I kept tabs on the directions we took, marking all the stairs and every twist and turn. I had mapped out the route from my bedchamber to the main rooms of the castle several times since coming here, always conscious of finding an exit or a means of escape should it present itself. If my calculations were correct, we'd just passed the dining hall and were now heading out into the gardens on the southern side of the castle.

"Watch your step, girl. We're near the cliff now." *The cliff?* I tried to scrabble back in alarm. Descending that rockface would be death even for most experienced climbers. "Easy," the male said with a chuckle. "We'll be going down some steps soon. Slow and steady and you'll be fine."

Steps, not slopes or rocks or ledges. Steps were Faemade, which meant there must be a secret staircase somewhere near the castle. Idiots might have kept that tidbit to themselves, but I would check it out later … if I survived whatever was to come.

Sure enough, we began the descent, and the males actually treated me with some level of care as we made gradual progress. It didn't escape my notice that if I fell, there was a good chance I could take them with me. Perhaps they had come to the same conclusion. I could hear the ocean lapping gently against the rocks and cliff face, and I focused on my breathing to steady the racing of my heart. My foot slipped on wet stone, and I jerked my arms in response, my stomach lurching. The guards immediately tightened their grasp, steadying me, and the second one cursed under his breath. *That one really didn't like me. Well, hey, the thought was fucking mutual, bud.*

A sudden scream sounded behind, along with a loud grunt and a curse, and then a horrible *smack* followed shortly after. The skin on my arms formed bumps as sick realisation set in. Another one down, this time lost to poor footing ... or someone pushing her. I tried not to dwell on the latter. If this was the Pentad's way of setting our teeth on edge and striking fear into our hearts, it was working. We started as 50, then we were 38 by the end of the first test. Portia had killed two more, and now a third was gone before the second test even began, leaving just 35 of us. I could almost smell the ripe stench of panic beneath the salt in the air, and an unhealthy portion of it was coming from me. *One step at a time, Aeris. Just keep moving.*

Thankfully, I heard no other females fall to their deaths, and I felt the blessed spray of water on my skin as we reached the bottom. A few minutes later, my captors dumped me in a boat and then began rowing. We didn't speak. Not until the strangest sensation washed over me. I swore and bent over as my stomach did a flip and my entire body zinged with energy. I gritted my teeth at my ribs feeling as though they were caving in on themselves, my heart slowing momentarily. Just as quickly as it had come, the feeling was gone again.

"What the fuck…," I said between sharp breaths, "…was that?"

"We've passed through a veil," one of the males answered gruffly. "From now until your return, your magic will remain dormant. No wielding in this test."

"Lucky me," I grumbled. Not that it made much difference for me personally. My power may have awakened but I didn't know how to effectively control it.

"You won't find any luck here," the second guard said with no small amount of satisfaction. "Not unless Brindere favours you with good fortune. Now get up. We're here."

Twenty-two minutes, give or take a few. That's how long it took to cross the body of water and reach our destination. The boat came to a bumpy halt, and the bag on my head was ripped off before I was shoved into the water rippling over the shoreline. A sharp shell sliced my hand as I fell to my knees on the sand. I hissed as I stiffly rose to my feet.

My heart sank as I took in my surroundings. We were on an island, with our only means of escape currently rowing back towards the castle through what looked like a graveyard of broken ships dotting the shallow waters. Stars still glimmered above, the moon bright in its seat, but the skyline appeared to be shifting. First light would soon be upon us.

One of the males grinned as he stood at the rear of the rowboat. "Don't make me regret my bet, girl," he called. Then he threw a shoddy blade. It moved in a straight line as it sailed overhead and thudded into the sand.

Even in the predawn darkness, it was clear what he'd tossed, and not just to my eyes. A line of females freshly shoved out of their beds and into boats followed the short sword with their eyes. I couldn't let them take it. I ran toward the lifeline the male guard had offered. But I slipped in the sand just shy of where it lay. Just out of reach, my fingertips nearly brushed against the hilt when someone pulled me back.

Portia's accomplice, Liv, and her triumphant face greeted me as I turned and kicked her in the stomach with my free leg. She shrieked and let go, and I scrambled through the sand towards the one thing that could end this fight quickly. But she grabbed me by both legs this time and dragged me back towards the water as I clawed for purchase, and sand scraped under my nails painfully. I was once again soaked as the shock of cold water hit my chest. The next thing I knew, my head was under the shallows, with Liv holding my face under with both hands, then dragging me back up. Salt filled my mouth as I struggled. I gritted my teeth and felt my nostrils flare as the water rushed over me again and again, giving me precious little air in between the steady in-and-out of the tide.

My eyes burned as the sea water clung to my lashes. All I could see when the water receded were flashes of bodies as females fought. Each time I lifted an arm, Liv would bat it away, until my very lungs threatened to collapse. I had no air, no breath, no strength in my veins. Her hand splayed over my cheek as I fought, her finger slipping over my mouth.

Panic gave way to fury, and I bit down hard on the slender bone. There was a sickening crunch at the joint, causing her to scream and jerk away. That quick movement alone caused me to rip half her finger clean off her hand.

I stumbled to my feet and spat the tip of her finger out in disgust, coughing and gagging as the taste of iron mixed with the salt in my mouth. Blood poured from her wound, but I didn't waste any more time. It was pointless to try for the sword, now half buried in the dredged-up sand and being fought over by several other females desperate for an advantage to stay alive. I pushed my feet through the soft sand past them all, doing my best to keep my balance without slowing down. I didn't look behind to see whether Liv followed. The dunes were so close. If I could just—

Pain erupted up my side as Liv suddenly attacked me yet again, this time with the sword in hand. I cried out as the salt water soaking my clothes touched the fresh wound. By the gods, did she ever quit?! Her pale face twisted in a sneer, her wet brown hair clinging to her cheeks. She raised the blade above her head with both hands, blood streaming from her severed finger. I prayed to Ryvia that this was not my end. I looked into Liv's frenzied eyes and said a silent goodbye. But before she could bring the blade down on my head, a long shard of steel impaled through her stomach. Liv's brown eyes widened as she looked down at the sword point. The bearer removed it, yanking forcefully and painfully, causing a spray of blood to mist over the shallow water. Her brows knitted together before she fell to her knees, dropping her arms to her sides. Her brown eyes turned black as her eyes dilated, and she was dead before her body hit the ground.

"Akira?" I gasped as I looked up at my ally standing behind Liv's body.

She smiled grimly, then plucked Liv's blade from her hand and tossed it to me. "Go," she urged. "Get somewhere safe. I'll come find you when I can."

"Where are you going? Where's Sherai?" I asked. I hadn't had a chance to really look, but it was too dark to make out distinct features anyway.

Another female charged at Akira before she could answer. She blocked the hit just in time, then adjusted her stance. I made to step forward, to help in any way I could, but a wave of dizziness washed over me and I winced, clutching at my side.

"Get out of here, Aeris," Akira hissed. "Now!"

Guilt weighed down my bones as I did as commanded and ran. It was odd that such an emotion could defy even the most base survival instinct. I'd only ever needed to look out for myself. I had made it this far in my life by keeping a low profile and doing as much as possible to avoid my father's wrath. I looked out for myself, which is how it had always needed to be. And yet ... leaving Akira behind felt like a betrayal. Like someone had plunged a knife into my heart and twisted. We'd only just met. Why did I feel this way? Maybe it was something my mother had said in her note. *We must stop allowing the males to divide us. We need each other.*

I shook my head and focused on scaling the soft terrain of the upper dunes. Blood stained the white sand as I climbed, but I ignored the pain as much as possible. Shouts rang out behind me, and I chanced one quick look over my shoulder before I cleared the rise entirely. Below, I could make out bodies scattered across the scarlet-stained beach. At least five females were dead, with likely more injured. I caught a glimpse of Akira finishing off her opponent and heaved a sigh of relief. She was okay.

The last thing I saw before I turned and disappeared from view of the beach was the wrath on Portia's beautiful face as she stood over Liz's fallen body. She would come for me, I knew that already, but now she had even more reason to. I would be prepared when she did. I would find both Sherai and Akira, and we would face her together when I was better equipped. I left the beach and didn't look back as I entered the strange thick of flora.

I ran through the shrubbery and cursed as spiky branches prodded and scraped at the flimsy, wet material of my pyjamas. Those fuckers hadn't even allowed us to change before stealing us away. My skin prickled, my whole body tense from the cold and the pain racking up my side. My soaked clothes clung to me, bitingly slowing my movements.

Just. Keep. Moving. I ran past more sandy dunes filled with needle-like bushes and into a forest populated with palms and beech trees until my chest ached and my salt-ravaged throat burned. Then I ran some more, until I found some ruins with half-crumbled pillars and landings. I decided that would make for a good vantage point and made my way up a broken column. I climbed, ignoring the bark of my limbs as my muscles strained in protest. My injury sent fresh waves of searing pain across my ribs, but I had to push on. I didn't think it was more than a flesh wound, nothing broken, nothing punctured; otherwise, there'd be significantly more blood, and I'd likely have passed out by now. I needed to make sure no one could abuse my vulnerability, though. Higher ground meant I would have an advantage against attackers, and I'd be able to see anyone approaching.

I groaned as I heaved myself up over the last ledge and rolled onto the stone until I was staring up at the midnight blue that was shifting to periwinkle, then slowly into pink. Dawn. When the real fun would begin. But first, I needed to tend to myself. My hand came back sticky and wet as I pressed it to my wound. The greatest threat right now was the blood loss sapping away at my strength. I could lose consciousness and be killed while I was completely helpless. Then there was the risk of infection ... If I didn't do something about the wound soon, I'd be lucky to see another dawn at all.

CHAPTER SIXTEEN

'There are two kinds of people in this world: the ones that fight, and the ones that take flight. One of them kills something inside you. The other gets you killed.'

I jolted as a shout broke the silence, then immediately regretted the sudden movement as my body flashed with pain. I'd taken the moment to rest and apply pressure to my wound while I could. Sticky, congealed blood trickled down my side to form a pool over the stone. I peeled myself off the stone floor with a wince, not daring to look at my injury. I strained my senses for any sound, but the forest was quiet, as if even the animals had fled into their burrows or taken flight. They knew when a predator was close, and this island was now full of them.

It was a shame we couldn't wield here. But then it wouldn't

do me much good anyway. My power had only just awoken yesterday, and I hadn't had any time to work out how to call it or use it. I recalled the sensation of my power blasting out of me. Shadow magic, just like the captain's. Spell Weavers from the Shadow Court were known for the ability to manipulate darkness and for casting dark spells, but to create shadows? A rare gift indeed.

I focused on my surroundings, skirting the edges of my vantage point to look for any movement in the trees. I must have drifted off for an hour or two, because the sun was now in the sky and trying its hardest to shine from behind a swathe of clouds. Good. An overcast day meant better coverage when using my surroundings.

"Aeris," a voice called. I flinched, then shuffled back into my corner, away from the edge where I was easily targeted. "It's Sherai and Akira. We're coming up."

Relief flooded through me as I recognised Sherai's soft tone. I slid back over to the edge of my platform and grinned down at them. "You're alive. Thank the gods," I said.

"Thank *me*," Akira said with a huff. "I found this one crashing through the forest practically *begging* to be found." She looked at Sherai and frowned. "We really need to work on your survival skills."

"For your information," Sherai said haughtily, "I've read several books about island survival and would do perfectly fine if left to my own devices. I was just a little panicked, that's all."

"You were about to fall into a pit lined with spikes," Akira said drily. "What did your books have to say about those?"

Sherai winced. "Don't fall in?"

Akira snorted and shook her head before turning her ire on me. "And you. *You* left a lovely little trail that led right up to the ledge you're sitting on. This area stinks of your blood, and if I found you so easily, others will too."

I cringed. "Yeah, well, it's not every day you get sliced up by a sword."

"Lucky I came prepared," she said with a sigh. "Get your ass down here. Sherai might have been willing to but I'm not bloody climbing that thing like a mountain goat."

Sherai assaulted me with a hug the moment my feet hit the ground. I flinched and stumbled back from the force of it, too surprised to say anything. But she was warm and her touch was cosy. Like a ball of sunshine in Fae form. My arms slowly lifted, then tightened around her frame as I hugged her back. It was nice. Comforting, if utterly alien to me.

"Let's get you patched up," she said gently as she pulled away. She took some strips of material from Akira's outstretched hand. "We need to clean the wound, but this will help stop the bleeding. Our bodies are designed to repair quicker than most other beings, you know. The perks of being Fae."

"Right now, I'd rather be a human safe and sound on another continent than having to fight off other females," I replied as I scrubbed my face. "Calendula and chamomile will help if we can find them. Hartsbreath, too, but the conditions aren't favourable this time of year."

Sherai smiled. "You know your herbs."

"I dabble," I said with a grin. "And you?"

She began wrapping my torso with the torn fabric. "I have studied herbology, but rarely applied my learnings."

I looked at Akira. "Do I want to know where you got this fabric?"

Her small nose pinched. "Don't ask questions you don't want the answers to. Now come on, we need to find another place to camp out."

"Akira, wait." I placed a hand on her shoulder and took a breath. "Thank you. I'm in your debt."

She cocked her head, then smiled. "You get one freebie. The next time I have to save your ass I'm writing a cheque to daddy dearest."

I scoffed. "Good luck getting him to pay up."

"Not even if I kidnapped you and held you for ransom?" Akira teased. Her light attempt at humour faded instantly as I tried and failed to smile.

"You're forgetting who sold me off to the Rite in the first place."

Sherai sighed. "Ah. Just another male trading for power. I bet the Pentad has them all drooling at the sight of their heavy purses."

"He doesn't even need the money," I said with an angry swipe at a palm frond blocking my way. "It's nothing more than a power play amongst the most elite males. A way to assert his dominance over key players in the Shadow Court."

Sherai and I followed Akira's steps as she led the way through the forest with her sword in hand. "But you are his only heir, no? He risks a lot by having you compete in the Rite."

"My father was cursed with a daughter when he wanted a son. I am worth precious little to him unless I marry a male of good stock and title. Marrying the captain, who also happens to be next in line as lord of one of the wealthiest estates in the Court ... Well, my father's lineage would continue so long as I produced an heir. His position as Merchant Mariner would remain secure, and any son I had would gain both estates, making his descendants even more powerful."

Akira stopped walking, and I halted a breath behind her. "Every male condoning this monstrosity is going to die. I am going to kill them all." She turned to face us. "We all are."

"What?" Sherai squeaked. "You want us to riot against the Pentad? We'd be signing our own death warrants."

I shrugged. "What's the difference between dying out here and dying at the castle?"

Akira grinned. "I knew you, of all females, would be on board."

Sherai's mouth dropped as she stared between us. "You can't be serious. Our chances of survival are slim to none. Beyond the Pentad, there are guards and other males of the court who would answer any call to arms to snuff out female insubordination. We'd be hunted down and killed for such a crime."

"Not if we had a certain captain on our side," I said after a beat.

Sherai gave me a long, hard look. "You need to be certain you can trust him. Because it wouldn't just be your life on the line, Aeris. It would be all of ours."

I placed a hand over my heart sincerely. "I would *never* put you both in danger if I weren't certain. Anyway, we're nowhere near that point right now. But I'm working on it. We can talk about this later. For now, we need to focus on our next move."

"Shelter first," Sherai said. "Then we need to find water and those herbs."

"And what do those books of yours suggest we do to survive this mess? What do we look for?" Akira said with a sly smile.

Sherai grinned. "Oh, you'll see."

An hour later, we huddled together in a small cave near a hill peak, its mouth partially hidden by foliage. It was cold and musty, but it was dry and offered protection from the elements. There was only one entrance, which meant we'd see any attackers coming.

"Do we risk a fire?" I asked Sherai. "I'm freezing my tits off."

She shook her head. "Even with the narrow opening, I wouldn't take the chance. Smoke rises. Besides, there might be more than females to worry about come nightfall. We don't want the light or smoke to attract anything."

Akira frowned as she whittled down the tip of a stick to form a makeshift spear. Somehow, she made it look easy with a sword, where I would have struggled even with a knife. She looked at her creation with a critical eye, then set it down on her growing pile. "At least now we have some tools to ward them off."

"And access to fresh water. Even beds," I said as I smiled at the palm fronds Sherai had gathered for bedding. Her knowledge would be a lifesaver in this place.

"It won't be enough," she said quietly as she sprinkled pebbles along the entrance. "This should act as a kind of warning system. A simple way to announce any unwanted guests when they step on them … Fresh water will be vital, too, which means the creek will be a magnet for all kinds of threats."

"We'll go morning and night to collect water, and I'll forage for food when I can. I know which mushrooms and plants are edible." I nodded at the spears as I addressed Akira. "Are you as good at using those things as you are at making them?"

"Stab them with the pointy end," Akira said. "Simple."

I cocked my head. "Your lack of concern given our situation is both oddly comforting and deeply disturbing. I'd better do some foraging and scouting before it gets dark."

Sherai perked up from the signal trap she was rigging at the door. "Are you sure that's a good idea?"

"No. But I don't have any other ideas, and we're not going

to be much use against whatever is out there without our strength." I patted the sword I'd tied to my waist with a makeshift vine rope. "I'm not alone."

Akira's eyes narrowed as she looked at my side. "I should go. You're in no state for a fight."

"You should keep each other safe," I replied as I made my way to the cave mouth. "Besides, I can be swift and stealthy when I need to be."

"Wait," Sherai said as she abandoned her task and collected something from a pile across the cave. She returned to my side and held it out to me. "Take this."

"You," I said as I looked at a basket woven from palm fronds and vines, "are a genius."

"Knowledge is and always will be our greatest form of strength."

"If I don't return by nightfall … don't come looking for me." My voice was quiet, but my gaze was hard as I looked between them. "I mean it. If I'm still out after dark, you stay put." I squeezed Sherai's arm, then stepped over her trap and out into the wilderness.

Outside, birds chirped in a nearby tree, and the soft sound of a frog warbling met my ears. Good enough for me. I made my way across the slope in the direction of the bird sounds, searching around tree trunks and dead logs for any sign of food or medicinal plants. A cluster of Fairy Inkcaps dotted a stump, and I leapt on them eagerly, placing them into the basket.

I spent the next couple of hours scouting the area, not only for food, but to get a lay of the land. The terrain was a mix of rolling hills that gave way to dense vegetation on all sides. The stream we'd found carved a snaking path down the hillside, likely converging with an outlet leading to the ocean. Maybe a river connected somewhere lower down, but I wasn't prepared to make the hike to confirm it.

There was food everywhere, if one knew how to look, and countless animals lived on the island as well. Rabbits and poultry, for the most part, though there could be pigs or goats. They'd be grazing somewhere safe and quiet, hidden away from predators, but I saw plenty of signs of smaller creatures. Burrows and nests, and the soft rustling of birds in the trees was a comfort as I went about my tasks.

I hadn't spotted anyone as I foraged, which was both a relief and a worry. Perhaps staying in one spot wasn't the best strategy. We could be sitting ducks. Worse still was the thought of new alliances forming among the other females, which could only make things harder. I didn't blame them, it's what I had done after all. I shook my head. Worrying was a useless notion that kept the body in a state ready to take flight. Fear and stress were detrimental to the body's function. And I needed mine in working form, which meant focusing on what I was out here to do.

Luckily, it didn't take much longer to find a healthy portion of morels and berries—the edible kind as well as those of the poisonous variety. A spear or a blade was just fine, but they weren't the only weapons that could come in handy. Knowledge, as Sherai had so aptly said, was the most pliable tool to work with. I filled my basket with chamomile and calendula, when shortly after, I heard something or someone running through the brush. I frowned, parting the leaves of some overgrown bushes, ready to flee or fight if necessary. I sucked in a breath as I saw a lone female running in my direction.

Her brows lifted, but she quickly took in my basket and my face, then voiced one word to me, "Run."

She didn't stop as she sprinted toward me. Blood was

splattered over her nightgown and pale face, and her red hair streamed behind her like a river of copper.

"Quickly," I urged. "Into the bushes."

Maybe it was foolish to try and help this girl. But I remained firm, holding out a hand and encouraging her to come to me. She looked at it like it was a beacon of hope, her legs pushing harder as she ran. *Too fast.* She stumbled over a rock, then fell forward, sliding over the grassy slope. She lifted her head, her pale blue eyes focusing on my face. They widened moments later when a dagger tore through her throat.

"No," I cried. My chest jolted, my stomach lurching, but there was no helping the female.

She tried to speak, but all that was heard was the sickening wetness of her blood drowning her. Gurgles and choking followed until her pupils blew out and she slumped to the ground, her hand still outstretched.

After her face hit the ground, I finally tore my eyes from her and saw the females responsible. Four bolted towards me, their faces slick with blood. By the swirling patterns and streaks, it appeared deliberately hand-painted. By the fucking gods. We'd been here scant hours and already they'd descended into madness. There was no winning against such odds. Not when it seemed the females were frenzied from the scent of blood and the promise of another victim to hunt. Perhaps it was due to some dark, fucked up ritual to honour Valere. I made a mental note to ask Akira later and was on my feet in seconds, running through the forest back toward the cave.

Down, down, down the hillside and around the many tree trunks and rocks I had passed. Once I saw a familiar gnarled tree, I turned sharply away from the direction of the cave, ensuring I kept track of how to get back. I would circle back when it was safe. Foraging had been easy … simple and slow. But this? My injury barked in renewed pain, and fresh blood seeped from the wound as I exerted my body.

Fuck. I couldn't keep this up for long. Couldn't keep running with no end in sight. Why were they so damn fast? I was small, and I was nimble, but I wasn't built for cross-country running. No, I had to bring them into new territory. One I was more than comfortable scaling. I searched, scanning the trees until I found a clearing. A small smile curved my lips as I looked up. Before me stood a towering tree that must have been centuries old, with how large its roots and branches were. The ancient tree's bark was gnarled and textured, giving me the perfect footholds and handholds to latch onto as I climbed.

Something came whistling towards me, and I let go of one hand, hanging from the other, as a spear slammed into the tree's flesh. I was momentarily awash with dizziness. I groaned as I refocused and swung my full weight back to grab the handhold. Just a little higher. A little longer … then I was swinging myself over a branch and lying on my back as I gulped in air. I leaned over the side, then immediately ducked as another spear came flying towards me. It missed the tree entirely, arcing through the air and landing somewhere off in the forest.

"Go after her," one said. She had a brown bob stiff with dried blood. "What are you waiting for?"

"I can't climb that!" the blonde she spoke to said. "She moved like a damn cat. I don't know how to do that."

"For fuck's sake, I'll do it myself. Here, kitty, kitty. Need someone to help you out of the tree?" A third, this one a darker brunette, said and moved slowly but surely. I cursed beneath my breath as I rolled and continued ascending. "Don't be shy. I'll get you down soon enough," she taunted.

I eased myself onto a branch directly above her, then considered. I had tried to avoid bloodshed and fighting with the other females. But I realised I wouldn't have a choice. They wouldn't stop. They were people like me who had been forced to enter the Rite after all—people like Akira, who had been dumped here by fathers and brothers—all males in a world that favoured blood and power and masculine dominance. Only they weren't all forced here. There were others who wanted to win the captain's hand for whatever reasons of their own. Maybe these four belonged to that group. Maybe they had been twisted one way or another into playing the game for the males. Maybe they didn't value their fellow female the way I, or Akira, or Sherai, or my mother, did. We were sisters, we were obstacles in a course designed for one victor. They wouldn't show me mercy. Just as they hadn't shown that girl any mercy when they cut her throat. But I was not a deer to be shot and strung up. I certainly was not a cat stuck in a tree.

I looked down at the brunette who was stuck midway up the tree, about two metres high, and took a deep, calming breath. I gauged the distance between us ... and stepped backwards off the edge. I grabbed a branch just above hers as I fell and quickly swung my legs with my knees slightly bent and pushed my feet forward. My feet crashed into her gut, sending her toppling off the tree branch with a scream. I swung up onto the branch with ease and crouched down to see her broken body on the forest floor. She hadn't landed well. Her limbs sprawled at odd angles, and blood pooled from the impact to her skull.

Her three allies stood over her, their faces a mask of fury as they looked up.

"You can hide in that tree all you like, but you'll have to

come down eventually," the blonde said with a sneer. "I can smell your blood. Without aid, your wound will fester."

"We'll be waiting when it does," a raven-haired one added.

I slumped against the tree's trunk and clutched at my side. Sure enough, that trickle of blood had turned into a blooming wetness. Sweat beaded my forehead, and I shivered, resting my head against the bark. It was going to be a long, hard night.

A shriek rent the air, instantly waking my body from the drowsiness it had slowly been succumbing to. The soft glow of dusk filtered through the canopy, signalling the end to what had been an exhausting day.

I'd come so close to falling asleep, but I'd kept my eyes firmly open and ignored the dull throbbing of my injury as I waited. The females below hadn't bothered with another attempt to climb the tree, but they did remain at the bottom as they'd promised. They even had a fire going, warming their hands by it and settling close. I watched the crackling embers longingly. What I wouldn't give to stretch out beside it and feel the heat in my bones.

I squeezed my eyes shut and rolled my neck as I shifted position. My ass was going numb from sitting for so long, and I was so tired. I needed medicine, just as those murderous assholes had said. Sherai was right—my Fae body was strong and sturdy, but there was only so much it could do to fight off bacteria and prevent an infection.

Another shriek sounded somewhere in the distance, echoed by several others. *Closer this time.* Instinct heightened my awareness, making me sit up straighter. My blood had turned cold at the sinister, mournful undertone of those cries, and I shivered on my perch. Aside from the cave, this might actually be the safest place to be if those cries belonged to land-prowling animals. The same couldn't be said for the females below me, however. They got up and stood back-to-back, spears in hand and on high alert, with the fire between them and the shrieks. Then the creatures came.

They were dark, almost wraithlike things with sagging skin and eyes of deepest black. Their hind legs were bent backwards, like a goat, but it was their movement that shocked me. They skittered, sometimes on all fours, sometimes on two legs, and they moved *fast.* I couldn't look away as one leapt at the females. But the blonde one managed to take it down with a calculated jab to the heart, and the gangly creature fell in a mess of tangled limbs. Its head lolled as it hit the ground, and I cringed at the mouth filled with sharp, spiky teeth as it heaved one final sigh.

The female with the blood-stiff bob plucked a stick from the fire, brandishing it with panicked waves. The monsters retreated to the shadows immediately, hissing at the light. *Interesting* ... but it was not enough. The creatures chittered and clicked in a way that seemed like they were communicating with each other, then scuttled closer in unison, flanking the females. It all happened quickly after that.

The bloodied-bob female launched her spear, missing her target as the creature darted slightly up the trunk before launching at her. The scream she uttered felt like it pierced my very soul, reverberating through me with a melancholy ring. Her limbs went flying shortly after, and her head was torn clean off with little effort. The creature held it like some kind of trophy, clinging onto the hair on her scalp as it dove onto her remains to begin feasting. The raven-haired female took one look at her dead friend and ran. She made it all of ten metres before the creature was upon her.

My stomach wanted to revolt. My bladder wanted to empty itself. But I didn't dare move a muscle or make a sound as the other two creatures turned towards the blonde and pounced. I didn't look. Didn't make a sound as she screamed over, and over, and over again. Her groans turned to gurgles that went on for what felt like an age as they tore her apart, and all I could see in my mind's eye was them taking their time, piece by piece, to dismantle her. Even after it fell silent, the grotesque eating sounds continued long into the night. All the while, I sat still and focused on my breathing. One sound, one single mistake, and they would rip me apart. They didn't look like they would have a problem climbing.

Tears welled in my eyes, the horror of what had just happened—what was still happening—washed over me. All I could do was squeeze my eyes shut, clamp one hand over my wound and the other over my mouth, and wait. I spent the night listening to the sounds that would forever haunt my dreams after that night.

CHAPTER SEVENTEEN

'There is sisterhood in death. Even as we're forced to destroy each other, there is camaraderie on both sides of the blade. I mourn the loss of my enemies, and I wish them well in the beyond.'

Journal excerpt, author unknown

I stumbled into the cave an hour or so after dawn, having retraced my steps to find my abandoned basket first. Calendula and chamomile would be my best friends, given the state of my injury. If I were anything but Fae, I'd probably be dead by now. A solemn reminder that while I was immortal, I wasn't invincible.

With the herbs in tow, we'd need to grind them into a poultice. I didn't think my wound was infected, so we likely wouldn't need to worry about adding clay or charcoal to draw out the infection. But we'd need to make sure whatever leaves we used to cover and keep it in place wouldn't cause my wound to turn toxic. Lucky for me, I had a friend who had studied all manner of subjects and therefore knew a great many things about survival and hopefully, what plants were safe to use.

As I stepped over her trap and into the cave, Sherai took one look at me before demanding I sit and eat something, then headed out while the day was still young. I ate my portion of mushrooms in silence while I stared at the cracks and veins webbing the stone walls. I could still hear their screams … still hear the flesh ripping and tearing as exhaustion finally took me and I fell asleep before Sherai returned.

I jerked awake some time later, my hand instantly lunging for my blade.

"It's just me," Sherai said quietly, leaning toward me. "Hush. You're safe."

I blinked back at her as she gently took my hands. The touch grounded me, settling the racing of my pulse. "Sorry," I whispered. "It was a long night. How long have I been out?"

"It's late afternoon. You've been asleep for a while, but I managed to dress your wound while you rested."

Gratitude, warm and bright, flooded through me. I looked at my side and saw the three large leaves held to my skin by a sticky poultice. I took her hands. "Thank you, Sherai. Really. You're a good friend." She had been since the moment we'd met. "I hope I can repay the favour."

Akira settled on a palm frond beside me. "What happened last night? We were going to look for you, but we heard the screaming echo in the distance and couldn't risk searching for you in the dark without knowing what was out there."

I swallowed the lump in my throat. "There are creatures out there. Things that are worse than any female on this island." Sherai's grip tightened on mine, but I squeezed back reassuringly. "They killed and ate three females with the kind of coordination I never would think possible for an animal. But I suspect they only hunt at night and rest during the day. They left before dawn."

Akira scrutinised me from head to toe. "You seem relatively unscathed. Did you fight them off?"

"Fighting is a death sentence. They're fast. So fucking fast. The three females only managed to take down one before the creatures reevaluated and adjusted their attack. I only got away unscathed because I was hiding up a tree. The females had chased me and cornered me..." A flash of limbs being ripped off assaulted my vision, and I focused on Akira's face to block it out. "They were waiting for me to come back down the tree when the creatures found them."

Sherai frowned. "This ... complicates things. We need a plan. A way to keep them at bay should they come."

"Fire," I said simply. "They didn't like the fire. I think their eyes are made to see in the dark, and the fire is too bright for them. Honestly, I don't know what drew the creatures to the females; it could have been the smoke or the light or something else. But the fire at close range at least gave them pause. We can use that. It might put us at risk of other females finding us, but honestly, I'd rather take my chances with a group of them than even one of those things."

"I'm just happy you got away," Sherai said. "Sleep more. We'll keep things covered."

"I'll take the first watch," Akira added.

"But—" I started to say.

"Sleep," Sherai demanded, her tone leaving no room to argue.

I raised a surprised brow at her, then looked at Akira, who

simply shrugged and tapped the side of her head. "I'd listen to her. The walking survival guide knows things."

A soft chortle escaped me, but I did as ordered and lay down on the makeshift bed. My eyes drifted shut immediately, and then I, too, drifted off not long after.

Three days passed, and we'd managed to survive without coming in contact with those creatures I'd seen the first night. We'd fallen into a kind of routine that kept us alive and relatively fed, all things considered. We also hadn't seen any other females, which either meant they'd all found a safe place to bunk down, too, or there were even fewer of us left than I thought.

On the fourth night, the island was silent and still when several horns blared in the twilight. Akira, Sherai, and I perked up immediately, our instincts on high alert as the long, sombre sounds echoed through the cave.

"What do you suppose that means?" I asked.

Long, piercing shrieks cut off whatever Sherai was going to say, causing us to block our ears. When the creatures were finished, she winced and then tried again.

"Our salvation. Or our end. It sounds like the horns are coming from the beach, which likely means that our ticket off this sand bucket is coming."

"We'd have to get past the monsters first," I said bluntly. "Goodie."

"The alternative is that it's a trap and one of the participants is trying to lure us all there," Akira said with a scowl.

"I'm not sure anyone would risk it with those things lurking about," I countered.

Another shriek sounded, closer this time. Sherai frowned. "I'm inclined to agree."

I sucked in a breath. In the flickering light of the small fire we'd made, Akira's lips had thinned, but Sherai's brown eyes were wide. The last thing I wanted to do was see those creatures again, not to mention what they could do to people, but if the boats were back … if this was our only chance to leave this place… We had to risk it. Judging by the looks on my friends' faces, they'd come to that conclusion too.

"My vote is we go, trap or not. If there's even the slightest chance we can get out of here, I want to take it."

"Agreed," Akira and Sherai said simultaneously.

"I know this is bad, but we can do this," I said as I rose. "We can't outrun those things, but we can ward them off."

The two got to their feet as well. Sherai shook her head. "How? We don't know how long the boats will wait, and you told us what happened to those females. There's no way we can survive those things and get to the beach in time."

"We can and we will," I promised as I put my hands on her shoulders. Her eyes darted between mine in a mixture of fear and dismay. "You are brave and you are strong. And that clever brain of yours hasn't failed us yet. I believe in you, Sherai. We both do. We've survived in the wilderness together for four days, and we can get back to the beach together."

Akira nodded. "Aeris said they don't like fire. So let's put on a damn good show."

A few hurried minutes later, we had several torches lit in our hands, spears at our backs, swords at our waists, and every ounce of courage we could scrounge from within. It had taken us a couple of hours to get from the beach to the cave, moving at a walking pace and stopping at the ruins I'd found when I was injured. I'd worked out the direction of the beach when finding food on the third day, so if we kept a steady pace and moved directly toward the shore, we'd make it in an hour or so.

"We run towards the beach and don't stop moving," Akira said. "If one falters, we pick her up together. If we're attacked, we fight, but no one gets left behind."

"We're all leaving here alive. Right, Sherai?" I said encouragingly.

She took a deep breath and closed her eyes, and I saw the conviction when she opened them again. The glow in those brown eyes wasn't from the firelight alone. "We're in this together," she confirmed. "Ready?"

"As we'll ever be," Akira said. "Quickly and quietly. Go."

I took point, given that I had become the most familiar with the terrain and direction of the shore. The night sky was clear, the stars twinkling on a midnight blue canvas as we filed down the hillside. I kept my eyes peeled, watching for any threats hiding in bushes or the trees as we slipped through the undergrowth. Sherai walked behind me, Akira taking up the rear as we crept onwards. I'd never felt so afraid. Not even when I was in that crypt beneath the castle. My heart thundered, and my skin became clammy from the trepidation crawling down my spine. Just breathing became a struggle as the cold air came short and sharp into my lungs. The only assurance was that I wasn't alone. Not this time. Not anymore.

In the distance, on either side of us, we saw glimpses of other torches flickering from between the trees and bushes, but no one attacked or bothered to approach. It seemed we all had one goal in mind: to get to that damn beach. We'd kept a good pace and had perhaps a twenty-minute walk between our current location and the beach. Suddenly, the echo of familiar shrieks rang out behind, too damn close for comfort. *Fuck*. Make that a 10-minute run.

Screams followed, bloodcurdling and bone-chilling as they

ended abruptly. I glanced to one side, seeing multiple dark shapes crashing through the growth. Seconds later, a torch along from us went out.

"Run!" I urged the others, breaking out into a sprint. "Fucking run!"

I focused on Sherai's panting breaths behind me as we put one foot in front of the other and high-tailed it. I held both torches high, not just for visibility but to ward off any monsters hiding in the bushes. Sherai in the middle kept her torches held lower, while Akira also held hers high in an attempt to make it look like the fire completely surrounded us.

"Fuck," Akira cried. "My leg!"

I glanced behind me, seeing my friend on the ground with something that had impaled her calf. Was that an animal bone or a Fae's? I clenched my jaw as blood dribbled out from the wound. Sherai and I backtracked, helping Akira to her feet with a grimace.

"Can you walk?" Sherai asked.

She attempted a step and cried out. "It's no use, I'll only slow you down. Go."

"We're not fucking leaving you," I hissed as I gave her a torch and slipped her arm around my neck. Sherai did the same on her other side. "Together, no matter what."

"So fucking stubborn," Akira said with a shake of her head, but the smile that followed revealed her fear.

I didn't need Sherai to tell me our chances of survival just decreased a bucketload. But there was no way in hell I was leaving either of my friends tonight. I meant what I'd said. Every damn word.

More screams from females, more howls from the beasts. We carried on, going as fast as we could with Akira slung between us. She held our torches with her own, creating an even more intense firelight on either side of us, while Sherai and I held her with one hand and our second torch in the other. And then it finally came. The sounds I'd been dreading since we'd left the safety of the cave. Thundering steps, shrieks and chitters.

"They're coming," I yelled. "Backs together!"

The torch shook in my left hand, but I held it high and took out a spear with my right. Sooner or later, I'd have to drop one, but for now, I'd take my chances. Sherai held Akira steady with her free hand and swept the torch with her other, trying to see which direction they were coming from. Akira held the torches and put her weight on her good leg, looking vulnerable but determined. We moved, slowly, ever so cautiously toward the beach, scanning our surroundings all the while.

The creatures' faces appeared in the light not long after. Three of them, all with large eyes like voids and sagging skin that stunk of rot and decay. Or maybe that was coming from their hideous mouths filled with endless sharp teeth. They circled us, hissing and chittering, as if unsure which angle they should attack from. Every time one of us would wave our torch, the creature would back away before getting brave again. Whether from adrenaline or pure desperation, Akira was managing to hop along without our help, but we'd only last so long. We were crawling at a snail's pace through the brush, constantly moving, circling to confuse our enemies and holding our firelight toward their eyes. Each time they were forced to look at the light, they squinted their eyes or turned away.

Finally, one got tired of waiting and trundled back, preparing to test our defences. "Spear up and knee down," Akira cried.

I did as commanded, dropping my torch at my feet, ready

to defend myself. But it shifted and suddenly lunged for Akira. *No*, I realised as the beast leapt high. It wasn't aiming for her, but *on* her. It was bigger than a large dog. She'd be crushed beneath its weight. Without thinking, I swivelled on my knee and tossed my spear at the creature's chest. It hit its mark, causing the creature to fall short of its target enough to prevent it from crushing us both. It wasn't enough. The monster was only momentarily inconvenienced as it got back up, but Akira shot forward, thwacking the thing over the head once, twice, with her torch until its flesh lit up and a scream that shook my very bones pierced through the night.

Akira had stepped too far in front of Sherai and me, and the other two creatures darted forward. Sherai grunted as she waved her torch madly, gaining one's attention. I yelped as the other came for me, so fast I barely saw its foreleg swipe at my limbs. Akira yelled, distracting it just enough for me to pick up my dropped torch and club it over the skull.

It backed up, disoriented long enough for me to give up on blunt force and opt for the sharp steel of the sword at my waist. The monster shook its head and hissed, then played a game of cat and mouse as it skittered back and forth, toying with us while Akira and I tried to corner it. My friend darted forward, attempting to club it again as she had the other. It caught the fucking torch in its mouth, bit down and *snapped* the wood in two. Then it cocked its head and leered at her. Akira's hand went for her sword … it was gone. Lost, most likely, when she had taken the fall earlier. *Oh gods.* I was too far away. I was so close, but I was still too far away to stop what came next. Akira looked at me, her face resigned, as if accepting what came next. And I saw what happened before it came. Saw the sad smile on her face before the creature leapt at her. She shrieked as it forced her to the ground.

"Akira," I screamed as tears filled my eyes and blurred my

vision. A grunting sounded behind me, and I gathered my wits enough to remember that there was another creature. I turned, my sword hanging loosely in my hand, then prepared to meet my maker as the last creature reared up on its hind legs, its spiky front legs preparing to swipe. Shock fired through me, just enough to jerk me back to reality. I pulled back to thrust my sword into its exposed belly when something else caught my eye.

A force so fierce and unstoppable that even the monster couldn't move in time. Sherai screamed, roaring her battle cry to the world as she sprinted forward. The creature turned to face her, right as Sherai plunged her spear into its stomach. I didn't know where the strength came from, but once she'd finished gutting it, Sherai lifted it into the air by the spear before crashing it down on its skull.

Silence.

I stared at the dead thing on the ground, then slowly turned my gaze to Sherai, who was panting with both hands on her knees. When she looked up, blood was splattered all over her face, and her eyes were wide.

"I killed it," she said quietly. "I actually killed it."

I couldn't muster any words as I just nodded stupidly. Gratefully. I realised it was too silent. The lump in my throat refused to dislodge, but I managed to croak out, "Akira."

Sherai ran towards the beast that had felled our mighty friend. It was still. My stomach twisted violently even as I smiled sadly. "Defiant even in death," I said. "Akira must have killed it. She was so fucking fierce."

"This can't be," Sherai whispered as she shook her head. "She can't be dead."

"Sherai," I said gently, reaching out a hand to comfort her. "There was nothing we could do."

A grunting sound came from where the creature and Akira lay dead.

"It's coming from the beast," Sherai said shrilly. "Quick. Help me!"

We cautiously checked that the creature wasn't about to tear our hands off, but it remained lifeless. Sherai gasped, and we heaved the carcass to the side to find Akira, covered in blood and gasping for air.

"Oh my gods," Sherai cried as she burst into tears and fell upon Akira in a giant hug. I stared at my friend in disbelief before joining them moments later. Nothing had ever felt so good as hugging a grumpy, dishevelled, wounded but very much alive Akira.

"Can't … breathe…" she huffed.

Sherai and I begrudgingly let her go as we rose. "But how?" I asked.

Akira's grin turned to a wince, but she simply wiggled her injured leg, as if too tired to explain. And she didn't need to. Her slim calf was bleeding heavily but was free of the object that had pierced it. She jerked her head to the creature, and as I followed her line of sight, I spotted a long shard of bone. Sharp and deadly as a knife. We shared a grin. Laughing a little, Sherai and I helped Akira to her feet. And then we hugged her once more, blood, sweat, and tears be damned.

"Let's go," I said to my friends as we all pulled apart. Firelights moved through the trees ahead, somewhere near the beach. "We've got a boat to catch."

CHAPTER EIGHTEEN

'In the event a bond is forged with one's fated mate, not even death can break it. To attempt to force such a terrible deed is to invoke the wrath of the gods themselves.'

Fake It Till You Make It: Romance Edition

We arrived on the beach without any further problems and half-carried Akira down the sand banks as carefully as possible, almost falling several times from the sand shifting beneath us. I searched the boats for a familiar face and was oddly disappointed when I didn't find Raithe amongst the various males manning them. Maybe it was the exhaustion of the fight, or the mental load of thinking my friend had died for a hot minute, but I wanted his company.

'He doesn't care whether you live or die,' a voice whispered in my head. *'He is just using you.'* The thoughts stung more than

they should have. The last time I'd seen him, I'd agreed to court him in the public eye, but that's as far as the arrangement went. Shortly before that, I would have killed him for botching my escape. It was safe to say things were complicated between the captain and me.

I should have been excited to get off the island. And while a large part of me was very glad to put it behind me, both literally and figuratively, another logical part of my brain knew that I was exchanging one prison for another. Still, I'd take any opponent over those *things*. And once I was back in the relative safety of my rooms, I'd be able to dive straight into my mother's journal, which I kept hidden in the bedchamber. I hadn't read much beyond a couple of pages, too focused on my earlier escape attempt and what to do about the imprisoned females of old Rites. I wondered at what I would find in its pages.

"I've never been more glad to return to the sea," Akira said with a grumble as we trudged towards the boats. "I need a healer, food, and a solid sleep."

"And a bath," Sherai said, wrinkling her nose. "You smell like monster soup and carcass."

Akira raised her brows. "Says the girl with chunks of guts stuck in her hair."

"Oh, gods. Ew. Ew. EW!" Sherai shook her hair like a dog, then combed her fingernails through her coils. "Get it off me!"

"Relax," Akira said with a grin. "I was just kidding. Sort of."

I laughed, even as I shook my head. "See you both back at the castle. Unless they still expect us to do chores, I don't plan on leaving my bed for the rest of the night."

We helped Akira to one of the small rowboats and said our goodbyes as we each hopped on a boat and made our way back to the mainland. There were significantly fewer females than the number that had arrived; many boats returned empty of any females.

"So, you survived after all," the male sitting across from me said with a toothy grin. The voice was irritatingly familiar, and I realised he was one of the guards who'd escorted me days ago. Without a bag over my head this time, I saw the fucker's nasty voice was a perfect match to his ugly mug, worsened by the break I'd given him days ago. The glimmering lantern hanging beside him did nothing to soften his appearance.

I considered the male opposite me. Once, I would have tightened my lips and simply obeyed. I would have done anything to remain unnoticeable. But the Rite was quickly teaching me how very capable I could be. Sherai and Akira were also teaching me how females could empower each other and lift each other up. I felt stronger for it—them. And because of that, I was quickly growing tired of bending to a male's will or staying silent. I was tired of being talked down to and treated like mud beneath one's boot. So, I decided enough was enough.

I smiled sweetly and leaned back on the prow, putting my feet up. "How's the nose? Not important enough to warrant a visit from the castle healer?" I clicked my tongue in mock pity.

A scar across his cheek puckered as he sneered. "You're lucky I'm under orders not to lay a hand on you. The bosses want you all pretty for yuletide."

"How thoughtful of them," I said drily. "Now, where's my money?"

He eyed me warily. "What're ye on about, girl?"

"The bet," I said matter-of-factly. "I believe you owe me 200 silvers."

"I owe no such thing," he spat. "Participants don't get the luxury of gambling."

"I gamble with my life every day. So much so that I've gotten a fair bit comfortable with taking the lives of others." *A lie, not that he needed to know that.* "My hand, you see. It can be a little … clumsy."

My hand drifted to my sword in emphasis. He tried to draw his own blade, dropping the oars with a thud, but I already had my blade placed against his crown jewels.

"Alright, alright!" he said, lifting his hands in defeat.

The tip of my blade cut into his pants ever so slightly, tearing them up from the seams. His jerky movement caused his cloak to flutter to the side, where a fat coin purse jiggled from his hip. Bastard was doing just fine from his so-called gambling.

"I'm thinking we might need to revisit the amount. Perhaps increase the price a little. Compensation for the grievance of throwing me on that damned island."

His face turned red, the scar puckering into a furious shade of purple. "You thieving—"

"Ah, ah, ah," I said, shoving the blade up higher.

His face drained of colour as he looked at me and realised I wasn't backing down. "Take it. Just fucking take the thing."

He didn't need to tell me twice. With a quick upwards stroke of the sword I slashed the drawstring of the purse and sent the bag up in the air towards me. It jingled quite nicely when I caught it, and I settled back down in my seat with a small smile. "So glad we could come to an agreement. Now row. I'm tired and in need of a bath."

The guard speared me with daggers the whole trip back. It didn't bother me. As soon as we were back on the mainland, he'd have a hard time getting vengeance. Especially if a certain captain was stalking around the castle.

I tried not to jiggle the purse and make him angry enough to retaliate before we even made it there. I tried *really* hard.

Fortunately, the ocean was in a mood today and the tides were choppy, forcing him to put all his concentration into the tedious task of rowing us back. I could have offered to help but … nah. This one delighted in the pain and suffering of others. He deserved much worse than a little petty theft.

It took a while, but eventually we were on land. Apparently, they didn't care if we saw exactly where we landed or if we were escorted back by the guards. I raced up the stairs, all too eager to go back to my rooms, and I didn't stop running until I was back behind my door and had turned the key. Only then did I allow myself to truly stop. I was safe.

Not just physically—my wound from that first day on the island was healing nicely, though I'd probably need to visit Margaery anyway—but mentally, too. All the horrors that I'd seen and heard and done … they came crashing down on me. I turned the tap and filled the small bath in the corner with hot water, and when I sank beneath its embrace, I didn't come up for air for a long time.

Akira and I had paid a visit to Margaery for some expert healing care, and we had planned to eat dinner with Sherai in my room that night. Unfortunately, the Pentad had other ideas. So, instead, I sat at a long table in the dining hall with Akira and Sherai flanking each side. I sipped on hot apple cider and sighed, nestling deeper into the chair. The scent of cinnamon sticks, cloves, and orange sailed up my nose. I relished the warmth as it slid down my throat to heat my belly. After the test of the island, I didn't even mind being forced to the dining room. I had hot food, hot drinks, and two beautiful friends by my side.

And that's what we were now. There was no point denying

the kinship I felt for the two fierce females beside me. Akira and Sherai had fought beside me like no one ever had—no one except my old mentor, Avadir, at least. I took note of the females seated at the table. There had been 50 of us to begin with. Now there were only 20, including my group of three. If Portia had anything to say about it, that number would dwindle even more before the next test. I tried my best to avoid her gaze, but she caught me looking in her direction. Her eyes narrowed as they moved from me to Sherai to Akira, then to the empty seat beside her. I could guess what she was thinking. Her right-hand ally was gone, and she'd come after my friends next as revenge.

"You know," Akira said as she leaned in. "Removing her existence would save us a lot of stress."

"Akira," Sherai admonished. "We do not go around the castle murdering people."

"What?" Akira shrugged her shoulders daintily. "It was merely a suggestion. One I would strongly encourage you both to consider. Without her, our odds improve significantly. I don't know about you two, but I'd feel a lot less comfortable if steak-knives-for-teeth over there found herself slipping on stairs one of these days."

"She does have a point," I told Sherai. "Maybe we could just file down her teeth. Get them back to butter knife proportions."

Sherai giggled and smoothed back her hair. "It *would* take the edge off."

I stared at her. "Did you … Did you just make a funny?"

Sherai fluffed her hair and grinned. "It's been known to happen on occasion."

Akira bumped her shoulder. "Brains, beauty, and brawn," she said wistfully. "Captain's got his decision cut out for him."

"Why choose? He could just keep us all. We could terrorise

the castle inhabitants forever," I said, fluttering my fingers as I whispered.

"Oh, gods, no," Sherai said with a snort. "No offence, but the two of you would surely send me to Ryvia before I was due." Her gaze swept pointedly to me. "And anyway, he's already courting this one."

I scowled at her. While alone on the island, we'd had plenty of time to talk about everything, including my escape attempt being foiled by the captain, followed by his proposal. "It's only for show. There's a difference."

"Is there, though?" she asked with a coy grin.

"There's a fine line between eye fucking and simply fucking," Akira agreed. "Besides, all the best romances start with some brewing tension. Maybe a little forced proximity."

"You're both insufferable," I said with an eye roll. "Romance is the last thing on my mind. Especially when I don't know where the captain's true allegiances lie."

"True," Sherai said with a sigh. "Still, it's fun to dream. Wouldn't it be ironic if he were a fated mate to one of the females here?"

"Come again?" I asked.

"Fated mate," she repeated. At my blank look, she let out a 'tsk' noise. "I read a fascinating book about the phenomenon. It's a rare thing, but every so often, a Fae will find their other half. A connection so strong, ancient magic literally binds their souls together in a love so strong nothing can break it. There's even a ritual of sorts for it. The female offers her throat in submission, and the male claims her with a bite. It's very primal."

"Lies," Akira said with a roll of her eyes. "I don't believe it for a second."

"Well, I like to think it's true," Sherai said with a huff. "Maybe Aeris will find that with the captain."

Talking about the captain made me wonder where he was. I felt her eyes on me, but I was too busy looking out the windows of the dining hall, somewhere towards the sea. I wondered if he was out there on one of his ships, surrounded by a fleet of the Shadow Court navy. Or perhaps across the border, visiting a different court altogether. Then a bigger question came to mind … why did I care where he was at all?

"Ladies, if I could have your attention," the sea serpent of the Pentad said from his position at the head of their table on the dais. The Pentad stood, wearing their usual black garb and golden masks. It was easy to imagine a mangled monster behind them when, really, they were probably handsome, maybe even captivating, to look upon. A juxtaposition to the cold and cruel hearts beating beneath. "We are so pleased to see you healthy and thriving before us, with another test under your belt. You came here as blooming petals from a rose, and with winter now upon us, we have seen you shed your skin and sharpen like thorns. Eat and drink with us tonight, knowing you are one step closer to our captain and all the responsibilities that come as the lady to our lord.

"While Captain Windaire cannot be present tonight, fighting for our land and seas as is his duty, rest assured he is aware of your progress and will return soon. Despite the harsher season, there are many triumphs to come. A toast"— He raised his wine, which had been freshly filled, along with all the glasses in the room—"to old blood and a new age."

The Pentad lifted their masks just enough to sip their wines. I had the distinct feeling that not drinking would be unwise, so I took a sip from the wine we had each been poured … and nearly spat the thing out. Akira didn't hold it in, however, unable to maintain her graceful composure as red dribbled down her lips. The sentiment was echoed by several others along the table.

"What is this?" she sputtered with red-stained teeth.

"Blood," Sherai said with narrowed eyes.

"To your good health, and the death of the unworthy," the sea-serpent said before he drained his glass and took his seat once again.

It took everything in me not to charge across the hall and stab the fucker in the throat. Instead, I put my glass down on the table and smiled prettily, as if pleased with all of the Pentad's empty praises. "Akira," I said quietly once I was sure no one was listening. "I think it's time we revisit that discussion about fighting back."

"Finally," she said with a huff. "I knew you'd come around."

"We're having this discussion now?" Sherai looked around and laughed softly, like we were discussing some big joke. And once, I would have laughed at the notion, too. But this wasn't a game anymore. Not one we could all win. Not on the Pentad's terms, at least.

"No more Rites. No more killing for the pleasure of males," Akira said under her breath. "Isn't that worth fighting for? I mean, fuck, don't you have a dream, Sherai?"

"Yes, of course, but I—"

"If you could do anything with your life, what would it be? *Who* would you be?"

Sherai was silent for a moment. "I've always wished to study at the Palantai Palace. To ensure our histories are remembered, and our future is never forgotten. I would be … me. A scholar and a dreamer, but still me."

"Don't waste a single moment on a wish," Akira said. "Dreams are a desire we can all afford, but goals are worth fighting for. That future? The three of us? We are worth fighting for."

Sherai smoothed back her hair and downed her cider in several long gulps. When she was done, she wiped her mouth with her sleeve and nodded. "Okay." She nodded once more. "Okay."

I shot a sly grin at Akira as she looked at me. "Do you even have to ask?"

My friend grabbed her mug and passed me mine, then lifted it into the air. "To us."

"To friendship," Sherai added.

I smiled as we clinked cups. "To a future worth fighting for."

CHAPTER NINETEEN

'Some of Mithria's greatest scholars and inventors hail from
the Soul Court. There is much to be said for Soul Speakers—
those wise seers and mediums. Though it is unfortunate so
many have gone mad whilst searching for answers in the
unknown.'
The Trials and Traditions of a Mithrian Fae

Not for the first time, I took my mother's journal
from its hiding place between the bedframe and
the wall and set it down to read. I stared out the window at
the thrashing sea. It was surreal, in a way, to meet her again
through this book. To get an insight into the female she was,
and the one she might have been if circumstances had been
different.

The scrawls on these pages were evidence of a clever mind
with a tendency towards kindness. Even as she faced the evils
within these halls and beyond them, she'd always remained

steadfast in her duty of care to others. Not just as an herbalist, but a healer. I felt closest to her through the annotations in the columns and footnotes of her entries and the random thoughts jotted down throughout her day. Notes on potion-mixing techniques or recipes that had been amended multiple times, the harsh crosses and violent exclamation marks speaking of her frustration or excitement.

And then there were the odd sentences where she expressed her fear and her sorrows. The further I read, the more I realised this place had begun to strip away that kindness and turn her into something harder. Stronger, maybe, but a harder shell of the female she'd once been. She had been a giver, but when others took and took until the bowl was fully empty, what more could a person give but their very soul? I didn't blame her for leaving the monster that was her husband. My father. And yet, the more I read, the more it sparked a stupid and pathetic notion. *Did she ever really leave?* Not mentally. Not on her own terms, at least. The more I thought about it, the more it made sense that my father had imprisoned her with the other females. He'd always hated her for never bearing a son. And I knew the things he had done to her behind closed doors. The beatings and the scrapes that chipped away at her piece by piece. I wondered if she left her true self behind all those years ago. If it was really here in these pages.

I sighed as I closed the book and set it gently on my lap. Against my better wishes, my mind drifted to Raithe. It had been over a week since I'd returned from the island, yet I hadn't seen or heard a peep from him. "Out at sea," one of the maids had said in the cleaning rooms a few days ago. "Fending off a flotilla of pirates in the Serpent Strait," a male servant had whispered in the kitchens not long after.

My pulse had quickened at the latter. I was afraid for him.

Something I had tried very hard not to analyse in the three days since hearing it. Raithe was nothing to me. Nothing beyond a means of protection and a shared interest in the imprisoned females. But if that were true, why then, in the quiet hours of the night, did I think of the way his lips curved when he smirked? Or how that sheer power he exuded frightened me, but excited me all at once. Despite myself, there was more to my feelings than just an alliance, and I was genuinely afraid something might happen to him on that ship.

Someone knocked softly at my door, and my head snapped toward it. Reality lifted me out of my ruminations, and I swiped my cheek quickly, realising tears had slowly trickled free and dried there. I shoved the book hastily down my pants, then rested an ear against the door.

"It's just me," Sherai said softly.

"Oh, thank the gods," I said as I unbolted and opened the door. I could use the distraction. "Come in."

"Hi," she said with a smile as she noted the fire crackling in the grate. "This is cosy. And ocean views, too. I could almost forget we were staying in a castle where everyone wants to kill me."

"Not everyone." I smiled as she moved to settle before the fire. I sat opposite her, grateful to see her. "How are you doing?"

She sucked in a breath. "You want the short answer or the long one?"

The firelight gleamed off her dark skin and hair, making it look like her coils were dusted with gold. She was so stunning, but the island had hardened her somewhat. She wasn't the scared and incapable female she'd thought she was upon arriving here. She was clever, kind, and strong. And so fiercely loyal. But I thought about the way the Rite had changed my mother, and felt more determined than ever not to let the same happen to Sherai. To not let that brightness in her go out.

"I want the truth," I asked with a smile. "Always."

She drew her knees up and hugged them to her chest. Her eyes drifted, seeing something I could not. "I'm terrified. All I can think about are those things. Or the feeling of my blade as it sank into that creature's skin." Her brown eyes flickered to mine. "I don't want to die here, Aeris." It sounded like she'd already resigned herself to that fact.

"We're going to get through this," I said. "You're going to get to the Palantai Palace where you'll be the most field-experienced scholar they've ever damn well had."

She laughed. "I suppose it's unlikely many of the academics there would have faced off a Waifling or one of the island creatures before." Her nose scrunched as she tilted her head. "I'll have to write a paper on them someday. Little is known about them, you know. It would be quite handy for the everyday traveller."

I grinned. "Or it might scare people off from hiking the countryside altogether. But I'll support you either way."

"We should capture one and set it loose on the Pentad. See how they like fighting for their lives." She frowned. "Gods, this place has turned me into a schemer. Or maybe that's you. You're a bad influence."

I stretched, yawning as I did. "And yet here you are, plotting the downfall of our masters as casually as if we were discussing the weather."

"Overcast," Sherai said without looking out the window. "And promising gale force winds."

Unlike her, I did glance out at the angry swells. Thoughts of Raithe battling on a ship somewhere out in those churning waters assailed me once more. The oily feeling of trepidation slid through my gut, which I quashed with equal fervour to the ocean beyond.

"You're thinking of the captain," Sherai said with pursed lips.

My eyes widened as I turned back to her. "How did you know?"

"You always look to the sea whenever you think of him, in whichever direction it's in. And you have a habit of stroking your forearm, right where his anchor tattoo is."

I blinked, having not even realised this myself. "You need another hobby because that's bordering on creepy. How do you know about his tattoo?"

She tapped her head. "I catalogue everything in here. It's not a bad thing, Aeris, to let yourself feel. To let someone in. Even better if that someone is motivated to protect you."

"Sherai," I said slowly. "I might have to court him under false pretences, but that's all it is."

"If you say so," she said with a knowing grin, followed by a cheeky wink of all things. "But just in case you need my approval or someone to weigh in, I am absolutely on board for things to progress further. Just be sure you're careful. Family is a tricky thing to navigate, and we don't always know the depths of that bond until we go to sever it."

"And I appreciate that," I said with a chuckle, but my amusement quickly died as I considered her words. "Does this have anything to do with rebelling against the Pentad and, quite possibly, killing his father?"

"Some," she admitted. "I keep thinking about what we discussed. I was hesitant before, but the more I think about it, the more I've realised that if we're going to die here, I want it to be on my terms."

I looked at the sincerity in her brown eyes and the

determined set of her jaw. "There's something I need to tell you. But first, we need Akira."

Sherai hunted down our friend while I called for some hot cocoa and biscuits. If the bastards running this castle were going to make us fight for our lives, then they could afford us a little luxury, too. Ten minutes later, the three of us were lounging around the fire in our pyjamas and indulging in our treats.

"Remember back on the island when I told you I found my mother's journal, along with a book on the Rite?" I said as I handed the journal over to the girls.

Sherai nodded eagerly as she sipped happily from her hot mug. "Yes, I'm so jealous. I would love to get a look at what's in the archives. Next time, I'll give you a list of rare tomes you could look for and bring out for me." She gave a cheeky smile and took another sip of hot chocolate. She was so much more comfortable with us now than even a week ago.

Akira's brows lifted as she turned through the journal's pages, wiping a hand on her skirts to remove any crumbs from the biscuit she had just eaten. "I'm still mad you snuck into the archives without me. Talk about rude. I love sneaking."

I held back a laugh at that. "Well, since we've been back, I've had time to read it. It details the Wedding Rite and what we can expect. But it also hints at weaknesses in the Pentad. The question now is," I continued, "are you sure you want to help me now that we have the information to begin?"

I knew what their answer would be. It was a massive, life-risking ask. But we were survivors, allies, friends. We had agreed to rise against the Pentad and the Wedding Rite, even if we were yet to plan out *how*. But we weren't doing it just for us. We were doing it to save the young females after us and free the previously captive females. Sherai and Akira were my family now. We'd created a bond on that island that could never be broken. If it were either of them imprisoned, I'd do anything to set them free. Just as my mother had tried to do with the females she'd fought alongside in her Rite. Those females the world had conveniently forgotten deserved nothing less than our best efforts.

Akira grinned at me, voicing what I'd said to her at the last dinner with the Pentad a week ago. "Do you even have to ask?"

Sherai took our hands, her eyes twinkling as she grinned. "I'm in, Aeris. All the fucking way."

CHAPTER TWENTY

'The most toxic herb known to Faekind is that of the lethal Faebane plant. Just several drops of this poison in the bloodstream means certain death. There is no cure, though some claim blood magic can heal even the direst of wounds.'

An Alchemist's Guide to Herbal Remedies

By Lord Windaire's request, Margaery went to Domeratt two days ago to tend to a member of his extended family. So, I was working in the apothecary alone one afternoon when I felt a presence approaching. A world turning in on itself as he was rushed in through the servant door with his arms draped around a male I hadn't seen before and Jaren. Blood oozed from an arrow embedded in his shoulder, and he slumped forward, his head lolling uselessly. *Fuck.* I couldn't have imagined the captain being hurt before.

Not truly. He was so confident and powerful, more than anyone I'd ever met. But seeing him like this … so hurt, so vulnerable … something in my chest twisted.

"What happened?" I asked Jaren as I cleared the table and motioned for them to lie Raithe on his side.

"We don't have time for particulars," he said through clenched teeth. "Where is the healer?"

The fact that they'd been forced to bring him to the castle for healing and had not had one of their ships' healers tend to him sooner told me something terribly wrong had happened. I looked Jaren point-blank in the eye. "You will make time because I need to know exactly what happened and how long ago. Margaery is not here, and I don't need to guess you're short of options if you've brought him here. The other castle healers are at the nearby outpost, so you're stuck with me."

Jaren's face tightened, but he nodded. "We've been chasing pirates down the south coast for the last few days. We believe they were headed for Cormoral with a cargo hold of slaves." He scowled at that. "Our flotilla had almost taken down their frigate when the sea serpents hit. We barely made it out alive. The captain was hit with an errant arrow."

My heart dropped like an anchor. The Strait of the Sea Serpent was avoided for good reason. Most of the time, those enormous beasts kept to themselves, but if a battle was taking place and blood hit the waters… "And the slaves?" Jaren shook his head, his expression tight. Sadness filled me, but I couldn't dwell on those lost lives now. "How many hours ago was the captain hit?" I asked as I rested a palm on his forehead. Sweat beaded over his brow, his skin burning to the touch.

"Why does that matter?" the other soldier huffed. "Enough questions and just save him already!"

"It matters," I said calmly as I hastily braided my hair back, "because depending on the type of poison the arrow was laced with, his life will be considerably shorter than you'd like."

Jaren's tanned skin paled several shades. "Poisoned? Are you certain?"

"The blood around the wound is congealed and blackening, and the veins are pulsing erratically. See the tip of the arrow here?" I pointed to the iron that was coated in a viscous black substance. "We need to get the shaft out before I can begin dressing the wound. I need bandages, gauze, hot water, and alcohol. And you better hope there's an apprentice healer or Blood Mage somewhere in this castle, or we're screwed."

"I'll find someone," the unfamiliar soldier said before rushing off.

Jaren waited, his voice low. "What are you saying, Aeris?"

"I believe the poison is Faebane, judging by the colour and the captain's symptoms."

Jaren asked, frustration evident in his tone, "Then why aren't we applying a drawing ointment to remove the poison? What about the antidote? Surely Margaery has synthesised one in the years she's been with us."

I lifted my head skyward and blew out a breath before pinning Jaren with my gaze. "There is no medicinal cure. So if we don't have any Blood Mages here…"

"No, that's not happening. I'll grab those supplies and a drawing ointment." As he headed for the door, he paused to look over his shoulder, his face a mask of determination. "Don't let him die, Aeris."

"Wasn't planning on it," I whispered after he'd left.

Raithe's body was deadly still on the countertop as I leaned over him. His eyes flickered beneath the closed lids, his breath a low rattle with every slow rise and fall of his chest. If not for the pain that pulled at his mouth and creased his features every so often, I could almost imagine he was peacefully sleeping.

I ran my fingers through his tousled black hair, pushing it back out of his face. The sunlight peeking through the stained glass apothecary window reflected like a prism on his face, the reds, greens, and blues dancing over his pale skin. An artist might have sculpted his face, handsome as it was. Chiselled and sharp, but soft in secret moments. His body was a wall of muscle, his features masculine and pronounced, but I had seen a subtle joy in his lips, if only for a moment. I had seen the sadness in his eyes when that mask had slipped. And I … I wanted to see more. Wanted to smooth out the wounds of the warrior to know the male beneath.

"You cannot die, Raithe," I said close to his face. "I will not allow it." There was little I could do except keep him comfortable until the other returned. Still, I looked around, feeling helpless, then reached a tentative hand towards his own. Thinking better of it, I began to pull away, just as Raithe's palm lashed out, grabbing my wrist so suddenly that I yelped in surprise. His eyes snapped open, finding mine immediately, and he visibly relaxed slightly.

"Aeris," he breathed.

It sounded like a prayer on his lips. "I'm here," I responded.

"If I don't make it…"

"Hush," I said softly. "You will. Of course you will."

"Promise me you'll find her," he said, his focus sharpening. "And live. Win the Rite or escape, but *live*."

I swallowed the thick lump forming in my throat. "I will. I swear. But remember, there is no Rite if you don't survive. I need you to live, too, Raithe. Besides, we haven't had the chance to fake court each other. We've got a ball to attend, remember?"

"It isn't … fake…" His words trailed off as he coughed

fitfully. The black that dribbled from his lips was alarming, but I wiped it gently with a cotton square from my pocket. His eyelids fluttered closed, and his thumb skated over my hand before he passed out. I stared at the skin he had touched. My brows knitted. It isn't fake?

Jaren came hurtling in with supplies in tow. I jerked my hand away from Raithe immediately. Jaren noticed, but he didn't say anything as he dumped the items on the counter. "What do you need?"

"I need a damn healer," I snapped as I scrubbed a hand over my face. I looked at my combat instructor sheepishly and shook my head. It wasn't fair to direct my fear and frustration at Jaren. He was Raithe's closest friend and was feeling much the same as I was right now. "Sorry. I'm sorry."

"There's no one else here, Aeris. Snap out of it and focus." His brown eyes held only conviction and hope. "Tell me what to do."

"Okay." I nodded and mentally got my shit together. "I need you to hold him firmly. He's unconscious and hopefully stays that way, but this is going to hurt."

Jaren set his hands on Raithe as I grabbed the arrow's shaft. "Ready."

I snapped the arrow and pulled it out in one quick motion. Raithe thrashed as blood poured from the wound, and I looked to Jaren. "Hold him still." I cleaned the site quickly with water, then alcohol, resulting in a hiss from Raithe. Then I covered the wound in drawing ointment and pressed gauze to his shoulder. I didn't think the ointment would do much. The poison was already in his bloodstream, but it gave Jaren hope. "Put pressure on it. All we can do now is wait."

"I'm here," a voice said behind me.

I turned, then stiffened as Portia walked in behind the

soldier. "You can't be serious," I said to the male. "No healer? No one else?"

"You asked for a Blood Mage and I delivered," he said gruffly. "We're in the Shadow Court, remember? Blood Mages are hard to come by."

Portia offered me a triumphant grin as she stalked up to the captain and stroked his chest like she was reuniting with a lover. The audacity—the possessiveness in that gesture—I saw red. Without meaning to, without knowing how exactly I even did it, my shadows sprang up, curling around my legs and torso in quick, fluid spirals.

She looked at the plumes, her eyes glittering with amusement. "You can go now. I've got him from here."

"I will not," I retorted. "Do you even know what you're doing?"

Her smirk faltered. "I..."

"That's okay." I forced myself to calm down, then walked to stand beside her. She stiffened at my proximity but remained quiet. I racked my brain, trying to remember everything I'd learned from *An Alchemist's Guide to Herbal Remedies* about Faebane. "The poison is in his bloodstream. I need you to ... purify it."

She looked at me with a raised brow. "You want me to do what now? I usually use my power for combat, you know, not healing. You'll need to be specific."

I winced, aware of how absurd and unconventional my request was, but I'd read about such things being done before. There had been rare cases of Blood Mages becoming healers despite the nature of their magic. It wasn't ideal, but ... desperate times. "You will need to filter out the bad blood. Can you identify the blood thickening from the poison and then separate it from his bloodstream?"

"Sure, if you want me to experiment with such a thing on

the fucking captain of the Shadow Court," Portia retorted. "If this goes wrong, it will kill him."

"If you don't, he's going to die. Take your time. Do it slowly and carefully if you have to," I said with a look at Jaren. "Where is Lord Windaire?"

"Meeting with dignitaries in Soul's End," he replied. "It's our call now."

I looked at Portia, who had the good sense to seem fearful at the prospect of wielding on the captain. And fair enough. If she failed, there was a good chance we'd be attending an execution ceremony arranged by the Pentad or the lord himself.

"Just think of the goodwill you'll receive for saving his life," I pressed as she looked at Raithe. "The Pentad will be eternally grateful. Maybe even forthcoming with protection or coin."

"You think I want money?" Her long, raven hair spilled over her shoulder as she tilted her head and laughed. "Of course you do. Whyever would you think otherwise? Power, money, territory, it's all that matters to you Lockharts. It doesn't matter who's standing in the way."

"For my father, yes. We can agree on that. I don't know what you think I've done to you," I said in a low voice, "but we will settle this another time."

"Enough," Jaren shouted as she shifted stance and faced me. "Wield, or leave, but decide now. Whatever happens, I will take responsibility."

My eyes narrowed as Portia bit her lip and stood rooted to the spot. Her eyes darted to Raithe as she did, until finally she squared her shoulders and straightened. "Fuck it." She stepped forward, resting her hands over the wound. "Give me some room. Here goes nothing."

Jaren and I stepped back. I held my breath as she closed her eyes and worked. Her perfectly arched brows pinched together as her hands floated over his body, searching, this time, as if gaining the measure of his health. When she finished her assessment, she made to place her hands on his wound, but Raithe's shadows snapped up, grasping at her wrists.

She grunted, her fingers flexing and hands shaking as she tried to pull away, but the shadows tightened further. "Do something!" she cried. "He's going to break my wrists at this rate. *Again.*"

"What's happening?" I yelled to Jaren.

He tried to step forward, but he, too, was pinned to the spot by those growing plumes of darkness. The whole room seemed to fill with black smoke, until all of us were consumed by it.

"It's like his shadows are protecting him subconsciously," Jaren said through gritted teeth. "I can't break free, and I can't wield without hurting him."

I took a tentative step forward. Then another. I could sense his shadows pulsing, but it didn't feel threatening to me. If anything, I was almost … drawn to him. My own shadows flooded the floor without thought, stroking at his tenderly as if to say, 'Come on, let me in!'

Portia shrieked something along the lines of not being able to work in these conditions, but I barely heard her as my power met his. The force of it, the primal strength of his magic, it felt like coming home, like being united with something I'd never known was missing until now.

The shadows stroked against me gently, and as I approached Raithe and set my hands upon his chest, I relinquished myself and let them in. They devoured me piece by imperfect piece until I was riding a wave of magic so strong I felt every inch of myself bow to its might. But I wasn't afraid. For the first time in forever, I felt wholly in control. His magic ripped through me, tearing me apart as if remaking my very being. It didn't hurt, but the sheer flood of it was so overwhelming I almost stumbled to the floor. When it was finished, his shadows receded with a soft stroke against my arm. I inhaled sharply as daylight once more filled the room. Raithe's face had softened slightly, and I'd never felt more inclined to trace his features. To soothe his hurts, inside and out.

"What in hells was that?" Portia said, breaking the silence.

I blinked and quickly withdrew my hands from his chest as reality came crashing down on me. "I ... I don't know," I answered honestly. As I turned to the others, Jaren was looking at me with something like awe and curiosity in his eyes, as if he knew something I didn't. But he didn't say anything, and Portia didn't allow me the time to ask what.

"It doesn't matter. He seems to have calmed down now," Portia said with a shrug. "I need some space. I can feel the poisoned blood. I don't think I can separate the poison and pull it out, but I can draw out the bad blood, leaving only the good blood behind. But I may need to make incisions to give the blood more exit points. I don't want to risk moving all that bad blood around his body again to pull it out of this one wound, and I have to avoid moving it too close to his heart or he'll die. Both of you stop hovering and get out so I have room to work."

"Do what you have to. But I'm not leaving," Jaren said firmly.

I wanted to echo that sentiment. *Strongly.* Every part of my being wanted to stay and ensure he was okay. The sheer strength of that feeling of our shadow magic combining had my head whirling. *What the fuck had his shadows done to me?!* The thought of not remaining by his side made my stomach twist. Like my ribs might cave in and my legs collapse if I didn't ensure he was alright.

"Out," Portia snapped at me.

It took every effort, but I forced myself to move and left without a word, almost stumbling into the door on my way out. It felt like the world had shifted axis, like it had changed somehow. Or maybe it wasn't the world that had changed. Maybe it was me.

CHAPTER TWENTY-ONE

Pros: He's handsome, he's amusing, and he can keep me safe
from the Pentad.
Cons: He's handsome, he's *annoyingly* amusing, and he might
kill me himself.

Journal excerpt, Aeris Lockhart

few days later, I sat in Raithe's chambers, drinking in
every detail that told me more about who he was. He
had been moved here to rest and finish healing after his
injuries had been tended in the apothecary. Despite his
advanced Fae healing abilities, the toll of the Faebane had
proven longer-lasting than expected. The surviving pirates
had been hunted down and exterminated since, but all those
innocent souls aboard their ships … they had been lost to the
serpents and the dark depths beneath. So, it had been all the
more surprising when I received a note under my door,

asking me to meet him in his rooms for dinner. It had also said to bring a book of my choice, which I took as code for my mother's journal.

Now, I was dressed in loose cream pants and a cream jumper, my hair braided into a messy bun. Akira would have lamented me squandering my chance to wear something sexy, but fuck it. If he didn't like this side of me, he didn't deserve my best. He'd already seen me at my best and worst thanks to the Rite. Besides, who said I wanted to impress him anyway?! It was all very confusing. And I was still a bit bewildered by what had happened with our shadow powers that day in the apothecary. Whether it was some subconscious trust thing or if it was simply the fact that I had the same kind of powers that allowed me to get close to him. I still had no idea what had happened between Raithe and me, but it had taken me a few days to feel somewhat normal again. Though I felt weirdly giddy and excited to see the captain.

It took every effort not to keep glancing at the giant four-poster bed taking up residence against the wall … or the male who was currently shirtless as he rested against the headboard and rotated his shoulder.

"You'd never know you were even injured," I remarked at the unmarred skin. All I could see was muscle and plenty of it.

He watched me like a cat hunting a mouse as he reclined, the very picture of laziness. "I hate to say it, but Portia knows how to use her hands. I owe her my life."

My eyes whipped to a stack of books, away from the amused smirk he gave me. Oh, we were *teasing* now, were we? "You are such an ass."

I flicked my eyes back to see his grin widen. "Is that a hint of jealousy?"

"It's a hint to be cautious around females who might stab you in the back if it serves them. Or maybe you wouldn't mind another injury for Portia to use her hands on you again," I replied, putting my hands on my hips. But there was no malice in my words or his. It felt more like … playful.

When had we gone from begrudging allies to flirting with each other? When had I let my guard down enough to play in the first place? Since our shadow magic had erupted? Or had there been a connection all along and I'd just been too stubborn and too scared to recognise it? I'd always thought he was handsome, but it wasn't just that. There was something … else. Something I felt it even more strongly now.

"You're cute when you're jealous," he said, leaning forward to gingerly get out of the bed.

I threw him an exasperated look before pacing around the room. More books lay in stacks across a lacquered oak desk, along with piles of missives and maps. A miniature board of the continent sat beside them, with little wooden pieces in red and white scattered across the various depictions of Fae courts. I lifted a piece and tilted it in my hand.

"I've heard power is shifting amongst the courts."

Raithe came up behind me, standing close. Very close. I didn't know when we arrived at this level of familiarity, but I wasn't about to reject it. His form was solid and warm against my back. It was comforting.

"Will there be a war?" I asked.

He took my hand gently and turned it over to take the piece I'd picked up. My skin tickled slightly at his touch. "There is always war among our kind. It's in our blood. Spell Weavers, Soul Speakers, Blood Mages and Bone Cleavers … our gods are giving, but they are not benevolent. Ryvia sees to that when she offers our ascension." He placed the red piece in the Shadow Court and sighed. "We are fighting a losing battle. The Soul Court remains neutral, but there are whispers of the Blood Court allying with the Bone Court. Too many seats of power have not changed for an age. I fear Ryvia grows restless, and blood will once again wash over these shores."

"It already is," I said bitterly. "If I live long enough to see it, I fear the future doesn't bode well. For any of us."

"Don't say that," Raithe said quickly, firmly, as he turned me around to face him. "Do not make space for doubt. Do not make space for the things that do not serve you."

I swallowed at the sincerity in his eyes. The way that earnest expression set my skin on fire and sent something fluttering in my stomach. The threat of war on top of everything else admittedly worried me. It made me want to seek out comfort and safety. Maybe I could let myself feel, as Sherai had not so subtly suggested. I could make space for new things. After what had happened the other day between us, my body was all but begging for it. Instead, I turned away and asked about the book he'd taken from the archives a month ago now. "Have you learnt anything in that book about the Rite?"

He dropped his hands and moved towards the old tome sitting in pride of place on a small table. Something like disappointment flashed in his eyes as he did, and I instantly felt the cold as he departed. I wrapped my arms around myself as I continued staring at the board, then found myself draped in a blanket not a few seconds later. Raithe lit a fire in the grate, then sat down at the table without comment, but the kind gesture warmed me. He patted the chair beside his. I walked over and took it gratefully, stretching out my toes towards the growing flames.

"From what I read, the tests always come in sets of three, though the length of the Rite itself has varied over the many years. What I can say with confidence is that the last one will be more of a spectacle. The Pentad—sometimes even other dignitaries—will all be watching." He slammed the book shut with disgust. "I am expected to be among them, watching the ladies of court slaughter each other for the honour of taking my hand."

My lips twisted. "We could just revolt. Chuck the Pentad in the arena instead and watch them turn on each other."

"Beautiful and deadly." Raithe leaned back in his chair. "We make quite a team." There was something in his tone I couldn't quite detect. A question, perhaps. Behind the slow curve of his lips, there was something genuine in that statement—in both of them.

"If circumstances were different," I said slowly. "If your mother wasn't being held as collateral, what would you do?"

He considered my question for a long minute. His voice was low and husky as he answered, "I would fight. I would find a way to take them down. If I hadn't been away in the navy for so many years, I would have tried to do so already. But once the Pentad is finished, I would ensure the Rite could never return."

"Even if it meant killing your father?" The question was soft, though my words were firm. This was dangerous territory, to be flirting with death in such a way. But I needed to know the lengths he was willing to go to serve justice. To see if the future and the court he was talking about was one I wanted any part in.

Raithe's face darkened. "He made his bed. I decided a long time ago that he would lie in it. Under his rule, the Shadow Court has been dying a slow death. Selfishness and archaic ritual keep us from moving forward. I would see it restored to the glory it once had. A place where both sexes are awarded equal opportunity and power. A place I can feel honoured to protect and serve. Not just as a captain or a lord, but a male. Just a regular, everyday male."

I laughed softly. "You are anything but regular, Raithe Windaire."

He regarded me for a long while after that, his blue eyes penetrating mine. The look he gave me ... I nearly shivered under the intensity of it. Not from fear but something else entirely.

"If circumstances were different," he repeated carefully, "if you could rebel against the Rite instead of being a victim of it, what would you do?"

I rose from my seat and walked to stand before the fire, staring into its crackling depths. "I would encourage the females to rise up. I would enlist a certain captain to help me. I would help those lost females and set them free. And I would kill the Pentad, one way or another."

Warm arms wrapped around my midriff. My stomach fluttered again at the touch. "And after that?" he whispered in my ear, like a soft caress from a curling shadow.

I sucked in a breath. "I ... I don't know." I smiled softly as he turned me and tilted my chin with that plume of shadow. "Someone recently ordered me to live. I suppose that would be a good start."

He looked at me in earnest, then pressed his forehead to mine. "Not an order, Aeris Lockhart, but a plea. A request for you to be happy and healthy and whole. I would see those eyes light with joy and those lips curve with a true smile. I would hear you laugh ... And I would hear you sing."

"Sing?"

The word was but a breath as he leaned in ever closer. I could sense every part of him from here. Could smell every aspect of his day, from the leather and musk of training and uniforms to the aroma of parchment and ink from his missives and maps to the rum that coated his tongue and left a memory on his lips. *His lips.* My eyes darted to them eagerly as all manner of coherent thought left my mind. All I had to do was close that gap, and I'd feel them brushing mine. I wanted to taste the rum, taste *him*. I'd never wanted anything more in my life.

"You have no idea how you tempt me," he said softly. "How your very presence steals all the oxygen from a room. How every smile and every laugh haunts my dreams. I am a ship, drowning in your seas. And I want to. Gods, do I want to, if you would let me."

I sucked in a breath at those words. "Raithe…" It came out like a whimper, and I was just about to close that gap when someone knocked at the door. I pulled away instantly, just as Jaren came barging in.

One look at us both and he instantly reddened. "We've got a problem," he said by way of hello. "The Pentad are back. And they've brought guests."

CHAPTER TWENTY-TWO

'He calls me little lark. I'd never admit it to him, but I like it.
And as the weeks go by and my walls begin to crumble, I find
myself wondering if this little bird might find herself ensnared
by a snake.'

Journal excerpt, Aeris Lockhart

"No fucking way," Raithe said as he placed white-knuckled hands over the back of a chair in his rooms the next morning. "There's no fucking way you're going tonight."

I sighed as I combed my fingers through my hair from my position curled up in the nook by his bedroom window. It was the next day, and we'd argued all morning, but had yet to find a solution to our latest conundrum. It turned out Jaren's 'problem' was a night of frivolity that the Pentad had decided to drop on the castle staff with no warning whatsoever. A gentlemale's club, of sorts, with invitations sent to only the most elite of guests. Raithe had informed me such events weren't uncommon, but the reason for the meeting … that had made my stomach drop.

The only staff who'd be providing service tonight were those serving meals. A select handful of females would be doing the rest, and I happened to be a chosen one of them. I'd received the note requesting my participation earlier today, left beside my door in a black box tied with red ribbon. Inside was the dress I was to wear tonight, if it could even be called such a thing. It was little more than a slip of sheer black material. More like a dressing gown, except it would hide absolutely nothing. The lacy undergarments provided alongside it were laughably flimsy, something that only a male could find appealing. The final item was a small, glittering black mask that covered the upper half of the face. The costume was clearly yet another way to objectify and demean females. Or potentially humiliate us and rattle our confidence. Seeing as it was only the most supposedly bride-worthy females invited, I didn't put it past the Pentad to use this as a way to remind us we were beneath them, no matter how well we did in the Rite.

Raithe had growled—actually growled like a cornered animal when he saw it. He'd pretty well acted like a grumpy bear since I'd come to his rooms.

"They've timed it this way on purpose, before I could announce a favourite and the protection that affords …If anyone touches you, if a single male lays a hand on your flesh, I will take my blade and make ribbons of their skin."

When had he gotten so violently protective? Something primal inside me liked the ferocity of his words. If it had come from anyone else, the words would sound possessive and petty, like a child unwilling to share its toy. But it felt right that he was the one saying them.

"They won't," I said calmly. "Because you're going to attend. And you're going to keep me safe."

Jaren folded his arms as he leaned against the wall. He'd accompanied Raithe to my bedchamber and been quiet during most of our discussion, letting the captain get his anger out. Since we were all together, and he could be trusted, Raithe and I had informed Jaren about the riddle my mother had left, along with what Raithe had learned from the book he'd borrowed. I wasn't sure when we'd gotten cosy enough to be so open about our intentions, but I didn't question Raithe's judgement.

"She's right, Raithe. If she doesn't go, the consequences could be great. They'd know you favour Aeris and would likely use that against you before the Yule ball. Besides, Killian is on the guest list. He can keep watch."

"No." I shook my head. "Don't drag him away from his duties. Finding Raithe's mother and the other females is far more important than one night of me serving nobles. Any progress on that, by the way?"

Jaren's jaw tightened. "Nothing. Killian busted a few slave holdings in Domeratt, but there has been no trace of Lady Windaire." His eyes shifted to me. "I can't make sense of the riddle your mother left, but something tells me she's closer to home than the city."

I nodded, thinking of the way my father never allowed my mother to stray far. Lord Windaire was likely much the same with his wife, even if he was the one who'd sent her away. "He'll want her close, so that if any threat arises, he can get to her quickly. What other villages are around here? Fishing ports or strongholds?"

"There's an outpost between the castle and Cormoral,"

Jaren said as he scratched his chin. "We've been focusing our efforts on the north, but maybe we should send some patrols down south. Spread wide enough to search any caves or hidden outlets along the bluff."

Raithe nodded. "Search the bluffs and scout the outpost, but there's no need to look beyond … My father despises pirates. Given Cormoral's affiliation as a hub for foreign ships, there's no way he'd send her there."

I fell silent while they discussed logistics and finished with my hair. As they talked, I drew my mother's note from my pocket and uncrumpled it. I must have read the lines over 50 times by now.

Go to the place where wooden teeth lead to still waters and look not at the ground but what's beneath it. There you will find them at the beginning of the end.

What lay beneath the surface? In a physical sense, she could have meant roots, soil, or sediment. I'd even considered bodies, fossils and, ultimately, bones. Was it a hint about necromancers? Perhaps something a Bone Weaver might understand? But then … that was a stretch given we were in the Shadow Court and Bone Weavers were rare in this province. I had dismissed the idea entirely, but maybe it was worth revisiting. I'd considered the idea of a graveyard, but even then … our kind burned our dead to prevent others from reanimating them for nefarious purposes. Did she mean a different kind of grave? My mind caught on the words 'wooden teeth' as I looked out the window to the crashing seas beyond. I stared at that gods awful island we'd been sent to and thought of all the things we'd endured there … and then it hit me. The rowboats that took us across had to navigate the ruins of shipwrecks lost to war and the whims of the sea. Wooden ships, their masts and prows looking like sharp teeth ready to cut the boats of any unseasoned sailors. Ships that had sunk below the surface. What was not on the ground but beneath it? The sea was deep and took you *beneath* ground level. The answer was the bay. The bay that led to a natural prison. I still didn't understand the end of the riddle, but this had to be it.

"Oh my gods," I said as I slowly stood. Any discussion quietened as two sets of eyes landed on me. "I know where she is. Where they all are."

I turned again, looking at the dark and stormy skies as rain began to pelt down on the window. Raithe's presence came up behind me, his hands warm and sturdy as he planted them on my shoulders. I didn't need to say the words as he followed my line of sight.

"The island," he said in a low voice.

"It's the perfect place," I said softly. "Nowhere to run, no way off the island, and a veil that blocked females from using their magic. I think they're underground. Perhaps in a cave system or a hidden bunker of sorts."

"It fits with the riddle. She's been right in front of me this whole time," Raithe said. Something in his tone wavered. I turned and took his large, calloused hand. "I've been looking for her—for all of them—in all the wrong places."

"You couldn't have known," Jaren said, coming up to look out the window.

"I should have known," Raithe said. He took a breath and closed his eyes. "All these years spent in his shadow, observing his every move, but he's still always one step ahead." Raithe's shadows curled out, as if enacting the rage quaking through him.

I placed my hands on his face and reached up on my tiptoes. "Look at me." The pressure from my fingertips turned his head just so until he could only see me. "You're going to find her, and we're going to save her. She's going to be okay."

He blinked, then placed his hands over mine before dropping them from his face. He gazed out the window once more and sighed almost regretfully. "We are going to find them. But not yet. Let's get through tonight, then we'll see about freeing those females."

I smiled softly. "I imagine the females might be a little pissed to see the lord's son looking back at them when we do. Especially when his father might very well be one of the Pentad."

Raithe smirked, and I felt my heart breathe a sigh of relief at the dark humour in that one subtle gesture. "Good. I'm counting on it."

CHAPTER TWENTY-THREE

'There is nothing so easily inflated as the male ego. When in doubt, praise and pamper it with everything you've got.'

Journal excerpt, author unknown

The den where the gentlemale's club took place was crowded with leering males at every turn. I tried my best to keep my chin up and shrug off the stares, but I could feel them skittering over me like a thousand tiny spiders. My skin itched from the weight of them, but I shoved the oily feeling of dread deep down into my stomach and forced a smile to my lips. The space was decadent and cosy, scattered with velvet lounges and cushions that took up every corner. The Fae lights cast a dim, amber glow over the room and its denizens, adding a sense of mystery and allure. I was never more grateful for the low light as I padded around in my scant clothes. Despite the fire crackling in one giant grate, it was cold, and the thin underwear and gown I wore did little to hide that fact.

Males laughed and gambled and drank at every turn. One group played darts with dark magic. Another pair played a game of five-finger fillet with a knife made from their shadow. *Idiots.* I served the males their drinks wordlessly and clamped my jaw to avoid any obscenity from slipping past my lips at their derogatory statements. The females in this room, alongside me, were not people to them. We were objects. Here to be looked at and not to speak or be spoken to. Here to entertain but not to partake in any joy.

I might have handled it better if Sherai hadn't been among the chosen females to serve tonight. It was bad enough to deal with on my own, but knowing she was forced to be here as well was almost unbearable. If they touched her … No. I couldn't think of that. I wouldn't think of that. The only saving grace was the fact that Jaren had assured me the males were forbidden from touching the merchandise—from 'spoiling' them before the captain had his bride.

It didn't end there, of course. Because this wasn't just a night of fun for the males, it was a means of surveying potential partners once the Rite was over. Jaren had informed me earlier that any male in attendance could have their pick from this curated selection, meaning if we were still alive at the end of the Rite and unpicked by the captain, we were effectively up for auction.

The females who weren't invited? They were destined for the island, presumably. I couldn't decide which was worse—being offered up on a golden platter, to be sold and used by these males as they wished, or to be imprisoned on the island for our immortal lives.

Every ounce of feminine rage rippled through me. Everyone in here, besides the females, was the very epitome of what was wrong with the world. If I could catalogue every name and face, I would, but they all wore masks to hide their identities. A rule of entry, it seemed. As if we females would ever have the chance to tell anyone about who attended. As if every one of the males in this room weren't bound by secrets and shame. I imagined most already had partners or wives—even families. Most were probably esteemed nobles, upheld by society for their various deeds.

They could all rot in Ryvia's realm of hell.

I searched for Raithe among the masks, trying to spot his bulky form amongst the unfamiliar patrons. It wasn't hard. My instincts led me to him, even if my eyes could not. It was like my body felt his shadows, his very being, and was drawn to him by something deeper than my senses. He lounged in a velvet chair against the wall, looking every inch a king on his throne as he crossed his legs and rested a lazy arm over the chair's back. His presence seemed to exude power, which appeared to keep the other males a healthy distance away. I approached him, taking care to keep my lips from curving, and bent, giving him a smirk as his eyes roved over the cleavage spilling over my lacy bra.

"Drink, Captain?"

A trickle of shadow caressed my ankle, then climbed my calf. "Should I check for poison before I take a sip?"

A sly smirk crossed my lips. "If it *were* poisoned, I could be persuaded into giving you the antidote."

"And where might I find such a thing?" he said, his eyes pinning me from beneath the bird mask he wore. A lark, I realised with a small ounce of satisfaction. "Here?" he asked as the shadow climbed up my thigh. I gasped at the cool touch of his magic. "Or perhaps here?" My body shuddered as that shadow slipped dangerously close to the junction of my legs.

"Be a good guard dog until this is over, and perhaps I'll let you find out …" I said breathlessly. Surprised by not only his forwardness, but my welcoming reaction to it.

"Continue teasing me, and maybe I won't be able to resist searching you myself," came his husky reply.

My core heated at the idea of him taking me into some corner and doing so many dirty things. His lips curled, as if sensing where my thoughts were headed, but I smiled again with rouge lips. "Aw, poor captain. If you can't wait, I might wonder at the endurance of your own ship … in rough weather. Now sit still and enjoy the view as I walk away." With that, I served his drink with a plume of shadow and turned on my heel.

The low chuckle that followed bounced around in my head as I continued serving drinks. And that damned shadow … I felt the phantom touch of it long after I'd crossed to the other side of the room. It reminded me of the moment we'd almost kissed and what it would be like to feel those lips on mine. What it would be like to feel all of him on me … inside me. The shiver that snaked down my body had nothing to do with the cold. The bastard would be having the time of his life if he knew how he affected me.

"Okay so far?" a voice whispered to my left as I waited at the bar for my tray to be refilled.

I didn't look at Sherai. Instead, I kept my focus dead ahead as I waited, careful to appear casual for anyone watching. "As well as can be expected, given the company. But all hands have remained to themselves. You?"

She huffed. "I had to fend off a drunk male and his obnoxious friends, but it was nothing I couldn't handle."

"'Atta girl," I said, collecting my full tray, and turned to again circle the room. "Stay safe."

I moved through the small crowd of privileged nobles, uninterested in calling attention to myself. A group of tipsy males seemed more animated than the rest, and I did my best to circle them without their notice. However, I was not so lucky as one of them lashed out and clasped my arm.

"What's the rush, love? Stay. Take a seat."

He yanked my arm, forcing me to fall rather ungracefully into his lap and knock several glasses over on my tray. The bubbly alcohol spilled onto the floor and one male's shoes, but he didn't seem to notice. I covered my nervousness with a small laugh and tried to bat him off with a polite smile, but his grip only tightened as he placed a firm hand on my knee.

"No touching the merchandise," I said with strained politeness. "Pentad rules."

"Fuck the rules," he said with a barked laugh. His friends snickered around him. "Rules are meant to be broken."

I shifted as his hand skated beneath my gown and higher up my leg. "We will both get in trouble for this," I insisted. "The captain—"

"The captain doesn't attend these events," he answered. "And I find myself wanting some company. Come," he said, forcing me to my feet and dragging me towards a dark alcove shrouded with curtains. "This will do nicely."

I looked around for Sherai or Jaren but saw neither of them among the rest of the party guests. My instincts screamed to escape—to find a way out of his grasp and back onto the floor. My head pounded as magic snaked through my veins, pulsing in time to the erratic thumping of my heart. "Keep your hands off me."

"Aw, what's the matter?" he said with a slur, pulling me through to the other side of the curtains, away from the view of the others. "Am I not good enough for you? Not as handsome or rich as the esteemed captain?"

I didn't bother to point out that I had no idea what he looked like beneath the mask, nor that I agreed the captain was ten times the male he could ever be. The roaring in my head was too loud to ignore, the blood pumping beneath my skin filled with the promise of shadows and death. But I didn't let them come to the surface. Didn't let them strangle the male holding me or shroud him in a nightmare of my own making. To do so would be looping a noose around my own neck.

He sat down heavily onto a couch, then pulled me onto his lap once more. A cold hand brushed my golden hair back, then strayed down my arm to my leg again. "You are here to entertain me. You are here to please me. That's all you're good for. You are mine," the male sneered into my ear as that hand rose ever higher.

I'd had enough. I couldn't take this leech of a male touching me anymore. Only a few weeks ago, I might have grinned and borne it. But something had changed in me since arriving. Something had changed in me since my shadows bonded with Raithe's. I was *not* his.

"I said, don't fucking touch me!" I elbowed the male in the gut before attempting to run, but his hand lashed out once again, grabbing my long hair. I almost used my magic—almost let it tear out of me to rip the male apart, but that would cause a scene and surely result in my death.

"You're going to regret that," he hissed. "Come here. I want to see your face before I paint it purple."

I flung an arm up, but he was lightning fast as he grabbed the edge of my mask and ripped it from my face. I gasped at the speed and force of his hand, as his eyes widened in what seemed like recognition. "You..." It was an accusation as much as a threat. Who was this male, and what the hells had I ever done to him? He raised his hand, pulling it back to strike when a shadow reached out and halted it mid-air.

"I believe the lady made it clear she doesn't wish to be touched," Raithe said, deadly quiet.

The alcove darkened, the room growing colder with each second. The sheer power that rippled from Raithe was like a maelstrom—impossible to escape and promising certain death. I welcomed it with a smile as I backed away toward him.

"And who the fuck are you to stand in my way?" the male snapped. Raithe removed his mask slowly, calmly, and turned eyes like black velvet onto the noble. The surface of his eyes rippled as his power seemed to *become* him. The male swore, then raised his hands. "Captain. Forgive me, I didn't realise—"

"That you were breaking the rules?" Raithe raised a brow. "Or that you were touching something that doesn't belong to you?"

The male gritted his teeth, then lowered his head in a mockery of a proper bow. "I meant no harm."

"Oh, but you did. Grievous harm, I believe. But I quite like her face the way it is." One second, both males were standing; the next, Raithe had the guy pinned to the couch with a weapon at his throat. "I also quite like the idea of sticking my blade down your throat and making you choke on it." He stepped back, and just as quickly as it had appeared, the blade slid home in its sheath. "Alas, I'm not as impulsive as you. Even though I don't like people touching what's mine. And make no mistake, she is *mine*."

"It won't happen again," the male said as he rubbed a hand over his throat. The skin had been nicked, and a small drop of blood trailed down the sensitive flesh.

"See that it doesn't with any females here, or next time we meet, the outcome will be much, much worse for you. But before I go, I'd like to mark the face of an abuser."

Raithe's shadows surged, plucking the mask straight off the male's face. I stiffened as recognition struck. Staring back at me, not Raithe, with eyes as cold as ice and hair of the whitest blond in all the court was my father's very own Bloodhound, Declan James.

"Are you okay?" Raithe asked once we were back in his rooms. After finding Jaren and asking him to escort Sherai back to her rooms, Raithe had all but whisked me away in a veil of shadows as we'd left the party. Only the Pentad's Lion had intervened, demanding to know where he was taking me. Raithe wore the lark mask instead of his usual kraken mask, so the Lion thought he was just another noble. Raithe used that to his advantage and said he'd paid handsomely for the night alone with one of the females, discreetly, of course. The Lion was all too willing to allow it, making a side comment about still making up his mind about which he wanted to indulge. I wanted to be sick, or claw his mask off, or both. But Raithe held me tight, and we were soon on our way undeterred.

It was only once we were in the privacy of Raithe's quarters that I realised I was shaking. His room was warm and surprisingly comforting, yet still, I couldn't stop shaking. "Do you know who that was?" I breathed.

"I know," Raithe said darkly. "I've heard many stories of the Bloodhound, even while at sea. He does not scare me."

"He should." I rested my back against the door. "Before my father had me brought here in chains, I tried to escape. On the way out, I saw something I wasn't meant to see. Something he tried to kill me for and likely still wants to. His wife is from a very powerful bloodline, from a highly regarded family. So, when I saw Declan with his mistress … If she found out about his affair, if her family knew—"

"It doesn't matter," Raithe said from his position perched

on the side of the bed. "None of it matters. He cannot hurt you. I will not allow it."

My heart tightened, like someone had pulled all the strings taut. "You can't promise that. The Rite is dangerous by nature. You can't protect me from all harm."

"Aeris," he said softly as he rose.

"Don't," I said with a shake of my head as I looked at him. "I don't need promises right now. I just need to feel something other than fear and anxiety. Everywhere I turn, something else appears to remind me that I'm not safe, I'm not free. I want…"

"Say it," he purred. He had his eyes intensely fixed on me, waiting, yielding. "Say it and it's yours, little lark."

"I…" He took one step, then another from the bed, his eyes darkening as he took me in, as they seemed to undress the near-naked state I was already in. My voice came out barely a whisper, "I want you."

"You have me, Aeris. You always did." He crossed the room in seconds, taking my face between his hands and consuming my entire being with a kiss. He pressed me against the door, his touch like fire, burning me as he held me firmly in his grasp. I melted into the embrace as he consumed my every breath. Then those hands shifted down my neck, tilting my head to the side where he planted heavy kisses in the sensitive curves. The smell of leather and rum washed over me, and I sucked it in until I was heady with the scent of him. His kisses trailed down my chest, his hands snaking over the thin fabric of my gown to settle firmly on my hips.

I shrugged the gown down my shoulders and unhooked the front clasp of my strapless bra, letting it drop to the floor. He eyed me hungrily, his gaze turning molten as he brushed my hair over one shoulder.

"Beautiful," he said, his tone filled with awe. "You are so beautiful."

His hands shifted my gown over my skin, used it to caress and explored me, gliding up my sides and front. He removed his palms from my skin, then gently caressed my nipples over the fabric, which scratched against my flesh, sending little waves of pleasure down to my core. I could feel my wetness soaking into my underwear, even as one of his hands resumed wandering until it brushed over the thong and pushed it to the side with his thumb. I gasped as his fingers slid down and replaced the space the thong had been covering. My gasp turned into a moan as he toyed with that flimsy strap once again and snapped it clean off my body.

"While this is sexy," he said, his voice deepening into a low growl as he grabbed the gown, "I'd much prefer you wear something I give you. Better yet?" He eased it down my body, kissing my collarbones as he went. "I'd much rather you wore nothing at all."

His fingers returned to their place between my legs, sliding home and eliciting another gasp of pleasure from me. He increased their tempo as his fingers slid in and out of me, then circled the tender bud until I thought I might combust. I whimpered, enraptured by the entirety of him as my spine pressed harder against the door which thudded with every stroke and pulse.

"Raithe," I whispered, his name like a prayer on my lips.

"Yes, little lark?"

A soft sigh escaped me as my walls began to mirror the rhythm of his fingers, contracting and building, my blood heating in response. "Make me sing."

"With pleasure." He lifted me, planting his hands on my ass as he carried me over to the bed, where he placed me gently and spread my legs wide. Then he fell to his knees and worshipped me with his tongue until I couldn't breathe, couldn't think.

"Oh gods," I cried, my spine arching as I pushed against his face, wanting more, more, more. He devoured me, so focused on his feast that he didn't notice my shadows that settled over the room like a fog. My legs began to shake, and then I was climaxing. My entire body released in a long breath of mumbled pleas and curses. There was only him. In this fucked-up world of Rites and dark power and cruel and wicked things, there was only him.

When he was done, he moved me gently so I was lying on my back and looking up at the stars through a glass window directly above the bed. I could have been floating up there with them, lost in a world without end. It was perhaps the first time I'd given myself so freely to someone, completely unguarded. And, honestly, the first time I'd ever wanted to.

"Raithe," I said, his name slow and lazy as a comfortable, heavy weight settled deep into my limbs. I wanted to explore him; to give him the pleasure he so easily wrought from me, but I was slipping away. Slipping to a safe place I hadn't known I'd yearned for.

"Sleep," he said as he placed a kiss first to my forehead, then another to my lips. "I am here."

Yes. He was here, and I thought for a moment I might like it to stay that way.

CHAPTER TWENTY-FOUR

'Any Bone Cleaver from the Bone Court can manipulate and guide the dead, but it takes a strong wielder indeed to reanimate multiple corpses for any significant time. In the right hands, such a powerful gift could turn the tides of war... or incite one.'

The Trials and Traditions of a Mithrian Fae

The next day, I was once again forced to take part in our daily combat training. Only this time, I was joined by the captain himself, if only for a short time. We had arrived early and decided to do some of our own practice while waiting. Raithe slammed me onto the training mat, his face a picture of cocky arrogance.

"Where is your head this morning? It wouldn't have something to do with last night, would it?"

I smiled slyly as I wriggled beneath his grip. "You mean the excellent sleep I had? I got so much of it, I'm sure I can't quite remember whatever exciting activity you're talking about."

He placed a hand over his heart. "Savage, little lark. I'll be sure to remember that the next time I make you scream to the stars. We can play beneath them all night if you'd prefer."

"The next time?" I shoved him playfully and swung my legs out, rising to my feet. "That's awfully presumptuous of you."

"I'm an awfully presumptuous guy when I know I can back my words up." He held his hand out and gestured in a come-hither motion. "Come at me and do not hold back."

I shifted to a low stance and grinned. "Wouldn't dream of it." I charged, jabbing twice before throwing an upper hook. The bastard smoothly angled out of the way with ease, but I wasn't done. I feinted, then twirled around his body to knee him in the balls. But he grabbed my knee before it could land, as I knew he would, and I lashed out with a punch to his throat. To my eternal surprise, this one almost landed. His eyes widened as he cleared his throat.

"Unexpectedly dirty ... I approve. But enough combat for now. Show me how you wield."

"Oh?" Excitement flared in my stomach, and I grinned as I shifted. "The big, bad captain is going to teach me magic now?"

Raithe widened his stance and crossed his arms, his expression shifting to one of seriousness. "Wield. If you're going to stand a chance against an opponent with powerful magic, you need to practise."

He had a point. I focused my attention on my inner strength, calling my powers to the surface. Since the incident in the apothecary, it was easier now. A strange phenomenon, but a welcome one, if this was the result. My shadows surged forward, pooling along the ground at Raithe's feet. He studied them with a keen eye before his piercing eyes landed on mine.

"Strong, but too slow. Your powers are an extension of yourself. If you must concentrate so hard to conjure them, you leave yourself vulnerable to attack." To emphasise his point, he tapped me on the shoulder with his own shadows, which I hadn't even noticed. "Strengthen your connection to your power and hone your instincts. Your magic is not separate to you. It *is* you. Now, attack me."

I didn't hesitate to send wave after wave of shadows crashing down on Raithe in an attempt to be quick and lethal. Only, when my power stopped surging, I realised the space he'd been standing in now remained empty. I blew out an exasperated breath as warm arms slid around my waist from behind me.

"You're just toying with me, aren't you?" I said with a huff.

"Maybe." A deep chuckle followed. "Keep practising and don't be disheartened. Your power is incredibly strong, considering your gift is newly awakened. You are already formidable … just not against me."

His voice was teasing, but I couldn't let him have all the fun, so I stepped out of his arms, turned, and responded with a quick whack of my shadows against the back of his head.

Raithe blinked, and I burst out laughing as the shock registered … right before a slow, cunning smile spread over his face. One that promised I'd be paying for my little trick.

As if confirming my thoughts, he said, "I'll be punishing you for that."

"Later," I said, even as my core heated at the thought of said punishment. I jerked my chin towards the small crowd of approaching onlookers. I smiled as I found Akira and Sherai among them. "We have company."

"Captain," Jaren said as he approached, a small squad of

females trickling along behind him. He nodded at me, then turned his attention back to Raithe. "How nice of you to join us for training today."

"I can't stay," Raithe said. At Jaren's questioning gaze, he elaborated. "Border patrol out at sea. I have some new information I need to investigate."

The island. It took everything in me to keep my soles planted firmly on the ground and not bob with excitement. Raithe didn't look at me as his hand grazed over the small of my back. I understood the gesture. We would do it together. Tonight. Just as we'd planned.

"I'll be back late, but I'd like to speak to you upon my return. I'll send word."

Jaren nodded, even if the words were meant for me. "Captain."

"Lieutenant. Ladies." Raithe nodded back, sparing a lingering glance at me, then exited the training field and disappeared within the castle walls.

"Right. Get to work, everyone," Jaren said. "I want to see you pushing yourselves today. Stretches, drills, then we're fighting one-on-one." Groans and grumbles answered him, and he waved an impatient hand. "Yes, yes, it's that day of the week again."

Everyone paired off and began their routines.

"What was all that about?" Akira said as she strode over with Sherai.

"We found it," I said excitedly, doing my best to keep my voice low. "At least, I think we have. We have an inkling of where they're keeping the females. Where Raithe's and my mother might be."

Akira and Sherai looked at me expectantly before Akira huffed when it was clear I wasn't getting the hint. "And? Spill."

I looked around at the other females, then pulled Sherai

and Akira to the side. "The island," I whispered. "We think they're being held there, underground."

The two considered this with a mix of thoughtful and frustrated expressions. "Of course. It fits the riddle, and with the veil in place, the females wouldn't have their magic," Sherai squeaked, her brown eyes lighting with excitement once she'd thought it over fully. She gripped my hands tightly, then gifted me a knowing smile. "The captain isn't really going on patrol, is he?"

I shook my head and grinned. "We're investigating tonight. Together."

"Aeris," Akira said softly. "You need to be careful. Don't forget what we saw on that island, and we only explored a portion of it. There could be more creatures guarding them, or worse. If you're caught—if the Pentad gets even a whiff of your movements, it'll be over. For everyone."

"I know." I sucked in a deep breath before blowing it out. "We'll be cautious, I promise. No matter what we find, we won't do anything rash."

Akira nodded, determination etched into her pale features. "Good. So, what can we do? Should we all go? No, that might bring too much attention … plus if something goes wrong, you'll need someone to bail you out."

I was beyond grateful that I wasn't alone in this, but we were still only a small number. I looked over at the females beyond my friends as the beginnings of a plan came to mind. "Akira, can you keep an eye on Portia and all the females? Maybe try to gauge where they stand on the Rite and whether they feel how we do or more like Portia? This is bigger than us, maybe too big. We might need help when the time comes."

"What about me?" Sherai said as she bobbed on her feet.

I linked arms with my friend and smiled, walking toward

the circle forming around the first one-on-one fight. "What do you know about veils and their magical properties? If all goes well tonight, I have a feeling we're going to need that knowledge."

CHAPTER TWENTY-FIVE

'The Pentad can eat a big, hairy [redacted] and shove it up
their [redacted], [redacted], [redacted]. If I die at their hands,
I'll still smile knowing some good soul will one day make
it so.'

Journal excerpt, Aeris Lockhart

We couldn't have asked for a better night. Clouds shrouded the moon, giving us the perfect cover under a blanket of darkness as we dashed through the castle. Raithe kept his shadows out, and I couldn't have been happier to be able to add my own to the mix. *Wielding.* It was becoming easier and easier, now barely requiring a thought to conjure them. Ever since Raithe had been injured and his power had sought mine, it had been significantly easier to master the darkness. Not that we needed much of it. This wing of the castle was dead, with most servants who slept here up and about still catering to the nobles visiting at the Pentad's request. I hated to think what they were up to tonight after seeing them last night. But I was thankful I wasn't forced to attend another party full of drunk males high on power and their own egos a second time.

Tonight, it was just the captain and I, two spectres who could become one with the night. Raithe led me to a hidden passage behind a statue in an alcove off the corridor, and then we began descending into the castle's bowels. I cringed as we headed deeper into the musty, poorly lit tunnel. "This isn't the same area the first test took place in, is it?"

"Not quite," Raithe said as he led the way underground. "That was the crypt. It was built many centuries ago, before our kind began burning our own, lest necromancers disturb the resting dead. The bodies of my ancestors were burned some centuries ago. Now it's a nest for those things you encountered. My father keeps them for … special occasions."

"That's horrible," I whispered. "I suppose I don't have to ask what happens to the bodies of females after they die down there."

Raithe's silence spoke volumes, but after a minute, he said, "Someday soon, when the Pentad is gone from this world, I will collapse those tunnels. None of those things will ever harm another living soul."

"If tonight goes well, it could be sooner than you think."

"We're just scouting, remember?" He halted at the bottom of the stairs. The flickering torch in his hand sent ripples of shadow over his face, highlighting the scar over his left brow. "I get it. You want to set them free and to look for your mother, but we need to be cautious, Aeris. They will be well guarded."

"I know." I sighed. "I just…"

"I know," he replied, taking me in his arms. I nestled

against his chest, grateful, as his body heat staved off the cold. Deep below the surface, the air here had a way of seeping into the bones. Even Raithe's warmth wasn't enough to ward off the chill, though that might have had something to do with the ominous silence down here. He ran a hand down my braid, sliding a thumb over the knot at the end, then tilted my chin and kissed me, long and slow. I savoured the sensual exploration of his tongue wrapping around mine, the way his lips fit so perfectly to my own. "We're almost at the dock," he said as he pulled away and looked into my eyes. "Are you ready?"

"Yes," I replied, though I made no effort to move from his embrace. "No," I admitted, looking up at his raised brow. He wrapped his arms around me again and pressed a gentle kiss to my head before cradling me under his chin. I allowed myself a few more quiet moments, then forced myself to peel away from his warmth. A long, steady breath, then I nodded. "Okay, I'm ready. Let's go."

The tunnel opened to a cave mouth hidden within a cove. Multiple small boats were moored to four rows of wooden docks, the salty spray of the sea splashing over the planking. Further down, a large ship bobbed on the water, its dark wooden hull gleaming. Accents of gold draped all over its impressive size, and a sea serpent figurehead snapped its jaws from where it curled up the beak. The figurehead reminded me of the Pentad member who wore a sea serpent mask. But this sea serpent was more detailed and somehow less intimidating.

"It's beautiful," I said of the wooden beast lurking beyond. "Yours?"

"My father gave it to me," Raithe said as he gazed at it. "He used to take me abroad on his journeys. They were some of the rare moments I had to bond with him in my youth. He was always away, always fighting a different war for territory and power. The fighting didn't stop when he came home either. Fighting is who my father is. My mother and I … we learnt that the hard way."

I swallowed the lump in my throat. My stomach curdled as the admission hit close to home. "My father used to beat my mother," I said softly. The confession seemed eerily loud in the vast chamber. "When she disappeared, he turned to me. When I tried to escape him—escape the Rite—he shot me in the leg. Fired on his own daughter with a crossbow."

Raithe's face darkened, his eyes flashing like an unforgiving storm. "He will never touch you again. Not him, not the Pentad. No one. They will have me to answer to. I swear it, Aeris."

I smiled. "I believe you. But if you think you're going to have all the fun, you're sadly mistaken, Captain."

He grinned. "That's my girl. Now get the line on one of those rowboats, wench. We've got some scouting to do."

I laughed and saluted him before I moved to untie the rope from the mooring point. "Aye, aye, Captain, but you're doing the heavy lifting when we're at sea." I stepped into the boat and raised my hood as he jumped in and pushed off with a burst of power from his shadows. "Show off," I grumbled as we began speeding along without him even lifting a finger.

"Why work harder when you can work smarter?" he said cockily. "It gives me time to spend on other more important, more fascinating things."

"Oh?" I raised a brow as his eyes travelled my body from head to toe. "Like?" I drew the word out playfully.

"Like little larks dressed to kill. Did I mention you look good in leathers?"

"You might have said so once before." My lips curved as he stepped over the bench toward me, but I held a black boot to his chest, preventing him from moving further. "Uh-uh." I pushed him away, then leaned back and opened my legs. His eyes turned molten. "You want to touch me?"

"Yes," he breathed.

"You want to taste what's between these legs?"

"Gods, yes," he said huskily.

I closed them and grinned. "The captain gets to plunder the goods *after* he's destroyed his enemies. Not a moment before."

A low growl rumbled from his chest, then he sucked in a sharp breath. "Fuck, Aeris. The things you do to me."

"Oh, I will do plenty of things," I promised. "After. Now increase the speed, wench, I want my dessert before it gets too late."

His answering laugh rivalled even the stars in its brightness and joy. I stared at him, a little bewildered by the rarity of such unrestrained amusement, and I thought the smile on his face was the most beautiful sight I'd ever looked upon.

"Yes, Captain," he said once his laugh quietened. But as I continued staring, he cocked his head, that grin still firmly on his lips. "What?"

"Nothing." I shrugged, my cheeks heating a little. "Just … just you."

"What about me?" he asked as he sat and planted his palms on the sides of the boat.

"It's just nice to see you so … free."

He looked at me for a long moment, the muscles in his arms rippling as he clasped the edge of the boat tightly. "It's easy to forget it all when I'm with you," he admitted. "Easy to imagine."

I rubbed my arms, fending off the chill of the salty spray combined with the cool night air. "Imagine what?"

His eyes were bright as he answered, "A better world."

My heart beat a little faster in my chest. "I know the feeling. But I don't have to imagine, Raithe. Not when I'm with you."

His stare intensified, and he leaned over, his face turning serious, almost imploring. "Aeris, there's something I need to tell you."

A tall, dark shadow appeared ahead of us, getting closer and closer with alarming speed. "The shipyard," I exclaimed, realising it was one of the masts jutting above the water. Beyond them, broken hulls and scraps of rotting wood littered the beach in the distance between us and the island. "We're here."

He withdrew quickly and rose, putting a boot on the bench as he inspected the water. The boat slowed as we approached, his shadows decreasing to a gentle trickle. "So we are. I trust you're a good swimmer, given our destination?"

I grinned. "I grew up by the beach and did anything I could to avoid my father as a child. I'm a decent swimmer."

"Good. I brought us some dry clothes and these." He reached into his pack and handed me some plain black pants and a long-sleeve black top in a stretchy, silky material. He also supplied a small chain with an orb pendant that glowed in the moonless night, followed by a mask. "They're lightweight and quieter than those pants, sexy as they are on you. The mask has a breather built in and will allow night-vision so you can see underwater. The pendant will provide extra light. These were all created by magic, so don't be afraid they'll fail."

I took them and undressed immediately, even going so far as to take my undergarments off as I turned. "You know, if you wanted to see me naked again, you could have asked." I could feel his eyes on me as I bent over. This teasing and tempting business was rather fun. I'd never enjoyed a male's eyes on me, undressing me, objectifying me, before. But I was quickly realising I never wanted to lose this effect on Raithe. I yelped as his hands were suddenly on me.

"You know," he purred in my ear, "if you wanted me to bend you over the prow and fuck you on this boat until you couldn't think straight, you could have asked." His hands curled over my naked breasts, pinching the already peaked nipples. Then his hands moved tenderly down my waist until he slapped my ass. I sucked in a breath, already wet with the idea of getting pounded out at sea. "You'd make a perfect figurehead," he added. "Naked and beautiful, wet for me and covered in my salty cum."

"Raithe," I breathed, barely able to stand as he pulled me against the impressive cock restrained only by his pants.

"'Tis a shame," he said with a sigh. "The captain runs a tight ship, so I guess that plundering will have to wait."

I protested his absence immediately as he shifted away. Bastard was enjoying teasing me immensely, not that I could blame him. I did start it, after all. Fine. Mission first, then he damn well better make those stars up in the sky seem like dull blips after he'd had his way with me. I grumbled as I dressed, then turned to see his amused grin. I rolled my eyes at him.

"Don't forget to equalise every few metres down by blowing gently out your nose. The mask will help. See you down there, little lark."

"Wait," I called. He stalled at the edge of the boat, looking back at me. "What were you going to tell me before?"

He smiled softly. "Later," he said, then dove into the water.

A winter breeze chilled me to my bones, and I was suddenly very unhappy about the thin material I'd exchanged my warm leathers for. Jumping in the water was about as appealing as stepping in a pile of dogshit, but I wouldn't hear the end of it if I complained about it. I frowned at the strapless mask Raithe had given me, unsure if it would fit or even work despite what he'd said. But as I pressed it to my face, the mask adjusted to my bone structure, compressing until there were no gaps between it and my skin. I kept the chain pendant tightly clasped in my fist as I dove off the boat ... and immediately regretted the decision. Water as cold as ice raked over my skin, nipping at my bones with sharp teeth.

As Raithe had promised, the mask adjusted to the pitch-black of the sea, switching to a neon blue that both illuminated the dark and allowed me a kind of night-vision. The pendant glowed brighter, too, somehow sensing the change of atmosphere.

I saw Raithe ahead, his powerful legs slicing through the water with ease. I followed quickly as thoughts of sharks taking a chunk out of me or sea monsters waiting to pull me to the depths flashed through my mind. *What was I thinking, going on some rescue mission in the dead of night out at sea?* I swore I could see shapes flashing at the edges of my vision, and I couldn't tell if it was my imagination or several somethings stirring in the depths.

My onset of paranoia caused panic to begin pulling at my limbs and chest, but I forced myself to pause and take the time to decompress the deeper I went. A lot could go wrong underwater. The deeper I went, the more the pressure of the water would affect me. At these depths, it wasn't exactly fatal, but if I didn't take the time to decompress, I could end up feeling dizzy and sick, unaware of any approaching creature coming to take a bite of me. If not a sea creature, the bones of the ships down here were just as likely to snag me with sharp teeth and claws. Their broken bodies scattered the sea floor, which was thankfully not as deep as I'd thought this close to the island. The sandy floor panned out below, dotted with sharp rocks that stood up like knives. It was no wonder so many ships had fallen or that the island remained unclaimed by the Fae ... at least on the surface.

Raithe had scouted the area earlier that day and found what he suspected was the most likely location for an underwater entrance. But it lay somewhere in the rocky wall dotted with coral, dead ahead. The naturally formed wall curved around the island, and I couldn't see a way through. I quickly joined Raithe as we scoured the face, looking for a yawning mouth to slip inside. Raithe would know the island better than I, but from what I'd seen, this was the only side of the island accessible by boat, which meant we had to be looking in the right location. I scanned the wall several times and—there. A narrow entrance partially covered by a small forest of seaweed loomed from within a hole in the deck of a sunken ship.

I gestured at Raithe, then pointed out the way. He gave me a thumbs-up, then proceeded into the drowned ship without hesitation. I felt less eager to enter the belly of that beast, but it was better than being a sitting duck in the open water. I clasped my hands in front of me and snaked my way inside, kicking my feet smoothly as I descended.

Inside, a skeleton sat by a bolted-down table, its bones clamped with shackles at the wrist. Whoever it was must have been incredibly hated or done something unforgivable to deserve such treatment. I wrinkled my nose beneath the mask. *Drowning ... what a horrid way to go.*

My attention turned to Raithe, who hovered below near a sizable hole in the rock wall. He gestured towards it, then sliced through the water until he disappeared from view. Butterflies fluttered in my stomach at the thought of what waited beyond ... this was it. *I might lay eyes upon my mother for the first time in years.* And if she wasn't there ... I shook my head and forced myself to move. I didn't want to go down that path. Not now.

The tunnel leading deeper into the cave beneath the island was dark, and it didn't escape me that we'd never have found it without Raithe's equipment. I frowned. At least one of us had their head on straight. Perhaps I was more nervous than I'd cared to admit. Still, I kept my eyes on Raithe and just kept swimming until the tunnel began to curve upwards and a light shone from beyond the surface.

Raithe waited for me a few metres from the top, gesturing once again, this time to tuck the pendant away. *Right.* We didn't want to announce our arrival before we even made it inside. I slipped the pendant under my collar and nestled it between the girls, safe and snug for later. With that, Raithe and I swam to the top, breaking the surface ever so slightly a few metres from the rocky shore. Torches rippled from sconces embedded into the rock walls, and a few crates and nets littered the cave nearby, but it appeared otherwise unoccupied.

We moved, silent and quick as we climbed out of the water and ducked behind the crates, both of our shadows in full play to avoid being seen. There was only one way through from here, so we crept forward cautiously, blending into the darkness where we could. I prayed to Brindere, father of luck, that no one would cross our path or notice the dripping trail of water we left. What I wouldn't give to wield fire right now. A little warmth, a lot of hiding any evidence of our being here.

But we were shadow masters, and, honestly, I wouldn't change a thing. Especially not as voices rang out from up ahead, and we were both able to wield our power to conceal ourselves within the darkness. I held my breath as Raithe tugged me to him while two guards approached … then stopped right in front of us.

Don't look, don't look, don't look.

The one on the left swigged from a canteen before smacking his lips. "So sick of being stuck on prison duty. Fucking Windaire has had it out for me ever since I witnessed him rutting that whore back at Domeratt."

The other snorted as he popped an herbal chew smelling of clove and cinnamon into his mouth. "You're lucky to still be alive if that's the case. I hear he doesn't take chances. I'm surprised he even bothered to stick his wife in this godsawful place instead of just killing her. Might have been the more merciful option."

"Hmm." Another swig of the canteen. "With the current Rite, I suppose we'll be getting more females sent here soon. There's already so many. Such a waste."

"You know the Pentad would rather kill them than risk anyone learning what really goes on in them Rites. Where do you think all the coin comes from? All those nobles placing bets and buying wives. And that's not even the worst part. All those females that are raped and impregnated, only for their babes to be stolen away and given to infertile wives." My stomach twisted at that statement. Violently. The male continued, "It's not right, even if they are females. They're still Fae, noble Fae at that, not animals. Am I right?"

The first one sighed. "Nobody asked, Barnes, and nobody ever will. They don't care about the females, and they don't give a shit about the males guarding them either. We're stuck down here for the foreseeable future unless Windaire carks it. They know where my family lives, Barnes. I can't talk or leave my post. It's my prison too. Best to just get on with it and look the other way."

"Fuck, I hate it here."

Silence for a moment. "Yeah, me too, mate. Me, too. Better get back to our rounds before the overseer notices we're missing, eh? Shift's almost over, at least. I still gotta finish up the cellblocks. I always need a break after walking through one before moving on to the other. Miserable fucking place. What about you?"

"Transit and the guards' ward," the other said. "Bloody mole work, checking everyone's junk for contraband. What do they think'll happen if a female somehow gets her hands on a book? She'll be mildly entertained? Gods forbid, eh?"

"Yeah … it's suffocating alright. Just don't wake Morren when you check his room, or he'll be pissed. The man's been doing doubles since Allen fell off that fucking cliff." The guards continued chatting as they peeled back the way they'd come, going their separate ways at a junction. I kept my eyes glued on the one set to patrol the cellblocks before he disappeared down the left walkway. *Bingo.*

A small part of me felt sorry for the guards. The Pentad weren't picky about who they manipulated or forced into doing their dirty work, apparently. But then … if no one dared to take a stand, nothing would ever change. And I was done being someone else's puppet.

"Let's go," I urged Raithe on, sneaking after the guard. He said nothing, but I felt his warmth at my back, never far from me. "Sounds like most of the guards are asleep. We should have a relatively clear path to the cellblocks."

"Keep your guard up," he whispered. "If anything happens, you take the first opportunity and you run, okay? They can't do anything to me. But if they catch you…"

"I'm dead. I know."

He grabbed my hand and squeezed. "I won't allow that to happen."

I squeezed his hand back, then we continued along the

quiet tunnel for several minutes, careful to hang back far enough that the guard wouldn't notice our presence, but close enough so we wouldn't lose him. My nerves fluttered in my stomach, anticipation and fear both vying for attention. I was close to suggesting we turn back when the tunnel opened into a looming cavern with a small opening at the top. A waterfall trickled in through the crack, dropping to a half-moon pool at the end of the cave. And before it were rows upon rows of cells, all filled to the brim with hundreds of females in varying states of distress. My blood ran cold at the sheer number of them, and this was just one cellblock. The guard had mentioned two.

We crept forward and ducked behind a rock to keep hidden as we took a better look. The closer we got, the more my heart plummeted into my stomach. The conditions of the cells were horrible. Dirty, dishevelled cots and nothing but cold, hard stone beneath the females' feet. And their clothes … scant more than ripped nightgowns and moth-riddled shawls to keep warm. There were braziers lit throughout the compound, but they would mean precious little in this colder weather. With winter here, they might very well freeze to death, unless there were other, more protected blocks that they switched between or a magical barrier of some kind. Some of the females I could see sported bruises and cuts visible even from afar as they held onto bars or paced their small living spaces. Other, more elderly females were curled up in their beds, not moving an inch. Tears pricked my eyes as I beheld them all.

"We have to get them out, Raithe," I whispered, my voice cracking. "We have to."

His white-knuckled fingers curled over the rock so hard I thought he might break it. "We will. And it kills me, but we can't act tonight, Aeris. We need to know what we're up against. As far as I can see, this is the only entrance and exit, and that's a lot of females to sneak through a small tunnel. There's no way we'd get them all out. Most of them are too weak to swim and would likely drown trying to escape. I don't have enough equipment for everyone."

I swore under my breath. "We can't leave them like this. We—"

A scream drowned out my words, and we both jerked our heads toward the sound as a female was dragged by her honey blonde hair out towards the crescent moon pool. The guard thrust her onto the ground, then backhanded her cheek. I couldn't hear what he was saying, but his lips were moving as he leaned in close. Then he ripped her nightgown open to reveal a back lined with red, raw lines. He raised a whip, ready to slash it against her skin. Another guard appeared from the side, dragging a female who thrashed against her captor. She was speaking, too, though it appeared her words were falling on deaf ears. She pulled and kicked, trying to reach the first female about to be whipped.

Raithe stiffened, his muscles forming a wall of impenetrable steel. I swore I felt the wrath emanating from him in waves, even though his shadows were locked away behind the invisible veil blocking our power.

"Raithe?" I leaned towards him and placed a hand on his arm. His eyes were glued on the females, on the one off to the side. I followed his line of sight, studying her dark brown hair and blue eyes, ones I knew so well in the male beside me. "She's your mother, isn't she?"

He nodded, almost imperceptibly, his gaze unwavering.

I looked back at the females, right as the whip crashed down on the first one's back. Another scream rang out as a new line of blood snaked across her pale skin. As she raised her head of golden hair, as she held out a hand to the other female frantically straining at the hands holding her back, I knew. I knew before she turned her head to reveal the face of the female who sang to me, told me stories, looked at me with a love and devotion I'd never truly let go of. The strength in my bones gave out as my body melted against my will.

Raithe caught me, his face the picture of concern as he held me close and tucked me to his side. He didn't ask, he just waited patiently as I collected my thoughts and pawed at my eyes before the tears could fall.

"You've seen your mother," I said quietly. "And now I've seen mine."

His face paled, his grip on me tightening. "Aeris..."

I shook my head. "We need to leave. I need to get out of here, Raithe, because if we stay for one more minute, one more second, I'll do something stupid and fuck this whole thing up." I locked eyes with his and saw the fury burning bright. The same fury that burned through my blood.

"We will save them, Aeris." He tucked a strand of hair behind my ear as he said the words that were anything but gentle. "We will tear this fucking place to the ground." Then he lifted me in his arms, surrounding us in shadow, and retreated down the corridor toward the exit with determined speed. I didn't look back as my mother's screams rang out once again. Nor did Raithe, as his mother shouted and snarled at the guards while she was forced to watch her friend endure more pain. Every time the whip cracked, I flinched, but I didn't look back.

CHAPTER TWENTY-SIX

'What is greater than love? Even the strongest foe cannot cleave through the bonds of fate. Even the most stubborn of Fae cannot deny what resides in their heart.'

Fake It Till You Make It: Romance Edition

"All this time," I said once we were back at the cove on the mainland and tying the boat to the mooring point. "I have been so angry at her for leaving for so long, and she was trapped there all this time."

"You couldn't have known," Raithe said gently as he gave me a hand up out of the boat. "You were a child, still innocent to the ways of our world and the people in it." He tucked a strand of hair behind my ear. "When we are young, we look for monsters in the darkness. We often miss the ones hiding in the daylight."

Monsters like my father. Both *our fathers.*

"Growing up, I always thought she'd chosen freedom over me. I thought she'd left me to rot under his care. Now I'm the one who left her to rot, even as they actively tortured her in front of us." My fingers curled, and my shoulders slumped. The tears came thick and fast, streaming down my cheeks before I could stop them. "At first, I mourned her loss, then I resented it—her. How could I have been so wrong?"

Raithe's hands moved to my shoulders, his touch firm, though they shook with the slightest tremor. His ocean eyes raged, and I knew he was only holding himself together for my sake. "Perhaps you were wrong, but you now have the tools to make it right. We'll be back for them. We will fix this. Together." He wiped my tears. "You're shivering. Come, there's somewhere I want to take you."

I hadn't even realised I was shaking, but he was right. My body quivered with cold even as the contents of my stomach lurched, as if by a wave made of guilt and rage, crashing over and over. I didn't protest as Raithe took my hand and guided me from the wooden docks over the slippery rocks of the cove.

"Where are you taking me?" I asked after the maelstrom of my thoughts became too much, and I needed the distraction.

Raithe's answer was a purr. "You'll see. It's not much further."

I wrinkled my nose as he led me into a tunnel, different from the one we'd used to get down here. The air was clear, if still salt-scented, and I breathed it in deeply, trying to calm my mind. I needed a hot meal and a bath. I needed to free our mothers. I needed to rip my enemies limb from fucking limb as I—

"Oh," I breathed as the tunnel opened into a small cavern. Glowworms gleamed from stalactites and stalagmites throughout the space, making the chamber look like a glittering starry night. Small pools of water littered the floor, with one larger crater dead ahead that had steam rising from its depths. "Raithe, it's beautiful," I said under my breath so as not to scare the glowworms.

"I come here to escape reality once in a while. It has always served as a place to think—and to bathe." He shucked off his clothes, the muscles in his back and powerful thighs rippling as he removed his garb and waded into the pool.

I stared at the male before me, closer to how I imagined a god than any Fae I'd ever seen. As he settled into the water and rested his arms around the smooth, rounded edges, his short hair curled up from the steam, and his eyes closed in momentary bliss. It occurred to me how ironic the Rite truly was. That I had been forced to fight for something I did not want, and was now fighting, in part, to lose someone who wasn't really mine.

I wanted Raithe to be mine. I didn't know when exactly it had happened. Maybe it was when our powers combined, but I had a feeling it was before even that. I didn't know why such things mattered at all, considering the weight of the tasks placed on our shoulders. Perhaps it was the looming threat of death that put things into perspective. Perhaps it was because, despite that threat, I had never felt more alive than I did now with him. I looked at the magic of the place we were in and the person who had wanted to share it with me.

With Raithe, I felt empowered and vulnerable all at once. Like he saw the deepest parts of me and had understood, truly, deeply understood the inner turmoil tucked away in a locked box in my chest. Or perhaps it was simply that when I was with him, I felt free. I could imagine a freedom spent *with* him. He had pried me open rib by rib and found a space to curl into by my heart. Warm and safe. My eyes found his from across the cavern, staring at me with a mix of curiosity, longing, and pain. The cold sapphires of his eyes burned as he gazed at me, and I felt myself drawn to their depths. My shadows stirred without prompt, floating up in swirling tendrils around me. His own answered, flooding the floor in a soft, rolling wave that caressed my power with gentle tugs.

It felt … intimate. Like we were crossing some kind of line I didn't want to go back from. Like I was scooping his very essence from his soul and bathing in it. And I didn't want to stop. Never wanted to stop. Maybe it was because we were both hurting, but I needed his comfort. Needed his steady hands on me and his distracting gaze.

I thought about the moment our power touched in the apothecary—at the notion I'd never heard of power melding together in such a way. At the same moment, something Sherai said popped into my head when she'd joked about one of us being the captain's true mate. I'd read about it, of course, but I'd never given much thought to such a thing, given the rarity. But it couldn't be … could it?

Raithe watched me carefully, and he could have been a statue for how still he was. How silent he breathed.

"Raithe," I breathed, unsure what I even wanted to say.

"Come to me," he demanded in a primal purr.

Something inside me delighted at that command. I stripped off my clothes and untied my hair, basking in the way he drank in every detail. No part of me was embarrassed or afraid. It just felt … right. I stepped over the lip of the pool and waded towards him, the water deliciously warm and soothing.

I stopped just before him, my breasts on full display, my hair now free of its braid and fanning around me. And I knew that he saw all of me. Not just the vessel but everything inside, too. All the chipped edges and the jagged holes. All the trauma and the pain. But every precious memory, too. Everything that shaped me into the person I am today and the person I could be.

"Raithe," I said again, my instincts were screaming at me to confess what I'd already guessed to be true.

"Say it," he said. "Say the words I've been wanting to share since the moment I felt my shadows connect to you in that apothecary, half-dead and on Ryvia's door. The feelings I could only share on a soul-deep level with one other in this life."

"You're my…" I swallowed, because once I said this, it could never be taken back. He lifted a large, warm hand to my cheek in gentle encouragement. And those eyes … they looked at me with all the endless depths of the ocean, full of sorrow and rage and courage and chaos and pure, beautiful joy. Any fear or doubt I had melted away as our shadows once again embraced, and a shiver skittered down my spine. Tears glimmered in my eyes, and I smiled with unrestrained happiness. "You're my mate."

He closed his eyes, as if hearing those words had eased some suffering inside him. "My mate," he repeated. "Those words from your lips could undo me entirely."

"You've known since you were wounded?" I asked softly.

"I suspected. It is a rare and precious thing to find one's mate even in our long lifetimes. I never thought I would find mine, especially under such circumstances. Truly, I wonder if it was the bond tethering me to this world—to you. The poison had long been in my veins … I should have died."

The idea of Raithe dying … I blinked away the unwanted thought and wrapped my arms around him. "You can't leave me. Not now."

"Not ever," he said. "There is nothing that could stop me from being with you. I would burn the world down for you and rip the very fabric of the realm apart from the seams if anything stood between us and forever. I am yours, Aeris. I always will be."

Pure joy and wonder rippled through me. How had something so horrific as the Rite also brought me something so precious? So rare? I was fated to be this male. This beautiful, brave, kind, *good* male. Every part of me wanted this. *Him.*

"Then kiss me, Captain, because I can't stand another moment where your lips aren't on mine. I need you—all of you."

He placed his hands on my waist and lifted me so I was straddling him. "Say that again," he replied huskily.

"I." A kiss on his cheek. "Need." A kiss on the other. "You." He claimed the next kiss for himself, hauling me in and tasting me greedily, like he couldn't get enough. I wasn't sure I'd ever get enough either as he curled a hand around the back of my neck, his fingers sliding up through my hair. The whimper that crawled up my throat was consumed, too, as his tongue twisted around mine in a reckless tangle of need. His cock pressed against me, nudging near my slick entrance as he shifted me and pressed kisses down my neck, my throat, my collar bones. I gasped as he then took my nipples in his mouth one after the other, his tongue flicking against their peaks.

"Please," I groaned as one hand disappeared beneath the water to stroke me. The water jumped as he worked, the heat of the hot spring only adding to his touch. Then the hand was gone, lifting me up by the hips and seating me over his cock. I gasped at the sheer length of it as it slid home, the water's embrace coaxing it fully inside me. "Oh gods," I cried. "It's—it's too big. I can't."

"Yes, you can," he moaned, and the sound alone made me melt around him. I felt myself stretch and devour him as he pumped deeper and deeper until almost all of him was inside me. My body responded, moulding to him as if in urgent need to be filled. "See, you can and you will," he commanded. "You said you wanted all of me. Take it."

I moaned as he slid deeper, then squeezed my hips deliciously tight as he bobbed me up and down. It was … Fuck. *He* was everything. He gazed into my eyes, that damnable smile on his face as he watched my every move. I grinned back and took over, riding him slowly as I ground on his dick, eliciting another moan from him. Then he gathered my hair in one hand, holding it firm as he leaned back against the pool with half-lidded eyes.

"You are my fucking salvation, Aeris Lockhart," he said with a groan.

"You are my mate," I replied breathily, still a little in awe. Our shadows reared up, circling us in a protective barrier. A tendril of his dripped into the pool, sliding towards me to land upon my clit. *Oh.* "Oh, fuck."

"The things I'm going to do to you, little lark," he sighed. "So many wicked things."

"Show me," I whispered as I rode him harder, faster, the air coming in short, sharp gasps as his shadows increased, flicking against me not just on my pussy now but stroking between my ass cheeks, too. "Oh gods, Raithe. It's too much. Too—"

"You can take it, baby. I want to fill you with my cum. I want you to writhe on me until you're so spent my shadows have to hold you."

Oh my gods. My body shuddered, my legs weakening as sweat beaded over my forehead and over my lips. I tossed my head back and arched my back, giving him access to every part of me as I rode and rode and rode until that wave of pleasure crested, then crashed.

Just before I came, he leaned in and bit my throat, claiming me in one final act of primal possession, just like Sherai had said a male would when claiming his mate. I screamed his name, and we were plunged into ecstatic darkness. That last surge of pleasurable pain was enough to shatter me into a million pieces. As the glowworms gradually alighted once more, they looked like flickering stars on the ceiling, a blur beneath the haze of shadows that swarmed all around us, mine and his, his and mine … together as one. Fire ripped through my mind and down my body, tearing through me in a blaze so bright I could barely contain the enormous power that shook our bodies and made the earth tremble at our feet.

When our shadows calmed and the fire stopped burning, there was only him, with his arms wrapped around me and my head buried in his chest. Because he was mine, and I was his, and he was…

"My mate."

CHAPTER TWENTY-SEVEN

'I've discovered the veil shrouding the adjacent island is not a natural phenomenon but that of Fae make. And whatever is Fae made can be unmade.'

Journal excerpt, Sherai Kiltain

I smiled to myself a week later as I strode through the forest just beyond the castle gates. After Raithe and I had joined body and soul, we'd spent each night tangled in the comfort of each other's arms and twisted in his bedsheets. It was relatively easy to keep from the rest of the castle occupants thanks to our shadow magic concealing us as one snuck through the halls to the other. We could afford to let our guard down or forget that the Rite was still very much happening and there were still 20 other females vying for his hand.

Tiredness and the ache of too much pleasure pulled at my

bones and muscles as I searched the castle gardens, but I'd never felt lighter. Raithe and I had been each other's comfort since seeing our mothers and the awful conditions they were subjected to. Despite the guilt of leaving them there, I'd never felt such hope for the future. My mother was *alive,* and I was more determined than ever to get her out. Unfortunately, logistics meant we had to be clever and calculated with our next move, and planning took time. Raithe continued my training, while Sherai, Akira, and I spent a good portion of each day studying various texts on magical veils, or more specifically, how to dismantle them. That task would be monumental, but Sherai—that incredibly gifted mind—had presented an alternative, which had led to my foraging this morning. And I was looking for something specific indeed to ascertain if her theory was true.

It was all coming together. With Raithe by my side, as well as Sherai and Akira, we could be unstoppable. We could save our mothers. Save all the females.

"We will be unstoppable," Raithe said. I stumbled as his words swept through my mind. We had discovered this telepathic connection almost immediately after he'd claimed me, and as much as I loved the ability to communicate like this, it was going to take some getting used to. Not to mention the shadows that had done a thorough exploration of my body last night and well into this morning. Gods. I clenched my legs together as a ripple of excitement wandered through me at the mere thought.

Raithe seemed to know the effect he had on me. *"Say the word and I can be there in five to do it all again."*

I snorted. *"Snoop. You and your shadows can stay put, thank you very much. I don't think I could handle the extra action right now."*

"Your body *says otherwise,"* he replied with some amusement.

Oh, he was so right. *"Can you really sense that?"* I wondered in awe.

His answering chuckle sent a jolt of happiness through me. *"I can sense your general mood. Whether you're feeling happy or sad. If you feel threatened or scared. The bond is still settling, and you are young. With time, you will get used to its power."*

I scowled, not wanting to wait that long. But I suppose I had only just begun to wield, and the gods had seen fit to gift me my mate at such an early point in my life. I smirked as I crunched through the powdered snow dusting over the earth. *"So, how does it feel to be a cradle snatcher?"*

"I ... what?!"

I laughed out loud. It was the first time I'd ever heard him so perplexed. I could just imagine the look on his face. *"Well, your mate is a hell of a lot younger than you. It should be downright illegal, really. I mean, I'm dating an old male."*

"Old?!" His disgruntled tone only added to my statement. *"I happen to be one of the most powerful males in the Shadow Court and one of the most influential. I am in my prime."*

"Uh-huh. Keep telling yourself that, buddy."

"If you consider me old and yourself as young, then you can think of this as an exercise in learning from your superior. I have so many things to teach you, little lark. Starting in the bedroom. And if you insist on being such a naughty girl, I'll be sure to exact a fitting punishment. For now, I have some villagers to appease and a rebellion to plan. Go back to picking herbs whilst the grown-ups do their job."

Oh, teasing or not, there would be no getting away with that. *"Sure,"* I replied sweetly. *"I'll pick something to help in the bedroom, just to make sure your old male parts can keep up with someone so spritely."*

"Someone so young has no business with my old male parts," he replied sassily. *"But I'll allow it. Later..."* His laughter echoed down the bond, then tapered off as he focused his mind elsewhere. Or maybe he just went out of range, if that was a thing. There was so much I still had to learn, starting with what the limits were on our powers. Given we both commanded shadows, what could we do if we used them against our enemies?

I tugged my cloak tighter around me and nestled into the thick fur of the hood as I walked through the castle gardens. Winter felt fully upon us now, with the first snows having finally fallen. They had been late this year, but the rivers and lakes would soon freeze over, and even the hardiest of herbs and flowers would give way to the winter frost. The only plus side was that, this close to the sea, the winters were more temperate than those of the Bone Court to the north-east. The castle gardens were more than strictly organised rose bushes and the like, but a vast stretch of woods up until that first wall that surrounded the entire property, the one I'd managed to sneak past that day in the cart. Surrounded by trees and flora, I could almost forget I was trapped in a vicious Wedding Rite.

I spied a sturdy black willow tree and hefted my satchel off my shoulder, plopping it into the snow. The peeling bark would serve quite nicely for medicinal stores over the season. I slipped my dagger from my boot and set to work, prying the bark gently from the trunk in long, vertical strips. I was so ingrained in my work that I didn't realise for some time the forest had gone silent. The hairs on the back of my neck prickled, and I turned just as someone lunged at me with a blade. I ducked as the weapon embedded into the trunk, the owner swearing viciously as they tried to pry it from the bark.

Panic flared through me, and then Raithe's voice was roaring in my mind. *"Aeris!"*

My shadows rippled out, clouding over the ground around me as my attacker turned. Declan's upper lip curled as he snarled at me, the pale blue of his eyes like ice. Murderous and hungry for blood.

"You again," I snarled while I shifted stance.

"Me," he responded as he abandoned the sword ingrained in the bark and charged with an axe forged from dark magic. I'd forgotten how fast he was. A mistake I paid for in blood as the tip of his axe nicked my shoulder. I cried out, holding a palm to the wound as I evaded his onslaught.

"Aeris!" Raithe cried again, his voice edged in panic. *"Hold on. I'm coming."*

"I'm okay! It's Declan. He's come to finish me off."

"Not if I finish him first," Raithe promised. *"He's a fucking dead male."*

I whirled around a tree as Declan came at me again. *Fuck.* I tried to remember everything Raithe and Jaren had taught me over the last weeks and use it to defend myself. But my cloak was too heavy and my steps were laboured and slow from the biting cold and little rest I'd had the night before. I was a sitting duck, but I wasn't helpless.

"It doesn't have to be like this, Declan," I said as I kept the obstacle between us. "I won't tell anyone about Melania. What you do is your business."

"You're right," he said gruffly. "And my business is for me alone. One word from those poisonous little lips and you could ruin me. I can't take that chance."

I stepped out from behind the tree with my hands up. "Be reasonable. I'm stuck in the Rite with a slim chance of surviving. Who would I tell? And let's say I do survive; your conquests will be of little concern to me. You can remain my father's Bloodhound. I will be Lady of the Court and never see you again."

"You will be Lady of Nothing," he hissed. "Even with such power, you will always be nothing compared to your male betters. I should have taken you the night of the party. I should have squeezed your slender neck until the air stopped flowing to your lungs."

I dropped my hands and grinned as I grabbed the neck of my tunic and the edge of my cloak to pull them to the side. His eyes widened as they saw the bite mark—Raithe's claim— still proudly etched on my throat. "No, Declan. You should have died. You'll wish you had when I'm through with you."

His mouth thinned as I dropped my hands and unleashed my shadows to their full extent. They flew at him, lunging at his arms and legs. When he sliced through one, another tendril would appear, and another, as he hacked and slashed. Soon, the sun was gone, and the world was filled with a darkness of my own making as my shadows raged around him in a tornado of power. A crash sounded beside me, and I realised it wasn't just my shadows at all but Raithe's, too. They dispersed, restoring my vision of the forest until it was just Declan before me, lashed down to the ground with multiple shadow bindings. And beside me … Raithe could have been a nightmare from another realm. Shadows formed smoky wings at his back, the membranes so incredibly lifelike and detailed for something intangible. His black clothes and thunderous eyes only added to his demonic countenance. His gaze shot to me, assessing my shoulder briefly, before flicking back to Declan.

"I told you not to touch things that didn't belong to you," Raithe said as he stalked towards Declan. "I told you not to touch what is mine."

Mine. Gods, he had said those words the night of the party, hadn't he? Had known even then that I was his fated mate, which meant those words were careful and intentional. I couldn't help the small smile that crept over my face. Yes. I was his. And he was mine. And no one could stand in the way of that. Especially not my father's Bloodhound.

"If you touch me, you'll have your father to answer to," Declan said as he backed away slowly. "Harming me is more trouble than it's worth."

"I'll take those odds," Raithe said with a shrug. "Right after I take your head off. But first…" He looked at me tenderly as he held out a hand. I walked over and took it, relishing in the feel of those callouses as they scraped against the newly formed ones on my own hands. "My lady, *my equal*, is more than entitled to shed first blood. If that's what she wishes."

Declan looked between us in disgust, and his face scrunched up in fury. "Females do not belong in positions of power. You disgrace your father's line by offering such."

"You disgrace the world with your very existence," I spat. I turned to Raithe. "Finish him. A lady does not diminish herself with the blood of a beast."

Raithe grinned. "As you wish."

I didn't watch. Not as the whine of steel came with the unleashing of his sword, nor as Raithe's power overwhelmed the Bloodhound's dark spells. But I heard it all. I stopped to listen to the sound of weapons clashing and males grunting before the sound of something thudding to the ground followed. Another heavy thud, then another, and Declan James was no more. To his credit, he'd lasted longer than I'd thought he would against Raithe. But I suppose one didn't get the title of Bloodhound for nothing.

I turned to find Raithe burning the body moments later, and then my captain was standing before me, laying his cloak around my shoulders and carrying my basket of herbs. He ran a gloved hand through my hair when he stopped at my side. "Are you okay?"

"He had it coming. I'm actually sorry I won't be there to see my father's face when he hears the news. He won't be so glad about his deal with the Pentad now. But what will happen to you?" The forest area hid what we had done from the guards and Pentad, but a missing male guest would not go unnoticed.

"I will deal with them," Raithe said. He nudged me playfully. "Being the captain of the Shadow Court navy has its perks, after all."

"And when will the captain take me for a ride on his ship?" I asked with a hopeful bob of my heels.

"The ship will have to wait," he said mischievously. He took my basket and set it down gently. "But I will take you for a ride."

I yelped as he lifted me into his arms and launched us into the sky. The breath left my lungs as his wings carried us into the cold air around the castle, taking me as far as the coastline. I realised his wings weren't intangible shadow anymore, but something else, something solid and real. The wings beat hard as they carried us higher. I clung to him for dear life, my knuckles white as I latched my arms tightly around his neck.

Raithe must have sensed my fear because he said to my mind, *I would make a poor captain if I lost my cargo so easily, especially something so precious.*

"I'd say that's romantic, but it's kind of hard to think when you're fifty feet in the air." I gritted my teeth and nestled in closer, but even as fear and adrenaline thundered through my heart, I risked leaning my head over his shoulder. It truly was beautiful up here. The rolling waves were white-capped and gleaming, and the sunlight filtering through the clouds glittered over the soft snow dusting the cliffs. Even the castle looked like a beacon when the light hit it just right. Castle Cliffscote was a picturesque place, if one could ignore the

company it kept. *"How do you do that with your shadows?"* I asked about his wings. *"How can the shadows turn solid?"*

"It took me a long time to master," he admitted. *"I spent a lot of time studying the wings of other beasts. Birds, obviously, but insects, too. Even the wings of a Jediri, on the rare occasion they have allowed my proximity."*

"You've actually seen one of the wyverns?!" My mouth fell open in awe. To see a Jediri was a rare sight indeed, much less to stand—and remain—alive in their company. I'd read much about them as a child, but I had always wondered what it would be like to be a rider. Most of the Jediri were born and bred in the Bone Court, giving them a great advantage in battle, but others rode the mighty beasts throughout the continent, too, if not as common.

Raithe chuckled. *"Like I said, on rare occasions. They are as magnificent as the stories say, but I'll take the sway of the sea and the feel of a wooden deck beneath my boots any day. At least the helm doesn't bite back."*

"You really do love the sea, don't you?" I asked as I looked at him. His face was relaxed, his eyes bright as we soared along the coastline. If I hadn't seen it, I would never have known he'd just beheaded a male without breaking a sweat.

"It is my calling. But you, mate, are my answer."

"Such a cheesy romantic," I answered with a grin. *"But I think I might keep you."*

I nuzzled deeper into his warmth and sighed as the world flashed beneath us. It would be so easy to keep flying, to start a new life together somewhere safe. But then he wouldn't be the male I had fallen for, and I wouldn't be the person I needed to be. The person I was growing into. Someone worthy. Someone fierce and powerful and feminine … *Someone free.*

CHAPTER TWENTY-EIGHT

'There is no Faemade concoction that cannot be countered.
For every creation, there is a cure. Start with an herb or
flower's base properties, then find something with the adverse
effect.'

An Alchemist's Guide to Herbal Remedies

"The final trial is in three days," Jaren informed five of us currently holed up in Raithe's chambers a few days later. "Whatever we're going to do, now is the time."

I glanced at our party and frowned. Raithe, Jaren, Killian, Sherai, Akira, and myself. Six people were hardly enough to stand against an island swarming with guards and a castle full of soldiers, female participants, and five powerful Pentad members. We weren't without resources, thanks to Sherai's impressive mind, but we certainly had our work cut out for us.

"Many of the guards will turn to our cause," Killian said gruffly from his position in front of the fire. "Say the word, Raithe, and they will obey your command."

"It isn't enough for the guards to form a coup," Raithe said as he ran a hand through his already messy hair. "We need to get hundreds of females off that island safely and securely. Many of them are malnourished and weak. They haven't lifted a blade or felt their power in years—centuries, even."

"They will fight for their freedom," Akira said quietly. "Not all of them, but enough will take up arms or fight tooth and nail to get out of that prison. I did. I did anything I could to escape mine. They will too."

Sherai rested her head against Akira's shoulder. "You got out. And you never have to go back there again."

"We can't ask them to fight for us," Raithe argued. "Not after being locked up for so long."

"We can, but we won't have to," Sherai said softly. "The Pentad have been allowed to continue this barbaric Rite for too long. They will never see a cell for what they have done, nor will any justice be served by those leading the Shadow Court. It is time for the oppressed to rise and finish this. When that happens, you'll see how deep their rage is. You won't be able to hold them back."

Her words filled the space, heavy and foreboding as they settled over us. I sat in one of the chairs by the fire and sipped my tea, barely tasting the sweet chamomile and honey as it warmed my throat and stomach. "It's their choice," I added. "All we can do is ask them. Whatever their answer, it still won't be enough. We need numbers and strength, and I think I know just the person to ask."

Raithe's eyes narrowed on me. *You're not seriously considering who I think you are, are you?"*

My silence was answer enough. He sighed, then scraped a

hand over his face, but he did not object. Taking that as acceptance, I continued, "We need to ally with the other Participants. Most of them will be too scared to fight … unless we get Portia on board."

Akira spat out a mouthful of tea. "Portia? She hates you. Why—?"

"Because she's strong," Sherai said. "She hates Aeris for a supposed injustice we have yet to learn. She may care enough to end a greater injustice that could affect her and any other female she's ever mildly liked. But more than that, she's a leader, even if most of them would follow out of fear. She's the most formidable opponent left, and if we have her on our side…"

"Then we might stand a chance," I finished. "We need to talk to her."

Akira sighed. "From what I've managed to find out from the other participants, their biggest motivator is survival. They're afraid of Portia, so they avoid doing anything to upset her or get in her way. But most are here against their will, and care more about staying alive than the captain's hand. No offence." She looked at Raithe with a shrug. "Like us, they've grown up with little say and little freedom. If we tell them the prison is their alternative to death in the Rite, they might just decide that's not an option. If we can convince them that siding with us has the best chance of survival *and* freedom, I think many would join us. Even if Portia doesn't agree."

"If it looks like we can't convince Portia, you go convince the others. I'll keep Portia busy and away from them if I have to. I'm sure she has a few things to get off her chest," I said. If Portia hating me was the reason she didn't help, then the least I could do was find out why she hated me in the first place.

Jaren raised his brow and pushed off the wall to rest his

hands atop Sherai's chair. "You understand that placing your faith in this person might jeopardise the whole plan, right?

"I don't like it either," Raithe said. "But I agree we need the numbers. Even with both groups of females on board, plus some of the castle guards on our side, we need to be ready for anything."

"So, let's go over the next steps, then," I said. "Sherai, Akira, and I will speak to Portia and try to convince the other female participants. Raithe, you will take a team of trusted soldiers to the island to free the prisoners there. Killian, you'll stand by with your troops positioned around the castle and open the gates to get everyone out if things go wrong." I glanced at Raithe. "That just leaves the Pentad."

He cocked his head ever so slightly as he sent a plume of shadow winding around my feet and up my legs. Both a question and encouragement. "I will stand against them."

"We will," I corrected. "They are not leaving here alive."

"You don't have to do it alone," Akira said. "We can help."

I smiled at her, then up at Raithe as he took his position behind me. "I won't be."

"We need to keep the females safe," Sherai said to Akira. "The last thing they need is more males to scare them witless. They will need us."

Akira nodded and placed a hand over her heart. "It will be done."

I blew out a breath. "In a perfect world, we'll get all females out of the castle with the Pentad none the wiser. If things go wrong…"

"Then we fight," Killian finished gruffly. "We all fight and finish this once and for all."

I nodded.

Jaren let out a low whistle. "All in a hard day's work. We do this at night under the cover of darkness. Maintain the element of surprise." He glanced at Raithe. "I hope your shadows can cover a whole lot of females. Not to mention a few ships."

Raithe's voice rumbled from behind me, "They will. They've never failed me yet."

"And what if everything goes to shambles?" Jaren asked. "What if the Pentad are prepared for an event like this and the final test goes ahead anyway?"

My lips curved into a wicked grin. "They aren't the only ones with surprises up their sleeve. And I've prepared a little something special just in case."

Jaren blinked at me. "Gods, help them then. With the odds we're up against? Gods help us all."

"So much for the Yuletide ball," Akira grumbled.

"If we're successful in killing the Pentad, we can still have one," Sherai said from her perch, her eyes glowing bright. "A real one, where we celebrate the things that matter."

"A Yuletide with our family," Raithe said to me, a soft smile on his face. *"Once we've brought them home."*

Home. I was beginning to understand what that meant and who would make it so.

"One more thing," I said, directing my attention to Raithe, Killian, and Jaren. "Where is the castle cellar and who is in charge of the stock?"

Jaren raised brow. "The cellar is accessed via the kitchen and through the storeroom. Most wait staff have access, but Harlan is your best bet. He's easily won over, especially if you bring him a sweet treat."

I nodded. "Perfect."

Akira tilted her head. "I'm always up for a nice red, but I'm guessing that's not why you're asking. Why do you want to know?"

My grin was nothing short of devious. "Oh, you'll see."

CHAPTER TWENTY-NINE

'Blackbell, a rare flower found along the coast, is known for its powerful properties in reversing spells and banishing evil. Treat with care and mix gently.'

An Alchemist's Guide to Herbal Remedies

I knew, as soon as I saw them, that the final test was upon us. Not on the third day, as Jaren had been informed, but tonight. They came in the night, once more ripping us from our beds like reapers come to claim their pound of flesh. I didn't say a word as a key opened my locked door, nor as the guards stood wordlessly at the end of my bed and waited. Did the Pentad know there were spies among them? That they had guards—even their prized captain—working against them?

Fuck.

"You are headed for combat," one of the soldiers said bluntly. "Dress accordingly."

I rose, calmly shrugging off the blanket, and padded to my wardrobe where I gathered skin-tight pants, a long-sleeve top, a cloak, and some boots. All black, of course. I also strapped on a thigh halter with several individual sleeves that would fit vials of a little something I'd prepared earlier. It was Sherai's answer to the veil theory, though yet untested. I had to hope she was right and that I hadn't botched my alchemy. Unfortunately for us, my little concoctions weren't in my room but back at the apothecary. A big problem, but one I couldn't dwell on.

"They're dragging us to the final test," I said to Raithe, doing my best not to let my panic drip through... *"The girls ... What if it's too late?"* We hadn't yet spoken to Portia or the other participants. It was a task I'd set aside for tomorrow, when we were all fresh and rested.

I braided my hair back, noting the way the soldiers shifted impatiently in the reflection of the mirror. I ignored them as I strapped the dagger Raithe had gifted me to my other thigh. That's it. That's the only weapon I had besides my magic. Of course, no armour was tucked away in the dresser. We had been given *nothing* to aid us other than what we'd killed for or been gifted—and it's not like everyone had a captain at their back to assist.

"Nothing has changed," Raithe remarked, the shadows of his mind stroking mine in a comforting gesture. *"You fight. You kill, if you have to. But you do what you must to stay alive, you hear me? You do not hesitate. Try to get them on our side, but don't let your guard down. We can't fully trust their intentions, and they may think you're just trying to sabotage them in the test."*

"People are going to die," I whispered. My heart beat rapidly,

and my stomach curdled as anxiety battled with adrenaline. *"This is not what we had planned."*

"So we adapt. We survive. We all have our parts to play." A brief pause, then I felt the conviction in his voice as he added, *"I will not fail you."*

I nodded to myself as I looked at the girl in the mirror. It was only a few months ago that I first stepped in here intending to escape. I'd thought this place had clipped me of my wings and my future, but it had awoken a resilience in me I'd not realised was there. I was not a meek and mild plaything to be bent and abused. I would not join the bones in the bowels of this place. I was not the weaker sex. And I would burn them all down before I allowed them to take me. They would learn to respect the name Aeris Lockhart, or they would fear it.

"That's my girl," came Raithe's distant whisper. *"Show them who you really are."*

"I didn't ... I didn't say that down the bond," I replied, a little bewildered. Could he read my thoughts, too?

A chuckle hummed through my mind. *"You didn't need to. I love you, Aeris. I never said that before, but I love you. I see who you are, and I bow to you. I would die before I let those fuckers take you."*

My heart swelled at least four times in size. *"I love you, too. Don't die for me, Raithe. Live for me. Fight with me. And be safe."*

A final caress against the walls of my mind was the only response I received before the bond fell silent. With any luck, Raithe would find a way to help or get those females out of the cave and away from the island. If I failed ... if I died today, I knew he would at least set them free.

The guards marched us all in single file down the corridors and stairwells. All 20 of us. My nerves jittered under my skin, my pulse beating in an erratic reminder that with every step, I might be walking to my death.

Through the passing windows, I saw snow blanketed the courtyards and crowned the castle turrets. The windows were frosted, and the air was sharp with a biting cold that burrowed beneath my skin and settled deep into my bones. It was a flurry now, but there must have been heavy snowfall in the last few hours, given its coverage. Not ideal for fighting in, though it did make for a picturesque battlefield. And they were sending us outside to die tonight, I just knew. I shivered, pulling my cloak tighter around me. That white sheet across the land would soon turn red, soaked with the blood of countless victims. From females failed by society, and the masked monsters parading as males. Regardless of what happened, I would make the Pentad bleed before my end. One way or another.

The soldiers shoved us out the great doors of the hall and into the bitter cold. My cheeks stung immediately. I flexed my hands and wished for gloves, but I was thankful to feel those fresh calluses against my fingertips. Raithe had helped create them, had helped to hone these hands into those of a warrior. They reminded me that I was stronger than when I'd arrived. That I'd already survived so much and would survive more still.

The snow crunched beneath my boots as we walked, and I held out a hand in fascination as a perfect snowflake landed on my palm. Its glistening edges shimmered briefly before melting into my skin. A beautiful anomaly in a world so rife with ruin. Just like Sherai and Akira … like Raithe.

We halted in a straight line at the garden's edge, in a space where the terrain lay open to the elements near the cliff's edge, rather than obscured by a wall. It now appeared to be an arena of sorts, with covered seating erected on either side of the snow-covered ground. Males occupied the space on one side, lounging in thick fur coats with servants standing by with delicacies and drinks. I wondered if they'd been up all night drinking, or if they, too, had recently woken for the event.

The other side housed only five seats, which were obviously for the Pentad. Seeing those five places sent anger bubbling beneath my skin. This was an arena, and we were the gladiators. Our deaths were passing entertainment for these elitist assholes. The only comfort was knowing I would make them squeal once this was done. I felt no guilt about that fact whatsoever. It warmed me, deep in my darkening little heart.

The crowd quieted as the Pentad took a step forward. Even the whistling wind seemed to pause, as if noting how important this moment was. The sea serpent stepped to the forefront, always the ringleader, and gestured at the arena.

"The final test," he exclaimed for all to hear. "A final farewell to the journey that led to this moment. We hope you enjoyed your stay." He paused, as if politely allowing for a cordial response. No one spoke a word. "The Wedding Rite is our most beloved ceremony, reserved for the most promising of females. You started this test in a blood offering to the beasts below, and we ask that you do so again. Normally, we end the Rite with some mercy. Allowing the losing females who made it this far to live and find another potential husband. However, tonight, we rein in a new era. One where only the strong survive, and the powerful Fae of this court take back what is rightfully ours. It begins with you. Become your wildest self—your most primal being. Take what is rightfully yours by blood. Claim it. Kill for it. And stand victorious over the fallen. Raulo, the wrathful God of War and Change, smiles on you tonight as you battle for the hand of the captain."

My heart plummeted as his words sank like a stone into my stomach. This was truly the end, then. I had never expected the Pentad to be merciful, but they were downright unhinged if this was the beginning of some great calamity to overthrow the court. *Rein in a new era? It begins with us?* I frowned. More like our deaths.

I looked at the five males with pure hatred filling my veins. It would be so easy to shove them off the cliff and end this insanity. The drop beyond promised a swift death on the rocks far below. The ocean roiled below, its waves foam-capped and angry. An ocean wind whipped through my hair, fluttering the braid and making me brace in my boots against the icy cold. But it wasn't the wind, nor the sea, that made me tremble. It was the five males standing in their black robes and their golden masks. It was the purveyors of death, looking upon their curiosities like we were priceless cuts of meat to be devoured.

I turned and caught my friends' faces down the line of females, noting the bravery in Sherai's honey-brown eyes and the resigned acceptance in Akira's nearly black ones. Two very different females who had proven their love and loyalty time again. Our friendship had been forged in the hottest fires to that of unbreakable steel, not iron or glass. We were sharp and deadly and fierce, and we were in this together.

Sherai smiled sadly at me, and Akira dipped her chin. I nodded at them both—a promise, and a shared order. We knew what we had to do. Even if it was too late, we still had to try.

The thunder of stomping boots came from behind me. I looked over my shoulder with narrowed eyes as row upon row of soldiers formed at our backs, effectively shutting off any hope of escape. Then they threw swords and spears to the ground between them and us. The weapons clanged as they thudded ominously onto the snow.

The sea serpent nodded towards the crowded stand of onlookers, where several servants rushed out with trays of goblets that they handed out to the females. The cups we received weren't nearly as fancy as those the guests were drinking from. I was betting the contents of ours was different, too.

"A toast," the sea serpent said as he and the other Pentad members raised their own glasses. "To the dawn of a new empire, and your brave sacrifice."

Most of the females raised their cups to their lips, but I took one sniff of the contents and subtly shook my head at my friends. Poison, most definitely.

"All females must drink," the lion purred from behind the sea serpent.

The guards stepped forward at once, combing down the line for any cups still full of liquid. Several other females hadn't drunk from theirs either. The guards forced the liquid down their throats. I wasn't surprised to see Portia among them, bearing her teeth and hissing as they yanked her hair back and forced her chin up. They did the same to Akira, who sneered at them from red lips before they forced it down her throat. Sherai complied, knowing there was no use struggling.

I took a sip from my cup and winced at the thick, syrupy texture and the acrid bitterness as I held it in my cheek. The lion broke rank, stalking towards me with all the intention of a predator. It was obvious he didn't buy that I'd willingly swallowed the cup's contents. He gripped my face hard enough to bruise, then dragged me forward as he ripped the goblet from my hand. I spat the liquid onto his mask, then was rewarded with a backhand to my face. Pain radiated through my jaw, and blood welled immediately from a tooth that cut through my lip. I staggered and wiped my mouth with my sleeve, glaring at the male with the full weight of my hatred.

Pure, undiluted wrath funnelled down the bond as Raithe's emotions welled down the connection linking us. He was the storm and the sea, waging war on all his enemies. The weight and force of his anger gave me pause, making me blink several times to adjust.

"We are intrinsically linked in a way that would be impossible to describe," Raithe answered with cold fury. *"When I get there, I am going to slice out his fucking innards. If he touches you again—"*

"I can handle myself," I promised, stroking the shadowy wall of his mind in reassurance. *"I need you to focus on your task. I'll be fine, Mother Hen. This may be our only chance. At least we have them all here where we can keep an eye on them ... and keep them distracted. I'll be fine."*

"I know you will. Doesn't mean I don't get to play the overprotective rooster when I have the chance. And if you don't kill that male, I swear to all the gods I sure as hell will."

"You will comply or you will die," the lion snarled, ripping me from my thoughts as his golden mask roared down at me. "The choice is yours."

"Okay, I'm thinking we can both rip this fucker to shreds," I whispered down the bond as power surged to my fingertips, barely held at bay as my anger nearly consumed me. I kept it in check. A sure death would follow if I acted prematurely. Worse, he may kill my friends for my actions. He grabbed me again, this time by the neck, and forced my head back before he poured the full contents of the cup down my throat. When the liquid overflowed out of the sides of my mouth, a guard behind me pinched my nose, and I was forced to swallow.

"My ruthless little—" Raithe's words cut off, and I blinked,

panic rising in me once again at the gaping chasm inside me that he usually filled. The bond was gone. *Raithe* was gone.

The lion grinned at my stunned expression. "A little concoction to even the scales," he said for the benefit of all. "Your ability to wield has been stripped from you, but don't worry, it will return … if you live long enough." He slid a hand over the small of my back, then round to my front, his fingers splaying downwards. Revulsion curdled in my stomach, but I said nothing, did nothing, until he pulled his hand back. He clucked his tongue. "You're the alchemist, aren't you? I'm surprised you don't come better prepared. Alas, there are no potions to aid you today."

Isn't there? a little voice in me wanted to say. Ever since Raithe and I had returned from our scouting trip to the island, my friends and I had pored over texts to find answers to the mystical veil. I'd wanted to remove it altogether—to give the females in the prison a fighting chance to escape—but such an obstacle was too large a feat to overcome with limited supplies. Instead, Sherai had suggested finding a more portable solution. A liquid cure to the Pentad's power-blocking magic. I now wondered if it would also cure the magic that was currently circling in our veins. I'd been gathering the herbs and testing the solution in the apothecary since. The ones I'd picked the day Raithe had taken me to fly had proven the answer. Blackbell. Our saving grace.-The vials were waiting … if only I could get to them.

My fingers curled into fists as the lion made his way, along with the other Pentad members, to the stand erected just for them. The sea serpent looked over us all, his golden mask swivelling slowly from left to right. And, after the wind shrieked its war song, he clapped his hands just once. "Begin."

CHAPTER THIRTY

'I used to help people. Now I find myself looking for ways to hurt them.'

I turned, rushing toward one of the swords they'd tossed to the ground, and rolled as I clamped a hand around its cool leather grip. I barely had enough time to shift and adjust my stance before a female, who had been faster, charged at me with a spear. I batted the spearhead aside with a clumsy block, still battling the lingering effects of being stripped of my other half. Since Raithe had essentially become a part of me—embedded in my soul and the very fibre of my being—having his presence blocked was like carving my body in two. The sudden loss of him was staggering … *wrong*.

"You have to keep moving, Aeris!" Akira shouted. "Defensive position, then fucking move!"

My muscles felt lethargic as I willed my body to obey, but she was right. I was a sitting duck right now. I needed to be the hunter, not the hunted. My heart thudded in my ears, beating like a war drum as I got to my feet and faced off against the female who cautiously circled me. She sneered, her hands white-knuckled over the spear. Her breath clouded out in plumes and snowflakes caught in her fiery red hair. It reminded me of Melania and the Bloodhound, adding further fuel to the anger already swirling through my veins.

"You don't have to do this," I said gently. "We can fight back. We can take the Pentad down." She jerked her spear in answer, and I swerved, careful to keep my distance. "Please," I tried again. "We can help each other—we can all fight *with* each other."

The look in her eyes promised that no amount of pleading or logical reasoning would get me anywhere. She was out for blood, and only victory would satisfy her. No more running. No more escaping. If it were kill or be killed, then I would choose the former, but I would disengage or disarm where I could.

I rolled my neck and adjusted my footing, then I waited for the inevitable. She charged head-on, swiping her spear. I ducked, sliding under the weapon along the frost-coated grass and slicing the tendons in her ankle with my sword. Blood spurted onto the ground, and she cried out, immediately falling to her knees. She may never walk on it again, but she wouldn't die. Not by my hand, at least.

I left her there in search of my friends in the arena, and there, in the middle of the fray, was Akira fending off two females with barely a blink. I could watch her fight for an eternity, her long hair swishing in a sheet of black, her twin blades in perfect synchronicity as she swung. She could handle herself. Sherai was balled up near the edge of the arena, but she was holding her own. Still, if the numbers added up, she'd remain stuck in that corner.

Fuck. We were all too separated for my liking, and we were stronger together. I ran, my boots stomping over the snow as I avoided skirmishes left and right.

A female jumped in my path and sliced upwards with her sword. I had to dive awkwardly to the ground, the blade narrowly missing my stomach as I fell. She was on me moments later, the sword driving into the snow behind my head as I shifted. Then, her fist grabbed my tunic and her other ploughed into my cheek, making stars burst behind my eyes. Another punch, then another. The blows caused the thumping already in my ears to dial up to a ringing that blocked out all other noise. I blinked, half dazed, as she drove down with her sword once again. It sank into the snow, pinning my cloak down. I wriggled out of it moments before a dagger appeared in her hand. My hands lashed out on instinct, clasping over hers as we each struggled in a power play. The blade teetered, dipping closer to my chest. My muscles burned as I gritted my teeth and grunted.

Swords whined and clashed all around us, the screams and cries of the dying drowning out the wind, but all I could see were green eyes and teeth. All I could think of was never seeing Raithe's face again. Never seeing that smirk or hearing the husky edge to his voice. The thought was too terrible to bear.

The blade wavered, and the scales began to tip in my favour as I hefted all my weight behind me and drove her over and down to the ground. Her arms bent, wobbling with effort as I gained the upper hand and began turning it against her. Those green eyes widened as fear and uncertainty flooded in, and I knew I had her.

She knew it, too, as her arms wobbled even harder. "Please," she spat out, her eyes darting between me and the sword. "Please don't kill me."

Would she give me mercy if the roles were reversed? I stared into those eyes, deep into the soul that lay beneath, and chose to trust her.

I chose wrong. The moment I lowered the blade and began to climb off her, she lashed out with a punch to my jaw. Surprised, I dropped the weapon, which clattered to the ground. We scrabbled towards it. I stretched, feeling the hilt scrape against my fingernails as I clawed for purchase. Pain flared in my leg, and I cried out as the female sank her teeth into my calf. *Fuck!* With a grunt I grasped the hilt and managed to horse kick the girl in the face. When I turned to face her this time, I didn't hesitate.

"May Ryvia rest your soul," I whispered, then I grunted as the blade slid home.

Her eyes widened, then a breath left her lungs as the pupils blew and the light went out. I didn't let myself dwell on that as I looked up at the warfare. I had tried to do the right thing, and that had to count for something.

My friends. I needed to get to my friends.

Blood soaked the crushed snow, now a sloshy, muddy field of dirt and death. I was still several feet away from Sherai when a squealing of rusted hinges sounded, and the very ground vibrated as hidden grooves at the four corners of the arena slowly slid open.

Not everyone noticed as the mechanisms underground screeched to a halt and the slots slid fully open, nor as those horrible beasts from the labyrinth we'd first been thrown into charged out all at once. The chains keeping them from roaming free clanged as they leapt at their victims. Blood-curdling screams rang out as the beasts joined. Fresh blood flowed freely as the Waiflings fed and ripped their victims limb from limb.

I looked away in disgust as the one closest to me leapt on a girl's back, immediately breaking her spine and tearing into her cheek. Bile rose up my throat, but I swallowed it down, focusing on Akira, who was far too close to one of those things for comfort.

"Akira," I shouted. "Push back to the middle. Don't let them corner you!"

"A little … preoccupied … at the moment," she yelled as a female opponent pressed her closer to the beast.

My chest tightened as I realised that the moment that Waifling was done with its current body bag, it would be upon her. "Sherai," I called over the din. "To me!"

Her eyes found mine through the throng of people, her gaze narrowing as she took stock of her surroundings. A muscle flexed in her jaw as I pointed at Akira and the deadly row of teeth at her back, but she nodded as I fought my way towards her, dodging or batting away weapons as they sang and whined through the night.

We met at the same time, then turned toward the female fighting Akira. "Leave or die," I hissed, my tone and our numbers leaving no room for argument.

The other Fae female took one look at us and turned tail. "We have to get to the middle of the arena," Sherai said to Akira as she grabbed her arm to steady her. "The leashes don't allow the Waiflings that far."

"I'd be happy to," Akira said as she panted. Her skin was white as snow and flecked with blood, but she was unharmed. "There's just one problem."

Sherai turned to follow her line of sight. My friend shouted, pulling Akira to the side, just as the massive jaws of a beast opened wide to devour me.

CHAPTER THIRTY-ONE

'Blood Mages are among the trickiest opponents to face. Their affinity for blood spells means even the hardiest of armour won't keep you safe. My advice? Avoid their bad side and have a healer on standby.'

The Trials and Traditions of a Mithrian Fae

"Aeris!"

My friends' screams clanged about in my head as I did the only thing I could and dropped, not away from, but towards the Waifling as it leapt. My boots slid over the cold, wet ground as the creature swiped where my head had just been. Its stench overwhelmed my senses as I lifted my sword, rending its stomach open, allowing its own weight and momentum to carve through its flesh. Guts and gore dripped over me, hot and heavy as it splattered over my face, my clothes … everything. It already reeked of death and the rot of an unkempt creature. Now I did too. My ears rang as it howled, long and mournful, while the Waifling's body slumped to the ground behind me.

I wiped the blood from my face and blinked at my friends, then turned to see the lump of the Waifling I'd just killed. It was even uglier in natural light, with dark, patchy, shaggy fur and welts leaking pus all over it. Most likely from frequent fighting with its kin and poor hygiene conditions. The milky eyes were wide, and its mouth full of razor teeth, yawned open.

Sherai cocked her head at the fallen creature, then at the chaos still surrounding us. "Our chances of survival just increased by 25 per cent. Care to repeat that three more times?"

I grimaced. "Not particularly. We need to stop fighting each other and start fighting back. We need *her*."

Akira looked at the female in question, then scowled. "That was when we had time and circumstance on our side. The end is near, and the only thing she wants more than victory is your head on a spike."

"She's all we've got," I said. "Watch my back."

I refocused my attention, then pushed on with Sherai and Akira at my back. We moved in formation, a deadly three-pointed shield as we guarded each other from every threat. Then I saw an opening, and I broke rank.

"Aeris!" Sherai cried, but I was already running, already halfway to my target as she roared her fury at the sky.

"Portia," I called through the din.

Her blue eyes swivelled to me, narrowing in contempt the moment they spotted me. She was a sight to behold, with her navy blue attire covered in blood and her long black braid snaking down her back. She stalked towards me slowly, not even phased as a chained beast snapped sharp teeth in her direction, stopping short only due to the limit of its restraints. She dodged a spear without even looking, then continued toward me.

"So, you've finally come to die." The sword in her hand gleamed under the moonlit sky, covered in fresh, dripping scarlet.

"I have a better solution," I offered with a hand up. "What if we both got out of here alive?"

Her perfectly manicured brow arched as she began to circle me. "I have no plans of letting you go. Nothing you say could change the way this ends."

Anger whirled like a tornado inside me. "What have I done to make you hate me so? I didn't choose this. I didn't want to be here."

"You think I did?" She lashed out with her sword. I parried, our blades shrieking as steel met steel. Surprise washed over me at the pure anger in her voice—in her eyes. She whirled away, then charged again, striking several times. I met her blow for blow, the weight of her sword clanging against mine. The jolt of the weapons clashing reverberated down my arm. "I *had* to enter the Rite."

"Am I meant to feel sorry for you?" I said in disbelief. "I was brought here in chains against my will. I didn't get a choice either. But you chose to murder those females when they were unarmed and vulnerable. You *chose* to remove anyone who stood in your way of the captain. Christine. That girl at the ball. Who knows who else? For what? Power? Position? The captain?"

Portia laughed, softly at first, then louder. "You really have no idea, do you? I couldn't care less about your precious captain, nor the Rite. I'm not here for a stupid love match. I'm here for *you*."

She launched, slicing down in one mighty blow as our

swords once again met in the middle. The blades slipped, the metal scraping until we were pommel to pommel, head to head. She snarled on the other side of our weapons, her face a mask of rage. "Your father ordered the execution of my mother and sister. He sent a raiding party to my home in Diever Downs. His men raped them, one after another, then strung their naked bodies up until the breath left their lungs. My ancestral home was burnt to the ground; my friends and neighbours were forced to flee the city or die. I watched it all as I hid. I was just a child. An innocent. He took everything that mattered from me, so I vowed to take everything from him."

Horror sluiced through me, my stomach plummeting at the thought of such monstrosity. My father gave that order. Had stood by as those males did such dark and terrible things. Tears pricked my eyes as my heart bled for her. I didn't understand before, but I did now. She was probably the only Fae in the world who might hate my father more than me.

Her rage slipped as she took in my face. "You didn't know."

I took that moment to shove her away and stand with my sword in a guarded position. "That my father is a monster? Yes. But I didn't think he was capable of … I never thought…" I shook my head.

What Portia had just told me was the tip of a giant, fixed iceberg. I'd already moved past the thought of ever forgiving my father for his wrongs, but this level of horror was unacceptable. There was no redeeming him in my eyes or the gods'. I looked at Portia and shook my head again, as if that might somehow erase what I'd learned.

"You can kill me, Portia, but he wouldn't care." I lowered my sword as she stared uncertainly at me. The females surrounding us, still fighting for their lives, were just a blur. Even Sherai and Akira, who I sensed standing stoically behind me, fending off any threats when they approached, said nothing. "Who do you think forced me to be here? Who shot me with a crossbow and chained me within the carriage that brought me here? I am not a beloved daughter. Just property with a hefty price tag, one that requires beatings and imprisonment when out of line. He does not love me. But I'm so sorry for what he did to you, to your family. No one deserves that."

I watched as her face crumpled with confusion, warring between anger, pain, and uncertainty. "You're just trying to get in my head," she insisted, raising her weapon once more. "It won't work."

"Portia, please," I said gently, softly. I threw my sword on the ground, the metal clanging, to show I wasn't going to fight her. Then I thudded to my knees and bared my throat.

"Aeris, no," Akira hissed. I flung out a hand, warning my friends not to interfere.

"You can rip my throat out if you don't believe me," I continued, "but trust me when I say we're more alike than you think. We're in this together. I will happily hold him still while you plunge your blade into his heart after we're out of this. But the only way to survive is to do so together. All of us."

"Stop," Portia snapped. "Stop trying to appeal to my soft side. I discarded that long ago."

"You didn't," I said confidently. "We're females, we are both unbreakable and soft. It's our greatest strength. No matter what, you could never lose that side of you. Or else you wouldn't be listening to me now. Wouldn't be seeing the logic in joining forces and fighting the people who truly deserve it." I let that sink in before adding quietly, "He took my mother too." Her eyes snapped to mine, and I nodded. "He took all of them—all the surviving females from Rites' past. They're alive, and they're trapped under that island. The captain is helping us. We can win this, Portia, and we can free them. We can end these Rites and the males' dominance over us. Together."

She was silent for a moment, her eyes flitting over the females surrounding us. Several had stopped to watch and listen to our conversation, their own swords lowering ever so slightly as they exchanged glances.

"And … the captain?" Portia asked slowly. "What of him?"

I grabbed my top and peeled it down my neck to show her the bite mark Raithe had given me. The Claim. "He's doing something that should have been done a long time ago."

She inhaled sharply. "I know what that mark means. My mother had one too, gifted by my father. So, the captain is your mate." A slow, bewildered laugh. "Of course he fucking is. I should have understood what was happening that day in the apothecary. So, where is he then? Making his girl do all the fighting?"

I grinned. "Raithe does not make me do anything. We are equal, and we both fight for the same thing." I raised my voice so the surrounding females could hear me. "Fight with us. Fight for your mothers and sisters, and friends. Fight to show these fuckers that we will not be slaughtered. No more females need to die needlessly today. Instead, *we* will do the slaughtering."

Portia looked at me like she saw me for the first time. Something sparkled in her eyes that I hadn't seen before. Something that looked suspiciously like hope. "Enough with the speeches already." She turned and roared at anyone listening. "You can die fighting for males who would enslave and abuse you, or you can fight for your freedom, for female freedom. No longer will we be oppressed. You choose how you will live and how you will die. Which one's it gonna be?"

"They have soldiers," a female called out. "They have power!"

Bells sounded, cutting off the outcry of females within the arena, effectively halting all fighting as everyone's head swivelled towards the other direction.

I grinned, my heart swelling about ten sizes. "So do we."

A flurry of movement caught my eye from across the way as countless soldiers swarmed from around both corners of the castle, Killian and Jaren leading each group. And at the main entrance, heading innumerable females dressed in varying states of dirty and dishevelled white, was Raithe. His shadow wings were out, his power streaking along the ground in pluming tendrils of black. My partner in everything. My mate. Here, with the females he'd freed from the island, just as we'd planned.

My smile dropped. Was that terror I saw in his eyes? In the paleness of his face? But then his gaze caught mine, and I registered the shockwave of relief as he realised I was safe and unharmed. Of course … the bond. The moment our connection was severed, he must have thought the worst. My eyes drifted from Raithe to the crowd beyond. I searched frantically for my mother, but I couldn't see her among the females.

"You're here," I breathed as Raithe ran towards me.

He pressed his hands to my cheeks in a loving embrace, pulling me to him tightly. "I never left. But when the bond went down, I was terrified, Aeris. I thought … I thought—"

"It's okay," I hushed. "I'm alright. Is my mother okay?"

"She's fine," Raithe said with a chuckle. "She is with mine. Turns out they're friends."

Relief flooded through me. I knew he would have taken them somewhere safe before joining me here. My heart leapt at the idea of reuniting with her, but it would have to wait. We had a Pentad to kill and a rebellion to lead. By the end of the night, this castle would be ours, and we would finally be reunited.

"What is the meaning of this?" the lion sputtered as soldiers and freed females flooded the grounds. "Stand down! That is a command!"

"These males do not fight for you," Raithe said as he turned. "And neither do I."

"How dare you interrupt this sacred Rite," a low voice said. The sea serpent stood slowly. "You, whom we have honoured so. How dare you lower yourself to their level and let the cattle out of their cage. You are a disgrace to your family name. Your title and rank will be stripped for this. No one shall remember the name Raithe Windaire after you have died a slow and miserable death."

"You're mistaken," Raithe said as the full weight of his stare fell upon the male. "There will be no trial. Only death. And I will not be among the fallen." As the lion and two other masked males began to edge away, he turned his wrath on them. "*Run.* See how far you get."

"Unleash the Waiflings," the sea serpent barked at the soldiers still standing loyal to the Pentad. "Protect the court and kill anyone who stands in your way! Reinforcements won't take long, Captain. And as a reward for their obedience, they may do whatever they please with the cattle. They were all just meat for slaughter, anyway."

"Like hell," I snarled. "You are all going to die. Every last one."

I charged towards the wall of soldiers blocking my way, Raithe and his males at my back. Renewed vigour filled my veins as the females surrounding me roared, taking up arms and turning against our captors. Pride rippled through me as we fought together, the way it should have always been. And as my blade sliced into the first male standing in my way, I didn't feel anything but pure determination.

The snow fell heavier now, reducing visibility as swords and bodies clashed. Fire rippled in my periphery as arrows soared through the night, and soldiers and females alike went down screaming. Mechanisms groaned, and then the sound of chains clanking along the ground followed as the Waiflings were set free. New, terrified screams echoed, drowning out the sound of steel. Even the Pentad's soldiers weren't spared as the creatures attacked. One Waifling turned to me, and my stomach lurched as its muzzle flared and it charged. It moved so fast I didn't have time to dive. The gaping mouth widened, revealing its razor-sharp teeth gleaming with blood.

Raithe's shadows lashed out, ensnaring the beast by its legs before it could launch at me. He grimaced as his boots slid along the ground, his brows scrunching with the effort of holding it back.

I didn't have time to breathe a sigh of relief as it snapped and raged against its leash. Portia snatched a spear from a passing female and launched it through the air. The point made its mark through the Waifling's left eye. The beast went down with a thud.

"They're getting away," I yelled as the Pentad made their way towards the castle proper. Typical. Powerful as they were, they'd rather let everyone else do their dirty work for them whilst they ran and hid.

"Go," Jaren shouted. "Killian and I will hold here."

"Do not let any Pentad soldiers through the castle gates," Raithe ordered. "Arm the battlements. Keep that gate shut at all costs!"

A boom sounded before Killian could answer, and my heart sank as I looked to the source. Reinforcements were already here. Was the nearest outpost really that close? Or had the Pentad sent for them ahead of time? I swore under my breath as soldiers poured in on horses, their long swords and spears making quick work of those in their way on foot.

Magic blasted from every direction. I halted, torn between chasing the Pentad and helping the others.

"We do not stop," Raithe roared. "They can handle themselves."

"The females—"

"Chose to fight. This is their story, Aeris. Let them decide how it begins and ends."

He was right. This was their choice. This was their moment. Because their choices had been stripped from them for so long. Because they deserved to fight, even if it killed me to see so many fall after being confined to that prison. But Raithe was right. I looked at the fighting one last time, then turned to see the final member of the Pentad disappear through the castle's doors. My power may have been temporarily put to sleep again, but a heady concoction of adrenaline and rage cycled through my bloodstream. It was time to change the narrative once and for all.

CHAPTER THIRTY-TWO

'Cinnamon, vanilla, or clove are perfect components to cover
the scent of poisonous potions. (And they're downright
delicious for a spot of freshly baked banana bread.)

An Alchemist's Guide to Herbal Remedies

Raithe and I raced through the corridors of the
castle, skirting panicked servants at every
turn. "We need to get those vials," I shouted over the booms
and battle cries of the chaos outside. "Without my power, I
won't stand a chance."

"Lead on," Raithe said as we ran. "I've got you, baby."

I grinned, wild and feral. I'd never felt so free. Never felt so
empowered as the moment those females rose up and fought
back. We just had to secure the castle and round up the
Pentad. Once they were dead, the battle would be over.

The way was relatively clear of danger, with an odd soldier

popping up along the way. One rounded a corner and faced us with a weapon drawn and a face of contempt. I threw my dagger, which landed directly in his heart. We continued, plucking the dagger up without ceremony as the soldier bled out on the floor. Raithe destroyed another soldier who tried to bar our way with a clean sweep of his sword, so fast I barely saw it happen. At last, we arrived at the apothecary, and I trudged downstairs into the small basement, while Raithe took watch above. I ran to the wall, removing the chunk of stone I'd gauged out and stuffed the vials in several days prior. I blew out a breath at finding them still there, grateful, then shifted as a floorboard creaked behind me. I palmed my dagger, gripping the hilt tightly as I spun to see the healer poking her head out from behind a stack of crates.

"Margaery?"

"Kill them, Aeris," she said firmly. Her eyes gleamed with fear, but there was resolve in them, too. Pain. "Offer no mercy." I nodded and placed a hand over my heart. No words were needed, but I did appreciate the quiet "Good luck" she added as I stormed back upstairs.

"Bottoms up," I said to Raithe as I unstopped the cork from one vial and took a small sip of the contents. Earthy, yet slightly sweet, thanks to the cinnamon I'd added.

His narrowed blue eyes raked over me expectantly. "Anything?"

I slipped my fingers between his and waited. We'd planned on testing the vials ahead of the trial, but this was it. The first test of my alchemy skills—one that could very well decide our fate today.

"Perhaps I need a bigger dose?" I whispered, thoughtfully. "Unless I got the mixture wrong. Oh gods, please work."

Raithe squeezed my hand at the same moment I squeezed my eyes shut. It felt like eternity passed me by until a soft warmth began to disperse in my stomach, slowly filtering out through my veins until the steady flow of power thrummed to the discordant thumping of my heart.

"*Aeris*," Raithe said softly in my mind. "*Look*."

I opened my eyes to see shadows spiralling across the room, licking up the walls in a plume of fluid black. I grinned, a sense of pride fuelling me. "It worked," I said aloud, a little bewildered. "It really worked."

"Of course it did," Raithe said with a laugh. "As if you'd allow any other outcome."

I laughed, still a little shocked, then sent a silent prayer of thanks to Sherai. Without her research, I'd never have figured out the compounds needed to make this happen. My boots thudded as I ran to the top of the stairs and called down to Margaery. She trundled up shortly after, her face wary and her steps hesitant.

"These vials contain a cure to the power-blocking magic the Pentad gave to the Rite participants. I need you to get this to them. Can you do that for me?"

Margaery's brown eyes widened. "You want me to go out there?!" She gestured at the battle unfolding beyond the walls with trembling hands.

"I know it's scary," I admitted. "But they need you now. We all do."

Her chin wobbled as she nodded slowly, still processing. Then she took the vials in my outstretched hand, her fist tightening around the tinctures. The floorboards creaked again as she turned and found a belt to stuff the precious bottles into, then she clipped it over her hips. "I won't fail you," she said, her voice steady.

I nodded and offered a grateful smile. "Stay safe and avoid any direct conflicts. Just get the vials distributed, then get out of there, okay? You can do this."

"I know," she huffed. "I've never let a few males stop me before."

I grinned. "One small sip, Margaery. That's all they need. Get it to Sherai and Akira if you can."

She ran out the door and didn't spare us a second look. A battle axe, that one. Even the kindest of souls could make the most formidable of opponents.

"Where to now?" I asked Raithe as we took off down the hallway.

"There's an underground bunker built for emergencies," Raithe answered. *"They'll be there; I guarantee it."*

He led me through the castle and down to a secret door that was hidden behind a giant tapestry hanging in the main foyer. I'd never noticed it before. We stepped through, and then we were twisting and turning in the bowels of the castle until we stopped before a large door. My breath shuddered out of me from both the running and the excitement snaking through me. Fear lined my stomach, trying to lock up my bones, until a tendril of Raithe's shadows caressed me, wrapping around my legs, even slipping up between them. I jerked at that delicious touch, then threw him an exasperated look. He grinned at me with pure mischief in his eyes, his white teeth gleaming in the low light. All the while, those shadows crept higher, stroking, encouraging. We arrived at the end of a corridor, standing before a large, bolted metal door.

"Together?" he asked as I took his hand and we faced the bolted door.

I scoffed and repeated his words from earlier. "As if I'd allow any other outcome. But how do we get through? The door must be at least two feet thick, and I don't suppose you have a key."

His grin turned a little evil, like he was enjoying the

thought of shredding the males on the other side. And to be honest, so was I. They deserved nothing less.

"Spread your wings, little lark," Raithe purred as he threw the torch down the hall, and we were plunged into darkness.

My stomach dropped as he whirled me off my feet in a wave of shadow and smoke. I couldn't see what was happening. One moment I was standing on solid ground, the next we were floating through the fabric of the world. My heart lodged in my throat as Raithe wielded his power to send us through the metal door and out the other side. *What. The. Fuck. Raithe could turn us* into *shadows, too?! Oh, I had to learn that one.* We rematerialised from the darkness into a low cave. Fire-lit sconces revealed we were now standing in a chamber. And inside that chamber were the Pentad.

"Boo," Raithe said as we solidified.

The males turned and tumbled out of their seats, their wine glasses tipping over in their rush. All but one, who simply leaned his elbows on the table and steepled his fingers. "You found us," the sea serpent said. "And now you're trapped, two against six."

Raithe grinned. "True. But I'll take my chances."

"I suppose you think you're clever," the Pentad leader responded. "Forming a coup and freeing the females. But even if you take this castle, you will never stop the Rite. We aren't the only males who celebrate traditions."

"Maybe not," I said as I unsheathed my blade. "But we'll make damn sure they die with you."

The sea serpent swivelled that golden mask my way, as if assessing my worth. "You can certainly try."

My power sizzled under my skin, begging to be released. I wielded my shadows with ease, the tendrils leeching out towards the males.

"You're not the only one with shadows, little girl," the bear said as he stepped forward. He turned his palms and … nothing happened. He tried again. "What?"

"Aw, can't get it up?" I asked with a pout. "That's the thing about you power-hungry males. You think you're invincible, so you forget to take note of the little things, like the slightest hint of vanilla and clove in your wine, or the fact it's a shade darker. That drowsiness you feel? It's the slow sap of power while your magic drains from your system. Wyrmwood, for stunting magic, and Faebane, for ensuring your immortal blood didn't work too hard to remove the effect. Nothing so obvious and primitive as that crap you shoved down our throats earlier."

"We didn't know which wines you'd drink tonight," Raithe said with a shrug. "So we poisoned them all ahead of time—including the batch you had served to your esteemed guests. It helps to have friends in low places. Lesser Fae, as father likes to call the servants."

The bear threw his cup with a roar. "If we can't wield, we'll just have to finish you off the old-fashioned way. My favourite kind."

I rolled my eyes and looked at Raithe. *"So emotional."*

"So dead," he answered with a smirk. Then he lifted a damning finger at the lion, who had made a show of moving toward a weapon, but had used the opportunity to cower behind the others at the rear of the cave. Raithe didn't miss the coward's act, though, singling the lion out. *"You.* I'm going to enjoy killing you."

The bear, the wolf, and the eagle converged, their blades unsheathed and glimmering from the reflection of the flickering fires in their sconces on the walls. Raithe and I stood side by side, our own blades raised high, our shadows swirling around our feet like a whirlpool. Not separate streams, but one flowing entity. The bear came for me first, raising his two-handed sword and crushing the space I'd been in before I hopped to the side. He growled as I spun around him easily. His mask was a clear reflection of the sheer strength he carried, but his heavy build combined with limited space for his greatsword meant he was clumsy and slow.

I sheathed my blade and assessed my opponent. Speed was my ally and my friend here. It would not fail me now. He came for me again, his sweeping arcs loaded with anger. I dodged them, then realised too late he was driving me towards the cave wall. My spine hit the rock with a thud, my eyes widening as the deadly edge of that sword came plummeting down. I shifted as it ploughed into the stone, causing a huge chunk to crumble. I lost my breath as a giant fist rammed into my stomach. The breath wheezed out of me as I felt a rib bone crack from the force.

"Do not falter," Raithe shouted down the bond. *"Do not yield."*

My body bent against its will, slumping against the wall until the bear grabbed me by the hair and punched me in the jaw. Stars burst behind my eyes, my vision wavering as darkness threatened to take me. But the darkness was my friend, and I was its master. I flexed my hand, willing my shadows to form vines that wrapped around the bear and kept his limbs in check. He grunted, snapping the tendrils with bulging muscles. His grip on my hair loosened enough for me to slump down the wall to a crouch, where I palmed the dagger still strapped at my thigh and drove up with a powerful surge, plunging that blade into his stomach. His cry of pain and fury was enough to make me tighten my grip and strike that blade into his body again and again. Blood dripped onto the ground, and he stumbled back a couple of times before looking at me once more.

I'd thought he would fall to his knees. Instead, the battle ram charged at me with his full weight and made it all of three steps before Raithe conjured his shadow wings, launched into the air—effectively batting his opponents aside—and used the bear's momentum to carry them both directly to the wall, where the male's head smashed under impact. Blood and gore slipped down the wall, and the bear's body crumpled to a pile at its base. I didn't have time to celebrate. Not as the wolf reoriented himself while Raithe's attention had shifted to the bear, and came at my mate's back with his sword held high. I didn't think, didn't act on anything but instinct as I held my blade and shadow-walked until I stood before him, my blade arcing up beneath the ribs and directly into his heart before he even knew I was there.

The male gasped as he stood before me, impaled and unmoving, as if my sword was anchoring his feet to the ground. He pulled his mask off, as if needing to take a final breath of fresh air, then his brown eyes glossed over me. He was incredibly handsome, with a chiselled face, welcoming lips, and hair to drag your hands through. The kind of face that females would swoon for—the kind that so often masked the monster beneath. How many females had fallen by his hands or his order? Just one was too many, so I put a hand on his shoulder and leaned in as I twisted my blade. A strangled gurgle sounded in my ear before I withdrew my sword and stepped away as his body fell.

Raithe had taken up a fight with the eagle. The pair moved so similarly, they could have been each other's mirror image. Shadows flared from both males, striking and blocking, arcing and soaring. Neither seemed able to gain the upper hand until the eagle rolled, grabbing some dirt in his palm before flinging it at Raithe's eyes. He grunted and raised an arm, giving the eagle time to land a cut in Raithe's side. My stomach lurched as the eagle then sliced at Raithe's thigh, causing him to stumble slightly. Blood flicked over the ground, but even then, my mate didn't falter. Instead, he wrapped a tendril of shadow around the wound and charged. I stared in awe at the two males as they fought.

Raithe's opponent was clearly war-trained and no stranger to a sword, but he was slower than my mate. Probably a lot older, too. Which was perhaps the only reason Raithe managed to charge through the eagle's guard to headbutt him on the temple before knocking the male out with a blow from his sword pommel.

I turned towards the two remaining members of the Pentad. The lion still cowered in the corner behind the table and chairs, while the sea serpent remained seated, utterly nonchalant. It was unnerving. My eyes flickered over his golden mask, his robes, then the cup before him. It was full and appeared untouched.

"That's right," the sea serpent said, aware of my gaze. "I didn't drink your poison brew, because I know who you are, Aeris Lockhart. My comrades, on the other hand … They were no longer fit for their positions. Lazy, whoremongering fools who became too comfortable with the luxuries afforded them. You've done me a favour, removing them, and will be rewarded. I want to build a new world, Aeris. I want to restore power to those worthy of it."

The way he said my name … it sent an oily feeling of dread through my veins. Even with the mask muffling his voice, my name on his lips felt overly familiar. I had suspected the serpent might have been Raithe's father …Trepidation warred with my anger, but I shook it off and focused.

"You mean you want to overthrow those ruling the Shadow Court and continue your barbaric traditions," I hissed. I looked at my friend, my lover, my mate, and smiled. "We will build a new world, but you will not be a part of it. Not for a second."

That snake mask swivelled to Raithe momentarily before the dark eyes behind it darted back to me. A low, muffled laugh followed. "So the lady has indeed fallen for the lord. A poetic turn of events, don't you think?"

"A poetic end, maybe," Raithe supplied with a cruel grin. "For you."

I gripped my sword firmly and stepped forward. "Stop stalling, snake, and meet your end with dignity."

Silence reigned for a few seconds, then he stood. "Very well. Let us begin."

Darkness fell over the serpent, as sudden as a lunar eclipse, and I blinked at the abrupt change in light.

My shadows seemed to shrink back at the sheer power vibrating from the other side of the room. *"Raithe?"*

"It's not me," he said. *"This male is strong, Aeris, the magic old and trained. Be on your guard."*

Light flared back into the room just as suddenly, and I found myself looking at six different sea serpents, all in a semicircle across the room. They each laughed in unison, the creepy sound sending a chill up my spine.

"Come," they said at once.

I grimaced but didn't hesitate as I charged with Raithe beside me. My blade cut through one of the illusions, sending it puffing into a plume of shadow. I turned just in time to parry the blade of another, then screamed as searing heat sliced through my back. My feet stumbled over each other, but I managed to right my footing just in time to block the blade of my first opponent and send my sword plunging through it.

Raithe did not fare much better. One by one, the wraithlike illusions went down, until it was just the original once more. The sea serpent clapped his hands, then a flurry of shadow daggers sailed through the air. We blocked them with our shadows, plucking them from the air and deflecting the strays as they made it through our shield.

"He's so fast." I vaulted back, then flung my shadows out in an arc, trying to slice at the sea serpent. He blocked with a lazy wave of his hand.

"Remember what I told you," Raithe said as he fought, this time blade to blade with the male himself. *"Every opponent has a weakness. Find it and use it against them."*

The metallic ring of steel clanged throughout the cave, echoing back to us as the duo moved about the chamber. I studied them from afar, watching to ensure my mate's safety whilst looking for something to use against the serpent. He was good, never missing a beat, always seemingly one step ahead of all Raithe's moves. And yet there was a slight hesitation, sometimes a subtle roll of a shoulder after Raithe attacked. His parries were seconds slower against certain angled attacks on the left side. Bingo. *"His shoulder is weak and stiff,"* I told him as I watched. *"Keep at it."*

"That's my girl," Raithe said as he battled.

I rallied my magic, sending my shadows in a cresting wave to smash against the serpent again and again to keep his wielding focused on defence instead of offence. He buckled but held his ground as Raithe closed in. As for my mate ... my shadows passed over him, through him, recognising the bond without question. I watched my magnificent male as he moved gracefully, his slices fluid and his steps perfect. We were so close. Just a little further and we'd—No.

I blinked, unsure I was seeing things right. The serpent dropped his sword and slammed his palms against Raithe's blade on the flat. The male's finger twitched, then shadow daggers slowly formed in the air at Raithe's back. Black as onyx and sharp as hell, they seemed to soak in the darkness surrounding them.

Shadows of my own lashed out in response, ready to pluck them from the air or form a wall of impenetrable darkness, but the serpent wielded vines that sprang through the earth. They grabbed my tendrils and squeezed, puffing out my magic like flames from a blown candle. I ran, slashing at those vines with both sword and shadow as I bolted towards my mate. But I wasn't going to make it in time. No, no, no, *no*. The daggers finished forming, their onyx tips glittering like stardust. Time seemed to slow as I extended my blade and sliced through three of the onyx daggers that I could reach, yet two remained.

"Raithe! Behind you!" I screamed both out loud and down the bond as my mate shoved the serpent back and turned towards me. He wouldn't block in time, so I did the only thing I could at that moment. I willed all my magic to obey and shadow-walked into Raithe's arms as he turned too late to see the daggers. Before he could have known what was happening, the onyx blades embedded in my back. The breath went out of me as I fell against his chest, warm and solid and safe. Raithe set me down gently, then turned towards the serpent.

He unleashed a roar that ripped through the room as he stood protectively over me. A hurricane of shadows lashed out in an explosion of fury, sending the serpent flying against the far end of the cave stone. A wall of impenetrable black formed around us as Raithe's shadows swarmed furiously now. He turned and crouched before pulling me to him carefully, his eyes liquid pools of sapphire as they searched my own. He ran a hand down my hair, his hand shaking and his gaze imploring. *"Why would you do that, Lark?"*

"Because I refused to lose you to a place I could not follow," I breathed.

Blood blossomed over Raithe's hand, which shook

violently as he tried to hold me still. "Silly little bird," he said softly. "There is no ship I could captain without you by my side. No ocean I wouldn't cross to reach you. You are the one thing I will never give up on and never let go of. Even in death. Even beyond it."

"That's quite the send-off," I said in a lame attempt at humour. Even smiling hurt, the muscles of my body barking with the slightest shift. Blood was beginning to pool over the ground, and my vision was wavering.

Distantly, I could hear the serpent's shouts of frustration as his magic repeatedly lashed at Raithe's shadow wall. But none of the blows broke through.

Raithe smiled grimly as he stroked a hand over my face. "You're not going anywhere, little lark. This dagger hit nothing vital," he said as he moved his fingers towards the one embedded to the left of my spine. "And this one?" He moved his other hand slightly as he supported me. "This one is an inch away from your heart. You are lucky, my love. And you are very much going to live."

"Good. Then I'll sit back and watch the rest of the show."

Raithe kissed me, long and slow and passionately as his mouth crashed to mine and his tongue curled most sensually. I could still hear the serpent trying to break through Raithe's shield, to no avail, but when my captain pulled away, his grin was savage. Oh, the serpent had it coming. Power rippled from Raithe in thunderous, vibrating waves as he rolled his neck and turned. The shadows exploded in a shockwave that made the serpent stumble, and when Raithe stepped out and plunged a shadow tendril deep into the serpent's stomach, I smiled. Raithe grinned as well, impaling that shadow deeper, ready to end this once and for all.

"Wait! Remove his mask. I want to see the mastermind behind the Pentad before he dies," I said down the bond.

The shadow halted. *"Aeris, you need a healer. The longer we delay—"*

"Please, Raithe." It hurt to breathe, but I kept the pain locked down. *"I need to know."*

"As you wish."

Raithe ripped that golden mask from the male's face in one swift movement. My heart sank—utterly plummeted. The world tilted on its axis, and I breathed in sharply as I looked upon the face of the male who'd long tormented me.

"You." I laughed in disbelief as it became all too clear why the serpent had felt so familiar. Why Declan had been here despite already having a wife. "Of course. It all makes sense now."

My father stared back at me with cold murder in his blue eyes. "Are you surprised?"

"No," I admitted. "Just disappointed. All that power and wealth. All that status. None of it was ever enough for you. The only time you felt powerful was when you were hurting those you deemed beneath you. I may not have the physical scars to prove what you did to me, but I wear them on the inside proudly." My vision dotted once more, but I blinked and refocused, determined to say my piece. "Despite your best efforts, I am no longer your captive. I am free."

"Free?" he said with a sneer. "You are chained to this male. You will never truly escape."

"Aeris can do whatever she wishes with her life," Raithe said darkly. "Even if that meant leaving me and never looking back. Unlike you, I do not keep my females bruised and chained. I am lucky to have her and damn proud to call her my mate."

"Mate?" My father snorted, then groaned at the weapon firmly embedded in him. "You are both fools. War is coming for this court, and you will bring it to its knees in the face of our enemies."

"I guess you'll never know," I said in disgust.

"I think we're done now," Raithe said with a hurried glance at my wounds. He shifted on his feet and moved to take the kill.

My father twisted, his pale face whitening even further. His eyes darted to mine. "No, you can't do this. Will you not have mercy on your father?"

"You're not my father. You never were in the ways that counted." I thought of my mother, Raithe's mother, and Portia's family. I thought of all the countless females he'd hurt by heading the Pentad and the Rite. I thought of how he would often be gone for months at a time during my youth, which now made much more sense after learning he was head of the Pentad. Finally, I thought of all the things I had learned in his absence and the female I had become because of it. Then, an idea formed in my mind. I relayed it to Raithe, who paused, his face tilting to reveal a raised brow.

Utter delight flashed in those ocean eyes, but he asked aloud all the same. "Are you sure?"

"Positive. They need to see this."

Raithe chuckled as he quickly dragged my father over to the table. He then grabbed a dagger from his belt and impaled my father's hand to the surface. The shriek that followed made my ears ring. It only worsened as Raithe grabbed another dagger and impaled the other hand in the same fashion. To the lion, who was still huddled in the corner looking like he might piss himself, he simply commanded, "Stay."

I snorted at the mocking command, then winced as the air rattled my chest. There was no chance that pitiful excuse for a

Fae was going anywhere, but I gathered my shadows around me just in case.

Raithe's eyes snapped to mine at the painful drag of air I took in, then he walked forward and kicked the unconscious male wearing the eagle mask. "My father," he said simply. "In case you hadn't guessed it already."

I had been too caught up in fighting the others to think about it, but Akira, Sherai and I had always guessed Lord Windaire was among the Pentad. We just thought he was its leader, not my own father's lackey. Raithe dragged him across the ground and said, *"Perhaps you should bind him to the table with your shadows as well."*

I did just that. "What are you going to do with him?" I asked as he made for the door, this time using the conventional method by unbarring it from this side.

"First, I'm going to find a healer immediately. But after that? Probably nothing," he said with a tilt of his head. "I'll save that for someone else. Someone with even more reason to finish him off than me."

CHAPTER THIRTY-THREE

'In spite of all the death, I never lost hope. I might be gone tomorrow, but someday someone will take up arms and end the killing. Someone will find a way to break the chains and set us free.'

My eyes immediately welled up when I saw her. This close, I could see her features clearly, and she was as beautiful as the day she'd left. Even covered in dirt and whatever other manner of filth, my mother's face was a beacon of light. Her blonde hair was braided much like mine, and her blue eyes—my eyes—gleamed. The state of her body, however … I gulped down the lump in my throat as I took in the obvious malnourishment and abuse she'd been through. Her body was thin and pale, her cheeks gaunt, and her eyes sunken in. Yes, the beauty was still there, even if trauma was visible in every line, or bruise, or scar. And I knew there were many of those lining her back alone.

"My daughter," she said, running to me where I still lay inside the Pentad's underground chamber. "I'm so sorry, Aeris. I'm so very sorry." She burst into tears as she beheld the state of me, all the blood now pooling over the dirt.

All I wanted was to hug her, but with the weapons jutting out of me and the blood trail, I was fading. Instead, I held out a weak hand for her to slide her own into, then tried for a smile. "It's okay, Mum. I'm okay."

"You've been stabbed in two places and you're bleeding out," she said with that familiar stern tone I remembered well. "You're anything but okay. Just as well, your mate brought some friends."

I turned to the door as Margaery hurried in, her face paling upon seeing the dead bodies and the Pentad males still alive. But she held her chin high and calmly set her satchel down with an anxious smile for my sake. She got to work on my wounds immediately and pointedly avoided her employer as he sagged atop the table across the room.

She removed the first dagger from my lower back and began immediately cleaning and dressing the wound. I couldn't help the shriek that escaped me as I felt it slide out. She repeated it with the other dagger, to which my scream was much more piercing. I almost passed out as my lids fluttered with exhaustion. But then another face appeared, and then another female was hunched over me, using her blood magic to stunt the bleeding and heal my wounds.

"Portia?" I rasped as her face came into view.

"I still don't like you," she huffed as she worked. "Just to be clear. But I guess I … I don't blame you anymore for what your father did. Or for doing what you needed to survive the Rite. And I suppose forming a rebellion was pretty badass."

I grinned, the motion turning to a sigh as relief flooded my bones and eased the tightness from my muscles. The searing pain that had turned to a dull throb slowly ceased, and I sat up a little straighter.

"I'm sure I can still win you over," I said.

"Don't hold your breath," she grumbled, but there was the slightest hint of a smile on her face when she said it.

I looked past the females to my mate, who walked towards us with a beautiful female in tow. "Is this…?"

"My mother, Lorelia," he said proudly as he placed his hands gently on her shoulders and ushered her forward.

She smiled nervously, but the gesture was warm and inviting. Her blue eyes—the mirror image of Raithe's—sparkled as she beheld me. To my surprise, she crouched and took my hands in her own. Her grip was firm, even with the angry red lines around her wrists left from shackles.

"Aeris," she said softly. "There are no words to repay what you and my son have done today. There will never be enough lifetimes to do that."

I squeezed her hands. "There is nothing to repay. We did what was right. What I wish someone could have done sooner."

"I tried," she admitted softly.

"We both did," my mother said as she patted Lorelia's arm. "But we're here now. We are here to see this done."

"And you will," I said as Margaery and Portia finished their work and nodded their okay for me to stand. My mother and Portia assisted me to my feet. I looked at Portia in the eye and jerked my chin at my father. "Consider this a gesture of goodwill."

She wiped her hands on her pants before she strode

toward the table for a better look. She bared her fangs as she looked upon my father's face. "Dariel Lockhart. I have been waiting for this moment for a long time."

He didn't even bother to respond. I took my mother's and Lorelia's hands and gently walked them towards the table. Raithe removed his daggers from my father's hands, eliciting a shriek, then grabbed him under the armpits before turning him and dumping him to his knees. After, he grabbed the lion, followed by his father, the eagle, and lined them up beside the sea serpent.

"Please," the lion mewed. "Please set me free. I'll give you anything. I'll—"

"You will cease speaking or I will rip out your wretched tongue," Raithe commanded.

Whimpers were the lion's only answer, and he did not dare move. Did not dare to try his luck at escaping. As for Raithe's father … My mate didn't say a word to him. The eagle simply held his chin high and stared with his brown eyes defiantly.

"For the Pentad," he said. "I have no regrets."

My heart sank for Raithe. Not that I'd expected any less, but I had hoped for some remorse from a father to his son. Wishful thinking, on my part.

When the three of them were on their knees before us, my mother, Lorelia, Portia, and Raithe beside me, I spoke. "Since the moment you married them, these males have done nothing but abuse, control, and coerce. They took your lives from you, so I think it's only fitting that you be given the chance to do the same."

"You want us to kill them?" Lorelia asked as she eyed her husband. It was a simple question without hesitation or fear. And the pain in her eyes … the rage swirling like storms … I knew she would do it, too.

"Kill them or let them rot for the rest of their long and

miserable lives as they would have done to you." I shrugged as I looked at the three pitiful beings before me, feeling nothing. "We will honour your wishes either way."

Lorelia, Portia, and my mother stood before the three males in perfect opposition. Oh, how the tides had turned.

"Give me a weapon," my mother said. Her voice was cold and hard, and her frame no longer shook. Instead, she squared her shoulders as she took the dagger I handed her. Portia joined her side, her dagger already palmed. Lorelia moved before her husband, which left the lion cowering on his own in a puddle of his own making.

"What do you want to do with him?" Raithe asked with a raised brow.

I looked at the lion in disgust, wondering how something so pitiful had once held the power to harm so many. *"We both know what he did to those females over the years. What he could have easily done to me if you hadn't been there. What he likely did to someone else that night. Make it hurt. Make him suffer."*

Raithe's lips cut a cold slice across his face. *"With pleasure."* He stood before the lion, sword in hand, and grabbed a fistful of brown hair from his scalp. "I told you I was going to kill you. And I'm very much going to enjoy it."

"Wait!" my father called out. "Have mercy on your father." He looked at my mother, pleading. "On your husband. Did I not take care of you? Keep you safe?"

"Safe?" she said, the voice ripping from her lungs with a vengeance. "You beat me, caged me, manipulated and gaslit me until I didn't know my own worth and questioned my own sanity." Tears filled her eyes, but she took a confident step forward. "You condemned me to that prison when I finally tried to break free and speak up. You took my daughter from me. Mercy?" She laughed, cold and mirthless. "You don't know the meaning of the word. The pain you're about to feel is but a fraction of the horrors you put me and countless others through. You deserve so much worse for what you've done. This death? This *is* mercy."

She stepped forward and sank the blade into my father's chest with a fierce cry. Lorelia took one look at her, then at her husband, and followed suit. Portia stood back, pure satisfaction and feminine rage glittering in her dark eyes as she watched. And then Raithe moved with cold calculation as he sliced his blade across the lion's stomach slowly, watching as the male's innards uncoiled to the ground.

The males' screams echoed off the walls, which suddenly appeared to be moving. I blinked as countless moths spiralled out of cracks and crevices, their wings rustling like the turning pages of a book. Gold glittered in every direction, the faces of a hundred skulls staring at me from the moths' backs. I held a finger out and marvelled as one landed on it, its wings flexing and its antennas twitching as it moved gently. They were a symbol of death and mortality—a reminder of the fragile lifecycle we lived through. But to me, in this moment, they represented balance.

They were the closing of a chapter and the promise of a new one. They were not death. We were. These females, my mate ... and me. Raithe finished the lion, then walked to my side. He intertwined blood-soaked fingers in mine, standing in silent solidarity as we watched the females before us.

The males weren't the ones screaming anymore. Just the females as they sliced again and again, their battle roars and mournful cries more cutting than any blade. The bodies had long ceased moving, but I didn't move an inch as they did what they had to do.

Raithe and I watched as the moths swarmed. We watched until the females turned around, covered in blood and gore. They each dropped their weapons to the ground.

"It's over," Portia said slowly, almost like she couldn't believe it. "It's done."

"What do we do now?" Lorelia said softly.

"Now comes the healing," I replied as I squeezed Raithe's hand. "Now we get to live."

CHAPTER THIRTY-FOUR

'There is no greater gift than love. It heals even the deepest of scars. It gives us hope when all is lost. But I didn't lose today, I won. I found a family, and I found my future. That's all I'll ever need.

Journal excerpt, Aeris Lockhart

The sun's rays streamed in through the floor-to-ceiling glass windows, painting the room in a halo of buttery light. I yawned, stretching my arms before nestling deeper against the warm body beside me. An arm wrapped around my ribs, tugging me closer as Raithe roused from his sleep. I smiled and pressed a kiss to the anchor tattoo over his forearm. It had been a week since we'd overthrown the Pentad, and Raithe had claimed the castle as its next lord. The battle had been short-lived once the soldiers received word that their master was dead. They had thrown down their arms after that and surrendered. They got to keep their lives, but Raithe sent them packing all the same.

As for the surviving males who'd come to see us die as mere entertainment? They remained under lock and key in the cells below the castle proper, but Raithe would have to let them go eventually. While they were despicable, wretched creatures who thrived off the pain and suffering of others, they hadn't directly harmed anyone. It would be a little too suspicious if any more blood were shed under the captain's orders. It would be seen as a coup for power over the entire court. As for their wives and families? Akira, Sherai, and I *might* have sent missives in the mail detailing all their extracurricular activities.

Most of the females from the past Rites had returned home to their families. Raithe had supplied provisions and protection for all on their journey home. Some remained, still healing from their wounds or receiving care that would better prepare them to rejoin the outside world. Others simply stayed because they had nowhere to go or no idea how to get there. We would house all of those who needed shelter for as long as they needed.

We. The thought was still so alien, so new. I wasn't just Aeris, daughter of Lord Lockhart, Merchant Mariner, anymore. I was the lady of Castle Cliffscote, even though I'd insisted on leaving the title off. Raithe wasn't having any of it, and I secretly loved him for that. Loved that he didn't want to place me on a pedestal, but instead ensured that we remained equal, side-by-side in all things.

"What's going through that beautiful mind of yours?" Raithe said sleepily.

"Just thinking about you, actually."

He curled my hair around his hand, playing

absentmindedly with the golden strands. "Ominous," he teased. "And what conclusion have you come to?"

I turned so I could see his beautiful face. The light gilded the planes of his cheeks and the striking cut of his jaw. The way the blue in his eyes turned a light shade of cerulean when the sun hit them just right.

"I'm thinking that I love you, and I can't wait to spend the rest of my life with you." I pressed a kiss to his forehead. "I'm thinking I want to know every part of you." A kiss to his cheek. "I want to explore the world with you." A kiss to his other one. "And I want to live every moment, knowing you will be by my side."

He kissed me on the lips, long and deep and achingly perfect. When he pulled away, he held my cheeks, then slid a hand down over my heart above the thin silk of my nightdress. "You hold in your heart my every intention and my utter devotion. I am yours until the end of time and beyond. I love you, Aeris. It was only ever you. It will always only ever be you."

Tears sprang to my eyes as his thumb brushed my cheek. I had never dared hope for such a love. Such an adventure as the one he promised me. "Show me," I said on a breath. "Show me your devotion."

His delicious mouth curved into a deadly grin, and he said seductively, "As my captain commands."

The hand over my heart slid down to cup my breast, my nipple pebbling as he ran a gentle thumb over it before he shifted and took it in his mouth. I moaned as he sucked and nipped, then laughed as he grabbed me and pressed me flat against the silky navy sheets.

"Hands up, baby," he whispered into my ear as he led a trail of kisses down my neck. I arched my back at the touch, then giggled again as he slipped the nightgown up my body. Which simply *had* to get stuck over my head, didn't it? I huffed as it finally tugged free and fluffed my hair. But I stilled at the utterly free laugh that escaped him, at the joy lighting up Raithe's eyes. "There," he said after he'd tossed the nightgown across the room. *"All mine to satisfy and surrender to."*

"But you're doing such a good job," I teased as I opened my legs. I wasn't wearing any panties, and his eyes darkened as he drank me in. *"I want you, Raithe. I want all of you with no holding back."*

"And you'll have me," he said as he lowered his head. "Right after I have my morning meal." With that, his shadows grabbed my wrists and ankles and stretched me out until I was all but suspended at his mercy. Then he was upon me, all lips and teeth and sweet, blessed heat as his mouth closed over my pussy and he began to feast.

I writhed, barely able to lean into him as his shadows turned me over and stretched me deliciously tight. His tongue lapped at my sensitive clit, circling and swirling until my nerves were zinging with pleasure. My body bent and arched, the silky sheets rubbing against my nipples only increasing my pleasure. I was coming undone and being reborn all at once as he devoured me. As he turned me over once again, his black tousled hair fell over his eyes, the muscles in his back rippling as he worked his tongue and lips on me. I moaned, fisting a handful of sheets as the pleasure built and built, threatening to overflow like a dam.

"Raithe," I breathed as he sighed into me.

"Fuck, Aeris," he said, running a hand up my stomach where he pressed down. "You're fucking beautiful."

Oh, gods. I was going to come. I was going to—

Pleasure rippled out of me in an explosive wave, my body shivering and pliant to his will. I didn't even have time to prepare before he moved up the bed and thrust into me. "Oh,"

I groaned as he slowly withdrew and slammed home again. He repeated the motion several times, and my eyes practically rolled out of my head as he filled me up completely. My inner walls stretched to his length, and his shadows eased enough for my legs to part even further and hook around him for a deeper angle.

He grabbed my ankles, kissing one tenderly before he raised them by his shoulders and seated himself deeper, moving achingly slow now as he hit my G-spot.

"Oh gods, Raithe."

His shadows moved, curling over my body to rub against my nipples, then down to my ass where they stroked against my other hole. I moaned at the sensation, my muscles flexing in response. Raithe hissed as my inner walls clenched around him. "Aeris, you're going to make this too damn quick if you keep this up."

I grinned, tightening my ankles around his neck and squeezing my legs. He groaned, the sound igniting a fire deep inside my core. His cock pumped in and out, slow and steady and glistening with my wetness. And it felt so good, so right, as we worshipped each other's very existence. As he pushed with just the right amount of pressure, a give and take of heady, sensual bliss. That wave began cresting again, ready to crash as heat filled my cheeks and a dizziness filled my head, like I was not on a bed of silk but a sea of stars. He looked at me, his eyes a mix of wonder and adoration, and his voice was like honey as he said, "Let go, baby. Let's go together."

My body obeyed, giving in to his thrusts as he pumped harder and faster, as our breathing quickened and our chests heaved, and we both came in a tangle of limbs and screams and shadow.

"Fuck, I love you, Aeris." The words rumbled against my

chest as he collapsed upon me. "I would die a happy male if life existed of only this. Only you."

I stroked his hair, his arms, his back, tracing little pictures with my fingernails. "I'd prefer you breathing, if I have any say in the matter." I smiled as he looked at me. "But I do want to start that life with you. I want so many things for us. For this court."

"Then let's start living it. We'll build that world we're dreaming of. Brick by brick. Stone by stone. Blood, sweat, and steel."

I pressed a kiss to his lips. "To a better world, my love."

He kissed me back, slow and lazy, like we had all the time in the world. And I supposed we did. It hadn't really occurred to me until now, but we did have time and plenty of it. Raithe looked at me knowingly, the light in his eyes my beacon. My guide.

"To a better world, Aeris."

EPILOGUE

'There is one word for happiness that sums it up quite nicely.
Him.'

Journal excerpt, Aeris Lockhart

The winter winds rippled through my hair and threatened to steal away my scarf. Freezing was an understatement for the weather today, and I was not looking forward to feeling its chill out at sea, even if I was *very* much looking forward to sailing it with the male before me.

Raithe helped the servants load the last of the supplies onto his ship, his black hair wind-tousled and his rippling muscles clad in a navy tunic and pants that brought out the colour of his eyes. He was taking me on a voyage, where there would be nothing but the sky and sea and the ship we sailed on for company. And a few servants, I supposed, but all of them were happy to escape the castle for a time, and all would be handsomely paid for their service.

I needed the trip. The reprieve from the business of the castle, and an escape from thoughts of brewing war and court politics. Despite the pure bliss that was Raithe, I was also struggling from the aftermath of the Rite. Dreams of Waiflings and bloodied females plagued me, and my body remained in a state of fight or flight. I needed time to unwind and decompress. And I needed time with Raithe before our attention turned to matters of castle and state. I wasn't quite ready for all that came with being lady yet, so a short escape would do wonders.

In our absence, Raithe's mother would stand in as Lady of Castle Windaire while we were away, with my own by her side, until things settled down.

It warmed my heart to see the two of them together. Bound by the trials and tribulations they'd faced, they created a friendship that had been cemented through hardship and despair. Family. A *real* family. The occupants living at Castle Windaire were in good hands.

Sherai, Akira, and our mothers had accompanied us here to see us off before we commenced our voyage. My friends stood beside me now, watching the males do the work and feeling zero guilt about it whatsoever. Sherai took my hand and leaned her head on my shoulder, and even Akira stepped closer, bundling up beside me. I didn't want to do it. Didn't want to say goodbye to the incredible females beside me. Both were so different, yet so utterly precious. Part of my family now. We'd been through so much, and still had so much to do. The court, the war, the fight for justice in these lands...

My eyes found Raithe's as he appeared at the end of the gangplank and winked at me. *"It's time, my love."*

His mother surged forward, and I watched a little longer as

they exchanged words just for them, before she hugged him tight. His face crinkled with warmth, even as a tightness pulled at his brows and lips. I knew it was guilt that surged through him. I knew he'd be conscious of her too-skinny frame, or the fact they'd just reunited, only for him to leave straight away. But he and I needed this. And I think they did, too. It would be something to keep their hands and minds busy while they readjusted. Something to stave away the terrors of what came before. I smiled at Raithe as he looked at me over her shoulder, and he offered one back. Such a simple gesture that filled me with such light.

I sucked in a deep breath and stepped away, turning to face my friends. "This is it," I said softly. "This is where we say goodbye."

"That seems so final," Akira grumbled. "I don't like it."

Sherai laughed. "It's not like we won't see each other again. Besides, I'll be expecting letters from you both. You can direct them to the Palace of Pantai."

My eyes widened. "You got in? I didn't know you'd applied!"

"I got in." She pressed her fingertips to her lips and squealed as she did a happy dance. Her eyes glittered with excitement. "I sent my letter last week, the day we revolted. Honestly, I'm surprised they got back to me so soon. I'm pretty sure they only do an intake twice a year."

Oh? *"You wouldn't have had anything to do with Sherai's enrolment, would you?"* I asked Raithe while Sherai continued to detail her excitement.

"I may have put in a good word for her character. The rest was all her."

"You know I fucking love you, right?" I sent back. The playful pulse of shadow he sent trickling along the bond was pure

triumph, smugness and joy. And I loved him for that. For always thinking of others.

Akira rested an arm around Sherai's shoulders. "Like there was any chance they wouldn't accept you. Guess our girl's gonna be a scholar after all."

I beamed at Sherai. She was beautiful in her joy, with her coils fluttering in the breeze, her tawny skin gleaming, and her honey-brown eyes shining bright. This was why we'd rebelled. So females as clever as her could lead the next generation. Educated, adventurous, unstoppable. Mithria would be all the stronger for it.

"I'm proud of you, Sherai," I said softly.

Tears prickled in her eyes, but she nodded softly. "Right back at you."

I turned to Akira. "What will you do now?"

She grinned as she looked past me. I glanced over my shoulder, only to find Raithe beaming in return. My head shot back to Akira, and I groaned. "What have you two cooked up?"

"Oh, nothing," she said innocently. "Unless you count me hijacking your little love boat to hitch a ride over open waters." Her face sobered, her lovely dark eyes flitting once more to the sea. "I want to find them, Aeris. They're out there somewhere, to lands rarely travelled by our kind of Fae. I'm going to find my family. I'm going home."

My heart swelled for her, for all the things she'd endured in a land that wasn't hers for a god she didn't recognise. But I knew in my heart she would find them. If anyone could, it would be Akira.

"You will," I promised. "And you can stay with us as long as you need."

Sherai screwed her nose up. "You do realise you've elected to join a newly mated pair on a voyage out at sea, right? Good luck with that."

Akira laughed. "I'll find a way to survive, I promise."

I rolled my eyes. "You're both ridiculous." My lips curved slyly. "If not entirely wrong."

"Let's never forget this," Sherai said. "This bond. What we've been through."

"Never," Akira agreed as she surprised us both with a big hug. "Some things will never die."

"To friendship," Sherai said.

I smiled at the two bright lights beside me. "To us."

WANT A SNEAK PEEK INTO THE
NEXT BOOK IN THE WORLD OF
MITHRIA? READ ON...

THE UNRAVELLING (Uncorrected excerpt)

It began with an execution. Not a swift and silent punishment, but a grand affair with tribulation and fanfare, the streets and stands teeming with citizens bearing a burning rage in their hearts.

I remember the oily feeling of dread that sluiced through my stomach, paired with a cold as deep as the lick of winter's first frost. Most of all, I remember feeling the kind of fear that haunts your memories and gnaws at you from the inside out.

I was eight years old when they took off his head. When the soldiers of the Soul Court gripped my shoulders with their spindly fingers and made me watch as the High Necromancers, their faces beautiful, their bodies ethereal, gave the order and condemned my father's soul to Ryvia.

A traitor's death: the ultimate punishment for his treachery and treason.

They took his magic first—sucked it from his body like

marrow from a bone. Then the High Necromancers removed his head, those brown eyes still shining bright, staring right at me while he died. As if imploring me to see truth, to see reason.

While his blood still wet the ground, they ripped me from my mother's arms and gave her a simple choice: Die beside her husband or live in eternal servitude. The last choice she ever made was *life*. To this day, I'm not sure I can forgive her for it—or them. For the utter disgrace of those Fae with their wicked smiles, as they stripped us of our titles and noble lineage. It wasn't the finery or the position that I cared about. No, it was the brutality that would come for the many years after.

In Mithria, we burn our beloved to prevent necromancers from conjuring their bones again. No such mercy is afforded to the bottom-feeders of our society. To die without magic is to die a human's death. To live as the offspring of such a male? It's not really living at all. It's surviving … hoping someone won't murder you in your sleep or slit your throat when no one's looking. I learnt that the hard way as they inked my skin with the traitor's mark, effectively sealing my fate forever.

And forever was a long time for the Fae.

ACKNOWLEDGMENTS

This book has been a labour of love. From the early concept to the finished product, the story sucked me in and had me enraptured. I am truly so excited for this new world and all the other stories I have planned within it. I hope this bite-sized taste has you wanting more, too!

When first outlining the skeleton of this novel, I knew I wanted it to be dark and gritty. *Courting the Fae Captain* explores themes of women living in a harsh patriarchy. In this Court, particularly with an ancient tradition so barbaric as the Wedding Rite, I wanted to explore the inequity of males versus females, and the outdated and gross ideals that many of its male Fae hold. We then have Aeris's feminine rage and her eventual desire to form a sisterhood and rise against their oppressors. I hope I did this justice, and you found yourself cheering on our girlies at the race to the finish! I also hope you enjoyed our main man, Raithe. I do love a shadow daddy, and thoroughly enjoyed giving him the perfect shadow mummy, too!

To be entirely honest, this book kicked my ass in many ways. From endless weeks of my child being sick, to starting a new job, to juggling another book release, as well as all the hurdles life threw my way. But if I had a chance for a do-over, I would still have written it. I'm so happy that you are here, reading this little heart-to-heart, and sticking with me through this funny thing called life. So, thank you, dear reader, for giving *Courting the Fae Captain* a chance and for supporting the other *Romancing the Realms* authors and me with our book babies. Thank you to the beta readers, the street teams, the ARC readers, and all the bookish babes and baddies who have cheered us on from the sidelines.

A special thank you to Jade, who had the amazing idea to make this incredible collaboration happen with Jordan, Michelle, Miranda and me. Not to mention the formatting! Huge thanks to Selkkie Designs for the beautiful covers, and Emily Morrison for the copy editing and incredibly helpful suggestions. As always, I'm so grateful to all the bookish businesses and artists who have worked with me over the years and continue to do so. Thank you, thank you, thank you.

And finally, thank you to my family. To Jason, for your support, the gentle nudges to keep on trucking, for the love and the strong foundation that you provide. And now I get to say thanks to my son, Kody, for bringing me love and joy and inspiration.

Thank you all so much. These stories are for you, so see you for the next one!

ABOUT THE AUTHOR

I'm Chloe Hodge, author of Fantasy Romance and Urban Fantasy. I write strong female characters with a penchant for the morally grey, dark, broody males. Don't forget dark, magical worlds with a dash of banter and tension!

When I'm not writing, you'll find me drinking copious amounts of tea, reading, playing video games, or spending time with my wonderful husband, baby, and two goofball dogs.

Stay in touch!
Instagram: @chloeschapters
TikTok: @chloehodgeauthor
www.chloehodge.com

Join my reading group!
https://www.facebook.com/groups/chloesreadingcoven

LOOKING FOR MORE STEAMY ROMANTASY? CHECK OUT THE REST OF THE ROMANCING THE REALMS COLLECTION!

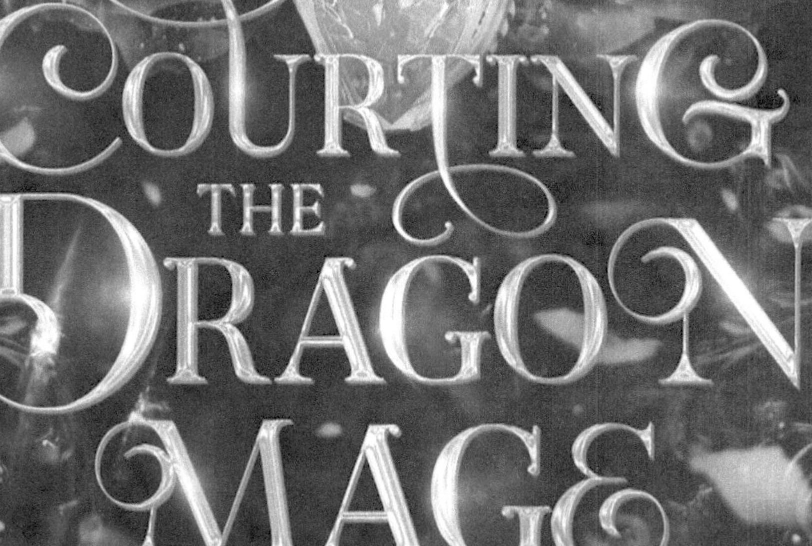

ROMANCING THE REALMS
JORDAN DUGDALE
COURTING THE DRAGON MAGE

COURTING THE DRAGON MAGE

My head slammed against the floor, and the shouting became distant.

Still, I'd never felt more alive.

Get up, Lyra.

"No one told me the Pit Viper was little more than a weedy little cunt. It's almost unfair, beating on a woman like that…" My opponent's words were invigorating as my anger sang through me like a numbing drug. The taste of copper was thick on my tongue as blood flowed through my mouth, and I spat it out as I forced myself to my feet. People surrounded me, shouting, though I could not discern their words. The man who had struck me waved his hands as if he had already won. I wanted to groan; the world swayed, but I refused to fall again as I launched myself at him. The people around me gasped, but I was quick and had my legs wrapped around his waist and my arm across his neck before he could turn to see me coming. I pulled my arm taut against his neck, crushing his windpipe, and he flung us around in a panic, scrambling with blunt fingers to pry me from his back. If I could just get him to pass out…

I cried out as he threw himself back. I hit the ground hard, and my vision went spotty as the air was ripped from my lungs. Gods, had he broken my rib? No, no, I could still breathe.

"Submit," I whispered, forcing my arm to tighten around his neck. I had managed to keep my arm across his neck by Nymera's miracle. My fingers locked around my wrist, and though he struggled, his thrashing was beginning to fade. I was lucky; they'd put me against someone suited to my size in this fight.

After a few tense moments, the man slumped against me, allowing my hold on him to lessen. The fighting rings of Kraeva were not to the death, and though my blood sang for violence, I yielded. I used what strength I possessed to push the man off of me, allowing the one in charge of enforcing fair fighting to drag me to my feet. My hearing was distorted; the crowd cheered as he lifted my arm, their screams distant and too loud all at once. Still, I smiled.

This was why I came down here.

"The Pit Viper takes another prey!"

"Thank *fuck*. I put a lot of sandyms down on her victory."

"Fucking bitch cheated!"

Their words surrounded me as my head thundered painfully. The headache I was about to have would be merciless, but I won, which was all that mattered.

"A small spitfire as always, my little viper." A man in noble silks approached with a large bag of sandyms. My head throbbed again, and the motion jarred against my swelling cheek. My tongue darted out, tasting blood on my lip, which had split on the right side. My opponent had done a number on me before I knocked him out.

"Some of us have to earn our suppers." The lie came to me quickly. I had more than enough sandyms to fill my belly, but the fewer underlings who recognized me, the better. The last thing I wanted was to get my father or brother involved with the fighting pits in the belly of Kraeva. Hence, I paid a local mage handsomely for a potion that would mask my features for a few hours.

The bag of sandyms in Faeva's plump hand was for potions I could only find in the lower districts, districts my father was too proud to purchase from, even if it was for medicine for his son.

The magic was beginning to wear off, though. It prickled against my skin, a warning that if I didn't hurry away, my cover would shatter.

I attempted to keep calm as I held my hand out, hoping, for once, that Faeva would be merciful and give me my dues with little trouble.

He was not.

"Come and speak with the others. They wish to celebrate your recent accomplishments. It's not common to have someone of your stature go undefeated in the rings." His eyes raked over me, and I suppressed the urge to shudder in disgust.

"I'm afraid I have other business to attend." Now that the fighting had won, my lust for the fight had diminished and slunk away to the hollow of my chest to slumber until it woke again and demanded blood. I had no time for the squabbles of nobles, no time to pretend to give a shit about their praises. I didn't do this for the validation. I did this to calm the ache in my chest. I did this to try to save my brother from the Blooming Dahlia, a plague that had swept through the streets of Kraeva in recent months. My brother had fallen ill with it a week or so ago, and my desire to seek his cure had consumed all of my efforts.

Faeva frowned but relented with little trouble, passing over the bag of sandyms and simply nodding. The weight felt good in my palm, and I made a mental note to stop by the bakery nearby in the morning to buy some warm gyras. They were my brother's favorite. He may be well enough tomorrow to eat one. His appetite came and went, and he hadn't been able to enjoy his favorite treat since before he got sick.

"Next time, then," Faeva said, and I agreed with a feigned smile. He said that every time. Sometimes, I indulged him, but not tonight. Not as my skin itched, and the magic began to liberate itself from my skin.

People murmured quietly around me as I made my way towards the door. Another fight was getting ready to happen, so most people paid me little mind, which I was grateful for. The room was small, and sweat collected on my brow from so many bodies pressed closely together.

The nape of my neck prickled like I was being watched. I glanced up from where my eyes had been trained mainly on the floor and met the gaze of a faerie.

She was of Eirwyn's Court. I knew that much. The fae from Neferíl's Court did not come here, not while they warred with the humans of the north. If the fae were here, it was from the Elven King of Southern Elvira, the forest of the fae.

She stared at me, her hair almost ethereal as it wove around her, embellished with intricate braids. Her eyes were cat-like, her ears as pointed as her canines when she flashed a wicked smile my way. It wasn't uncommon for the fair folk to attend these fights; they had a simple curiosity for human affairs and could only breach the forest's edge at night.

Another faerie stood next to her, a male. He was tall and

lanky, with dark hair that was longer than hers and draped over his shoulders. He was pale, eerily so, his eyes dark voids of black.

I ducked my head, ignoring the anxious patter in my chest, and strode past him.

The male faerie said something, but I couldn't understand him. Some folk from Kraeva braved the faerie food and wine to understand the fae, diluting it to avoid the consequences of too much of its consumption. I was not one of those people, and I smiled apologetically as I met the faerie's gaze.

He didn't say anything else, and I barreled into someone in my eagerness to escape them.

"*Shit*. I'm sor—" My words died as the stranger flinched away from me in disgust.

It was the crowned prince, Nasir, someone I was all too familiar with during my time growing up in the castle. His hair was slicked back, and his dark eyes raked over me in disgust. Luckily, he didn't seem to recognize me. His attention turned towards the front of his shirt, now covered in ale. I must have knocked his glass from his grasp.

What was Prince Nasir doing at the fighting pits?

"Stupid cunt—these silks cost more than your worthless life. They could throw you back in the pits, you know—all it would take is a snap of my pretty little fingers." He raised his hand, his fingers poised at the ready. Like a snake, ready to strike. "Next time, I'll see you fight someone you cannot win against."

I sneered, but my words lodged in the back of my throat as my skin prickled again. *Last warning. I need to get out of here before the prince recognizes me.*

"My apologies, Your Royal Highness." I curtsied and then turned on my heel, fleeing before the prince could rebut.

I spilled out into the alleyway. The air, while warm, was a

welcome relief against my aching skin as I pressed myself against the wall and sighed.

That was too close. I would time things better next time.

Still, the thrill of it all sang through me, and breathless laughter escaped my lips as I pressed a hand to my face. I clutched the bag of sandyms in my other hand as I hurried from the alley, eager to be home. The fighting pits were located in the lower districts of Kraeva, but I had learned which alleys and side roads to take to reach the royal districts more quickly as I tucked my sandyms inside my shirt, hiding the bag from wandering eyes. I knew better than to flash currency in the struggling parts of the city.

Wind trailed through the deserted streets as I stayed within shadows, hidden from anyone who might be out. Knights patrolled the city in their light leather armor and khopeshes, but I managed to stay out of their observant gaze as I hurried up the cliffs towards the Royal Keep.

A low whimper echoed to my right as I passed by an alley. It was so soft it could have been the wind, but as my eyes adjusted to the dark, I flinched and ducked away as a fist swung past my left shoulder.

"Beat it, little rat," a man hissed, his eyes glowing in the darkness. Fae, perhaps? I couldn't tell as I scrambled away, my heart a wild, untamed thing in my chest. I couldn't see well enough in the dark, but it looked like there were two of them, and one had someone pinned up against the wall further in the alley, their shirt wrapped around his fingers. "Before you end up in'a sit'a'tion you don' wanna be in."

"What did he do?" I asked, gesturing to the man pinned to the wall. "Because if there's something I hate, it's pricks that think they can beat on someone half their size."

The man who had nearly punched me growled and lunged,

his bald head gleaming in the moon's light. I swung out of the way just in time and then let go. Headache be damned.

The ache in my chest rekindled as it sang in excitement. I swept to the side and turned, instantly swinging out to grab the man's wrist as he lashed out at me with a curled fist.

Dodging the man's attack, I sank low. I needed to take him out quickly. I was already exhausted from my last fight.

He was quicker than I thought, though, and he laughed. "Tired, street rat?" His words were meant to poke at me, tug at my resolve, and make me reckless, but I had learned long ago that anger only led to mistakes and loss.

Somehow, I managed to get behind him as he darted past me.

Gotcha. Like the man from the pits, I latched myself onto the man's back, wrapped my legs around his waist, and slipped my arm across his windpipe. Tugging, I did not hold back as I had in the fighting pits. Here, there was no one telling me to show mercy.

The man struggled for several moments before he eventually gave up, his body slumping. I released him and managed to stay on my feet, my attention turning towards the others in the alley.

The other man cursed in a language I did not recognize and spit on the ground. "Not worth the trouble," he said in a heavily accented tone, pushing the man towards me and bolting.

Chest heaving, my legs gave out. I had borrowed too much time tonight and fought the odds stacked against me. The man they'd been bullying rushed over and knelt, his face swimming in my blurry vision. Oh gods, I was going to pass out. I couldn't pass out, not here. Not now. Someone would find me. Someone would…

"Breathe." The man's voice washed over me, and I inhaled sharply, forcing the darkness encroaching at my vision's edge to retreat. It was as if by magic, and I blinked rapidly as my eyes fell upon the stranger.

"Thank you for saving me," the stranger said, his eyes burning with the flourish of magic. It was otherworldly, and I immediately flushed as he smiled at me. The alley was too dark to reveal his features, but I knew he wasn't human. No human looked as he did now, with the soft glow of magic brushed against his skin.

"You shouldn't be out at night unless you know how to handle yourself. Or at least keep away from dark alleys. There's a fucking war going on," I scolded, but my voice was weak, wavering from exhaustion.

"Yes, well..." the stranger's thumb brushed against the sharp line of my jaw, and the tingle of magic returned. Suddenly, I didn't feel quite so weak, as if I could stand if I tried. Pain pulsed through my face, a reminder that I had taken quite the beating *before* I had fought the men in the alley. "They caught me off guard as I was leaving."

"What were they bothering you for anyway?" I trailed off, distracted by the man's thumb against my cheek.

He pulled away, adjusting his jacket as he rose and offered me a hand. "Wrong place, wrong time, I gather," he muttered as I allowed him to pull me to my feet. Yes, I could make it home now, and a startling clarity overcame me.

Not many knew how to wield magic, which meant this man was either a fae or a mage.

Both prospects made me uneasy, and I watched the man limp over and pick something up off the ground. A cane, one he leaned heavily against as he turned to meet my nervous gaze.

I shouldn't have been so frightened; I had seen him

incapable of defending himself, but the idea of what he was capable of magically didn't sit right in my stomach, and I sidled towards the lip of the alley and cleared my throat.

"I'm glad I could help, but I should get home."

"Let me accompany you. As you said, it's dangerous at night."

I sneered, trying to tame the flurry of my racing heart in my chest. "And as you saw, I know how to care for myself. Good night…"

A low, breathy laughter escaped the man's lips. "Alistair."

I turned and fled the alley, sticking to the main roads towards my flower shop. The magic had worn from my face, freeing it from its disguise, and while I was usually one to stick to the shadows to avoid recognition, the whole night had left me rattled.

No one was out anyway. The warring kingdoms had left the streets of Kraeva silent; everyone was too fearful of Bracaea flying their dragons to lay waste to the cities and villages to dare brave the nightlife. No one knew of the sickness that festered in the belly of their city. Not yet. I knew it was only a matter of time, though. The Crown couldn't silence it forever.

Chilly sea air brushed my face as I rounded the corner, and my flower shop appeared. It was near the keep, which loomed high up on a cliffside edging the ocean, and relief overcame me. Everything that had transpired tonight left me rattled. It was becoming increasingly dangerous to travel the city at night.

A shadow blotted out the moon, and my blood ran cold as I looked up and met the sight of a dragon soaring overhead. It wasn't close enough to discern its size or what it looked like, but there was no mistaking it as it sailed over the city and bells began to sound, an alarm signaling that the city was under attack.

I quickened my pace and did not look up again as I found myself safely inside my shop, my heart thundering in my ears.

What the fuck was a dragon doing in Kraeva?

Continue reading now on Kindle Unlimited: https://mybook.to/6lFQ1

ROMANCING THE REALMS

JADE CHURCH

COURTING THE TIGER KING

COURTING THE TIGER KING

"Fucking fuck!" He shook out his hand to ease the sting, squinting against the dusty darkness in the tunnels that had them all stumbling around like blind idiots. If the witch would hold still for just two seconds, then maybe she'd know that they weren't there to harm her.

It was difficult to communicate that while being struck with her sparks of silver lightning though.

They'd hunted her down over the course of weeks until his men had received word that the witch had been spotted in the forest that precluded the shore. If she left his kingdom now there was no telling when they'd be able to find her again, and he didn't have time to waste. Not with the curse breathing down his neck.

"I don't have time for this," he muttered, following the sound of the witch up ahead around the curve in the tunnel. How she'd known the tunnels were here, he wasn't sure. There were not many secrets that his kingdom held that he did not know about and yet she'd managed to evade them for an impressive amount of time. Louder, he called, "For the last time, Sonnet. We're here to—*Ouch!*" The pain sparked his anger, the beast within snapping at the reins and Wren decided he had no reason to hold it back.

The change was a warm cascade over his skin. Heavy paws hit the dirt floor as his senses sharpened, the tunnel no longer appearing pitch black. A metallic scent tickled his nose and he chuffed, suddenly understanding why the witch hadn't utilised anything more than sparks to dissuade them from following. She was injured, which meant she likely didn't have much more magic in her reserves since it depended on the life energy of the user.

He moved quickly, his stride long between his paws, and he caught up to the witch easily. She spun, silver eyes widening as she lifted her hands between them and only the faintest flicker of magic answered her call. Blood coated her side and the pallor of her face was chalky, panic overtaking any logic she may have had until Wren knocked her to the ground with the press of one large paw.

Perhaps it was the pain that jolted her out of the panic, or maybe being face-to-face with a tiger knocked the sense back into her, because she stopped trying to fight and instead breathed a sigh of relief. "Your Majesty."

Sensing it was safe and that the witch was at last in her right mind, Wren let his beast fade away in favour of the man. With barely a thought, the magic of the change reproduced his clothes and he offered the witch a hand, frowning when she grasped it weakly. She couldn't die. Not when he needed her. She was the only known lunar witch left of her line and, consequently, the only one who could perform the spell he needed.

"Sonnet," he acknowledged. "What trouble have you got yourself into now?"

The infirmary was largely empty, affording the witch privacy as his team of healers worked to cleanse and erase the wound that stretched from her hip to her ribcage. Sonnet had fallen unconscious on the journey back to the palace and Wren could only pray to the goddess that the witch pulled through.

"Thank Selene you found her when you did. The worst is over now." Gabe clapped a hand on Wren's shoulder, making him grunt. He wished he could believe that his friend was right, but the ceremony he needed Sonnet to perform was only the first step in thwarting his curse. Gabe sighed, like he could see the doubt churning in Wren's mind behind his eyes. "Come, let her rest. There's nothing you can do here while the healers work."

That much was true at least.

Wren accepted Gabe's hand up as he stood from the uncomfortable wooden bench that lined the outside wall of the infirmary. He'd been out on the hunt for weeks and was desperate for a bath, whiskey, and bed. Not necessarily in that order. He didn't like to spend so much time away from court, but needs-must and this wasn't a task he could let fall to anyone else. Only his most trusted soldiers had accompanied him in an effort to keep their task under wraps.

He followed Gabe out of the room and into the stone corridor, their footsteps muffled by the green runner that wound through the halls. Wren must have looked worse than he'd thought if the unusual tightness of Gabe's jaw was anything to go by.

"Tell me," he said quietly and Gabe nodded, scrubbing a hand over the blond stubble on his jaw before heaving a sigh. His amber eyes were weary when they met Wren's.

"More of the same. Whispers mostly, that the king would

rather be out fucking and hunting than looking after his court."

Wren snorted. If only that were true.

The hour was early, most of the castle hadn't yet stirred as the sun began to stream weakly in through the windows that lined the corridor. But still, he was careful to guard his words lest someone be lurking unseen. In a kingdom full of shifters, you couldn't trust anything you saw—sometimes the fly on the wall was a grown man in disguise.

"Someone is going to a lot of trouble to sow discord," Gabe continued, the early morning light washing over him and dyeing his white skin momentarily gold. "But whoever it is, they're being careful."

"Well, hopefully this should be the last hunt I'll have to go on for a while." Then they would have no reason to complain or spread rumours.

The entrance to his chambers was a welcome sight and he nodded in greeting to the two guards who stood sentry before he turned to clasp Gabe's shoulder.

"I need to rest, will you and Skye—"

"We'll keep an eye on your witch," Gabe confirmed, voice pitched low enough that the human guards wouldn't have picked up the words. "Rest, brother."

Wren smiled, the look fleeting as Gabe nodded and walked back the way they'd come. Gabe wasn't a brother by blood, but he had grown up with him and Skye and the three of them were close. The doors opened quietly beneath Wren's palm and the familiar scent of his rooms tickled his nose and relaxed his body automatically.

The hearth was cold but Wren couldn't be bothered to heat it, instead he wandered to the small golden cart in one corner of the room and poured a healthy measure of the amber liquid into a crystal glass. He sat down heavily into one of the plush armchairs arranged around the low, large oak table as he sipped.

He had his witch and had collected all but one of the ingredients Sonnet would need for her spellwork. This curse had been in his family for generations, so he was well versed in what it would entail. Lunar witches like Sonnet were beyond rare, they specialised in matters of the soul—a magic that many felt was too powerful to be allowed to exist. As a result, they had been hunted. His family had done what they could to protect the witches, but they were a stubborn lot and Wren was forced into secrecy; any hint of his curse could be perceived as a weakness that the court and their adversaries may pounce upon.

Worse, Wren wasn't sure that he could blame them for questioning his fitness for the throne if they discovered the truth. He'd only learned of the curse himself that same year. The ceremony Sonnet would perform could only be done during the cursed's twenty-fifth year. Now he had less than a year to find and bond with his mate, or the curse would take effect.

The only comfort was that Wren wouldn't know that he'd failed if that happened. Trapped in his animal form, Wren wouldn't know much of anything. He couldn't say the same for the kingdom and the throne. The chaos would leave them weak, scrambling for his replacement, perfectly poised for their enemies to close in.

He swallowed back the last of the drink, frowning in the darkness at the morbid turn his thoughts had taken. The glass thunked as he set it on the table, the sound loud in the quiet of the room as he stood and walked to the drapes and tugged them open until a small slither of light cut through the gloom.

His parlour space was where he did his best thinking, aside from when he was in the bath, it was also where he spent the most time with Gabe and Skye. Normally accompanied by drink and cards as they worked to clean out his coffers.

Dust motes swirled in the small beam of light, returning some warmth and brightness to the room as he turned and walked into his adjoining bedroom. A balcony waited to his left, the drapes shut to keep the sun out while he slept, but despite the security risk he often liked to sleep with the doors open, enjoying the smell of fresh air that carried the scents of the forest below up to his room. He pulled open one drape, leaving the one closest to the bed closed to keep it in shadow, and opened the door, breathing deeply and enjoying the hint of earth on the air.

The bed took up most of the room, carved wooden posts forming the vague shape of trees and birds guarding the bed below like a woodland canopy. A copper tub sat in front of the empty hearth, steam curling up from the water within and he hesitated, gaze flitting between the promise of the bed and the heat of the bath calling to him.

His simple tunic and trousers hit the ground, discarded next to his boots and the small horde of weapons he'd had hidden on his person. The need to be clean was too strong to be ignored and he slipped into the water with a groan. After the rough sleeping of the hunt, endless days spent in the underbrush of the forest and the odd tavern, the opportunity to soak in the bath was heavenly. One of his attendants had even added his favourite jasmine oil to the water and the scent had his eyes falling closed.

Water slipped over his nose and he spluttered, jerking upright and blinking the moisture out of his eyes. Fuck. He'd spent all this time trying to break the curse, only to nearly drown in his bath.

Wren dunked his head and reached for a bar of soap, lathering his hair and body and rinsing quickly in the rapidly cooling water. How long had he been asleep for? He wasn't too pruney yet so he had to assume it hadn't been a long time.

A large towel had been placed onto the fabric seat of the wooden chair beside the hearth and he reached for it as he stood, toweling off roughly and pushing the dark fabric over his hair so the semi-long strands wouldn't drip down his back. There was also a small pot of cream on the chair, scented similarly to his favored jasmine, and he scooped up a portion with two fingers before working it across his face and hands. Spending so much time outside would leave him with weathered skin as thick as a bore's hide if he wasn't careful.

Mostly dry, he stumbled over to the bed and promptly collapsed atop the sheets face first. He was asleep before the sun finished rising.

Continue reading now on Kindle Unlimited: https://books2read.com/u/4EjdZl?store=amazon&format=EBOOK

MICHELLE MORAS

COURTING THE SWAN PRINCE

COURTING THE SWAN PRINCE

The air is heavy with the Autumn Realm's constant amber haze, sunlight filtering through the oak trees' branches. I close my eyes, relishing in the warmth as it seeps into my skin. It's a perfect day for archery practice with my best friends. Best friends who are the princes of the kingdom.

"Ready to lose, Odette?" Odin asks, taunting me with his playful voice. He knows just how to provoke me. Ever since our earlier years in primary school, he was always teasing and toying with me, relentless in his pursuit to make me laugh or get a rise out of me. Ever the troublemaker, but I love him for it.

I open my eyes and shoot him a glance. "You only wish," I say, pressing my shoulders back and adjusting my bow. The target stands across the clearing, bark chipped where we've already missed a few times. "Besides, we all know Siegfried is the best shot," I say, looking over my shoulder at Odin's twin. Siegfried's cheeks flush after I wink at him. If Odin is the jester, Siegfried is like the royal librarian, wise and quiet.

Odin's smirk deepens, his gaze flicking between Siegfried

and me. "Well, then let's make it interesting," he says. "Whoever lands a bullseye first gets to marry Odette someday."

Freezing in my spot with heat rising in my cheeks, I glance toward Siegfried. His face is turning red too, but he tries to laugh it off, rubbing the back of his neck. I know it's just a silly game, but I'm baffled he'd wager such a bet. We're just friends, and to suggest we'd be more someday makes my stomach flutter with a thousand butterflies. Neither prince has ever dared to even hold my hand, let alone kiss me. Although, I've daydreamed of Seigfried doing those very things.

"Odin, that's…" Siegfried says, rubbing his temples. "Odette's too good for either of us."

"That may be true, but one of us will be king someday, so maybe she'll want to be queen. Besides, it's just a bit of fun, right?" Odin asks, flashing that charming, dangerous, gorgeous smile of his.

The twins couldn't be more different in personality or looks. Odin, with his dark, curly locks, wide jaw, and dimples, and Siegfried with blonde hair, a long nose, and high cheekbones. Their only similarity is in their stunning blue eyes that are now staring each other down. "Or are you too afraid to compete?"

Siegfried stiffens, the flicker of rivalry between them sparking as it always does when we do anything competitive. Neither wanting ever to appear weak, especially not in front of me. I'm not sure when things became this tense between them, this shift in their relationship to prove themselves. It's hard sometimes, balancing between them. Odin and Siegfried —they're like fire and water, and I'm caught right in the middle, tugged between their differences. But I don't want to choose. I prefer things to remain unchanged.

It infuriates me, especially when they should know they

have nothing to prove. I'll always be their friend and refuse to be something that comes between them.

Siegfried squares his shoulders, staring at me for a moment before nodding. "Fine," he says, tightening his grip on his bow.

My heart stutters at that, and my face burns at the idea that they would bet on me. This is silly, and we all know it's not serious. They could never marry me anyway. I'm just a simple elven villager and not future queen material, I remind myself. It's expected that their future partners will hail from the royal families from the other kingdoms.

"Hey!" I say, my voice rising to match their intensity. "And if I win? What then?"

Odin cocks his head, a glint in his eye. "If you win, Odette, both of us will give you a kiss."

"A kiss?"

My voice comes out in a squeak, and Odin grins wider, pleased with himself. Siegfried's face goes pale. We've always been close friends, but never outright flirted. My stomach twists and the sun feels too hot. If I'm being honest, I've daydreamed of what it would be like to mean more to Sig, but Odin? We might kill each other with how we argue about the silliest things. Besides, it's inevitable we won't see one another once they turn eighteen and go off to the royal college. I want to enjoy their friendship while I can and not complicate things.

"Well?" Odin asks, gesturing to the target. "Ladies first."

I shake off the nerves, focus my eyes, and raise my bow. It's just a game, I tell myself again as I steady my breathing and let the arrow fly. It sails through the air, swift and true, and lands…just outside the bullseye.

"Close, but not close enough!" Odin taunts, chuckling to himself, before setting up his own shot.

I roll my eyes and step back, pretending I don't care, but I feel my pulse quicken. Odin pulls the string back, his eyes narrowing as he lines up his shot. There's a confidence in his stance that makes me flustered, as if he already knows he'll win.

He lets the arrow fly, and with a dull thud, it sinks into the bullseye, dead center.

"Woo!" Odin shouts, throwing his hands up in victory. "Looks like I've won myself a bride."

"Just a lucky shot," Siegfried says, muttering under his breath.

"Luck?" Odin asks with a scoff. "Maybe you're just jealous because you're not as good as I am."

Siegfried's jaw clenches as he stares at the target. I see the way his hands grip his bow, his knuckles turning white as he lets go and his arrow soars towards the target. It misses its mark, just outside the center circle. He glares at Odin, and for a moment, it's as if there's nothing playful left in their rivalry. His eyes flick toward me, but he doesn't meet my gaze.

Siegfried's face darkens, and before I can say anything, he breaks his bow in half, turning and walking away, his steps quick and tense.

"Siegfried!" I yell, calling after him, but he doesn't slow down.

I round on Odin, fists clenched. "Why did you have to say that?"

Odin shrugs, unfazed. "It's just a bit of fun, Odette."

"Fun?" I glare at him, heart pounding with frustration. "You're being a jerk."

Odin raises an eyebrow, crossing his arms. "He'll get over it."

"You'd better hope so," I say, shaking my head. "I'm going to go find him." Without waiting for his response, I turn and hurry off in the direction Siegfried went, leaving Odin alone in the clearing. The sun dips lower, casting long shadows as I follow the path toward Siegfried's favorite spot—a tranquil lake where he goes whenever he wants to be alone.

I find him there, tossing stones into the water, each one making a ripple that spreads out across the glassy surface. His back is to me, shoulders hunched, his posture radiating frustration.

"Hey," I say as I approach him. He doesn't look at me, but I can tell he knows I'm here. "You shouldn't let him get to you."

He's silent for a moment, watching the ripples fade, and then he sighs, picking up another stone and hurling it into the pond. "Odin always wins, Odette. Always."

I step closer, reaching out but stopping just short of touching his shoulder. "It doesn't matter. It was just a joke. Besides, I'm not some prize to be won. And we both know I'm no one's future queen."

Siegfried's jaw tightens, and he stares down at his hands, as if the stone he holds contains all the words he can't seem to say out loud.

After chucking it into the lake, he meets my eyes. "You don't realize how special you are, do you?" he asks, shaking his head. "Odin always gets what he wants, Odette, especially if he thinks it's something I want."

I'm surprised by his omission. Does that mean Seigfried likes me more than a friend? I feel warm all over and bite my lip, searching for the right words. "Odin wasn't being serious. We all know neither of you can marry me," I say firmly. "We will be lucky to be able to stay friends. You both will move on to bigger and better things without me."

Siegfried glances at me, his eyes dark and full of something I can't quite place. "It won't be long before everything changes, and I dread it."

I shake my head, trying to brush off his words, but a small part of me feels unsettled knowing that they'll leave for the Royal College when they turn eighteen in a couple of years. "I don't want things to be different, but I know you're right."

He almost smiles at that, but it fades. "I wish… I wish I weren't a prince."

"How can you say that?"

Siegfried glances back at the pond, silent again. He tosses the last stone into the water, and I watch it skip once, twice, before sinking beneath the surface. "Compared to Odin, I just don't feel cut out for royal life. I'd much rather live in the village, like you. Enjoy a simple existence."

"That's why you'd make a great king. You understand your people and our way of life, and I know you'd fight to protect it."

He looks me in the eye as he takes my hand in his. "Thank you, Odette. You always know the words to say to make me feel better." He squeezes my hand before releasing it.

"Come on," I say, tugging his sleeve. "Let's go back. We can make Odin charm Madame Fallow for cookies as punishment for being an arse."

That earns me a genuine smile, and he follows me away from the lake, leaving the ripples to settle in our wake.

Two Years Later

"I wish you were coming with me," Siegfried says as he packs the last of his favorite books into his trunk. "You could fit in here and I'll sneak you into the college."

I let out a sad laugh at the visual of that. "Tempting, but

what would I do once we've arrived? Hide in your room all day while you're attending your courses?"

Sig lets out a frustrated grunt, grumbling under his breath about stupid royal rules. "I should have pushed my mother harder about convincing your uncle to let you enroll."

"It would have been no use. My uncle tested my abilities, and I'm not powerful enough to study further. Besides, I'm content with making teas and elixirs with my flora magic. You are meant for more. You'll have an amazing time, even if I'm not there."

"Doubtful," he says as he latches the trunk closed and turns to face me. His eyes are full of sorrow, and it breaks the false bravado I've been mustering up today. Despite trying to be happy for him, I'm hating this. I don't want him to leave; I want us to stay in our happy little bubble that we've been in the past year. Somewhere along the way, our friendship evolved into something more. Something deeper. Something I think might be love. But alas, all royals and nobles' elflings must go away to the Royal College at eighteen.

"You know this is hard for me too. I'm going to miss you so much, but it would be selfish of me not to want you to learn to harness your moon magic." Siegfried's powers emerged a couple of years ago, but it's been difficult for him to learn to wield them due to how strong they are. The moon's energy can flow into him, which he says will allow him to use it as a weapon and a shield. So far, he's only been able to use it to create light orbs and small beams. He needs to go to college.

"It's going to be the worst four years of my life. Every moment away from you will be absolute torture," he says as he steps closer, reaching a hand out to cup my face. I lean into the warmth, savoring his touch while I can. "But, I vow I will write to you every day, so expect a hawk delivery daily."

I smile up at him, bringing my hand up and resting it on

his chest. "And I'll write back just as often, but I don't want you to feel pressure to keep in touch. You need to focus on your studies and advance your magic. Don't worry about me." We've known this day was always coming, and sometimes I wish I hadn't let myself fall for him. Everyone knows there's an expectation that the royals find a suitable match while at the college. As deeply as I care for Sig, I know it's futile to hope he'd wait for me.

He drops his hand and frowns down at me. I'm much shorter than him, my head coming up to his chest. He's gotten so tall over the past couple of years, and so handsome, even when he looks at me in dismay.

"You really think I could forget you?"

"I'm just trying to be realistic, Sig. Our paths are going in different directions, and I don't want to hold you back. Our kingdom needs you — you could be the future king someday, and I'll just be making tea."

"But, I need *you*," he says with a hint of desperation in his voice. "Odette, maybe I haven't made this clear, but I... I love you. I always have. Going away to college will not change my feelings. You're what I want. All I want."

I gasp at the words I've been longing to hear, but a little voice deep inside me reminds me he's leaving and we're too young to be making such claims.

I reach out and clasp his hands in my own. "Sig, you know I love you too, but it may not be enough. You must make the kingdom a priority, and I won't ever blame you for that. Promise me you'll focus on yourself while you're there."

He looks away from me, his jaw ticking. "I don't agree, but I will promise you that, if you promise me one thing before I leave?"

"Okay... what?"

"Just tonight, let us be enough. Stay with me. Let me love you fully, wholly."

"Okay."

"Are you sure? You want me as much as I want you, right?" he asks, and I can't help but blush. We've come close so many times to letting ourselves go all the way, but something has always made it nearly impossible to get enough alone time. If this is our chance, I'm taking it.

"Of course I do, Sig, you know that. I'd regret it if we didn't, but I'm also scared it'll make telling you goodbye that much harder," I admit, looking down, trying to hold back the tears that threaten to spill out.

He lifts my chin with his fingers, forcing me to meet his beautiful icy blue eyes. I think they might be what I'll miss the most.

"I know, and you may be right, but I can't leave without showing you just how much you mean to me. My heart, my body, my soul — they all burn for you," he says before crashing his lips to mine. I let him pour all his love and angst into me as I kiss him back with everything I have. He may not be mine forever, but he's mine in this perfect moment, and I'm going to savor it.

We kiss. And kiss. And kiss some more, before he lifts me into his arms, my legs wrapping around his waist as he carries me over to his bed. He lays me down so gently that my chest aches. I try to steady my breath so that I can commit every touch, every kiss to memory.

"You are the loveliest elf in all the realm, Odette," Siegfried says, standing over me. "I'm the luckiest elf in all the realm to be loved by you. I'll never take your love for granted." A tear falls from the corner of my eye and slides down into my hair. He wipes it away with his thumb and then takes his time undressing me. First, taking off my leather slippers, then rolling down my stockings and tossing them on the floor. He kisses his way up my legs, teasing me with one quick press of his lips to that magic spot above my entrance before pulling my pantaloons off. I can't help but groan in both frustration and need. My middle feels like it's burning up in anticipation, and I'm sure he can see the evidence of my desire.

Just when I'm about to demand he hurry, he leans over me, our bodies perfectly aligned. I moan at the delicious feel of the weight of him against me. He hikes up my chemise and dress, teasing my core with his fingers. We've done this part so many times that he knows how to make me explode, playing me like an instrument.

"That's my girl, soak my hand so that you're ready for me," he croons over me, making my toes curl.

"Oh stars, Sig. I'm so close, don't stop," I say, my breathing turning ragged as I lose myself to his touch. It doesn't take long before I'm shaking and coming undone beneath him. He bends lower, kissing me hard to cover my cries as waves of pleasure flow through me, eventually ebbing away into mere ripples. And yet, I'm ready for more. Craving it. Craving him.

Siegfried rolls onto his back, pulling me with him. Sitting, straddling his hips, I lean down to kiss him while holding his face in my hands before trailing kisses down his neck. I push myself up, sitting atop him, so I can unbutton his trousers and slide them off. He sits up to take off his shirt, and I help pull it off. Then he does the same to my dress, loosening the tie in the back and lifting it over my head. There's nothing left, just our burning bodies, begging for each other.

"Are you sure you're ready?" he asks as he brushes my wild red curls back behind my shoulders.

"I've been ready. Make me yours," I tell him.

"You've always been mine, and you always will be," he says right before he lines himself up and nudges my entrance. I'm still so wet and warm that he slides in easily. There's a pinch of pain as he stretches me wider than I've ever felt before, but it dissipates into pleasure as Sigfried moves slowly in and out of me.

"You feel better than I could have ever imagined," he groans above me, as he pinches his eyes closed and bites his bottom lip.

It feels so good that I can't form words, so all I do is nod in agreement. Chasing the friction I'm craving, I lose all sense of time getting lost in the electric feel of him. Our bodies collide over and over as I ride him. When Sigfried brings his lips to my breasts, zings of lightning zap through my body. His teeth pull at my hard peak, and I come undone once again. "Yes, yes, yes," is all I can say as I get lost in the pleasure flowing through me.

Next thing I know, Siegfried flips us over and pulls my hips up, pressing into me from behind. "You have the most perfect body," he says as he caresses my backside before holding onto my waist. He feels so deep at this angle that I think for a moment maybe I can't take it. I grip the sheets beneath me and hold on for dear life as Siegfried enters me faster and harder.

Nothing has ever felt this good and this right. I squeeze around him, eliciting moans from his mouth before his movements get erratic. "Odette," he whispers like a prayer over and over, except it's me he's worshipping instead of the woodland spirits. Turning my head to look over my shoulder, I watch in fascination as he stills inside of me, only feeling a slight twitching before he wraps an arm around my middle and collapses against me.

We both roll onto our sides, facing each other with heaving chests, trying to catch our breath. Siegfried interlaces my fingers with his and kisses the back of my hand.

"Thank you," he says and kisses me. He stares into my eyes so reverently, like I'm the most precious thing in the world. I've never felt so cherished, so adored, so worshipped. "Do you feel okay? I didn't hurt you, did I?"

"I'm perfect. I'm sure I'll be sore, but that's to be expected, I think. Don't worry," I tell him and I mean it wholeheartedly.

"I hate that I'm leaving in the morning. I want to stay here with you and love you over and over and over again."

"I hate it too," I whisper, my voice beginning to shake with all the emotions I've been holding in. I've never felt so happy and sorrowful at once. Burying my head in the crook of his neck, I try to breathe him in and fight back the tears. But as he pulls me into his embrace and runs his hand down my locks, I can't hold them back.

"I know, I know," he says into my ear, consoling me. "It will be pure torture being apart from you. I swear to you that when I return, we will be together again."

"I hate their stupid rules. How can they keep you secluded for four years and not let anyone visit? It seems cruel to keep everyone away from their family and friends."

"I'll see if I can get my mother to get them to allow me visits, but it may not happen. That has been the rule for centuries upon centuries, unfortunately. Are you sure you don't want to hide in my trunk?"

"Wishful thinking won't get us anywhere. I'm just not ready to say goodbye," I tell him, wiping my eyes.

"Stay the night then. Let me show you the depth of my love until the sun rises."

"I'd like that," I say, as we crash our lips together once again. This time, our movements are not slow and sweet, but frantic and full of the desperation we feel to cling to each other.

We stay tangled up together, loving each other with

everything we have until we are both too spent for more. When the first rays of sunlight stream through the cracks of the drapes, I can't bear the thought of saying goodbye. So, I kiss him one last time before slipping out of his arms. Out of the castle. Out of his life for the unforeseeable future.

Every step away from him feels like wading through mud. I know he'll be upset that I left, but I refuse to say goodbye. My heart already feels like it's shattering, and I don't want him to feel any worse about leaving than he already does. He needs to focus on honing his power and not have me as a distraction.

So, I'll do the same. I'll build my life here, contributing what I can to our kingdom. And I'll hope that the next four years go by like a flash of lightning and pray he'll come back to me.

Continue reading now on Kindle Unlimited: https://mybook.to/NKPMHD

ROMANCING THE REALMS

MIRANDA JOY

COURTING THE MOON PRIEST

COURTING THE MOON PRIEST

SORAYA

Everyone on the island holds their breath, eyes locked on the night sky. We wait patiently for the twin moons to overlap, forming a single supermoon as they do one night every thirty days.

"Almost," Mariel whispers, gripping my hand tightly in both of hers.

The moons overlap, almost entirely consumed by one another. The moment the second moon is gone from sight—fully nestled into the other—a roar of appreciation rises from the beach. The conjoined moons' glow intensifies, sending radiant waves of iridescent light streaking through the dark sky.

In response, the jungle brightens, glimmering with the gifted power of our goddesses.

"Praise the moons," I whisper, excitement bubbling up in my chest.

The bright silver light casts an ethereal glow across the

island. The rivers shimmer, running down the single verdant mountain and through the jungle like narrow arteries. They all feed into the ocean around us. The currents pulse softly, as if alive. Along the banks, all through the island, the plants harbor the same magical light. Their usually vibrant green coloring mirrors the ribbons of blue-green streaking through the sky beside the newly formed supermoon.

A smile overtakes my face, and my shoulders soften. Mariel drops my hands, throwing her arms around me.

"Blessed Union, Soraya," she squeals in my ear. I squeeze her back, and she pulls free. Music starts playing, and the gratitude of the villagers is palpable. "I'm going to snag us some nectar. I'll be right back."

She bounds off toward the hut at the edge of the sand, waving animatedly at everyone she passes. Most of us were born and raised on the Isle de Lunith, and we're a fairly tight-knit community.

Strong arms snake around my waist, startling me. The scent of salt and earth, mixed with a familiar musk, invades my nose, and I chuckle.

"This dress does things to me," Joss murmurs into my neck, invading my personal space.

Swatting his arms away, I turn to face him. Moonlight dances on the droplets lining his deeply tanned chest. He runs a hand through his short brown hair, slicking it back. It glistens from his dip in the ocean. His lips raise into a teasing grin, and my expression softens, mirroring his.

I playfully roll my eyes. "We're all wearing the same thing."

Gesturing around the beach, I take in the various celestial servants scattered on the beach, mingling with the rest of the island's population. Everyone drinks, dances, and feasts tonight, celebrating the moons' union.

The priests and priestesses are easy to pick out, all dressed in similar wispy, lightweight garments in the color of the moons—pale silvers and off-whites. Some don cascading gossamer gowns with thin straps, others have flowy pants with billowing arms, but they're all variations of the same look with cascading layers.

"No," he says, arching a light-brown brow. "You certainly are not." His fingers trail up my covered collarbone until his hand lands on my exposed shoulder. "I like *yours* best."

Planting my hands on his bare chest, I gently push him back. "We talked about this!"

"I thought we were friends." He fake pouts, running his fingers through his wet hair.

"Exactly—*friends*."

He gives me a broad, charming grin. "And I'm honoring your wishes… by being very friendly."

I can't help but laugh and roll my eyes, amused by his quick quip. "You know damn well what I mean, Joss Thalor!"

"It's impossible to keep my hands off you." He groans. "I miss you already."

It's my own fault for blurring the boundaries between us. I might've ended our official relationship, but I haven't kept him out of my bed.

I shake my head, scanning the beach for Mariel. She's out of sight, likely having made her way into the hut for our drinks. As much fun as Joss is, I ended things for a reason. No matter how handsome, kind, and funny he is, I just don't want *more*.

Not the same way he does.

My eyes flit to the moons. I want a love like *theirs*. Lore says the two moons were previously goddesses who sacrificed their mortal forms and cursed themselves, all to spend eternity together, hung in the skies side-by-side, only kissing once per month.

They're forever suspended overhead, only shifting to touch on Union Night and separating by morning.

I don't necessarily want their fate, but the thought of a passionate, all-consuming, eternal love lingers in the back of my mind. With Joss, things are comfortable, but the thought of being without him doesn't steal my breath.

When I glance over at him, he's staring out at the dark ocean, all the previous humor gone. My heart spasms violently. We've been there for each other our whole lives, including when he lost his mother to the very sea he loves.

The guilt gnaws at me, and I step beside him. I nudge him with my elbow. "Wanna go find some silverdew?"

The flower, indigenous to the Isle de Lunith, only opens at night. Though it sprouts in abundance, it's a cherished flower, mainly because it's our primary export and the source of our island's income.

It can be tapped for nectar—the delightful, fruity brew we enjoy for a buzz. It also provides a more intense, euphoric high when the petals unfurl and the pollen is snorted.

Joss shoots me a crooked smile. "Later? I'm going to catch another quick dip with the other tideborn—before they get too nectared."

Squeezing his hand in understanding, I nod. When he leaves, I dig my feet into the cool, packed sand, watching the water gently lick the shore. With my back to the revelry, I take this moment to myself to just *be*.

My lungs fill with fresh, salty air with a fruity tinge. It smells like home—like *everything*.

I love Union Night. Not only for the obvious—the energetically charged revelry, the merriment, the magic—but because I feel as if I'm truly one with the island. Fingering a strand of teal hair, I smile down at the color, feeling less like an outcast because of its unnatural hue and more like I'm an integral part of the ecosystem.

Shoving my hair over my shoulder, I squint, catching the faint ring of the smaller moon as it nestles in front of its larger counterpart. One night a month, when the moons align, the Isle de Lunith comes alive with magic. Even though I've experienced it twelve times a year for twenty-six years, it never ceases to fill me with awe.

Amazement tickles my insides, and my heart pulses in time with the flickering fireflies lighting up the beach.

Familiar faces play the shell horns, blowing merrily into the seashells as they sway to the music. Drums and stringed instruments accompany them, blending into a tune that instills a need to move. It's melodic and hypnotic. A group of celestial servants throw their limbs around as they release pent-up energy in dance. Others chant in groups, leaning into gratitude mantras to thank the goddess moons for their protection.

Every soul dances barefoot on the sand, connecting intimately with the land, and celebrating another night—another month—of life-sustaining magic.

Every soul except for one.

I gaze toward the temple atop the tallest hill, which settles into the trees far beyond the village. It's where the celestial servants live and work—the point of the island closest to the moons. Even from this distance, I glimpse a hint of light sparkling from the top where the moonstone lives, absorbing the energy on this powerful night as it does during every Union.

Sparkling waters crest over the stony side, feeding into our rivers.

"You'd think out of everyone, *he* would be down here celebrating," Mariel yells, thrusting a drink at me.

"Where have you been?" I graciously accept the beverage, wrapping my lips around the bamboo straw peeking out of the coconut shell. The fruity, slightly sour tang of nectar washes over my tongue, and I close my eyes to revel in it for a moment.

"Maybe one day he'll stop thinking he's too good for us," she says bitterly.

A soft sigh escapes my lips as I open my eyes and face my best friend. "You know how he is, Mariel."

"*Reclusive*," she says sarcastically.

My lips press into a thin line as my head swivels toward her. "Hush." I glance around to ensure no one's eavesdropping on her talking poorly about High Priest Raziel Kasper. Granted, I've heard enough whispers to know many of the villagers think the same way. "He's our Moon Priest."

"Exactly." She lowers her voice, but the way she slurs tells me she's already had a little too much fun during tonight's celebration. "With how up the moons' butts he is, you'd expect him to show face during the most sacred night of the month."

"I'm sure he celebrates in his own way." I squint at the temple, unable to understand why he'd choose to skip the Union. The High Priests before him were known for flashing their magic on this sacred night. He's an enigma for hiding his powers from the islanders.

She snorts. "I'm not the only one who notices his attitude."

Mariel isn't wrong about him being a bit of a recluse, but he's our island's Highest Keeper. *The* Moon Priest. The Goddesses' Anointed. The moons chose him to oversee the magic and, thus, the life of our island.

Yet, he snubs every ceremony.

Mariel raises her drink to the moon, and her bracelets clink together noisily overhead. She throws her head back, closes her eyes, and lets out a *whoop*.

"To the moons!" she yells.

"Praise the moons," I say with a soft laugh.

"Hey, there's your man." Mariel nudges me with her elbow.

I turn to catch Joss heading toward us. He charges the last few steps toward me, and despite his bare feet sinking into the soft sand, it barely slows him down. His muscular arms wrap around me, squeezing me as he playfully nibbles on my neck.

"Joss," I chastise, swatting at him. "You're getting me wet!"

"I wish," he murmurs.

He spins me around, and some of my nectar splashes over the side. The sheer, wispy bottom half of my gown floats around me, the slits parting to reveal my bronzed legs, toned from my daily treks up and down the temple's archive stairwells. The delicate silver chains crisscrossing my midsection hold the dress in place with effortless grace. The tiny star and moon charms tinkle with the movement.

I laugh. "Put me down!"

He obliges, placing me back on my feet. I stumble, quickly reorienting myself and adjusting my neckline to ensure my chest is fully covered.

"What are you two talking about?" Joss's green eyes twinkle with jest.

I'm glad to see he's swum his previous sorrows away. The grief hits him from time to time, and though I can't relate in the same way, I know what it's like to miss a mother. Unlike him, I never knew mine, though. Where he misses a person, I miss the idea of one.

Mariel, having refocused her attention on us, smirks with amusement. Her dress matches mine, but where mine is high in the front and plunging in the back, hers is the opposite, showcasing her glorious cleavage. The pale coloring contrasts beautifully with her brown skin and dark curls.

The outfits are symbolic, marking us as priestesses of the moon—a reminder of who we are and who we serve.

The Moon Priest.

My eyes flick back in the temple's direction. I find it rather blasphemous to talk poorly of him or the moons he protects. That *we* protect. Mariel, on the other hand, loves instigating and stirring up the 'monotony of our island'—her words, not mine.

"We're not talking about anything," I tell a waiting Joss. "Hey, would you mind grabbing me another nectar? Please?"

Joss gives me a broad smile and then glances at Mariel.

"Make that two?" Mariel says, twisting a curl of dark hair around her finger.

Joss thumbs us up, then jogs off toward the Nectar Hut—our beach tavern.

His muscles flex with power, only the tiny fabric of his hemp water shorts covering his ass.

"Your boyfriend is a delight," Mariel says. She grabs my hand, tugging me through the sand, closer to where the band plays their live instruments.

"You know we broke up." I raise my voice so she can hear me over the melody.

She whirls toward me, rolling her hips to the tempo as she raises a brow. "I saw him sneaking out of your bed this morning."

"Yeah, but we're not—"

"You *always* find your way back to each other." She spins, arms overhead, and her face tilted to the sky with glee.

"This is different, Mar." Shaking my head, I give up and let the music sink into my bones. I move naturally, matching Mariel's steps.

"He would've bonded with you in a heartbeat."

I flush at the thought of completing the Union ceremony

with Joss—on a night like tonight, when such bonding events occur. I'd be lying if I said I hadn't imagined it a thousand times over.

I shake my head, and a few tendrils of hair fall into my face. "I don't want that—we're better as friends."

"No," she says sternly, gesturing from me to her as she dances. "*We* are better as just friends. That man is better as a husband, and you know it, Soraya."

"It was never serious." I stop moving to the music and dig my toes into the sand instead.

She snorts. "He loves you something fierce."

I kick a hearty amount of sand at her legs. She squeals, kicking sand back at me.

Joss appears with our drinks, cutting the conversation short. Mariel teases him about something, but his eyes stay locked on me. I flush under his attention, hating that I'm letting both of my best friends down with my decision.

Not wanting to think about it, I fiddle mindlessly with my straw and return my attention to the temple, catching the light refracting from the moonstone atop.

Everyone around me is focused on the music, the moon, or the drinks, socializing and dancing in spades. Though the source of the magic comes from the sky, the moonstone nestled in the temple's summit is the heart of our island. It absorbs the pulsating magic sent down from the goddess moons, after all. Without it, there would be no magic. No island.

Suddenly, the gleaming light flickers out, and the top of the temple goes dark. My heart trips over itself, and I nearly drop my nectar.

"Joss," I yell, grasping his arm tightly with my free hand.

He stops mid-conversation, turning to me with concern etched into his features. "What is it?"

"The moonstone." I turn back to the temple, raising my hand to point, but the soft glow has returned, wavering hazily above the temple.

"What about it?" The worry leaves his voice, and he gives me a curious look.

"She's obsessed with that thing," Mariel says, giggling. "Overcome by its sheer beauty from time to time."

"I can understand what that's like," he says wistfully, his gaze boring into me.

Mariel giggles.

Sighing, I glance down at my drink, shaking my head. I take a long pull, finishing it off in one go while my friends cheer.

"Nevermind," I whisper, blinking stupidly in the direction it sits. It flickered for a moment—I swear it. Or maybe I had too much nectar, and my eyes are playing tricks. My lips stay sealed, not wanting to rouse unnecessary fear on a sacred night, but sweat beads on my spine.

My hand rises to the center of my chest, mindlessly hovering there.

Joss and Mariel laugh at something, talking animatedly. None of their words stick in my brain. Instead, my eyes stay glued to the temple as if I might catch the moonstone winking again.

"I should check on the High Priest," I say in a rush, interrupting their conversation.

Mariel looks at me as if I've lost my mind.

"Is he sick?" Joss asks with a frown. "We have our island assembly tomorrow."

I shake my head. "Something just feels *off*." The words are weak—strange—even to my own ears.

"Ooookay." Mariel takes the coconut out of my hand, tossing it onto the beach. "No more nectar for you. Let's dance it off." She grips my hand and tugs me closer toward the shore, where waves gently caress the packed sand. "Come on, Joss!"

We navigate the merriment, smiling and nodding at everyone we pass.

A pit of dread builds in my stomach, but I don't fight my friends. I can't make sense of my feelings on my own, let alone verbalize them. Instead, I allow Mariel and Joss to sandwich me as we sway our hips in rhythm to the drumbeat.

We drink more nectar, and later, when Joss's hands snake around my waist, threatening to steal me away to the bushes, I let him.

My eyes continue to flick toward the temple, and the unsettled feeling lingers, even though I try my best to let Joss *distract* me.

Continue reading now on Kindle Unlimited: https://mybook.to/lmxJAj